Right on Walton

sands press
Brockville, Ontario

Right on Walton

Book 2 in the Heart of Madison Series

By Crystal Jackson

sands press

sands press

A Division of 3244601 Canada Inc.
300 Central Avenue West
Brockville, Ontario
K6V 5V2

Toll Free 1-800-563-0911 or 613-345-2687
http://www.sandspress.com

ISBN 978-1-988281-81-0
Copyright © Crystal Jackson 2020
All Rights Reserved

Edited by Laurie Carter

Publisher's Note
This book is a work of fiction. References to real people, events, establishments, organizations, or locales, are intended only to provide as a sense of authenticity, and are used fictitiously. All other characters, and all incidents and dialogue, are drawn from the authors' imaginations and are not to be construed as real.

No part of this book may be reproduced in whole or in part, stored in a retrieval system or transmitted in any form or by any means, without the prior written permission of the publisher.

For information on bulk purchases of this book or any book published by Sands Press, please call 1-800-563-0911.

1st Printing

To book an author for your live event, please call: 1-800-563-0911

Sands Press is a literary publisher interested in new and established authors wishing to develop and market their product. For more information please visit our website at www.sandspress.com.

To Jenni, for letting the bathwater get cold and yelling at everyone to go away so you could finish reading the first draft

And to David, for passing through the seven layers of the candy cane forest, over the sea of swirly twirly gumdrops, and through the Midtown Tunnel to meet me for pizza

Acknowledgments

I would be remiss not to acknowledge, first and foremost, Luna and Linus who beautifully tolerate having a mother with her head in the clouds. I love you, I'm proud of you, and I appreciate you.

To Jessica, who has always believed in me. To Stephanie who has encouraged my work and helped me hone it, and to Sarah, Carmen, Michael, Anna, Brandy, and Lieselle who cheered me on. To Josh & Amanda for your love and support. To Caroline of BooksBecause and Linda at In High Cotton for your enthusiastic support. Thank you to the Madison Writers Group for your unwavering support and superb feedback.

A heartfelt thank you to my original readers—Shannon, April, and Mary. To Laurie Carter, my editor, with my appreciation.

But most of all, to my readers. Every day, I get to wake up and do what I love. Thank you.

"You don't have a right to the cards you believe you should have been dealt. You have an obligation to play the hell out of the ones you're holding." ~Cheryl Strayed

Chapter 1

Lindy Carver stepped out of the enclosed shower with a sigh, letting out a thick cloud of steam as she wrapped herself in an oversized bath sheet. She knew today would be the day she'd have to come clean to her mother, and she wasn't exactly looking forward to it. She got dressed in black leggings and a gray sweatshirt that said "I'm too clumsy to be around fragile masculinity" and paired it with sweater socks. She dried her long, thick brown hair quickly, wondering if she should cut it. Then she twisted it up into a messy bun and decided that a shorter style might just end up being more trouble than it was worth.

She looked at herself critically in the mirror. She was taller than most of her friends at five-nine, and slender still. She studied her face. Sure, she had lines around her eyes when she smiled, but she was almost thirty-six now. That was to be expected. She was told that she had her father's eyes in her mother's face. Her father had left when she was a toddler, too young to even hold a single memory of him. She shrugged one shoulder carelessly, shaking off the thought. Water under the bridge now. She didn't need him. Or any man. No, she'd decided she'd do just fine without them.

Lindy went down the stairs quickly and slipped into a pair of Uggs, caring more about speed and comfort over style so early in the morning. She grabbed a couple of brochures as she headed out the door of the carriage house she called home and crossed the large garden to the historic home she'd grown up in. She'd never expected to settle down in the small town of Madison, Georgia. She'd assumed that she'd travel after college, perhaps settling in some far-flung cosmopolitan city. It had surprised no one more than herself that she had chosen to come home with her double major in art and education to open up a painting studio in town. She'd moved into the carriage house on her mother's property as a matter of financial necessity while she'd gotten the business off the ground. After a while, it had simply become home.

She used her key to let herself into the big house. Her mother wouldn't get up and stumble sleepily into the shower until she heard Lindy start the coffee grinder. As a single mom, her mother had spent plenty of years having to be the early bird to get up with Lindy and her brother Seth. Now, they agreed that she could sleep a little later while Lindy started breakfast prep.

First step? Coffee. Lindy ground the organic fair-trade beans that she'd ordered online and heard the first sounds come from upstairs. Right on time. She poked her head into the fridge and decided she would make omelets today. She lined the ingredients up on the counter: ham, cheese, eggs, milk, and spinach. She dug around in the cabinet and found a jar of sundried tomatoes. She added that and chopped onions to her assembled ingredients and got to work.

She glanced over at the brochures she'd brought and wondered how she would begin the conversation. She'd practiced it a few times in her head, but what she could never predict was her mother's reaction. Of course, Lindy thought, her mother was never one to overreact. Surely, she'd see the logic in her decision. She reached for her phone and selected a playlist they'd both enjoy. Worrying about her mom's reaction wouldn't change it, she thought with a shrug as she tucked the brochures out of sight and turned her attention to the ingredients.

*****

Keely came down the stairs to the smell of coffee and … omelets, if she wasn't mistaken. She stopped in the doorway and smiled widely at her daughter. Lindy was at the stove, turning an omelet. She was the mirror image of Keely except for the large brown eyes she'd gotten from her father. And of course, Keely's thick dark hair had gone silver some time ago. But their faces? They could have been twins rather than mother and daughter. It still gave Keely an odd sort of thrill to see it.

Right now, Lindy was singing loudly to Springsteen's "Dancing in the Dark" and dancing at the stove. They both loved The Boss. Keely leaned against the door and wondered how her heart could contain all this love. She could still see little Lindy singing loudly and dancing around this kitchen as a small girl wearing a pink tutu and a superhero cape, begging her grandfather to dance with her. Watching the two of them had cracked her heart open, but in the good way that only a parent could fully understand.

She waited until Lindy turned around and returned her smile before heading into the kitchen. Lindy didn't stop singing or dancing until the song was done. Keely added her own voice and a couple of dance moves that made Lindy stop singing long enough to laugh. The playlist switched to "I'm on Fire" and Lindy reached over to turn the volume down.

"I didn't want to interrupt," Keely said with a smile. "Looks like you've been busy, what with performing a concert and making us omelets."

"I've been up painting since four. I just couldn't sleep. I thought I'd go ahead and get started on breakfast."

"Well, I'm glad you waited until now to start. I wouldn't have been happy if I'd stumbled down here before dawn."

Keely picked up the mug Lindy had made her in art school. It said, "I can't decide what pants to put out today: smarty or fancy." She looked over and noticed Lindy was drinking out of the one she'd made for herself: "Blood of my enemies (Just kidding; it's coffee)." Lindy had always had plenty of sass, but Keely could admit that she came by it honestly enough. Of course, her own sass and pure grit had seen her through her husband leaving without a word. It had gotten her through single parenting two toddlers and going from a stay-at-home mom to a store manager and then store owner. Sass wasn't the worst thing.

"If you don't have to be in too early today, I wondered if we could talk," Lindy began, fingering the brochures she held in her lap beneath the table. She tried to keep the nerves out of her voice, but her mother didn't seem fooled.

"Well, of course, we can. What's on your mind, baby?" Keely asked, her brow wrinkling in concern. When Lindy looked down into her lap and paused, her mildly concerned expression gave way to one of alarm. "Okay, now you're worrying me. Pass me my omelet, and then tell me what all this is about." Keely sat down carefully and offered up a prayer that nothing was wrong with her baby.

"I've been thinking a lot lately about what I want for my life. I'm going to be thirty-six soon, and I really haven't met anyone I want to spend my life with," Lindy began.

"Oh, honey, that will happen when it's time," Keely assured her.

"Just hear me out, Mom. I just don't want to put my whole life on hold on the off-chance that Mr. Right is just around the corner. I've decided I'm going to start a family on my own." She took out the brochures she'd picked up at the fertility clinic and sat them down on the table in front of them. When her mother simply looked puzzled, she continued. "With science. I can get a donor since I'm healthy enough, and if that doesn't work, I can look into adoption next."

Keely abruptly dropped her head to the table, and Lindy jumped up in alarm. She'd expected questions but not shock and certainly not whatever this was. She came around to the side of the table and knelt down beside her mother. It took her a full minute to realize that her mother was laughing, not crying. She sat back on her heels, perplexed. Well, that wasn't the reaction she was expecting, she thought.

"I'm sorry," Keely said, wiping tears from her eyes. "I think I've just seen one too many movies. For a minute there, all I could see was you carrying home one of those turkey basters from the hospital." Choking out a startled laugh, Lindy looked up at her mom. Relieved and a little sheepish, she stood slowly and went to sit back down.

"I'm so glad you're finding this entertaining," Lindy said wryly. "Do you know how long I've practiced telling you this?"

"I'm sorry, baby," Keely said, choking on a last laugh and clearing her throat. "I don't mean to make light of it. I think it's a wonderful idea. You'll make such a wonderful mama," she said with a grin. "My baby is going to have a baby."

"Well, not quite yet," Lindy said with a smile. "And there will be no turkey basters involved, thank you very much," she returned with a roll of her eyes.

"I think it's very brave, and I couldn't be prouder. Now, look at me." Lindy looked up. "It's going to be hard, what you're doing. So hard. But we'll be right here. Me, your brother, Libby. We'll all be here." Lindy knew that she meant it. Her brother lived just down the street, and Libby was practically living with him these days. They would all be there for her and the baby when the time came.

"Thank you, Mama," Lindy said gratefully. "Just let me tell Seth, okay?"

"Of course you can tell him," Keely agreed. "Although I'd love to see his reaction. Do you think you could get that on video?" she asked with a grin. "Now I know all this is supposed to be expensive. Do you need any money?"

"No, it's affordable enough. Do you mind if I stay in the carriage house a while longer? I'm still saving up for a house, and with the studio expansions I have in mind, I'm hoping that I won't have to be here for more than another couple of years."

"You stay in the carriage house as long as you like. It's plenty big enough, and you'll be right here so I can play with the baby." Lindy leaned against her mother's shoulder, and Keely breathed in the citrus scent of her hair. She held her daughter tightly and wondered if she knew how hard her choice would be. Well, she'd done it alone and so could Lindy. She knew her baby would be a wonderful mama.

Chapter 2

Dean Walton woke up groggily and knocked his alarm clock to the floor. He'd worked a late shift at the fire department where he was subbing in part-time, and he had an early shift at his full-time job with the fire department in town. He loved his work, but he was only working the two jobs for extra money.

He was restoring a cabin on the lake, and it was taking every dime he had, and then some. It was throwing good money after bad, he often thought. Still, he loved it, and when it was livable in a few months, he planned on moving in and roughing it while he fixed it up. It would save him rent, and he could use that money to fix up the place.

He picked up his phone and scrolled through the messages. Naomi from Brews & Blues in town, their local coffee shop, had already messaged him. He never should have slept with her. She was college-age, fresh-faced, and cute, but he hadn't been serious about her. Now she worked practically across the street from him and wouldn't take no for an answer.

Not that he ever said no, exactly, but surely she knew that if he wasn't trying to spend time with her, it meant that he didn't want to. It was obvious to anyone with a brain. He rolled his eyes. Well, she was persistent, that's for sure. He had a couple of other messages and a few matches on one of the online dating apps he used. Not that he had much time for that these days, but he still liked to play the field.

He took a quick shower, making it as hot as it would go, and then wiped the steam from the mirror and studied his face. He had just turned thirty-three, and he was showing a few smile lines around his eyes. His blond hair was still thick, and he could still get away with spiking it up a bit in the front. It was starting to get a little long, but he didn't mind that much. He wondered if he should shave, but the short beard he'd grown for the hell of it had seemed to suit his face. Plus, with working so much, it was easier not to have to worry about shaving every day. His green eyes stood out with long lashes that some girlfriends had referred to as "pretty." Hey, he didn't mind the pretty boy label if it kept them coming back. He was tall and in reasonably good shape from spending time at the gym—well, when he had time to spare. Of course, working on the house was at least as good a workout these days.

He left the house with a large thermos of coffee to walk to work. He lived off Walton Street, which he liked to tell the ladies was named after his family. Of course, it was a lie. His family may have shared the same name, but they wouldn't have been able to afford any of the antebellum houses that lined his street. Not even the small ones or the carriage houses. He was lucky to be able to afford the rent in the duplex he was living in right now. He'd gotten a good deal because his best friend's mom knew the owner. He took care of his own lawn and hers, and she gave him a generous discount.

No, his family wasn't from Walton Street. If there was a wrong side of the tracks in this town, that's where Dean's family had lived. They'd been blue-collar people who barbecued on the weekends and saved for a vacation in Panama City every few years. Not that there was anything wrong with that. He liked a good BBQ and beach vacation as much as the next guy. They just didn't have anything in common with the people who lived in this neighborhood with their manicured lawns and social engagements. It could have been worlds away rather than just a handful of miles. He'd always felt that he didn't quite fit in here, but a little charm could go a long way to smoothing over any awkwardness, so he'd developed charm in spades.

After his parents' divorce, he'd split time between living in

Madison during the week and spending every other weekend with his dad out in Macon where he'd moved. Back and forth. But it was better than the fighting he'd had to put up with when his parents had been married. Not that they fought any less, but they certainly had less occasion to do it. He'd grown up to the sound of his parents screaming at each other. Walton Street didn't have people like the Waltons living on it, which is why Dean liked it. It was quiet and peaceful, and no one ever looked at him like he didn't belong.

Home had always been Seth's house more than his own. They'd been friends since elementary school, and that was one thing that had never changed. Seth's mom still lived in that same house. It was just around the corner from his duplex. He'd had the privilege to spend most holidays with them, although he was always sure to wait for an invitation. He didn't want to intrude, but Keely treated him just like another son.

Dean was still single, but he was the kind of single that meant he could take a different woman home every night if he wanted to. He had a few friends with benefits if he ever got lonely. The last thing he wanted to do was end up like his parents, married and bitter as hell that they'd settled for less than they wanted. He didn't think the thing he wanted existed anyway. Might as well enjoy life.

Dean jolted as Lindy stepped in his path. They often walked the same way to work, but their schedules rarely synced. It was a surprise to see her, and he wasn't sure if it was a good surprise. She'd been avoiding him since they'd exchanged some heated words last year. Of course, he'd been avoiding her, too. They had both been pissed, but now Dean was just embarrassed that he'd let her get to him. He stopped to see what she would do. She stopped when she saw him and shot him an appraising look.

"You're not usually up this early," she commented, coolly.

"I could say the same," he said with a shrug. "Your mama okay?"

Lindy softened. It was hard to hate the bastard when he so

clearly loved her mama. "Yeah, she's good. She's perfect."

They fell into step with each other awkwardly. Dean wondered if he should apologize, but the argument was so many months back now that an apology might just be weird. If she wasn't bothered by it, why should he be?

"You alright? You look like you've been crying," Dean said, noticing a trace of tear tracks on her face.

Lindy sighed heavily, annoyed. He was too damn observant for his own good. There had been a few tears after the big announcement. At least, there had been once the laughter had subsided. "Onions. Omelets," she said shortly, waving her hand in dismissal.

"Omelets!" Dean sighed wistfully. He'd had a granola bar for breakfast. He didn't remember buying it so he was pretty sure one of the women who stayed the night had left it there, though he couldn't think which one. "Now I'm hungry."

"You're always hungry," Lindy said with some irritation. She'd known Dean as long as he'd known Seth, since they were little boys tagging along behind her and her friends, annoying them. She had no desire to have an awkward conversation with him this morning. She'd hoped for a little time to herself on the walk to work to think of and plan for the future.

"I've got a healthy appetite," Dean said with a slow, flirtatious grin.

Lindy cut her eyes toward him, picking up on the innuendo. "So I hear," she snorted.

Dean stiffened and nodded, the smile disappearing. Usually, her snarky comments wouldn't have bothered him. Normally, he didn't take what she said to heart, but she'd thrown his reputation in his face last year during their argument. It was the reason he hadn't spoken to her until now. He didn't appreciate the reminder any more than the insinuation. Damn, judgmental harpy, he thought.

Lindy sighed as Dean picked up the pace toward town. She and Dean had always had friction. They'd been arguing since the day Seth had first brought him home to play. They'd just been little boys, and Dean had nearly white-blonde hair then that stuck up in every direction. They'd aggravated the then pre-teen Lindy to distraction. Since then, arguing was just this thing they did. She had to admit, to herself at any rate, that she'd been in the wrong the last time they'd argued. It didn't sit well with her to be wrong in the first place, but she wasn't usually so judgmental. She lengthened her own stride to catch up with him.

"Hey, I'm sorry. That was out of line." Lindy reached out and rested her hand on his arm briefly until he looked at her.

"It's fine," Dean said quietly, shooting her a quick glance.

"It's really not, and I am sorry, Dean."

"Just forget it," he told her. An apology from Lindy was rare enough, particularly a sincere one. "Want some coffee?" He offered his thermos to her in a gesture of peace.

"No. Thanks though. I filled up at Mom's. Plus, I had some when I first got up at four. I think I'm over-caffeinated already," Lindy commented wryly. She thought about how she would handle the switch to decaf. She was about to find out. Now that she'd begun taking the prenatal vitamins and had appointments lined up to speak to the fertility specialist about potential treatments, she was cutting out the caffeine. She wasn't pregnant yet, but if she had her way she would be soon. She wanted to be ready.

"Yeah, same," Dean admitted. "Late shift followed by an early one."

"I didn't think you did that."

"Well, you don't know everything, Lindy Carver," Dean replied with a wolfish grin.

"Hmm," she replied noncommittally. "I've got to head into work. See you," Lindy said, turning toward her studio.

"Later," Dean said with a wave, watching her walk away.

Those long strides sure did eat up the pavement. She always seemed to be in a hurry, but that was just Lindy. All that energy in that willow slim package. He sighed. He remembered watching her as a teenager, his first serious crush. It had embarrassed the hell out of Seth, but Dean had grown out of it. Well, at least they were back on speaking terms. That was something. He headed toward the fire station when he saw Naomi waiting outside. He rolled his eyes and then headed that way, dreading the confrontation. He put on his smoothest smile and walked toward her.

"Well, hey, Naomi! Don't you look pretty as a picture today?"

Chapter 3

"Sorry I'm late," Naomi called out to Elle as she rushed into Brews & Blues.

She knew that waiting for Dean would likely make her late again, but it had been worth it. She'd left her work shirt unbuttoned just enough to show off her ample cleavage and had worn a necklace that drew the eye right down to it. It had been worth it when Dean had taken notice. She'd needed to remind him of what he was missing. With her thick chestnut hair curling down her back and her expertly made-up doe eyes, she knew that she had the girl-next-door look down to a science. Shooting a quick glance over at her boss, she buttoned her blouse back up before Elle could give her hell for it.

"How's Dean doing?" Candace asked with a cool quirk of her brow.

"He's just fine," Naomi said primly.

"If he was interested, you wouldn't have to hang around there," Candace said pointedly.

Naomi ignored her and went to wipe down a couple of the tables. Dean used to come into the coffee shop all the time when they first started seeing each other. She'd flirted with him pretty heavily then. She'd even given him her number on the back of his receipt. That's how it had all started. The texting had been pretty hot and heavy. Well, I guess you'd call it sexting, she thought. He'd taken her out for a drink, and then they'd headed over to his place after. The sex had been hot. Like ridiculously hot. She didn't date a lot of older men. She really went more for guys her own age, but Dean had that sexy firefighter fantasy thing going, which was kind of rarer than most firefighter calendars would lead a girl to believe.

After a few nights of mind-blowing, Earth-shattering sex, he'd stopped returning her calls—or texts—no matter how hot they were. He'd made comments about what a good friend she'd been to him and how busy he was, and that seemed to be that. Naomi went back through it all in her mind. She couldn't quite figure out when or why he lost interest.

But Naomi was no quitter. She kept tabs on his social media accounts. She made sure to park near his work instead of her own so she could walk by every day. And she still dated other men. She even made sure to bring them around town instead of going out in Athens or Atlanta, just to show him she could still have any man she wanted. She had some feelings for him, and she wasn't going to be ignored.

If she'd learned anything from men, it was that showing that you didn't care at all usually worked to bring them back. She'd been steadily ignoring him the last few months—to no avail. Now she wanted to remind him of what he was missing, so she'd shown up in the short skirt with her mouth painted a lush and wet pink and flirted with him just enough to make him think of her before she crossed the road slowly to head into work. She was a year older now, older and wiser. She was ready to remind Dean Walton that she was still here and still interested.

*****

Candace watched Naomi saunter over to wipe the tables and turned around to straighten the bags of coffee beans on the shelf behind her so that she could roll her eyes in private. That girl was going to stalk Dean until he told her that no really means no. She wished one of them would grow up. Candace rolled her shoulders, trying to work out a kink that had settled in sometime around midmorning. She had too much on her plate between problems at home, a full load at school, and working extra shifts to pick up Naomi's slack. Actually, she'd had a conversation with Elle Lewis-Lawson, Brews' owner and manager, this morning about cutting back her hours for the last couple of months of school. Candace didn't want to slack off before finals, not with graduation looming.

Of course, the pain in her shoulders and extending up her neck was probably about Michael. He was, after all, a pain the neck, she thought wryly. She'd decided to cut him loose, and soon. It had gone on far too long, and with graduation and potential career opportunities ahead, she had no interest in letting him continue to drag her down into more debt. She'd meant to do it last year, but then he'd started applying for jobs. She'd had hope he'd get his act together. Of course, he never did. And never would either. At least not as long as she was footing the bills.

"I heard Tammy got engaged over the weekend," she said, making idle chit-chat with a long-time customer while preparing the vanilla latte he'd ordered.

"Thought that girl was never going to get married," he returned with a grin. "Of course, June keeps telling me y'all don't get married anymore quite as early as we did."

Candace kept up the conversation easily as she made the latte and worried a little about the situation with Michael, making a mental note to herself to study at the park rather than at home when the weather was right.

"Probably best," she told him as she handed over the latte and rang up his order. "It'll just save her a divorce."

He barked out a hoarse laugh in agreement that ended in a cough. "You seem to have avoided a messy divorce yourself."

"Well, that's because no man in his right mind would marry me," she told him with a laugh.

Of course, it kind of felt true. She'd thought her current relationship might go the marriage route, but now she was glad it didn't. She cut her eyes over to Naomi who was taking more time daydreaming than bussing those tables. Candace reminded herself that at twenty-two, Naomi was still plenty young. She'd made her own share of mistakes at that age, Michael being one of them.

"If I was younger, I'd marry you myself," he vowed, taking his receipt.

"I think June might have something to say about that," she replied with a warm smile. She loved her customers. She actually loved her job most of the time. When there was a lull, she walked into the kitchen to get a few more pastries for the front display case. Elle was making some notes but then looked up as Candace walked in.

"Is Naomi working the counter?" Elle asked.

"She's out there," Candace said shortly. She had a great working relationship with Elle, but there was no love lost between her and Naomi. She was getting tired of picking up her slack.

"I hope Dean doesn't decide to wash the firetrucks today. The last time he did that I couldn't get the girl to do much of anything productive," Elle said in exasperation.

"It wasn't a bad view," Candace said with a grin.

"I don't disagree," Elle said, her mouth quirking up at the corner. "Just not during our busiest hours. It might have been entertaining for the customers, but it left me short a server." Elle had noticed Candace checking Dean out a time or two. It was only natural, but at least she had the good sense not to take his flirtations seriously. She wished Naomi could have done the same.

"She'll figure it out eventually."

"It would help if he'd just tell her he's not interested," Elle commented. "But Lord knows men rarely seem to do the sensible thing."

"I guess I can't really judge," Candace said uncomfortably.

"You'll leave him when you're ready," Elle said soothingly, looking up from where she'd been writing down supply orders. "I guess Michael still doesn't have a job."

"Nope. But I'm sure he has some new video games to play, so

that's something," Candace said bitterly. "I need to just do it. I don't even know why I'm still holding on."

"Love can be a powerful motivator," Elle commented knowingly. She'd been there, too. Who hadn't?

"I think I need to love me more and him less," Candace observed wearily. "I just miss the way things were."

"So does she," Elle commented, nodding toward Naomi who was looking toward the firehouse and didn't even notice that a customer had walked in.

"Yeah. I guess I should cut her some slack. I'll go out and help," Candace said quietly. She sighed as she moved out to the counter. It was hard to fault Naomi for refusing to let go when she wasn't doing such a bang-up job of it herself, she thought.

*****

Across the street, Dean was getting ready to wash the firetrucks. He pulled them both out and was about to get started when he noticed Seth walking up the street. They'd been friends all their lives, ever since they'd bonded over dinosaurs and race cars in primary school. He grinned and headed his way.

"You're out early," Dean commented.

"I went for a run with Libby," he said with a smile. "I decided to get a jump on the day."

"You picked a good one there," Dean commented. "Too bad I didn't see her first," he said with a grin.

"Well, you can't have them all," Seth said philosophically.

"Speaking of which, I saw your sister this morning."

"Oh yeah? How'd that go?" Seth asked with a raised eyebrow. Dean and Lindy had been having some long-drawn-out fight for a while now. Neither would say what it was about, but every time he asked, he got treated to character assassination of either his best friend or his sister. He'd decided just to enjoy the show and let them work it out.

"We're good now," Dean said shortly. "I think we called a truce."

"Well, with Lindy, that won't last long," Seth reminded him.

"You're probably right," Dean said with a sigh.

"Are you coming to the book signing tonight?"

"What signing?" Dean asked in confusion.

"At Utopia. I told you last week. Beth scored some big deal local author. I gave you the book a week ago," Seth reminded him.

"Yeah, I read it. I forgot that was tonight," Dean said, glad he had the night off but already watching his plans for a lazy evening go up in smoke. "I guess I better go support my best girl."

"Yeah, Mom's counting on it," Seth said with a smile. Dean had flirted with his mom since he was a teenager. "You better hope Naomi doesn't show up."

"I don't think reading is her thing," Dean said with an uncomfortable shrug. "Besides, I talked to her earlier. I think she understands now that I'm not interested."

"Did you tell her that?" Seth asked, impressed.

"Well, not in so many words ..." Dean stopped as Seth let out a long laugh.

"That's what I thought. Good luck with that," Seth told him, patting his shoulder. "I'll be there with Libby if I can get out of that auction in time."

"Lunch later?"

"Yeah, let me know if you want to grab wings or pizza," Seth called as he walked back toward Lost Horizon Antiques.

Chapter 4

Keely unlocked the back door of Utopia Tea, Books, and Gifts and quietly made her way to the kitchen. This was one of her favorite places to be. It had long been her dream to open up a tea room and bookshop in town, but she'd never imagined that the reality would be even better than the idea. She walked into the kitchen and smiled. Amie was already there, making the fresh scones and desserts they would serve today.

"Good morning," Amie said with a warm smile. "I'm adding a new tartlet to the menu, and I'll prep the quiche in a bit."

"We'll likely sell a lot of the chicken salad croissants this week now that you've put them back on the menu," Keely commented, as she took off her coat and went to the counter to grab the kettle. She filled it with water while chatting with Amie about the week's menu and last week's boisterous bridal shower. Amie was an inventive chef, and Keely felt lucky to have found her when she did. She might have started out as an employee, but she'd become a good friend.

While the kettle was heating, Keely checked supplies and wrote out the specials in calligraphy, as Lindy had taught her to do. When the door opened, the tea was already brewing, and Amie had the scones in the oven. "Hey, Beth," Amie called down the hall.

Beth came into the room with the bounce in her step that only morning people could successfully master. It made Keely smile. "You look like you had a good weekend," she commented. "Hot date?"

"Ha! Thanks, but no thanks," she said scrunching up her pert nose. Then, she took a dramatic sniff of the room. "Oh my God, tell me those are the chocolate coconut scones," she said, reaching across the counter and grabbing Amie's hands.

"Girl, you are too much," Amie told her with a laugh. Beth only gripped her hands tighter. "Fine, you're right. I made them." Beth sat back with a grin, and Keely shook her head at both of them.

"You've only been nagging the hair off her head for a week," she commented wryly, pouring for the three of them. They sat down at bar stools at the counter and sipped their tea. They always started the day that way. It was the most relaxed staff meeting that any of them had ever known. Amie brought out a tray of extra scones, including the chocolate coconut ones, and sat them out with clotted cream and lemon curd.

"What books are we promoting this week?" Amie asked. She was the chef, but they all took an avid interest in each other's work.

"We've got a best seller, a local indie release, and the one by the beekeeper I told you about. He should be around later," Beth reminded them.

"Wasn't that a charming book?" Keely asked. "Powerful, too. It wasn't what I was expecting."

"That's the general consensus. We should pack a full house for the signing," Beth told her with a grin.

They were slowly establishing a reputation for being a welcoming atmosphere that could provide significant book sales for authors. The beekeeper lived a little outside town where he kept bees and ran a modest farm. Keely had him slotted to come in around 5 p.m. to start signing a few copies of books and to go over the schedule for the night. Beth had picked his book out as a book club read so the full group would be there for the signing, in addition to members of the public who were interested. Keely had been fielding inquiries all week about the event.

"Abby and Maureen are serving today," Amie told them. "Abby might run just a smidge late after she gets out of class, but Maureen said she could handle the flow for an extra 20 minutes. They'll both pitch in for the signing later, too."

"I can pitch in if I need to if Maureen gets busy," Keely said easily. These days, she mostly acted as hostess and general manager, but she didn't mind serving tables. It gave her a chance to talk to the customers and get to know them.

She was glad that she had opened the tea room. She knew it was a risk. The rent in the historic district was high, and many businesses had tried and failed to make a go of it downtown. Besides, she'd only had the experience of working in the antique shop, which was quite different from running a tea room. Still, she'd enjoyed the experience of going out to tea, and at home, she'd sampled various full leaf teas and recipes to serve with it.

She'd plotted and planned in a little notebook that she kept on hand while she watched her son and waited until he was ready to take over the antique store and leave her free to start a new venture. She'd studied and crunched the numbers and waited until the right building downtown had opened up. She'd dreamed of the day when she would run a tea room and bookstore that could complement rather than compete with other businesses downtown. It would provide an upscale specialty tea experience, and it would also include the first bookstore to open in the area.

She'd had her eye on her niece, Beth, for that spot. Beth brought out the plans for the signing, proving to Keely she'd been the perfect choice for local bookseller extraordinaire. She put it beside her own notebook, a new one now. It was filled with all the plans for the future, plans she'd barely even dreamt of when they'd gotten started. Nearly five years later, it had all worked out better than she could have dreamed. They'd even been written up in a couple of local magazines, and Utopia's reputation had also spread by word of mouth.

"Earth to Keely," Amie said with a grin. Keely looked up to find Amie and Beth watching her curiously. "What are you daydreaming about?"

"Oh, I was a million miles away. I was just thinking how far we've come here."

"Business has gotten a boost since we added the book clubs and author events," Beth pointed out. "And it doesn't hurt to have a damn good chef on hand," she said with a nod to Amie.

"It's a team effort, but today's going to be busy. I guess we better get to it," Amie said with a smile. "Just leave the tea things. I'll take care of that," she told them, shooing them away to get started on the day.

It passed quickly. The bookstore had a steady stream of visitors from locals and tourists, and the tea room was booked fairly solid for most of the day. A small local company had reserved a few tables in the back for an informal business lunch. She had a couple of showers—baby and bridal—and then there were the regular lunches of individuals and small groups.

Abby and Maureen handled serving while Keely played hostess. Amie kept the kitchen running smoothly, and Beth chatted up anyone who came in the door, often convincing them to buy that book she'd noticed they had looked at with interest. By 4:15, they'd ushered the last guest out the door and had started to straighten up. Abby and Maureen had left for a break before their shift later in the evening. Amie was washing dishes in the back with the volume turned up on a country station that had Beth loudly objecting. They argued about music amicably while running through their end of day tasks.

Keely listened to it all with contentment from her office where she was going over her notes. When she heard the knock on the door a few minutes before five, the music had been turned off, and the refreshments for the evening's event were being placed out on tables. Beth had already taken care of gift bags, which they provided at each event, and set up door prizes and was now stacking the author's books on the table to be signed. Keely went to answer the back door where they instructed their authors to enter. She'd worn a simple sheath dress in a soft violet with a gray cardigan and ballet flats. She'd kept her silver hair pulled up through the day in an elegant twist, but she'd pulled it down for a softer, after-hours look.

She'd dyed her hair for years to keep out any sign of aging, but when she crossed the line at fifty, she decided to stop fighting the gray that kept insisting on creeping in. She'd decided to go silver all at once rather than waiting for the streaks to take over. Eight years later, she didn't have to do more than the occasional touch-up. Her skin was still smooth from a combination of good genes and a daily moisturizing routine she'd used since she was a teenager. Her eyes were a bright blue, and her features were sculpted. She'd always thought of them as too sharp as a young girl. Sharp cheekbones, straight nose. She was five eight in her flats and had always been tall and on the slim side, although she'd put on a few pounds in the years after she'd had Seth and Lindy. Still, she was slim enough for her own liking and made sure to walk regularly so that she could eat all of Amie's desserts guilt-free. If she was thicker than she'd been before, it didn't bother her.

She opened the door with a welcoming smile. And everything froze for just a second. The door was open, the warmer air spilling out to mix with the cool. Keely stood eye to eye with Theodore Westerman. She'd seen the book jacket with his photo but hadn't really taken it in with more than a glance. Now that he stood in front of her, she quickly sized him up. They were the same height, and he was wearing a gray tweed jacket and slacks with a gray vest with a light blue button-up shirt underneath.

"Hello." It came out a little too breathy, and she tried to calm herself.

"Hello," he answered back easily, making no move to enter. His hair was full and silver with a few streaks of black still left. He looked like he could be in his sixties or seventies, maybe younger. It was difficult to tell. His eyebrows were thin slashes of black in a tan face with a well-kept, short silver beard. His eyes were dark, a blue that bordered on gray. She took in his small ears and square chin and noticed that he had a woodsy sort of scent that was subtle and not overpowering. She felt her cheeks flush at her frank inspection and the rudeness of keeping him waiting, although in truth it had only been seconds since she'd opened the door.

"Please, come in," she invited, flushing with embarrassment at the way she'd been staring. "I'm Keely Carver, the owner of Utopia." She stretched out a hand to shake his. She felt the warmth and firmness of his grip and found her eyes holding his.

"Theodore Westerman," he said with a shy smile. "I hope I'm not too late."

"Not at all. You're just in time. If you'd like to come through here, I can introduce you to the staff and show you where you'll be setting up. Guests won't start arriving for a while yet, but we're fully booked for the night."

Theodore looked around the large open room with admiration. "It's a beautiful place you have here," he stated simply.

"You should see it in the spring. The garden area is beautiful even now, but it's magnificent then. We're really quite proud of this place, and we're so happy to have you here for a reading." She felt a little more in control, even if the blush hadn't quite left her cheeks.

"I have to admit that I'm a little nervous about that," he said quietly. "I've done signings, of course, but this is all very new still."

"You're welcome to keep the reading short, and you can always take a quick Q&A from the guests and simply talk about your work more informally," she offered. "We've had a few of our authors take that approach. Your book was the pick for our book club, and they've all been simply charmed. They'll just be happy you were so gracious to come out tonight."

He smiled and looked more at ease. She took him around to

meet the staff and then set him up at a table to start signing books. "Would you like any tea? Or coffee perhaps?" Keely asked him as he began.

"Tea would be wonderful. Just whatever you recommend," he said simply. As she walked away, he watched her with undisguised admiration.

"She's lovely, isn't she?" Beth asked him proudly.

"Yes, she is," he admitted, embarrassed that his own observations had been noted.

"It's hard to believe sometimes that she's still single," Beth said innocently, carefully watching Theodore sign his name to another book.

"Hmm," Theodore answered noncommittally, grateful that he hadn't had to find a way to ask.

It always seemed too obvious to inquire after a husband or boyfriend. He'd been widowed in his late thirties and had raised his daughters on his own. He'd always thought he'd remarry, but he never had. He'd dated, of course, but no one really stood out to him. Plus, he'd had his girls to finish raising. They were in their teens when Mandy had passed. After that, he'd become interested in beekeeping and travel. He'd enjoyed his solitude more than he ached for company, and it had been a long time since he'd met anyone with whom he'd felt a spark of connection. He thought back to the handshake with Keely and how it had seemed to warm and pulse between them.

"Here's your tea. I'll just leave it on the burner to keep it warm. Would you like milk or sugar?" Keely asked him, placing a china cup down in its saucer beside him. "Or honey perhaps?" she asked with a smile. She sat his own farms' honey on the table beside him.

"Milk and honey, please," he said with a smile.

"We've been selling your honey out of the gift shop, and I think it will sell like hotcakes tonight with the book. One of our door prizes will include a personalized signed copy of your book, a large jar of honey, and a set of our teacups." Keely paused. "I know you must hear this a lot, but I was completely charmed by your book. I couldn't put it down," she admitted.

"I never intended to write a book, to be honest. I started making notes when I began working with the bees, and it just kind of flowed from there," Theodore explained.

"They're really lining up out there," Beth announced.

"That's our cue to open up," Keely said. "Are you ready?"

"Do I have a choice?"

"You'll be great," Keely told him warmly and then headed to the door while Theodore watched her go with a bemused smile.

He really should just ask her to dinner, he thought to himself. If he could stand up and talk to a room full of people, he could gather the courage to invite her out on a date.

Chapter 5

Lindy was one of the first guests to arrive. She went over and introduced herself to Theodore and shook his hand. They had a short conversation before she went to find her mother in the kitchen helping Amie with the tea.

"Now *that* is a silver fox!" Lindy declared.

"What?" Keely asked distractedly.

"Theodore Westerman, silver fox," Lindy declared dramatically.

Keely looked over at her curiously. "I thought you were done dating older men." She wondered if Theodore had flirted with her very attractive daughter. She wouldn't have blamed him. Perhaps he was just one of those men who made every woman feel beautiful and seen.

"I didn't say I wanted to date him, but he is gorgeous. Just look at him." They stood in the doorway to the kitchen and watched him chatting with Beth and another of the book club members. "Besides, he was quick to mention he has a daughter about my age so I don't think he's one of those older men who date younger women."

"That's a rarity," Amie said behind them. "Maybe you should ask him out, Keely," she suggested.

"Yeah, Mom. You should get on that before someone else does. The book club is practically salivating out there," Lindy told her frankly.

"You're being ridiculous," Keely said shortly. "He's a very nice man who wrote a beautiful book, and we're going to be polite." She walked out of the kitchen carrying a pot of tea for one of the tables. Behind her, Amie and Lindy exchanged a smile.

"Did you notice she was blushing?" Amie asked her.

"I did notice. It would be nice if she dated more. And he is hot."

"They'd make a stunning couple," Amie agreed. "Think she'd go out with him?"

"Oh yeah. I hope he's smart enough to ask her. Wait—he *is* single, right?" Lindy checked.

"Widowed, I believe," Amie informed her. "The book is good. Did you read it?"

"Of course. Between Beth and Mom, I couldn't escape it. But it's good. Not at all what I expected. And neither is he. I think he might be a little shy."

Lindy watched him glancing over at her mother and wondered if her mother even noticed. She dated, but there hadn't been anyone serious in years. Or even regular. Her mother was beautiful, and more than that, she was kind. Lindy had held out hope that her mom would find someone to love her in the way that she deserved, but the more she dated, the fewer hopes she had about men in general. Which she knew was even more pessimistic than usual.

Still, maybe it would happen for her mom. She'd given up on finding it for herself. She went and got a glass of the Bee's Knees they were serving in addition to tea. It was a Prohibition Era drink made from gin, lemon juice, and honey from Westerman's farm. It was good, a mix of both sweet and sour. She looked around the room at the gathering crowd and quirked an eyebrow when she saw Dean walk in, wearing that leather bomber jacket that would have looked ridiculous on almost anyone else. How he could be cold in this weather she would never understand! It was sixty degrees out. Long sleeves would have sufficed. She crossed the room.

"I didn't think I'd see you here," Lindy said dryly.

"Beth talked Seth into the book. He read it reluctantly and then talked me into it. Anyway, I liked it. Plus, your mom's sweet on me," Dean explained with a grin. "I had to come by and see my best girl," he said loudly as Keely walked by, pausing to kiss his cheek and pull him in for a long hug.

"Lindy, you get my boy here a drink and maybe grab a broom from the back closet to keep the girls at bay," Keely said with a laugh, walking off to greet another group who had just arrived.

"Want a drink?" Lindy asked dutifully.

"What's that you're drinking?" Dean asked.

"It's the Bee's Knees," she told him.

"That's cute, but what's the drink called?" he asked with a grin.

"Ha. Ha. Ha," Lindy said sarcastically. "Here." She thrust her glass at him. He took a sip and then gave it an appreciative look.

"Not bad," he commented.

Lindy reached to take her glass back. "And you can get your own."

Dean tried not to notice her lips drinking from the same spot on the glass where he'd just taken a drink. Those kinds of thoughts were not productive. He tried to focus on something else as he obediently poured himself a glass.

"How were the classes today?" he asked curiously. He'd never taken one of her painting classes, but he'd heard enough about them around town. Naomi had taken one with some friends and enjoyed it.

"Hectic," Lindy said, shortly. Then she softened. "We had a group in from the primary school. We did storytime and then let them paint little canvases so it was very messy. We actually ended up with more clean-up time afterward than prep time beforehand, but it was fun. They were really sweet. We didn't have an evening session since it would have conflicted with this, but I've been getting ready for one tomorrow night." She looked over at him, curiously. "Put out any fires today?"

"No, it was pretty tame. Not even a single cat to rescue from a tree," he joked with a heavy sigh, shaking his head. "I'm going out to the school in a few weeks for a demonstration. Actually, working with the little kids is one of my favorite things. They always get a kick out of it."

"What kid doesn't love a fire truck?" Lindy commented. "You don't seem the type to like working with kids. I figured it'd cramp your style."

"Well, like I said. You don't know everything, Lindy." She shrugged, and he watched her walk off absently to strike up a conversation with the author.

Dean watched the two of them critically. He was just Lindy's type. Older. He figured it was probably because her father had never been around, but he still didn't like it. He watched Theodore Westerman's slow smile at something Lindy said and decided that the book hadn't been that great after all. Lindy laughed, and Dean felt his nerves jump. Never mind her, he thought, looking around at the growing crowd in the tea room.

People were milling about, and the crowd was primarily female with a few men scattered throughout. He thought he saw Naomi come in. She wasn't a reader, at least she wasn't when they had dated, so if she was here it was for stalking purposes. He rolled his shoulders in frustration and looked for a distraction. He caught sight of Beth's red hair disappearing into the kitchen. He followed behind her.

"Hey, Beth. How's it going?" he asked with his best, most charming smile.

"Dean," she said coolly. She still hadn't forgiven him for that time he'd invited her to the movies and then flirted with literally every woman he'd spoken to on the way in and even out of the theater. She'd thought it was a date, but apparently, she was just a stand-in, a friend, a warm body to sit beside his own at the theater. Of course, he and Seth both had tried to smooth things over with her, but she was still hurt and embarrassed by the whole thing. "The reading is taking place out there." She pointed out of the kitchen dramatically.

"I thought I'd come say hello to my favorite bookseller," he said with a smile, leaning on the counter.

"You mean you're avoiding Naomi," Beth said bluntly. "I saw her come in right before you followed me back here."

"She's crazy," Dean said, dismissively. "I'm going to hide until I can escape," he said with a laugh.

Beth turned and looked at him seriously. "She's not crazy actually. She's just really young. She probably believed you meant whatever it is you said." She sailed out of the kitchen on that note, and Dean sat down on a stool at the counter and thought about it.

He sighed. He never lied to the women he dated. He told them exactly what he was about: He just wanted to have fun, he didn't want anything serious, and he wasn't really into the relationship thing. The problem is that most of them heard what they wanted to hear. He poured another drink and waited for the crowd to settle down. He'd hear this guy speak, and then he was getting out of there before he had to endure another awkward conversation with Naomi.

"Well, hey, you," he heard from behind him. Shit, he thought. He turned around slowly.

"Hey, Naomi," he said cautiously. "I don't think they allow guests back here." She looked at him pointedly. "Oh, well, I was just back here talking to Beth."

She frowned, her perfectly groomed eyebrows drawing together. "Are you and Beth seeing each other?" she asked coolly.

"No, we're just friends." He shrugged uncomfortably, as Naomi smiled and moved closer.

"Well, then," she said, her manicured fingers tracing a path up his arm. She leaned toward him in what she likely assumed was a seductive manner, and might even have come across as seductive had he been remotely interested, when they heard a throat clear at the door. Lindy stood in the doorway with one hip cocked and her arms crossed.

"Beth sent me to tell you that the coast was clear, and Theodore is about to speak," she said shortly.

"The coast was not clear," Dean said wryly, extracting himself from Naomi's half embrace while she shot evil looks toward Lindy. "Anyway, thanks for letting me know. I'll just head out now. Later, Naomi," he said, backing out of the kitchen in relief.

"Did it occur to you that you were interrupting something?" Naomi hissed at Lindy.

"You embarrassing yourself? Yeah, I caught that," Lindy said with a roll of her eyes. She wasn't normally mean, but Naomi managed to work every nerve that she had. "Dean's not interested. If he was, you wouldn't be able to keep him off you."

"You're just jealous!" Naomi spat out. "You want him, and he just ignores you."

Lindy looked at her and burst out laughing. "Okay, sure," she said sarcastically. "That must be it."

She walked out of the kitchen with a smile and saw Dean settling in between two young women on the back row. They were both turned toward him, and he had on his biggest smile. She rolled her eyes, something she did often when Dean was around, and turned back to the audience. She headed over to sit with her mother and didn't notice Dean watch her walk to the front and take a seat.

Chapter 6

Dean showed up at Seth's early on Saturday morning. He'd talked Seth into coming out to help him with the lake house for the day. They were going to get an early start so Seth could spend the rest of the day with Libby. They were going to do something overly adorable like go on a hayride or roast marshmallows together. If he was honest with himself, he could admit that he envied their relationship. It hadn't been easy for either of them. They'd met when Libby was still going through a divorce, and Seth had massive baggage where relationships were concerned. There was a moment when he was sure they weren't going to make it. But they had.

Libby opened the door in her running clothes with a huge mug of coffee. She passed the mug to Dean with a smile, "I figured you could use this." Even in her running clothes and no makeup, Libby was pretty, Dean thought. Her long dark hair was pulled back in a braid, and she already had her earbuds in for her run. "Sorry I can't stay and hang out, but I was just heading out to run." She leaned over to kiss his cheek as Seth came downstairs.

"Just remember that's my girl you're kissing," Seth said loudly as he walked downstairs with a grin.

"Hey, she's kissing me. I can't help the ladies think I'm irresistible," he winked at Libby and grinned at Seth.

"Try," Seth said shortly. "And where's my coffee?" he asked Libby, pulling her in for a kiss.

"On the table," she said with a laugh. "Y'all are distracting me. I need to run. Don't work too hard. I packed your lunch and left it on the table, too." She smiled at Dean, gave Seth another kiss, and headed out the door.

"Let's go see what she made us," Seth said with a grin.

"She made us a picnic?" Dean asked, walking in and looking at the wicker basket. "Do we have to eat it out of that?" he asked, looking at the picnic basket skeptically.

Seth smiled. "It's sweet. Anyway, it won't wound your masculinity to eat out of a picnic basket. Besides, I'm pretty sure there's chicken salad in here. And thermoses of what might be sweet tea. Plus, chips and cookies. I know she made the cookies. She swatted my hand when I tried to eat them last night."

"You've got a good one there," Dean said, sitting down and drinking deeply from his mug. She'd even made his coffee the way he liked it. He sighed, happily. "I've got to be honest with you. Things don't work out between you two, I'm asking her out."

Seth laughed. "I'll keep that in mind. Hey, if you're ready for a relationship, Libby could set you up with one of her friends," he offered over Dean's look of annoyance.

"Stop trying to pair us all up. I don't mind the single life. I got numbers even at that book club thing the other night," Dean reminded him. "Plenty of fish in the sea, brother."

"Yeah, I heard about that from Libby. I had inventory at the store to do so I missed it, but my mom snagged me a signed copy. I heard the author was nice," Seth commented.

"Yeah, your sister sure did think so. Just her type. Looked like he was pushing retirement," Dean said in disgust, draining the last of his coffee.

"I talked to Lindy yesterday, and she didn't say anything about him. But you know she's always been tight-lipped when it comes to dating," Seth said with a shrug. "I think she dates in her own age group these days, but who knows with her."

"She say anything about walking in on and me and Naomi?" Dean asked curiously.

"Don't tell me you were hooking up with Naomi at my mom's bookstore!" Seth said in surprise.

"No, I was ducking Naomi when she cornered me in the kitchen," Dean said with a roll of his eyes. "So, there I was, hiding in the kitchen …" Dean began with a grin.

*****

Lindy stretched out in bed with a sigh. It was early, but it was going to be a full day. The studio had parties booked this afternoon and evening. She'd lead one and help out with the other. She turned over on her side and wondered if she should go ahead and start the nursery. You know, just in case. It was early, but she could definitely get the painting part out of the way. She didn't want to invest in a crib and everything just yet. If she wasn't able to get pregnant, she'd adopt, and that might mean an older child. She was ready. God, she'd been ready for years now.

She remembered the first time she'd realized she wanted a baby. She'd found herself daydreaming about a family, the kind she'd never had. Her mom had been great, but she'd always envied the families where there were two parents. Her grandfather had been like a dad, and when he'd died, when Lindy was only eleven, she'd been heartbroken. Her mom had quietly stepped in for the father-daughter dances or coerced her uncle into taking her, but she'd gone from not missing a dad in her life at all to realizing how much her grandfather had done to fill that void.

Lindy sighed. Having a child on her own wasn't the original plan, but she was tired of waiting. She could spend all this time looking for a partner and miss the baby boat. And who knew if there was a Mr. Right out there for her at all? It didn't look that way.

She'd thought Tyler was the one if she were honest with herself. She and Tyler had started dating just after she'd turned thirty-two. They'd met at one of those school art shows that her alma mater occasionally hosted for up and coming artists. She'd had a few drinks and then wandered around the gallery. There were sculptures she knew were made by Damian, the artist she'd come to support. She looked them over and then walked around, silently assessing the art on display. She liked to think that her own art was good, but what she really loved was teaching. She had just opened up the painting studio a couple of years before, and things seemed to be going well.

She'd nearly run into Tyler when she'd taken a couple of steps back from a painting that she couldn't quite decide if she liked. She'd spilled her drink on him and clumsily apologized. He'd smiled at her with that flashing grin and insisted on getting her another drink. He was taller than her by a few inches, even in heels, and he had thick black hair and dark eyes. He was pale and brooding with a beard that was longer than what she usually found attractive on a man. The smile changed his face entirely, and she'd been drawn to him. She'd noticed the sleeves of artful tattoos and admired them as they talked.

He was a tattoo artist who was studying art part-time and had a friend whose work was on display. They'd talked for hours into the night—first leaving for dinner and then going out for drinks. Over the next weekend, they'd spent time not talking at all. She'd passed the weekend in his loft, getting out of bed only long enough to answer the door for takeout or jump into a hot shower together. After that, they were inseparable.

They'd dated a couple of years, and everything looked like it was moving in a serious direction. The dreams of a family started to include Tyler. The more she wanted that kind of permanence, the less interested he seemed. When he'd finally left, after distancing himself for months, Lindy had been heartbroken. Since then, she'd only dated intermittently. Lately, she just hadn't been interested in making the effort. All of the men that she met either had kids already or didn't want any at all. Then there were the men interested purely in a hook-up, and Lindy was tired of sex without the slightest hint of intimacy.

She sighed. She tried not to think about Tyler. She hadn't heard from him in a few years now. She'd blocked him on social media just to keep herself from checking up on him. When friends tried to mention what he was up to, she steered the conversation away. She just didn't want to know. She'd been in love with him, and she wasn't sure if she was still. She only knew that whatever they had was over.

Lindy slowly got out of bed and decided to head into town for coffee today. She silently prayed that Naomi wouldn't be at Brews. She had no desire to have her coffee spit in, and she was sure there was no love lost there after the run-in at the book signing. Hopefully, Candace or Elle would take—and make—her order. Her mother was having breakfast with her friend Vera, and Libby would be out for a run about now. Lindy thought she'd stop by and see if she could interest Beth in coming along for a cup. She'd probably be up and out walking Mr. Darcy if she wasn't at home.

Beth was her cousin, but they were also close friends, despite the age difference. They were in agreement that the single life was preferable to a bad relationship, and Beth had chosen pet ownership with her little bull terrier Mr. Darcy over chasing Mr. Right. She decided to walk over and see if she could talk her into an early cup of coffee and a walk.

Chapter 7

Beth woke up early to take Mr. Darcy outside. She stood at the back door of her home and watched him run around the small fenced-in area, looking for the perfect spot to do his business. She watched him consider and discard several options before finding a spot that suited him. Beth rolled her eyes and grinned. She kept an eye on him while he made his morning rounds. He'd been known to be a flight risk, although she still hadn't found the hole in the fence that he escaped through each time. She wondered sometimes if he'd managed to tunnel his way out under a bush or something. She was tired of getting calls from the neighbors that he'd escaped again and wreaked havoc in someone's garden in the five minutes that she'd gone inside to make coffee. So, she watched and waited and then called him in with a treat.

When the doorbell rang, she quirked her eyebrows in puzzlement. Early morning visitors were a rarity. It could be her friend Jamie, stopping in to pick up the jacket he'd forgotten last night, but usually, he'd just grab it later or she'd take it by his work at the antique shop with Seth. When she opened the door and saw Lindy on the other side, she cocked her head inquisitively.

"What brings you out so early?"

"I need coffee I didn't make. Want to run over to Brews with me? If you want to bring Mr. Darcy, I could grab the coffee. We could take it over to the park," Lindy suggested.

"That sounds great. Let me just get his leash. Come on in while I throw on some shoes. I'll just grab a light jacket." The weather was slowly getting colder, and mornings tended to be the coolest part of the day.

"How were the book sales the other night?"

"They were great. We almost sold out of the title, and we sold a jar of honey with almost every book. We had to send him home with another order," Beth said with glee.

"I thought he was really interesting," Lindy said casually.

"Ha! You mean hot!" Beth laughed. "Yeah, he was eye candy for sure. But the talk was great, too. I'm just glad it went so well. I kind of thought he was interested in your mom," Beth said with a smile.

"Is that so? Hmm ..." Lindy thought about it. "Think he asked her out?"

"I may or may not have mentioned she was single. You know, in case he was wondering," Beth said with a sly smile.

"Oh my God. Are you trying to pimp out my mom?" Lindy asked with a laugh.

"Hey, he's attractive; she's attractive. And he's literate. Laugh all you want, but I've dated a lot of men who never read anything more than their Twitter accounts so an actual reader ranks up there pretty high for me. Plus, I caught her checking him out."

"It would be nice if she met a good man. She hasn't really dated much in the last few years," Lindy said thoughtfully.

She wondered, not for the first time, if her mother might have liked to remarry or have more kids. It was part of the reason she had decided to go ahead and have a baby on her own. Her mom was young when Zeke had left. She could have had a big family if she'd wanted to, but then no one else ever really stayed in the picture. Lindy admitted that she had been a handful after her grandfather died, and a single mom raising two young children wasn't exactly in high demand in the dating world. Still, she'd dated regularly but not seriously for some time.

"I'm perfectly happy with Mr. Darcy here, but I do love a good love story," Beth said with a grin as they headed over to Brews & Blues. Mr. Darcy cocked his head at the sound of his name. "Good boy," she told him affectionately. "Speaking of which, how are Seth and Libby?"

"They're good. They seem happy now. Libby's been slowly moving in, but I think she practically lives over at his house anyway. They're just waiting until her lease is up to make it official, but that should be by the end of next month. It's good to see Seth so happy."

"I really like Libby. I'm glad they worked it out." They were both silent for a minute, thinking of the months when Seth and Libby had parted ways. They had all been surprised by how swiftly it had happened and how long it had taken them to find their way back.

"So, did I tell you I caught Naomi and Dean making out in the kitchen at the signing?" Lindy asked.

"No! That can't be right. Dean told me he was literally hiding from her," Beth said in confusion.

"Huh. Well, they were awfully cozy when I walked in." Lindy remembered that surge of annoyance when she saw Naomi all but throwing herself at Dean. She thought back and remembered the look of frustration on his face, but she'd assumed at the time that he'd been bothered by the interruption rather than by Naomi herself. "Naomi hates me."

"Naomi hates anyone she thinks is in competition for Dean. She gave me a word of warning when I came out of the kitchen." Beth laughed. "I hate to tell her, but Dean is not interested in me." She nearly blushed when she thought about the date that wasn't a date. God, she'd been a fool!

"Are you interested in him?"

"No, Dean's not my type. It's not even the fact that he dates around so much," Beth began.

"You mean sleeps around," Lindy interrupted.

"Well, yeah, that, too. But I don't judge anyone for that. It's not any of my business. But we don't really vibe on the same level, you know? I mean, he's not exactly going to drink tea and read with me or curl up and watch an old movie. We're not really into the same things at all," Beth said frankly. "I'd like someone who was interested in doing some of that with me."

Lindy thought about how Jamie did those things with her but kept her peace. They claimed to just be friends, but Lindy wondered. Still, it wasn't her business after all, and she wasn't about to play matchmaker with two people perfectly able to determine who they wanted to date and who they didn't. She shrugged.

"I can see that. Common interests can get you pretty far." She thought about her relationship with Tyler. They'd both been artists, although of a different type. She'd loved his moody intensity and knew that they shared it. It made their fights rough, but the making up was spectacular enough to clear the dark mood for a while. Still, common interests and even chemistry hadn't been enough.

"Yeah, but common interests can be hard to find." She sighed. "Do you want to go in and grab my coffee since I've got Mr. Darcy?" Beth asked. She noticed Lindy look inside first.

"Um, Naomi's on duty. Think you could grab the coffee, and I could hang out with the dog?" Lindy asked. "That girl will spit in my drink if you say it's for me."

Beth laughed but agreed. "Just hold on tight to the leash. I'll be right back. I'll just say it's for Seth or something, but head over there where she can't see you so my coffee doesn't get spit in, too." She sauntered in with a wide grin while Lindy walked a little further down the block with Mr. Darcy. She sat down on a bench and patted his head. He immediately dropped to the ground to expose his belly.

"You are a good dog," Lindy told him.

"What are you doing, Lindy Carver? Beth manage to rope you in as a dog walker?" Seth asked her as he walked up the sidewalk with Dean.

"She's getting me coffee," Lindy said. "Naomi's on shift, and I didn't want her to spit in mine." She looked over at Dean evenly.

Seth laughed. "Okay, I get it. Well, I'm leaving Dean out here so

I can go in and pick up some muffins before we head out. We're on our way to the lake in a bit, and I'm still starving."

"Does Libby not feed you?" Lindy asked.

"Number one, you'd be the first to tell me that's sexist."

Lindy laughed.

"And number two, she already packed us lunch so I can't have her making breakfast as well. And before you say anything, I'm taking her out for dinner tonight."

"Fair enough," Lindy said, leaning back on the bench. "Just keep in mind that Beth is telling Naomi the coffee is for you so try not to ruin her cover. Say you forgot to ask for the muffins and bring me my coffee on the way out," she said with a grin.

"You women sure are complicated." Seth walked off with a sigh.

Dean sat down on the bench beside Lindy. "Well, hey there, Mr. Darcy," he said, giving the dog a quick stroke. Mr. Darcy turned over again to show his belly, stretching his paws in the air. "Is Naomi giving you trouble?" he asked Lindy evenly.

"Not any more than she's giving you and with considerably less reason," Lindy said calmly. "You're just going to have to tell her you're not interested."

"I don't want to hurt her feelings," Dean explained.

"Why do men think lying doesn't hurt our feelings? Look, if you're not interested, you're allowed to say just that. You don't have to protect us from feelings. And the girl is damn near obsessed so you aren't doing her any favors by letting her hold out hope," Lindy told him.

"Jealous, Lindy?" Dean asked with a grin.

"What, of your stalker? Not a bit," she said wryly, reaching a hand down to pat Mr. Darcy. Her hand brushed against Dean's. She moved it quickly and didn't notice Dean carefully sit up and look at her. Now wasn't that interesting, he thought.

"So, what's going on with you and Westerman?" Dean asked

casually, sitting back and stretching his arm over the seat.

"What, you mean the writer?" Lindy asked in confusion. She sat up and turned toward him. "Nothing. Why?"

"Well, I noticed you chatting him up, and he seemed like your type."

Lindy rolled her eyes. "You didn't seem to have any trouble collecting numbers at the same event as I recall," she shot back.

Dean grinned. So, she'd noticed that, huh? Very interesting.

"I surely didn't. But I'm pretty sure Westerman collected more than I did," Dean said, needling her.

"So what if he did?" Lindy shot back. "Why does it bother you?"

"No reason. And I didn't say it bothered me. I was just thinking out loud." Dean watched Lindy as she settled back in the seat with a huff. She didn't even notice at first that she was leaning back into the arm he'd settled around the back of the bench. He watched her in amusement and decided to test out a theory. He scooted a little bit closer to her.

"What are you doing?" Mr. Darcy raised his head up at her sharp tone and circled around to the other side of the bench where he stretched out and closed his eyes.

"Not a thing. So how are you doing these days, Lindy?" He leaned a little toward her.

"Fine. Same as usual. Why are you acting so weird?" She shifted in her seat. She seemed to notice suddenly that his arm was nearly around her, and he was so close she could see just how green his eyes were under his lashes. His hair was getting long, and he was still wearing the trim beard he'd started to grow when the weather turned cooler. It changed his face and made him seem older somehow. She looked away.

"I'm not acting weird, Lindy." He grinned at her, watching her discomfort and the careful way she scooted forward and away from him. He saw Seth coming out of the coffee shop and withdrew his arm. "I was just being interested is all," he explained to her.

"A little too interested," Lindy huffed out under her breath, rolling her shoulders. Dean's grin stretched wider. He'd heard what she said, but he stood up to say hello to Beth and to pass Lindy the coffee Seth was gingerly carrying.

"Well, she didn't throw us out on our ear, but I'm not sure we were entirely convincing," Seth told them. "She asked about you," he said to Dean.

Dean rolled his eyes. "What did you say to her?"

"Oh, I told her I'm sure you'd be giving her a call, pretty girl like that." At Dean's exasperated sigh, he said, "I'm kidding. I told her you were fine, just busy with work. You know, the usual line." Beth and Lindy exchanged an eye roll.

"Well, we've got stuff to do," Dean began.

"And muffins to eat," Seth concluded holding up the box. "You ladies want one before we go?"

"You don't have to ask me twice," Lindy told them, reaching in to take a double mocha muffin.

"We don't have to ask you once," Dean muttered, earning a dirty look from Lindy, which made him grin.

"I'm just going to relieve you of this peanut butter one so I can share with Mr. Darcy. Y'all have fun now," Beth told them and waved them on their way. They laughed and walked to Dean's truck while Beth and Lindy headed downtown.

Chapter 8

"Hey, what are you doing right now?" Nina's voice down the line was the verbal equivalent of jumping up and down with enthusiasm.

"Looking at donors," Lindy said absently.

She was just starting to really look through the cryobank website that the clinic had directed her to during last week's appointment. The process was truly fascinating. She was able to read full health reports from donors, listen to interviews, and even see their baby pictures. She could choose what qualities she wanted and simply complete the process from there.

"Wow. Okay, I wasn't expecting that," Nina said with a laugh. "So, you're definitely doing this?"

"I'm definitely doing it. They said I'm good, and I've got my cycle down to a science right now. I've even got an ovulation tracker on my phone." Her fertility wasn't the problem, and in all fairness, they said she probably had a few years left if she wanted to wait. That was the point though. She didn't want to wait. She was ready now.

"Damn, girl. So, you start ovulating and your phone plays Let's Get It On or something?" Nina asked, fascinated.

"Um, no. It's I'll Make Love to You," Lindy said without a hint of humor in her voice. When she heard her friend gasp, she started laughing. "I'm kidding, Nina. It just sends me an alert. But I'll have an appointment set up on one of my cycles, just as soon as I pick a donor."

"Like Tinder for baby daddies? Do you get to swipe left or right?" The amusement in her voice brought a smile to Lindy's face. She might as well find the humor in the whole thing.

"Something like that."

"Are you nervous?"

"A little. It's a little daunting. I mean, I won't have a partner to hold my hand through the whole thing. I guess I always thought I would." It would just be her and the baby bump. Not that her family wouldn't help, but the responsibility would rest solely on her shoulders.

"I'll hold your hand," Nina said stoutly.

"Honestly, I'm not worried about it. So, what's up anyway? You sound like you're over the moon."

"Okay, get this. You know the new guy I'm dating?" Lindy didn't have time to confirm before Nina was moving on. "He's got to work this weekend, but he said I could come to the gig on Friday. Come with me?"

"You're going to ditch me the second you see him," Lindy pointed out, closing the laptop with a firm click and getting up to get ready for work.

"I won't," she said earnestly, but Lindy knew that was a lie, however well-meaning. "And the band might be great."

"Or it might be awful," Lindy pointed out.

"But the drinks will be good," Nina wheedled.

"You have a point. And my drinking days are very nearly done," she said quietly. "For a while anyway."

"Consider it a last hurrah. Besides, it's not like you've picked a donor and can do the turkey baster bit."

"Oh my God, Nina," Lindy chuckled. "Like I told my mom, no turkey basters. This isn't a Pinterest project or whatever."

"Fine. Friday. Don't forget."

"I won't."

She'd been hoping for a quiet Friday in, but going out with Nina was guaranteed to be fun all the way up until the moment she was ditched for the new boyfriend. Of course, she could always pick someone up herself, but she'd just been tired of the whole thing lately, and "I'm about to get intrauterine insemination" didn't really make great first date conversation.

As she prepared the sample canvases at the studio, she thought about the profiles she'd read. Maybe she'd go with a donor with musical talent since she could sing but couldn't play a note. She definitely wanted to find a donor who seemed intelligent and reasonably attractive. She wasn't worried about height. She had that from her own side of the family. Her number one concern was to find someone healthy who would give her child the best possible chance at a healthy life.

She reminded herself that it didn't matter what qualities her child was born with; she'd love that baby just the same. Her friend Marnie, Seth's high school sweetheart, had asked if she was considering more than one child, but right now Lindy had decided just to try the one. If she could handle it, maybe a sibling would be in the cards down the road. She just wasn't ready to decide.

Her mom had been a peach about it. She'd offered to help in any way she could. The process wasn't really very expensive, at least not compared to adoption or to artificial insemination, which she hoped to avoid. Keely didn't seem to be creeped out by the scientific factor, and she'd even made a secret Pinterest board to share nursery ideas. They'd talked about it privately, but Lindy knew that she would soon have to tell Seth.

That was going to be awkward, but she wanted to be open about what she was doing and why. She knew Libby would understand. After all, she'd had her own fertility challenges in the last few years. She cringed at the thought of explaining it to her brother. It was going to be unavoidably awkward. Lindy went through the workday on autopilot, considering when she should tell him. It would have to be soon. She wanted to pick out a donor within the next couple of months so she could start the process.

*****

Keely sat in her office in the back of the tea room reviewing a few suggested menus Amie had left in her box. She also had a box of teacups Jamie over at Lost Horizon had salvaged for her from an estate sale. Seth had told him to send any over to her first so she could pick what she wanted to use, and they could sell the rest at the store.

She'd loved Lost Horizon Antiques. It had saved her when Zeke had left so casually. Her father had sat her down while she was weeping buckets and helped her figure out a budget and how much money she would need to bring in to survive. Then he'd asked her to help out around the store, just until she found what she wanted to do. It had saved her. She'd enjoyed managing it, and her father left it in her capable hands. When he died almost a decade later, he willed the place to her.

Her mother Olivia had been quietly disappointed when Zeke had left. She'd always found him charming, and he had been kind to her. She hadn't offered any advice, but she'd quietly hoped that Keely would be able to find a father for her kids if Zeke would grant her a divorce. Oh, he granted one alright. He ran off with his secretary and remarried later. She'd even heard they had a big family out in Arizona where they'd gone. That was the last thing she'd heard, some years back from a mutual friend. Keely's mother had spent her life suffering from one ailment or another, but it was cancer that finally got her in the end. She'd passed only a couple of years before her husband Graham's heart attack. She'd gone as quietly as she'd lived, in her own bed at home where she'd spent so much of her life.

Keely held the fragile teacups in her hands and remembered her mother. Her father had been her rock. He'd been the one to show up to her school plays and to sit at the football games by her side. He'd encouraged her and even given her a part-time job in the store during school so she'd have a little extra money to spend. They'd lived comfortably but not extravagantly. Her father had inherited an antebellum house from his mother's side of the family and then the business from his father. They lived modestly, a large portion of their income going to keep the house in order and much of the rest going to help her mother's failing health. Most of Keely's memories from childhood were of her father.

But the teacups made her think of her mother. She'd loved them. She'd held them in her hand, the teacups as fragile as her own failing body, and taught Keely how to brew tea. She made herbal tea from the garden she tended when she was feeling able, and she taught Keely to love and appreciate the art. On a good day, Olivia Sanderson would even cut up small tea sandwiches and bake cookies and serve them on an elaborate tea tray Graham had found for her at an estate sale.

Having tea with her mother was one of Keely's fondest memories. When she'd opened Utopia, she'd felt deeply connected to her mother. She also felt like passing on her father's business to Seth was the right thing to do. The store would continue as it always had in Seth's capable hands. He'd idolized his grandfather and had loved the store since he was small. It was nice to know he would continue it, and perhaps one day a child of his own would take it over.

She'd been thinking about children a lot, of course. She was excited that Lindy wanted to start a family, but she was also worried about her little girl. She'd always been headstrong, and Keely had hoped that she would find a partner to share her life. She knew from experience that being single and raising children could be wonderful, but it was also very difficult. There were many nights over the years of raising her kids that Keely envied those happy, nuclear families—those women with partners who didn't have to carry the full load on their own.

Of course, she knew plenty of women who still did it all, even with a partner available to help. But she had spent a number of years hoping to find someone to fit that role. There had been a few contenders, but none had seemed like they would make good fathers for Lindy and Seth. She didn't want them to have a stepdad who would treat them like some other man's children. She had hoped she would find someone who could love them like they were his own. She never did, but she'd built a happy life in spite of it. Her children had a happy childhood and the stability the store provided. It had been enough.

Keely heard the knock at the door and looked up distractedly. In the doorway, Theodore Westerman held a bouquet of wildflowers. He smiled when she looked up, and she invited him in.

"I don't want to interrupt your day, but I wanted to thank you for hosting my book signing. I don't think I've ever sold so many books in one place, and so many pots of honey were sold that Beth sent me home with another order. This is just a small way of saying thanks. They came from my garden." Keely took them from his hands with a smile.

"That's so kind of you! It's completely unnecessary, but I appreciate it." Theodore thought that her voice sounded like the honey he loved, slow and smooth.

"I left bouquets for your staff with Beth," he added. Keely tried not to feel disappointed that he hadn't thought only of her. After all, it was a sweet gesture. He was standing in her office dressed more informally today with a pair of slacks and a long-sleeved shirt with a sweater vest. His shoes looked more worn than polished as if they saw a day's work rather than a night of book signings.

"That was very sweet of you," Keely told him. "Can I get you a cup of tea? Or coffee if you would prefer?" she offered, hoping he might stay a few minutes longer.

"I'm afraid I can't stay. I have a few errands to run before I have to get back to the farm." He looked at her steadily for a minute, summoning his courage. It was now or never. "Would you like to have dinner with me this weekend? Friday, perhaps?" he asked, holding her eyes with his.

"Yes, I would," Keely answered, surprised at her own forthrightness and not hesitating for a second. She'd said it calmly, but she could feel the heavy thump of her heart inside her chest. She was still holding the flowers and could feel the slow blush light her cheeks.

"Would Park Bistro suit? I can reserve us a table any time you'd like," he offered courteously.

"I love Park Bistro," she replied with a smile. "How does seven sound?"

He smiled at her. "Should I pick you up, or should I meet you there?"

She couldn't remember the last time that she'd had a date ask to pick her up. Most of them simply met her at a designated place and time. It was certainly safer when she didn't know them well. Still, she'd gotten to know a little of him, and she lived nearby. She even knew the owners of Park Bistro well enough that she wasn't concerned about her safety there. "If you don't mind picking me up, I can give you the address."

Theodore waited as she wrote it down for him. When she handed him the card, he took it with a slow smile. "It was nice to see you again, Keely. I look forward to Friday."

He walked out of the office, and Keely sat down heavily in her chair. She wasn't sure she'd even said goodbye. She hadn't expected him to ask, and she certainly hadn't expected to say yes. He was very attractive, of course, and undeniably intelligent. His book had been fascinating. She was sure the conversation would be interesting, but then she wasn't sure how to date anymore. She did go out for the occasional drink or dinner or even a movie, but they were with men she knew or at least knew through friends. In each of the most recent cases, they had felt casual to the point of boredom. But this? Keely leaned back in her chair and breathed in the scent of the wildflowers.

"Hey, Keely, look what Theodore brought me!" Beth called from the door. She came in with a small bouquet of daisies wrapped sweetly in burlap. "Well, look at that," she said, glancing from her small bouquet to the large profusion of wildflowers in Keely's hand. "I wondered who those were for. My money was on you."

Keely smiled sheepishly. "It was certainly a nice gesture for him to bring us flowers."

"Mm-hm. We got these daisies. They're beautiful, but look at your stunners! I think someone has a little crush," Beth said with glee, flicking her bright red hair over her shoulder.

Keely looked ruefully at Beth. She'd loved this girl all of her life. She was wearing a bohemian dress with lots of jewelry today. She'd kept her hair down, her makeup minimal, and her eyes were sparkling behind the horn-rim glasses she'd acquired over the last few years. She was a bit eccentric, but she had the best heart of almost anyone Keely knew. "I think we're too old for crushes."

"No one is too old for crushes!" Beth declared firmly. "Tell me he at least asked you out on a date?" Keely colored to the roots of her hair. "Oh my God, he did! He asked you out, didn't he?" Beth squealed.

"It's just dinner. I'm sure he's just being kind," Keely said in embarrassment.

"Hmm ... kind ... sure," Beth said in amusement. "Okay, we'll leave it at that, but I want details! Hey, want me to put those in water for you?" She took the large bouquet and headed to the kitchen. It would be the perfect opportunity to show Amie the flowers and fill her in on the date while she was grabbing a vase.

Keely watched her walk off with a laugh. She'd give them a few minutes to gossip before she headed in to check the specials. She looked at the clock and wondered how long they would need. She smiled to herself to think of Theodore stopping by with flowers and an offer of dinner. If she didn't know better, she'd think he was courting her! But of course, that tradition was long gone even by the time she'd started dating.

Zeke had never courted her, that was for sure. His idea of dinner was a greasy burger wrapped in paper and a Coke, or maybe a beer if money was good. He'd had charisma though. She shook her head. That was a long time ago. She paused for a moment and then headed to her computer to Google Theodore. After all, if she didn't, she knew Beth would.

Chapter 9

Dean was doing a walk-through of the lake house, going over it with a critical eye and making more notes to add to the ones he already had. It wasn't an easy job, but it made for a good distraction. His ears weren't burning, but they might as well have been for the thoughts being sent his way.

*****

"No, wait, I'll show you a picture."

Emma Wells stopped idly scrolling through her Facebook feed and instead pulled up the search bar. She typed in Dean Walton and easily pulled up his page. His name popped up so at least he hadn't blocked her, she thought. She scrolled through the few public posts she could find and then pulled up the photos. Most of them were private, which was frustrating. She was sure all the ones she'd been in were deleted. Not that he'd ever shared them publicly anyway. She rolled her eyes in disgust. This wasn't Emma's first time searching for Dean or even looking through his posts, and she doubted it would be the last.

"See? Hot," she told her coworker who was wiping down a counter and looking bored.

"Mmmm ... why'd you let that one get away?"

"Well, I didn't do it on purpose. He just sort of ... lost interest," Emma said, still baffled at how it had all happened.

Emma had met Dean at a club. He'd been at the bar drinking with friends when she'd caught his attention. She'd seen him from the moment he walked in. It wasn't an unattractive group of men, and she'd have noticed them sooner or later, but Dean had stood out. Maybe it was his swagger or that slow smile with that wink of dimples. Or maybe it was just the way he perfectly filled out the t-shirt and jeans he'd carelessly thrown on for a night out drinking with friends.

Emma knew that she could dance. She'd been told often enough before that she had a way of moving that conjured up bedroom fantasies. She wore an outfit that put her full curves on display, and she knew that she had his full attention while she moved her hips to the beat of the song blasting into the crowded club. He'd left the bar and headed to her across the floor, never taking his eyes from hers. They'd danced, and when the club was winding down, they headed back to her place. It was closer than his anyway, and she didn't want to wait.

After that, she'd gone to his place a time or two, but mostly he'd come to hers. They'd even gone out a couple of times, but she'd suspected that he was still seeing other women. Not that he'd come out and say that. She just noticed that there were nights he wouldn't respond to texts and times when he claimed to be working but probably wasn't. She'd taken to checking his phone when he was in the shower and checking up on his social media accounts.

He'd called her crazy, but she knew that she was right, and he just wouldn't come out and say it. Instead, he deftly avoided defining their relationship at all and skillfully maneuvered any conversations around the idea of exclusivity or future planning. Emma should have known what he was doing. She'd done it enough herself. But she typically wasn't on the receiving end, and she didn't like feeling like a fool.

"He's still single," her new friend pointed out, nodding at the relationship status.

"It always says that. Even when we were together," Emma said grudgingly. If he was dating someone, he wasn't publicly acknowledging her either, which didn't make her feel any better or any worse really.

"Oh, that type."

"Yeah. There's no way he's not seeing anyone." Emma put down the phone. She didn't like being rejected, but she absolutely hated being played. She thought back over the months she'd spent with him. There had been something about him that had made her dream of a future. He'd made her laugh, but mostly he'd made her weak with desire. Well, at least they'd had a few hot nights, which was all you could get from someone like Dean, Emma thought as she typed another name in the search bar.

*****

"No. Nope. Not him. Absolutely not," Kristin Yuen laughed as she swiped left on yet another potential match. Nope. Nope. Nope.

"What's wrong with that one?" her sister asked. They were lying on the bed together in her room, half-watching Netflix and half swiping. They'd endured breakups around the same time, and they'd both agreed to give online dating a try.

"No shirtless gym selfies. Just no."

"Look at that six-pack though," Lacy pointed out.

"I know, but I've done the whole gym rat thing. Pretty but vain."

"And that's your job," Lacy said with a giggle.

"Shut it," Kristin shot back, elbowing her. "I wouldn't mind being worshipped a little," she mused. She scrolled through pictures of shirtless men at the gym and men holding up fish and men laying in their beds. She sighed. She just wanted to meet a nice guy. Maybe this app wasn't exactly the best place to do it, but she hadn't really met anyone in real life in a long time. Ages!

Every now and then, she met a good guy on here. She stopped swiping a second. Dean Walton. There he was. She'd met him on here, and it wasn't really a surprise he was still on. Kristin paused in her swiping. They'd met and had dinner and exchanged tons of texts over the handful of months they'd dated. He'd kind of fallen into the friends with benefits category, though. I mean, he'd carefully avoided talk of being exclusive, and Kristin wasn't interested in exclusively dating someone who was seeing other people. She'd been okay with seeing him on and off when she wasn't out there looking for a serious relationship.

Dean was fun. Plus, he was seriously sweet. Did he have commitment issues? Without a doubt! But Kristin had enjoyed him. They had ended things amicably when she started dating Brian exclusively. Clearly, that hadn't worked out, or she wouldn't be swiping now. She sighed.

"Tell me you're swiping right on him," Lacy said with a grin stretched wide across her face. "I mean, I'd do him."

"Been there," Kristin said with a laugh. "But no. And you shouldn't either. Girl, just swipe left if you see him."

"No good in bed?"

"I am not discussing that with you. We're not that close," Kristin laughed. "It's not that. He's just not serious, and he's definitely not the one-woman type."

She was tempted to give Dean a call. He was always game, but she knew that if she was going to get serious finding a real relationship, she'd have to stop wasting her time with guys like Dean. They were great for the casual but not so good with the serious. Kristin blew her thick black bangs back with a heavy sigh. She'd cut her hair after things with Brian went south. It now hung around her face in a glossy fringe, which was cute, but a little more high-maintenance than she liked. She updated her profile again and went back to swiping.

"Let's keep looking," she suggested.

*****

Shelby Kent turned over in her bed to stare at the ceiling. She wasn't working today. She hadn't actually worked for the last couple of days. She'd had bouts of depression since she was a kid. She managed them. It actually took a hell of a lot of therapy over the years to get her to the point where she could present a happy front and be functional. She'd held down this job for a couple of years, and she knew she could afford the sick days to take care of herself. It had just been a rough few months, and this week she'd been unable to get out of bed for more than just the basic tasks of caring for herself.

The frustrating part was, Shelby thought, that it wasn't just one thing. She couldn't just point to a cause and then fix it. She was just sad in a way that felt endless, and the thought of getting out of bed to even take a shower seemed overwhelming. When she was at her best, she was lively and vivacious with a sharp sense of humor. She dated and worked and went to school and really enjoyed her life. Then she'd fall into the darkness again. Friends helped. She'd had a couple stop by—one with soup and one who just sat with her and watched Netflix. It meant the world to her.

And then there was Maddox. She'd met him a few months after the thing with Dean had busted up. She'd been miserable and hadn't even bothered to hide it. She went to a friend's party out of obligation, but then had sat in a corner and tried to be invisible until a reasonable amount of time had passed where she could just go home. Maddox had sat down and struck up a conversation with her and refused to be deterred by her negative mood. He'd even asked her out, which floored Shelby. She figured he just had a thing for women with a dark side and shot him down. She didn't like this version of herself and couldn't see how anyone else could. But he texted her and kept in touch and eventually wore her down with pure sweetness.

When he wasn't at work, he would curl up with her and just stay through the darkness. He'd make sure she had enough to eat and would even take her out on walks with him through the woods.

They'd started hiking together, and slowly, she found that there were more good days than bad again. Of course, she knew that she'd probably have more tough days in the future, but they would get through it.

Maddox had been amazing after Dean, Shelby thought as she flipped through her watchlist. Dean had been great at first. He was charming and fun and kind of sweet under all that flash. But then she'd had an episode. She'd gotten weepy and emotional in front of him. It had only taken one time, but as soon as he sensed actual, real emotions under the surface, he'd ghosted so fast her head had spun. He had avoided her calls and texts without even a single response. She didn't think he was trying to be unkind, but that's how it felt. Actually, it felt cruel.

She'd been so angry and sad when she'd met Maddox, and he loved her anyway. She could look back now and even feel glad that Dean had run away like a scared little rabbit at the first sign of emotion. After all, it had brought her to a true relationship. But she didn't appreciate the ghosting. It really stung, and it had taken her a while to deal with it. She chose a show that made her feel a little better and curled around the body pillow Maddox had bought for her. She wrapped herself around it and knew that she would be okay.

*****

"Hey, baby, I've got to get to work," Naomi told the man in the bed. She'd met him at the bar last night. She'd tried to remember his name, but then she decided that she could always go with "baby". That never failed.

Hell, she'd picked up that little trick from Dean. She'd thought it was sweet at first, the way he'd called her baby and sweetheart and honey with that butter-wouldn't-melt Southern accent. She'd grin and grab him by his silky blonde hair, wrapping it around her fingers, and pulling him down to meet her mouth and back into bed. Later, she'd wondered if he simply had trouble keeping track of the names. After all, she was hardly the first or even the last, although she'd like to be.

"Can't you stay a little longer? Maybe take a shower with me?" he asked sleepily, stretching out and reaching for her. She nimbly stepped out of his grasp and pulled on her pants.

"I can't be late to work," she told him, which was true.

What was also true was that she was still hung up on Dean. She wasn't an idiot. She knew that he was dating other women. He was barely ever home. She'd driven by a number of times and noticed he was hardly there in the evenings at all, and he was gone most of the weekends, too. Plus, if he wasn't sleeping with her, he was certainly banging someone else, she thought in disgust.

She flicked her eyes over to the man on the bed. He was hot. He'd said he was a professional boxer, and she believed it. He certainly had the build for it. She leaned over and kissed him, the hot deep kind that had him reaching for the button on her pants. She slapped his hands away but allowed them to settle on her ass and hold her firmly. She ran her fingers through his spiky blond hair, but it was nowhere near the silken texture of Dean's.

"You've got to go, and I've got to get to work," she told him. He sat up lazily and started throwing on his clothes in a haphazard sort of way.

"You got any coffee?" he asked her.

"I can make some," she said, annoyed because she did that enough at work. She went over to start coffee and then came back in the room to finish getting dressed.

The hair had reminded her a little of Dean, but the resemblance ended there. This guy's hair had been hardened with gel, and he'd lacked the finesse that Dean had managed so easily in bed. It wasn't the worst sex she'd had, but it certainly hadn't been worth her time. She glanced over to her bedside table. There were a number of toys in there that could have taken care of things much easier. She sighed. That's not what she wanted. What she wanted was Dean. And if she had any say in it, she'd have him in the end. She waited for the coffee to finish and dug out a to-go cup so her date could leave first chance. For herself, she grabbed a soda out of the fridge and sat down on the couch to think about how she could get Dean back.

*****

In the lake house, Dean brushed his arm absently. For a second, it felt like a hand had brushed against him. Probably damn spider webs, he thought absently, scowling down at the lengthy list he'd made. He didn't have anywhere to be until later in the evening. It gave him a few hours to kill so he was trying to assess what work had been done and what still needed to be addressed.

He looked it over critically. It had seemed like such a good investment, but he'd been a fool not to have had a more thorough inspection before he'd sunk his savings into this wreck. Of course, he'd thought he could fix most of it himself, but he'd already had to pay an electrician to fix the wiring and a plumber to repair the bathrooms. Nothing in there seemed to work right. Not the toilet, not the sink, and certainly not the shower over the large claw-foot tub. Sure, it was all rustic, and he liked rustic. But he wasn't about to use an outhouse. That was overkill, in his opinion.

He had no idea that the women he had dated recently had thought of him during the day. Mostly, he didn't look back once a relationship was done. There was the occasional woman he thought about reaching out to, but the truth was that there were always new women to meet if he got lonely. Lately, he'd been spending too much time on the cabin and working to earn enough to fix up the cabin to really date. Though he hoped to change that over the weekend. A friend of his had invited him out for drinks with some of his work buddies so he thought he'd head out with them.

A little bar hopping around Athens was usually successful. Of course, they'd have to stick to the 21 and Over places. It was a college town and having to flash ID at the door ensured that any women he met were legal at the very least. He wasn't interested in dating some high schooler masquerading as a college girl, and he couldn't even tell anymore just by looking at them.

He headed back inside to grab a Coke from the fridge. At least the fridge worked. He'd bought it new to replace the hunk of junk that had broken down within weeks of the closing. He knew that the kitchen needed to be gutted, but the expense was outrageous. He sat down heavily. He'd already learned how to lay tile and restore a hardwood floor. Thank you, YouTube. Plus, Seth was happy to pitch in for a six-pack and a pizza. When the weather was right, he could dock a boat here and even swim in the lake.

It would be a pretty sweet home if he could ever get it livable. He was pretty close to just pitching a tent on the property and saying goodbye to rent payments. But not just yet. He wanted to make sure the bathroom was at least in working order, and he really did need to finish the kitchen. After that, he could move in and rough it until the last few repairs were made.

He headed back out to the porch to look at the lakefront. The view was the whole reason he'd bought the property. It was secluded enough for the sake of privacy without being creepy. Plus, it would be great for water sports later on. He looked at the cabin behind him. There were two large bedrooms and a large open loft overhead. The kitchen was spacious, if a little rough, and the bathroom would be great once he had the showerheads installed that he liked. It wasn't luxurious, and it certainly wouldn't fit in on Walton Street, but Dean felt for the first time like he'd come home.

He drank deeply of the cold Coke in his hand and leaned back against the railing. At least the railing was sturdy since he'd repaired it first thing. The porch had been a death trap, and he'd fixed it up one long weekend with Seth, repairing the stairs and railing along with it. It looked good if he did say so himself. He knew he'd have to head back to town in a little while, but for now, it was nice just to have the peace. He'd left his cell phone on the counter inside so he couldn't get messages and felt a little relief. Naomi had sent a few drunk texts the night before. The whole situation was making him uncomfortable, and he dreaded the inevitable confrontation when he told her he wasn't interested. He looked out at the lake and put that conversation off a little longer.

    He thought about Lindy and how she'd reacted to him the last time he saw her. He knew he should steer clear of her. She was his best friend's sister after all, but he'd always been curious. He knew that she dated, but she kept it all fairly private, a fact he respected and appreciated. He didn't know what it was about him that riled her up, but he'd never been able to keep himself from poking those soft spots just to see how she'd react.

    He thought about swinging by her studio, but he couldn't think of one reasonable excuse he could offer for doing it. Not one, in all the years they'd known each other. Dean sighed. He just needed to hook up with someone tonight and forget Lindy altogether. She was complicated anyway, and complicated was fun in the short term but usually ended up being trouble in the end.

Chapter 10

"It's silly to be nervous. It's just dinner," Keely said as she discarded one dress in favor of another.

"Who are you trying to convince?" Vera asked her.

Keely stood in front of the full-length mirror and evaluated herself again. It had been a long time since she'd accepted something as simple as a dinner date. It's not that she was uninterested in dating. She'd simply been busy. She looked again at the dress with its low neckline and a long slit up the thigh. She was closer to sixty now than fifty, but she had kept in good shape over the years.

"It's too much, isn't it?" she asked her closest friend. She thought that she looked damn good in it if she did say so herself, but maybe it was a bit forward for a first date. She sighed heavily, kicked off the pair of strappy high heels she'd paired with it and started looking through her closet again.

"Not for Vegas," Vera said with a laugh in her voice. She sat on her bed and shook her head no at the latest dress selection. "It's not the one. Try something else."

Vera Jamison had been a friend for nearly twenty-five years now. They'd met through the local Chamber of Commerce when Keely was still managing Lost Horizon Antiques and Vera was just learning the ropes of innkeeping. She was now the innkeeper and baker for one of the premier bed and breakfasts in town and also was known to squeeze in an occasional catering order for clients. She was a few years younger than Keely and several inches shorter. She was petite, and her curves were considerably more pronounced now than when they'd first met.

Her skin was deeply tanned, a legacy from her Mexican mother. Her dark coloring was flatteringly set off by the red blouse she wore over charcoal slacks, her business-casual ensemble for the day. She'd pulled her luxurious salt and pepper hair back at the nape of her neck where the curls cascaded down her back. She'd always thought of her features as uniformly brown: brown eyes, brown skin, brown hair, but she was proud of the thick curls she'd inherited from her mother. She'd been a love child of the sixties so she didn't know her father, but she'd been told that he had been an insurance salesman with blonde hair and dimples. Although she'd never had a real chance of inheriting his hair color, the dimples winked out of her cheeks in a way that her mother still claimed reminded her of that young man.

Vera's guests at the inn were off on tours so she had made a little time for this fashion emergency. She'd been Keely's closest friend for a long time, and she'd never seen her so nervous about a date. She regretted that she'd missed the book signing and the chance to meet this author who had her friend's nerves frayed. She suspected he might be someone special, or at least had the possibility to be. She looked at another selection speculatively.

"I love those shoes, but not with that dress," she said decisively.

"I feel like I've tried everything on that I own!" Keely declared. She looked at the pile of discarded dresses in distress. "I don't have time to buy anything new."

"Well, now, don't panic," Vera said with a smile. "You're a bit of a clothes horse so I'm positive you haven't tried on everything. Let me take a look." She strode to the walk-in closet with confidence and came out bearing three dresses that Keely had yet to try on. "What's wrong with these?" Vera asked.

"Oh, I haven't worn that blue one in ages. I'm not even sure it will fit anymore. And the peach is really just a sheath. I thought it might be too plain for a dinner out. I must have overlooked this one," she said, looking thoughtfully at the black dress she'd bought with the exact thought that you could never go wrong with a little black dress.

"Try them all on, and we'll see." Vera sat back on the bed and began putting clothes back on hangers while Keely changed. "So, tell me about this man again."

"I don't really know much about him," Keely said, her voice muffled from the closet. "I loved his book. He seems a little shy."

"And he's attractive?" Vera asked curiously. She'd never met Keely's first husband, but she'd seen pictures. He'd been long gone by the time they'd met. It was something the two had in common—husbands who'd deserted them with children still at home.

Vera had lived in Madison for near-on thirty years now. She'd come here as a bride of twenty-four, and she'd stayed even after her husband departed. Of course, he hadn't departed the Earth or anything tragic like that. He'd simply decided he'd liked men better than women and had forgotten to inform Vera of this prior to their nuptials. But Vera didn't judge. She was angry at the lies, but she wasn't interested in keeping a man who didn't want to be kept so she helped him pack up and go. Last she heard, he'd moved to Atlanta and then some years later down to Florida somewhere. They didn't exactly keep in touch, although her son Garrett kept her informed from time to time.

Garrett was still in diapers when she met Keely. She'd been struggling to balance her part-time responsibilities at an inn in town with parenting on her own. They'd recognized in each other that grit that seemed particular to certain Southern women. They'd both been left, but they were carving out the lives that they wanted. Of course, they'd done so differently. Vera had dated a number of different men over the years while Keely had accepted the occasional date but seemed to be steering clear of relationships and had for as long as she'd known her.

Right now, Vera was trying out online dating, to her son's horror. Still, it was her life and not Garrett's anyway. She had been on a few interesting dates and had even dated a dentist for a few months. She'd never been quite comfortable smiling in his presence though. She felt he'd be looking at her overbite or examining her for crooked teeth. She knew it was paranoid. After all, she didn't assess her dates as potential inn guests. But she just couldn't get around the discomfort. Perhaps if there'd been more chemistry she wouldn't have cared what he did for a living. But there wasn't, nice as he was.

Keely had accused her of being too hard on him, but that was a bit like the pot calling the kettle as none of Keely's dates stuck around for long. Not because they were unwilling, of course. In their youth, some might have called Keely frigid, but she was simply very clear in what she wanted in her life and unwilling to tolerate a relationship that didn't suit the life she was leading. Vera admired that attitude but couldn't seem to adopt it for her own. She seemed to fall into one disastrous relationship after another, although none had tempted her to make it official in some years.

She watched quietly as Keely tried on all three dresses. They both dismissed the peach as somehow being too plain, although Vera argued that she could dress it up with jewelry. The blue dress fit like a glove and was almost perfect, but when Keely put on the little black dress, they both smiled. It was form-fitting enough to be flattering without running the risk of revealing too much. It fell to about mid-calf with a flare in the skirt that would swish if she turned. They both sighed. Of course, it was the last dress she'd tried on. Didn't it always work out that way? Vera selected simple hoop earrings and passed them over while Keely redid her makeup carefully.

"Do you think it's wise that he's picking you up here?" Vera asked nervously.

"Well, normally you know I wouldn't. But his face is on the cover of his book jacket, and Beth has his home address at the store. If things go South, I trust you both can give the police all the necessary details," she said with a flippant smile. "I thought, just this once, I'd let him pick me up."

"It's so close you could walk if you weren't wearing the heels," Vera commented with a nod to the modest shoes Keely had selected. "Is he tall?"

"He's about my height," Keely explained, looking at the heels. She wondered if she wouldn't do better wearing flats. After all, some men were self-conscious going out with tall women. But the heels were truly better with the dress, and she wasn't willing to forego the shoes she loved for the rest of her life for any man. It was better that they realize that upfront. "I might be a couple of inches taller than him in the heels."

"This is a problem I never have," Vera said smugly. "There's something to be said for being very short. I've never had to worry about height when it comes to dating. I could wear four-inch heels and still not be at eye-level of most of the men I meet."

"But you never wear heels," Keely pointed out dryly.

"But I could," Vera said with a laugh. "And I do wear heels sometimes." She looked down at her feet in the vibrant red ballet flats she'd paired with her outfit. "Just rarely on workdays."

"Every day is a workday for you," Keely said with a smile.

"I don't mind it. You can't beat the benefits." Vera had moved into the carriage house on the property of the bed and breakfast a few years back. It was one of the perks of her position.

Keely finished getting ready and then sighed. "He's not due to get here for at least another hour. I shouldn't have started getting ready so early," she reflected.

"Want to play a hand of cards while we wait? Or Scrabble maybe?" Vera asked. They both enjoyed card and board games and had spent many nights over the years amusing themselves this way. "Or watch a little television?"

"Have you seen the last season of *Grace and Frankie*?" Keely asked, curiously.

"Yes, but I'm always game for that. Do we have time?"

"We can squeeze one in. I'd play cards, but I'm too distracted. Scrabble is definitely out. It'd be far too easy for you to cheat," Keely said with a laugh toward her friend as they walked down the stairs.

"Ha! I never cheat. I just have an extensive vocabulary," Vera said.

"And access to Google," Keely pointed out, kicking off her heels and curling her feet under her on the sofa.

"Hey, house rules," Vera countered, sitting down with a grin. They turned on Netflix and selected their program. Vera suspected that Keely was just trying to calm her nerves so she chose a particularly funny episode and sat back for a few laughs.

*****

Theodore arrived at the door a few minutes after Vera left for the inn. Had he taken a different route to pick up Keely, he would have passed her on the road, humming a song she'd had stuck in her head all day. He arrived at the door promptly at seven, afraid for a moment that being too punctual was as bad as being too early or too late. He rang the doorbell and tried not to hold his breath.

"Hello," Keely said nervously, but he didn't have any words. For what seemed like a full minute, but was really only a matter of seconds, he just stared. Then, his common sense came back along with his words.

"Hello. You look ... extraordinary," he decided. Keely lit up like a firefly, a blush rising in her cheeks that was quite becoming.

"So do you," she told him. "Shall we?" she asked, as he'd made no move to leave. "Or would you like to come in for a drink?"

"I've made reservations," he told her. "It would be better if we weren't late. I'm afraid I'm not very good at this."

"At what?" she asked, a smile in her eyes.

"Dating," he said simply.

"Oh, that's okay. I'm very good at it," she told him with a smile that put him immediately at ease.

He escorted Keely to his truck, which he'd had cleaned for the occasion, and opened the door and helped her in. As he walked around to his side to drive to Park Bistro, he hoped that his jumping nerves wouldn't spoil the night. She looked perfect, but it had been so long since he'd met anyone he'd felt any real interest in.

"I'm a fast learner," he offered, once they started the short drive into town.

"You're not doing badly at all," she told him with a smile.

Chapter 11

Just down the road, Dean was stepping out of a hot shower. He'd worked later on the lake house than he intended, and he'd had to cut his shower short. He'd wanted to stay under the hot spray of water as long as he could stand it. He was already feeling the strain of a day spent rehabbing the place. His plan for the night was to have a few medicinal drinks and maybe meet someone new.

He pulled on a clean shirt and buttoned it up while carefully inspecting his face. He considered the beard again. To shave or not to shave. He'd been trying a new look, and he decided he'd give it a few more days before he changed it up. He pulled on a pair of slacks and looked for his good shoes. He'd left his work boots outside the door of his place. He'd have to take some time to clean them tomorrow. He grabbed his keys and headed to town to meet his friends. He'd leave his truck there and pick it up tomorrow. He was hoping he wouldn't be coming home alone, but he could always grab an Uber if all else failed.

*****

As her mother headed toward Park Bistro with Theodore, Lindy was walking out to the ancient Jeep she called Frances. She'd owned it since college, and it had definitely seen better days. She thought that a paint job wouldn't be a bad idea. After all, with all the new parts on it, Frances was practically a new car. It was about time she gave her exterior the attention she'd given her inner workings. She unlocked her car and climbed in with a sigh. She really didn't want to go hear whatever awful band was likely playing, but she didn't want to stay home all night watching TV either.

Nina's new boyfriend was a bouncer at the club so Lindy

strongly suspected that she'd be spending the evening fending off advances or drinking alone while Nina hung around the door chatting up Rick. Or was it Nick? God, it might have been Mick. Lindy reminded herself to pay better attention. Nina went through boyfriends on a semi-regular basis, and Lindy hadn't exactly been paying the closest attention when she'd announced the newest one.

"I'm parking," Lindy said without preamble as she pulled into a parking spot downtown and called her friend.

"Are you hungry?" Nina asked.

"I can always eat. Mexican?"

"Yeah, I'm a couple blocks away. If you get there first, snag a table. I'll tell you all about Rob when I get there."

The Mexican place had both good food and strong drinks, a combination that they agreed was rare these days. Over dinner, Nina told her all about Rob and how they'd met, and Lindy was grateful she hadn't asked about Rick. Clearly, there was no Rick. They stretched dinner out with drinks while they killed time before the show, and Lindy was glad she'd put a little extra effort into her appearance.

"How do you do that?" she asked her friend with a combination of suspicion or admiration.

"Do what?" Nina asked knowingly, leaning back in her chair. They'd had this conversation before.

"You can throw on jeans with a top and boots and look effortlessly fashionable," Lindy said in mock annoyance. "It isn't right. I'm pretty sure you're a witch," she accused with a grin.

"Nope. Still can't fold a fitted sheet. That's the true test of the witch," Nina said with a flashing smile. She ran a hand through her short blonde hair, ruffling it a little. She'd made her brown eyes extra smoky for the evening. Lindy leaned closer.

"Did you get eyelash extensions?" she asked.

"I told you that I got that stuff to grow them out," she said innocently. "But yes," she answered with a laugh. Even in college, when her budget had run to thrift store chic, she'd been able to come up with the perfect outfit for any occasion.

"Are you sure you can't fold a fitted sheet?" Lindy asked, taking a drink of her margarita.

When Nina laughed and launched into another story about Rob, Lindy was glad she'd chosen the tight jeans and form-fitting open-backed shirt with the plunging neckline instead of her usual uniform of leggings and snarky sweater. She'd paired the outfit with stilettos so sharp they could double as a weapon and dangling earrings. She wore her hair wavy and loose down her back.

"Hey, don't abandon me when we get to the club," Lindy reminded Nina when she could get a word in edgewise.

"Would I do that?" Nina asked and then laughed. "Okay, I'll try not to stay with Rob the whole time. He's working anyway."

"You know I'm not going to have many wild nights left."

"Did you pick a donor? And can I see pictures?"

"Girl, this is better than that dating app I tried. Much better selection anyway," Lindy said with a grin. Some of the entries had been as comical as the dating app, but there were a good many of them that warranted a closer look. She leaned in and started to fill her in.

*****

Keely and Theodore were lingering over dinner, and neither was eager for the night to end. They decided to split a slice of carrot cake. It was hardly the most elegant of dessert choices, but they'd found they had many common interests including a good strong cup of tea, reading selections, and a mutual fondness for carrot cake. Both were curious as to what other things they might have in common as they sipped from glasses of wine and talked about their lives. They tread lightly around serious topics, saving those for another time—each hoping that another time would be on the table.

Keely's nerves had settled during the night. Good food and good company helped. She was grateful that the staff kept a discreet distance throughout the meal, checking on them without ever interrupting the easy flow of conversation. She was well-acquainted with their server, and indeed the hostess, but they had handled the date as smoothly as with any other guest. At other establishments, she'd had the awkward chat with the local friend while waiting for a table, and it seemed like it made her more nervous on her date rather than less. It was hard to live in a town for so long and be such an integral part of the downtown business community without getting to know most of the residents.

"So, you have two daughters?" Keely asked, sipping her wine.

"Yes. Presley and Layla," he said with a grin.

"Elvis and Clapton?" Keely asked, raising an eyebrow.

"It was their mother's idea, but I liked it. It was different than their friends growing up."

"It must have been hard to be widowed so young."

"I guess no harder than being left to raise two babies on your own," he returned evenly. "Although, I did get the chance to say goodbye. Maybe that made it easier in some ways."

"I doubt any of it was easy."

"Would you have wanted a chance to say goodbye?"

"Oh, if my ex-husband had told me what he was about to do I might have thrown a shoe at his head," Keely said with a grin.

Theodore sat back and looked at her in appraisal. She was as elegant as a film star and just as poised, but there was fire in her eyes. He grinned at her.

"I can believe that," Theodore said. "I can't say I'd have blamed you." The shared smile held, and the server almost chose that moment to stop by with the check before she thought better of it and detoured to another table.

*****

Dean and his friends headed out of their second bar of the night. The drinks had been alright, but the music left something to be desired. The first had been a bit of a disaster. His friend Allen had run into an ex-girlfriend straightaway, and Dean had spied one of Emma's close friends loitering near the bathroom. He'd done an about-face and headed straight for the door, signaling Allen and their friend Lucas that they needed to head out.

The last thing he needed was one of his ex's friends giving her the heads up on where to find him. It wouldn't be the first time she'd tracked him down when he was out with his friends. The last time had resulted in a marginally embarrassing scene that made him look like a jackass and had lost him the chance to get the number of the woman he'd been chatting up, who'd looked at him like pure scum after Emma had finished her tirade.

He had no interest in replaying that whole scene, and Allen's ex wasn't much better. She wouldn't make a scene, but she'd come over and start reeling Allen back in. He might not have learned his lesson from the last time so it was a good time to find somewhere else to drink.

"Well, that was close," Lucas commented. "Did she see you?" he asked Dean.

"I don't think so. Best not to chance it though," Dean said as they walked.

"Is Emma still bothering you then?" Allen asked.

"Not so much these days. But anything could set her off." He shrugged his shoulders. He wasn't really feeling the bar scene tonight. He just felt restless, although he wasn't sure why. "Naomi's been the problem lately."

"Want me to take her off your hands?" Allen asked.

"I wouldn't mind it, but she might have something to say about it," Dean returned with a sharp grin. Allen fancied himself as more of a playboy than he was, and he figured Naomi would chew him up and spit him out if he even attempted it.

They nearly walked past the next small club when Lucas stopped to talk to the bouncer, some guy he used to work with. The guy let them in without a cover charge and tipped them off that the upstairs bar might mix the drinks a little stronger than the downstairs. They decided to check out a few bands. If they weren't any good or if the scene was boring, they could always move on.

Most nights, they were in and out of half a dozen bars before the end of the night, depending on how they felt. Allen had already made his way over to order drinks, and Dean and Lucas exchanged grins when they noticed how heavily he was flirting with the bartender. She could have been a double for the woman they'd just dodged at the last bar and looked equally like trouble.

"What do they call that?" Dean asked facetiously.

"The word you're looking for is *dopple-banger*," Lucas said with a laugh. They were laughing when Allen brought the drinks over.

"What?" he asked in confusion. Then he glanced back at the bartender with a grin and heard the laughs behind him. "Y'all, shut up," he said, his North Carolina accent deepening as he turned red and dropped the drinks on the table.

*****

"Good night," Theodore said again, as Keely softly shut the door.

She leaned against it for a moment and smiled. The drive from the restaurant back to Keely's home was a short one, and Theodore had gotten out to walk her to the door. She wasn't sure he'd make a move so early, but he'd kissed her in a way that was both sweet and smoldering. She couldn't stop smiling.

She walked through the house and into the kitchen to pour herself a glass of wine. She noticed Lindy's front porch light was left on, but the interior lights were off. She was likely still out for the night, and Keely felt a little relief. It was too soon for her to feel like dissecting the date. She'd tell Vera all about in the morning over breakfast. For now, she just wanted to revel in it.

It was a damn good first date if she did say so herself. He'd already secured her agreement for a second date, a community theatrical production he'd been invited to in a neighboring town. She walked lightly up the stairs to bed and replayed that goodnight kiss. It had been a long time since she'd felt that connection with anyone. Maybe not since Zeke—and hadn't that been fleeting, she thought to herself. Still, Theodore was in a class above Zeke, in every way. She sipped the glass of wine slowly and let the night replay. Tomorrow, she'd have to talk about it, but tonight she just wanted to hug the memories close and savor them alone.

Chapter 12

Lindy shook her head as she watched Nina head back over to the door to talk to Rob for "just a minute." She was under no illusion that a minute of talking would actually be comprised of sixty seconds. She signaled to her that she was going to head upstairs. There was a terrace on the second level so it wouldn't be quite as stuffy. Besides, she'd been here before, and she knew that the drinks were better upstairs. The Long Island Iced Tea she'd ordered when they'd first walked in was too weak for her tastes. She climbed the stairs and hoped that Nina would eventually remember that she came with a friend and wander back over. The last thing Lindy wanted was to be that person who sat at the bar surfing Facebook all night. Or, worse, fending off college-age guys she had no interest in dating, much less hooking up with.

She made her way to the bar, feeling largely invisible in this sea of early-twenty-somethings. Sure, she'd caught a few appreciative glances her way, but she was under no illusion that the night would lead to anything more than a few drinks and a laugh with Nina if she ever came back from chatting with the new boyfriend. She ordered a drink and took it to a small table near the terrace. Her back was to the bar, and it was just warm enough to come out of her jacket and still get a little bit of a breeze from outside. She sipped her drink and checked out the stage.

The first band was due to come on soon, and Lindy just hoped they would be bearable. She knew of a few local bands that were incredibly talented, but she remembered a night here with Tyler—oh, ages ago—where they'd listened to a band that was incredible only for how awful it was. They'd had to squeeze through the crowd of drunk college students celebrating a football win to make it out of there. They'd both joked that their ears had rung for days afterward.

Lindy sipped her drink, thankfully mixed stronger than the last, and turned her attention away from memories with Tyler. That was a past she didn't care to revisit. She felt the cool air on her open back, a welcome relief from the heat of the room. She'd already easily rebuffed a couple of interested looks from men who seemed barely old enough to drink. It was easy to simply turn away from an open stare or smile blandly, although smiling at all could be construed as interest. In fact, she noticed one open stare that she'd actively avoided returning had not faltered. In fact, she could see from the corner of her eye that he was heading her way.

She sighed. When Resting Bitch Face didn't deter them and active avoidance of eye contact didn't get the message across, there was bound to be an unpleasant confrontation. She sipped her drink, a little liquid courage for the altercation to come. She could tell by his swagger that he wasn't the kind to take no for an answer. She knew the type.

Hell, every woman knew the type. They were the bane of the dating world and still thought they were God's gift to women. He walked toward her table with what he likely thought was a sexy grin and she thought looked smug as hell when she felt a familiar hand on her back. She turned, puzzled but unworried and found herself looking straight into Dean's eyes as he put another drink down in front of her.

"God, Lindy, I'm sorry that took so long. I ran into a couple of guys from work," Dean said, nodding to Allen and Lucas who were talking to a few women at the bar. They nodded back and returned to their conversation.

Dean could see the guy who had been making a beeline for Lindy break his stride and watch them with narrowed eyes. Well, hell, Dean thought. Might as well be hanged for a sheep as a lamb. He moved in as Lindy's eyes widened, and he hesitated just enough to make sure that she was on the same page. She closed the distance for him, her lips meeting his in a long, slow kiss.

Dean had meant to make the kiss just convincing enough to steer the guy clear of her, but then he forgot what he was doing. He got caught up in the taste of Lindy and her mouth moving on his. It took him a moment to recall himself and even longer to break the contact. He leaned back and watched her slow grin.

"Is he gone?" Lindy asked with a smile, keeping her eyes on Dean's.

"Yeah, he's heading back to the bar. It's nice that you're so quick on the uptake," Dean said admiringly, thinking of how fast she'd caught on to his play.

He didn't see where the guy had gone after he'd turned toward the bar, but he kept his hand resting on her back for good measure. He liked how soft her skin felt there. She was lean and strong, and he hadn't expected the silky softness of her skin or how warm it felt even with the cool breeze coming in from behind them.

"Of course," Lindy lied smoothly. From the moment she had turned around and found Dean's eyes on hers, she hadn't thought at all. She'd simply responded, to his hand on her back and his mouth meeting her own. She hadn't meant to go along with any of it, but she also hadn't been able to resist. After all, she knew she could easily handle confrontation. It was just too tempting to allow Dean's way of defusing the conflict. She could admit, if only to herself, that she'd been curious. Now she tried to slow her racing heart and project only calm confidence. "I appreciate it."

"Oh, no. My pleasure entirely," Dean said with a slow smile. Now, that was a sexy smile, Lindy thought. He could give that other guy a lesson or two on charming the ladies. She smiled back and realized that his hand was lightly stroking her back in movements so small she almost didn't notice. She cast a glance over her shoulder to where his hand rested, and he lifted it, to her regret. "I wanted to make it convincing."

"Was he convinced?" she asked, not taking the time to even glance in the other direction.

"I guess so. It looks like he found some other woman to bother," Dean said with a shrug.

"Thanks for the drink," Lindy added, sipping the Long Island he'd brought over. "Can I buy you one? It's the least I can do."

"I wouldn't say no," Dean told her. "Jack and Coke?"

He watched her head over to the bar and took a deep breath. When he'd first noticed her, he hadn't realized just who he was checking out. He should have, of course. It's not like he hadn't spent half his teen years studying Lindy in minute detail to Seth's unending embarrassment. But he'd noticed the open back of her top with all that smooth skin above tight jeans. When he'd seen the other guy move in despite her obvious disinterest, he'd thought he might make a little interception.

As he walked toward her and realized who she was, he'd quickly changed his approach. He figured she might be a little steamed at his methods, but he was surprised that she'd taken it in stride. His own heart was still racing, and his fingers could still feel the softness and warmth of her skin. He watched her walk up to the bar and order a drink, as cool as you please, and he wondered how she could be so unaffected by a kiss that had sent him reeling.

She walked back to him and set the drink down in front of him. "This doesn't exactly seem like your scene."

"It's not exactly yours either."

"Nina's downstairs. The bouncer's the new boyfriend."

"Which one? Rob?"

"You know him?"

"No, Lucas used to work with the guy. He seems nice enough. That's how we ended up here."

"Well, don't let me keep you from your friends. I'm sure Nina will be up … sometime," Lindy said with a shrug.

Dean looked over at his friends and turned back to Lindy. "I think they're doing just fine on their own. No need to play wingman at the moment."

"Do you do that?" Lindy asked, curiously.

"Do what?" Dean asked, taking a sip of his drink and trying not to focus on her mouth as she sipped hers.

"You know, play wingman. I figured it worked the other way around."

"Well, we take it in turns," Dean said with a grin. "Lucas has a girlfriend, but that won't stop him from collecting a handful of numbers tonight, and Allen is always on the hunt." He shrugged. "He already struck out with the bartender so he's trying to recover his mojo."

"Is that right?" Lindy rolled her eyes but laughed.

They talked for a few minutes, passing the time and batting the conversation easily back and forth with talk of home and work. When the first band started playing, they exchanged a look. It was loud, and it was, well, bad would be a generous way of putting it. Dean motioned Lindy outside, and they moved out to the terrace where the music was a little fainter. He picked up another drink on the way out, but Lindy declined another.

"I'm driving later," she explained. "Actually, if the next band is as bad as this, I'm driving sooner rather than later."

"Why don't you and Nina drink somewhere else?" He didn't want her to go, but it was a reasonable question.

"She won't leave with Rob downstairs. We're here for the night. I told her I might cut out early though, depending."

Dean used the volume of the music to lean in closer. They were mere inches apart, and she didn't seem to be nervous like she'd been the other day when he'd sat beside her on the park bench in town. "I was thinking the same. It was kind of a long day."

"Did you drive here?"

"No, I rode with Allen. I can take an Uber home if he drinks too much. I don't think he plans on going home tonight," he said with a glance at Allen and the woman he'd cozied up to.

"I can give you a ride home if you need one," Lindy offered casually. She knew she was playing with fire, drawing out their time together, but she could still feel his mouth pressed against her own and how easily she'd opened to it. It was tempting fate, but she was just this side of reckless tonight.

"Frances is here?" Dean asked skeptically. "Is she even roadworthy anymore?" He knew Lindy had bought the car in college. She'd taken to calling her Frances after the main character in *Dirty Dancing*. He'd been amused. It was just one of Lindy's quirks. She'd probably drive that beat-up old Jeep forever.

"She's good as new. I mean that literally. I think I've replaced every part on her at least twice," Lindy said with a roll of her eyes. They stayed out talking until the next band started and then exchanged a look. Without a word, they both headed for the door.

Dean stopped to let the guys know he was on his way, and Lindy found Nina hovering near the door. They both said their goodbyes and headed out into the cool air. Lindy slipped on her jacket as they walked, and Dean nearly sighed in disappointment. They commiserated on just how bad the band had been as they walked to her car. When they got in, Lindy slipped off her jacket and slid into the driver's seat. Dean climbed in with a grin, happy to see the jacket discarded in the back. He leaned his seat back and watched Lindy drive. He liked how confidently she did everything. He wondered what it would take to shake that confidence a little.

"I'm sorry, but I really need to cleanse my listening palate. I'm not kidding. I don't want that band stuck in my head for the next week," Lindy told him. She plugged her phone in and selected a playlist. "Any requests?" she asked him before she hit play.

"No, I'm good with whatever," Dean said with a smile.

He'd had a few drinks at the first bar and a few at the last, and he was just this side of drunk. But not quite. All of his senses were heightened, and the focus was on Lindy. He planned on enjoying this rare time alone with her. It would take a little over half an hour to get back home. He put on his seatbelt and smiled when Bruce Springsteen blared from her speakers. She started to turn it down, but he reached out and stopped her hand, holding it in his own. He leaned across the seat and told her he didn't mind the volume.

When he let go of her hand, she missed it and then nearly rolled her eyes at how ridiculous she was being. It was just Dean, after all. Dean, who she'd known forever. Seth's best friend. It wasn't a date or anything like it.

They drove to the sound of The Boss on the speakers, and when they made it to town, Dean turned down the volume for a minute. "Just drive to your house, and I'll walk from there."

"Dean, it's almost three in the morning. I don't mind driving you home."

"I'd rather know you got home safely. And I'm just up the street," Dean pointed out. "I'm not drunk, Lindy. I can make it home from your place."

The playlist switched to "I'm on Fire," one of Lindy's personal favorites, but not exactly what she needed when she was already keyed up from an evening in Dean's company. He exuded sexiness. It was in everything he did. It wasn't always noticeable in their quick interactions in town, in the daylight. But tonight, she couldn't help but notice the cool confidence or the slow smile. And she couldn't quite forget the feel of his hand on her back and his mouth fused to her own. They pulled up at her house and sat in the dark driveway for a minute. Lindy turned off the car and took off her seatbelt slowly while Dean did the same.

"I just need to check something," Dean said casually.

Lindy turned toward him, and he moved in. His mouth was on hers before she could even draw a breath, and she found her hands fisted in his hair. She drew in a sharp breath and broke contact just long enough to meet his eyes. Then, slowly, she moved in. He hadn't expected that. He'd just wanted to test the waters a little, to see if the kiss before had been a fluke or good acting on Lindy's part or something more. He hadn't expected the heat of the response. Hell, he'd almost expected anger or derision but not this. He pulled her in closer, his entire body straining toward hers on the other side of the console.

"Inside," she murmured.

He pulled back and looked into her eyes. She held his stare without blinking, and he could see that she was serious. He wasn't going to ask questions. They got out of the car quickly, and when she fumbled with the keys, he took them from her and carefully opened the door. Then, when she closed it, she found herself pressed up against it, her body fused to Dean's. His hands were stroking her bare back and diving into her hair. She was starting to unbutton his shirt when he pulled back and leaned against the door.

"Lindy, look at me." She dragged her eyes from her fingers on the buttons to meet his own, but her hands didn't stop. He put one hand over hers, and asked, "Are you sure, Lindy? I know you were drinking earlier."

"Dean, I was sober enough to drive us both home. I know what I want." She left those words hanging in the air for a minute, and then his mouth moved back to hers. There was no more hesitation, and she had just a moment to savor the sweetness of him making sure that she was okay first. Then there were no more thoughts and only sensation.

*****

Lindy woke up desperately needing that first hit of coffee. She didn't move though. She wasn't sure how to with Dean's arm wrapped firmly around her body and their legs solidly intertwined. She could feel him nuzzling his face against the back of her neck. "It's too early," he said groggily. "Did we even sleep?"

Lindy glanced at the clock. "Maybe an hour. Just over."

"You need room darkening shades," he muttered.

"So noted," she said with a slow smile.

With no coffee, her brain hadn't yet begun its busy spinning, which she was sure it would do later. Right now, she just felt languid. Exhausted, yes, but perfectly content. She was afraid that the first sip of coffee would jolt her back to her senses with all of the reasons why this wasn't right. She closed her eyes and pulled the sheet up a little higher, not for warmth as much as coverage.

She was all too aware that her clothes were lying in a heap somewhere near the front door. She had no idea where she'd left her shoes. She would have been both delighted and embarrassed to know that one still lay outside at the door and the other lay just inside where it had been kicked carelessly aside. Her shoes weren't used to being treated so cavalierly.

Dean began softly kissing the back of her neck, a kiss that moved around and down the line of her shoulder and then traveled up to her ear. She found herself turning toward him, exhaustion be damned. She'd think about the consequences later, over the strongest coffee she could make, but right now, she just wanted a little more time. Her mouth found his easily. After all, she'd found it again and again during the night, between short bouts of sleep.

The sun was up quite a bit higher when they woke again, and Lindy realized that she was lucky that her mom had made a breakfast date with Vera earlier in the week. The timing could not have been better. Usually, she'd be up and maybe even reading in the garden by now, which would have proved awkward for all of them. Not that her mother would judge her in the normal course of events, but this was Dean for Christ's sake. The same playboy who had charmed half the skirts in town and who her mom had watched grow up. He was practically family. Thankfully, she'd never felt particularly familial toward him in any way, but it would undoubtedly be awkward if anyone were to find out.

They'd stumbled, bleary-eyed, into a shower that got quite a bit hotter than Lindy had been expecting, and then she stumbled downstairs to make coffee while Dean got dressed. She wondered, bemusedly, if he'd be able to find all of his clothes. After all, they seemed to have come off in stages throughout the house the night before. She'd thrown on his shirt and sauntered downstairs wearing little else.

Over that first sip of coffee, she thought about the situation. Clearly, they'd need to be discreet. Either it was a one-time thing they never spoke of again, or they would need to be very careful. And very casual. Lindy didn't want to become one of his starry-eyed groupies he had to ghost. They were adults, after all, and there was no reason they both couldn't handle a sexual relationship maturely.

She looked up and saw Dean watching her from the doorway. He'd found his slacks, but as she was wearing his shirt, his chest was bare. He was watching her intently, and when she looked up at him over her cup of coffee, he smiled. As he walked over and took the cup from her and took a sip, she wondered why it felt like so much more than just a casual fling. But then, they'd known each other forever, she reasoned. It was bound to feel different.

"I have other cups," she pointed out, taking hers back. She got him a mug down from the cabinet and turned to find him a step behind her and their bodies aligned.

"Thanks," he said, taking the mug and sitting it on the counter. He took her own mug and sat it down, too, and kissed her softly.

She could see, easily, how other women fell so hard for him. She returned the kiss and then picked up his mug and gave it back to him and picked up her own pointedly and started drinking. He laughed and went to pour coffee into his mug. She'd just have to remember to keep her wits about her. The last thing she needed to do was fall in love with someone like Dean Walton.

Chapter 13

Theodore Westerman picked up his cell phone and checked it once again to make sure it was fully charged. It was, of course. Just like it had been five minutes ago when he checked it and ten minutes before that. He shook his head ruefully. He hadn't waited around for the phone to ring since he was a moony adolescent, and he was pretty sure it was a phone with a curly cord attached to a wall. Or maybe even a rotary phone.

God, he felt old. And he felt older still as he checked his messages and wondered about the current dating protocol. Was he supposed to call her? Send a text? Send an instant message filled with emojis? He wasn't sure how this worked anymore.

He drank his coffee and tried to return to the *National Geographic* he'd been reading. Okay, trying to read. He hadn't read, or at least absorbed, a single word. He sighed and picked up his phone. He knew one person he could ask, but he was afraid it was an awkward thing to do. Still, he didn't have a lot of options. Most of his friends were either confirmed bachelors or had been married for so long that they couldn't be of real help. He selected her number from his speed dial and sat back and listened to it ring. He knew that at five rings it would go directly to voice mail. Presley never did have any patience.

"Hey, Dad," Presley answered, sounding breathless.

"Did I catch you on your morning run?" he asked, already knowing the answer.

"I've just finished. I'm nearly up to eight miles now." Theodore knew that she was training for a half marathon. It was still a few months off, but she was determined.

"That's impressive." He waited a beat. "Which donut are you getting?" he asked, tongue in cheek. Presley started her run downtown and always made sure she hit the donut shop on the walk back home. She called it balance, but he thought of it as one of the many whimsical things about his daughter.

"I'm going to grab a Bearclaw this morning," she said with a smile in her voice.

Presley had been like that as a girl, too—a contradiction more often than not—always the one to make the unexpected choice. In fact, he'd fully expected her to become a doctor or a researcher after her keen interest in medicine. She'd collected medical knowledge while other girls were collecting nail polish or dates or college applications. She'd gone after a nursing degree and then gone on to become a midwife. She'd also gotten certified as a yoga instructor, and she led a class once a week at the local gym. She still surprised him sometimes with her ability to switch gears and keep finding new goals to embrace. The half marathon was the latest in a line of goals she'd set for herself.

"That sounds good," Theodore replied, stalling for time. "How's work?"

"Same as always. What's up, Dad? Is everything okay?" she asked, sounding worried. He heard her cover the phone with her hand for a moment and call out, "Bear claw and a skinny mocha latte. Thanks."

"I just had a question, and I wasn't sure who else to ask," Theodore began.

"Medical?" Presley asked, curiously.

"Um, no," Theodore said. "You see, I had this date the other night ..."

"Oh, Dad." Presley sighed. "Did it not go well?"

She worried about him. Presley took her Bear claw and latte over to a small chair in the back. It was warm in the café and a bit chilly outside. Presley looked down at her running clothes and wished she were a little more warmly dressed. Not that the hipsters here would pay her any mind. This place was mostly that sort of establishment, with the occasional business person rushing off to work.

Presley sat in her workout clothes with her black hair pulled up into a ponytail. Her hair was fairly short these days so it only made the shortest of tails in the back, and she had a straight fringe of bangs over light blue eyes. When she wore makeup, she could look quite striking, if she did say so herself. But in yoga pants, a racerback tank, and a fresh face, she considered herself pretty average. She didn't notice an appreciative glance that slid her way quickly and was gone. She was too busy watching the door. People watching wasn't exactly her hobby. She was really just watching for one person.

"No, it went fine. Actually, it went great."

"So, what's the problem?"

"I don't know what to do. Do I call her? Do I text her? Do I need to send those emoji things? Am I supposed to send her a friend request? What?" Presley laughed at his befuddlement.

"Dad, you've done this before."

"I know that," he said in exasperation. "Just not with anyone I really like."

"Oh." Presley thought about that. "Do you want to call her?"

"Well, yes, but I wasn't sure if that's what's done now."

"Look, if you want to call her, call her. If you want to send a text, do that. Do not, I repeat do not, send her any emojis. Some of them don't mean what you think they mean. Just do what feels natural."

"None of this feels natural."

"You'll be fine, Dad. I'm glad you met someone nice. What's she like?"

She'd always thought her dad would remarry after her mom died. As a teenager, it was something she feared. Just the whole idea of a stepmom had creeped her out. But then she'd watched her dad handle everything and do it all alone. She'd wanted him to find someone nice. He'd dated. Even she could acknowledge her dad was a good-looking man. But he'd never met anyone he'd wanted to commit to long term.

She could relate, she supposed. She'd only ever truly fallen in love once. And that hadn't turned out great. In fact, she'd met him right here. They'd shared a cup of coffee at this very table. She sat there and watched the door, but she rarely saw him. She suspected that when he'd left her for someone else that he'd found somewhere else to buy coffee. Still, she wanted to see him, if only to know if she would still feel the same when he came through the door. She drank deeply of her latte and knew she probably would.

"I think you'd like her, Presley. She's very smart and well-read. She has great taste in music. She's beautiful but in a sort of classic way. Anyway, she owns the tea room in Madison. The one where I had my book signing?"

"Aha! I thought you seemed particularly pleased with how the signing had gone. This explains it," Presley said with a laugh. "Does she have any kids?"

Presley thought she'd have liked siblings. Well, other siblings than the one she actually had. She had Layla, who was only a couple of years younger than her. They hadn't been close since their Mom had died though. That was about when Layla had gone off the rails. First, smoking and drinking. Later, the drugs. She'd sort of cleaned up her life these last few years. She'd gotten a steady job and started taking classes at a community college. She'd even met a guy who didn't sound like a total loser, like all the rest of the men she'd dated. Still, they hadn't quite managed to make the leap from sisters to friends.

"She has a son and a daughter. The son is about your age, and the daughter is a few years older," Theodore explained. "I met the daughter at the book signing, briefly."

"Well, call her if you're going to call her. Just don't stress about it," she said breezily and then stopped.

The door had opened, admitting a blast of cool air and her ex—with his new girlfriend. She felt her stomach drop and suddenly wished she'd gone someplace else or at least left immediately after getting her coffee. She picked at the bear claw and turned away from the door, hoping to go unnoticed. She'd been about to get off the phone, but she didn't want to look like some loser sitting here at "their" table, in workout clothes no less, and makeup-free. At least a phone conversation made her look busy.

"I will. I'm sorry if it's awkward. I wasn't sure who else I could ask."

"It's not a problem, Dad. Really," she said quietly. "Dating is stressful."

"Are you dating anyone, pumpkin?"

"I don't really have a lot of time right now. With work and the marathon. I am picking up an extra yoga class though. This one is just a couple of times a month for some of my patients."

She chatted a little about her plans for the class and about work. Her dad liked to hear about the most ridiculous baby names she heard, and she heard a lot. She amused him for a little while with those stories and then glanced around to see if the coast was clear. She looked up just in time to make eye contact with Derek. He held her eyes for a beat and then looked away, abashed. He was steering *her* out of the shop quickly.

Presley doubted that Amber had even noticed her back here. She wasn't the type to notice anyone but herself really. It was unfortunate that Presley had been the one to introduce them. Not that she'd had much of a choice. Derek had come by to have lunch with her at the hospital cafeteria and Amber had inserted herself into their conversation.

Still, Presley had never seen what was coming. She hated that it had made the rounds of the rumor mill before she found out. She looked back and wished that they'd had lunch outside, even though it had been pouring, or back in one of the private lounges. Somewhere an entry-level nurse working part-time would be unlikely to visit. Amber had seen Derek, wanted him, and made sure that she got him.

Presley sighed before she remembered herself. She knew her Dad heard it, just that brief pause in what he was saying. "Is everything okay?"

She wanted to say no. That she still loved someone who didn't love her back. That she was lonely. That she was training for a marathon so she'd be too tired to think after work. Instead, she replied, "I'm fine, Dad. I just realized I'm going to be late for my shift if I don't head back now to get a shower. Can we talk later?"

"Of course, pumpkin. I love you."

"I love you, too. And don't forget to call her."

She heard his chuckle before she hung up. She rubbed her chest, over her heart. She'd caught her breath but still felt the tightness around her heart. She ate the last bite of the bear claw and took a last sip of the latte before she tossed the cup away. She headed outside in the chilly air and decided that she'd try that other coffee shop. After all, they gave a discount if you brought in your own cup, and she'd heard that they had quite the pastry selection. Maybe it was time to stop haunting "their" old spots and find some new ones.

*****

While Theodore was listening to Keely's phone ring, Dean was walking to work. He'd made it out of Lindy's with no one the wiser. He'd slipped out the back way. He already knew it wasn't visible from the main house. He'd taken a girlfriend there once when he and Seth had been teenagers. Seth had given the okay, but then he'd warned him that his mom was going to start fixing the place up to rent out so he'd found other places to go. Dean walked home and changed for work and then headed over on foot. He'd go pick up his truck after work or ask one of the guys to drop it off in town.

He was distracted, thinking of Lindy still lying in bed. She'd made him coffee and an omelet, and they'd sat in her little kitchen and talked over breakfast. He'd been distracted by her long legs while they'd talked. His shirt came to about mid-thigh, and she'd only buttoned it up part of the way. He wanted to kiss her collarbone and let his hand move up her smooth thighs. But instead, he'd eaten the best omelet he'd had in ages and drank coffee and watched Lindy move easily around her kitchen.

He'd never seen her like this, at least not as an adult. She seemed more relaxed and less guarded. He enjoyed the snarky version she'd always shown him, but he liked this, too. He leaned forward while she was still talking and kissed her. She went still and then leaned in to return it, running her fingers through his hair. He rested one hand lightly on her waist and drew the kiss out slowly.

"Keep that up, and you're not going to make it to work on time," she told him evenly.

He sat back with a grin, "I can be ... very efficient."

"I'm sure you can," she grinned ruefully. "But if you stay much later, you might run into my mom coming back from Vera's. How would that look?"

"I'd imagine it would look like what it is," Dean replied evenly.

"Will you explain that to Seth, too?" she asked him curiously, raising an eyebrow.

"Okay, point taken. So, this is just between us?"

"I don't see a reason to take an ad out in the paper about it. We're adults after all," Lindy told him with a shrug. "It was fun, and maybe we can do it again sometime."

Dean looked at her, putting the mugs into the dishwasher along with their plates. "Sometime ... like later tonight?"

She looked up, quickly. "Okay," she said simply.

"I left my phone upstairs," Dean told her. They walked up the stairs together, each thinking about the situation.

"I guess you'll need this back." Lindy slowly unbuttoned his shirt and shrugged it off. She handed it to him, and he stood frozen for a full minute before he moved into her.

"I can be quick," he murmured.

"Normally, that is not a commendation, but under the circumstances …"

Now, walking to work, he remembered how she looked stretched out beneath the blankets. She'd been nearly asleep when he left, which is probably why she hadn't objected when he'd kissed her again. She mumbled something about locking the door on the way out, and Dean had just grinned down at her. They really hadn't had much sleep. He decided to grab coffee on the way into work. He was still thinking about Lindy, sex, and coffee—in that order—when he nearly plowed into Seth and Libby.

"Hey!" Seth called out with a laugh. "Wake up!"

"Sorry about that. I guess I'm not fully awake yet. I overslept," he replied shortly, feeling awkward.

"Are you on your way to work?" Libby asked him.

"Yeah, I'm covering a guy for a couple of hours. We're taking shorter shifts today so I'll have the afternoon free," Dean explained. "I was just heading to pick up some coffee if I have time."

"We're doing the same. Why don't we grab you some coffee so you can get to work on time?" Libby asked him kindly. "We're heading over there anyway."

"That's sweet of you. You got a good one, Seth," Dean said with a smile. "Better treat her right."

"I'm just lucky I saw her first," Seth said with a grin. Libby rolled her eyes at the two of them and got Dean's coffee order. "I'll bring it over to you in a few," Seth told him. "Hey, you need any help on the lake house later?"

"I could stand to put in a few hours tomorrow if you're available. Not tonight though. I didn't get much sleep." Dean tried not to look as awkward as he felt.

"Yeah, you're asleep on your feet today. You must have had a good night," Seth said with a grin. "Late night in Athens?" he asked in an innocent tone.

"Mind your business," Libby told him, poking Seth in the stomach. She looked back at Dean with a smile. "Don't mind him. Go ahead and get to work, and we'll bring the coffee by shortly."

He nodded appreciatively and tried not to wonder how Seth would react if he found out what had happened. It's not that he was overly protective of Lindy or anything, but she was still his sister. He was relieved that they had decided to keep what happened quiet, even if the suggestion had annoyed him at first. Still, it was probably best for now. He couldn't help but marvel that it had happened at all.

Chapter 14

Seth dropped coffee off for Dean at the fire station and then headed back to Brews & Blues. He dropped onto the couch beside Libby and gratefully took his coffee. "It's starting to get cold outside," he noted.

"It really is. I'm glad we brought jackets," Libby said, sipping from her mug. "I'm about ready to get the fireplace going. I know it's a little early, but it's that kind of day."

She looked out at the gray skies and wondered if it would rain later or just stay this chilly gray. She was taking the day off from writing, and Seth had Farrah and Jamie minding the shop so they were spending the time together. She wouldn't mind a lazy day reading in front of the fire or curled up watching movies.

"Do you want to go ahead and walk home, let the coffee keep us warm?"

"Sure."

Seth held the door open for her, and she started to go back the way they came. "Do you mind if we walk this way instead?"

Libby looked at him curiously but agreed. "That's fine with me. I don't think any of the shops are open yet though."

"I just thought it would be nice to take a different route home," he said noncommittally.

"You're being weird, but okay. What do you want to do today?"

"Whatever you want."

"I really don't care. I'm glad we have the whole day to do whatever. Even if it's sleep. It seemed like a long week."

Libby had gotten an article in for the paper, added a few entries into her blog, and had taken a day trip and done a quick travel writeup for an online journal. She wasn't about to work this weekend. That was the luxury of being a freelancer after all. They'd also spent most afternoons boxing up the rest of her apartment and slowly moving it across town to Seth's house. They'd agreed to move in together after a lot of consideration. And therapy. They'd had things to work through, after all. But it seemed like the next step. Her lease would be up soon, and they'd managed to get the last couple of boxes out last night.

"I've been thinking," Seth said, as they approached the park. "It's been a year since we met, and I know this year didn't start out great for us. My fault, I know." He sat down on the park bench. Libby sat beside him and covered his hand with her own. "I know it hasn't been long since we've been back together. But I've been thinking a lot about it, and I just don't know that moving in together is the next step."

"Wait. You don't want to live together?" Libby asked him, withdrawing her hand, quickly.

"No, that's not what I'm saying. I'm saying this wrong," he replied in frustration. "What I'm trying to say is that I don't think it's the only next step." Libby looked at him curiously. "I fell in love with you probably somewhere into our second date," Seth admitted.

Libby reached over and took his hand again.

"Me, too," she replied quietly. "I didn't want to. I wasn't ready yet."

"Me either. Are you ready now?"

"I'm happy with us. I love us."

"So do I. And I don't want to ever be without us. I know you haven't been divorced long, and I know that neither of us counted on the other. But ..." He stopped for a moment and stood up, motioning Libby to stay seated. He knelt down, and Libby stopped breathing. He reached a hand in his pocket, and Libby went completely still. He brought out the box slowly.

"Marry me, Libby. Spend the rest of your life with me. I love you, and I can't imagine the future without us." He handed her the box, which she slowly opened. The ring inside was clearly vintage. "It was the ring my grandfather gave to my grandmother, and he gave it to me in his will to give to the woman I spend my life with. There's no one else I want wearing this ring but you."

Libby reached out and touched it, still silent. Seth looked at her face and noticed the silent tears falling down.

He quickly got up from kneeling and sat beside her. "Too soon?"

"No," she said softly, reaching out to touch his face. "Just right." She smiled, and he slipped the ring on her finger with shaking hands.

"I'm taking that as a yes," Seth said with a laugh.

"Of course, I'm saying yes," Libby laughed, leaning her head on his shoulder. "But, baby?"

"Yes?"

"It's really cold out here. Can we go home now?" Seth laughed and pulled her to her feet. They walked home with her left hand held tightly in his, the vintage diamond winking in the light.

*****

Lindy woke up and reached for her phone to check the time. She couldn't remember the last time she slept so late. It was nearly noon. Of course, she hadn't gotten much sleep the night before, and she didn't have to be at the studio today. She could stay in bed all day if she wanted. She sat up and stretched. She felt like she'd run a marathon, but that made sense given the night's activities. She got up slowly and pulled on leggings and a sweater featuring a vintage 80s cartoon and headed downstairs.

She made herself a sandwich while she booted up her laptop at the kitchen counter. She slathered ciabatta bread with savory honey mustard and piled it high with thick slices of ham she'd bought at the butchers in town a couple of days ago. She added lettuce and a slice of tomato and scrounged around until she found the package with a couple of slices left of provolone cheese. She layered it with swiss and sat down to look through potential donors. She tried to focus on their medical histories and various talents. It felt like reviewing job applications, but she knew it was a necessary part of the process. She poured herself a glass of orange juice and took the fertility drug that they'd given her. Since she was over thirty-five, they suggested it to increase her chances of conception.

Her phone rang, and she nearly jumped. She looked down and noticed the local number pop up. She suspected it was Dean, and it was. She answered the call, feeling awkward, and closed the laptop. "Hello."

"I just wanted to make sure it was still okay if I came over later," Dean said casually.

He'd grabbed a slice of pizza on lunch before calling Lindy. He wasn't exactly sure how to handle this. After all, this was Lindy. It wasn't just some woman he met who he could casually text when he got around to it. Number one, her temper was notorious. He'd been on the receiving end of it a time or two. And number two, he wasn't sure exactly what was going on between them, but he didn't want to screw it up.

"Yeah, that's fine," Lindy said, wondering what else to say. "I was just having lunch."

"Yeah, me, too," Dean said, walking back to the fire station. "I'm out of here in a couple of hours."

"Did you want to come over then?"

"Yeah, if you don't mind." Dean paused. "Should I maybe just walk over? So my truck's not parked outside?"

"Oh, good thinking. Yeah, that would be great. Or I could pick you up when I come through town? I've got to run to the grocery store in an hour or so anyway."

Lindy remembered how empty her refrigerator seemed. She'd had enough for an omelet and a sandwich but not much more. She'd need to feed him, right? They could always order in, but she liked to at least be able to offer to cook. Then, she reminded herself that it wasn't an actual relationship. Just casual sex with an old—friend. She'd never really considered him a friend before, but they'd been a part of each other's lives, at least peripherally, for ages.

"That could work. Maybe pick me up over at the park?" Dean asked, relieved that she wasn't going to blow him off. You never could tell with Lindy. Her moods could change like the wind.

"Sure. I'll call you when I'm on my way," Lindy told him and hung up.

She opened the laptop back up and tried to concentrate. She thought she'd mostly figured out her cycle, and she was taking the medicine they'd prescribed. She'd even gotten it filled at a pharmacy out of town so she didn't have to deal with the gossip that would surely result if she filled it locally. She needed to make her mind up about a donor. She saw one she liked with blonde hair and green eyes and the cutest baby pictures, but then she checked herself. She could have been describing Dean. Clearly, she was just distracted.

She tried to shake it off. It was just healthy sex. A lot of healthy sex. But that was good for her. After all, she wasn't going to be celibate just because she was planning a family on her own. Eventually, she might even meet someone she could have a serious, long-term relationship with. Not necessarily marriage. Just someone she could love who would love her baby, too. But if that didn't happen, she had no intention of missing the boat on starting a family.

Forty was looming large these days. A good friend of hers from school had just turned forty and announced her pregnancy. But Lindy didn't want to wait. If this thing with Dean wasn't casual, she'd probably just tell him about it, but she didn't want to make it weird. Anyway, they'd been very careful last night, and she'd just have to make sure that they didn't have any accidents. After all, she was determined to plan her little family. She skipped over the donor with the eyes so like Dean's and looked at a few other options.

*****

Dean looked at his phone in amusement. He'd always known she could be abrupt. What he hadn't known was that she could be soft. She could wake up quiet and move with him slowly. He heard his name being called and nearly sighed. He should have walked back to work the other way.

"Hey, Naomi. How's it going?" You couldn't just pass someone on the street and not acknowledge them. At least, not in Madison.

"You know, Dean, living the dream," she said with a smile.

He noticed that she'd paired her short skirt with tights in a nod to the cooler weather and was wearing a leather jacket over a tight-fitting plaid shirt that was open to expose a generous amount of cleavage. At one point in time, he'd thought she was the sexiest thing. He'd been curious, and he'd indulged his curiosity. Now, she showed up at work and drunk texted him whenever. He really wished he'd remembered that curiosity killed the cat. Though he thought he remembered Lindy saying that the expression didn't mean what he thought it meant. He'd have to ask her about it later.

"Good. It was good seeing you, Naomi," Dean said quickly, stepping around her. "I've got to get back to work."

Naomi lengthened her stride and caught up to him. "I was just going this way myself," she told him. "Want to hang out after work?" Sure, he'd ignored her drunk texts the other night, but that was to be expected. She would have, too. But maybe he needed a more direct approach.

"I can't. Sorry. Thanks for thinking of me though. It's just that I've got plans already," Dean told her with a helpless shrug.

"Oh?" Naomi asked, nonplussed. "What kind of plans?"

"Um, well, it's sort of a date," Dean admitted. God, he was usually much smoother than this. He mentally kicked himself for being so damn awkward. "I have a date, Naomi. I'm sorry."

Naomi stopped and gave him a cool look. "Well, your loss, Dean." She turned on her heel and walked away.

He figured she'd be steaming so he hurried in the opposite direction back to work. He'd have been surprised to know that she walked away with tears in her eyes. Sure, she was mad, but she also felt humiliated and hurt. And very, very angry.

Chapter 15

Lindy reached over to unlock the door. Her Jeep was so old that it didn't run to automatic locks. Or automatic anything, really. Dean slid in with a smile. "Thanks for picking me up." He noticed that she'd picked him up on the opposite side of the park from where her mother ran the tea room. They even went back to her place without passing it. Well, he'd always known Lindy was clever.

"No problem. How was work?" she asked him, trying not to feel awkward about this whole situation in the light of day.

"Pretty tame. No fires. No emergencies at all actually. I did get a call about doing a kid's birthday party so I put that on the schedule."

"I didn't know you did that," Lindy replied glancing over at him. "I knew you did the school thing and the parades."

"Yeah, it's a community thing we do. It's actually pretty fun. There's a good chance of cake anyway," he said with a grin.

"Well, you do have a notorious sweet tooth," Lindy said with a roll of her eyes, parking in her driveway.

"And as I recall, you always had a thing for sour over sweet," Dean replied as they headed inside. She looked over at him curiously. "Hey, I pay attention."

"Hmm…" she said, noncommittally. "I've just got to get the groceries inside."

"No, I've got it," Dean told her, heading back out to the car.

He was glad Lindy didn't know just exactly how well he knew her. Or at least, how well he'd known her in high school. He'd made it his business to study her then, but that was some time ago. He didn't know the all-grown-up version of Lindy very well. Sure, he spent most of the holidays with her family, but she'd always sort of avoided him. He figured he annoyed her as much as he had as a kid. She treated him like Seth's little friend, not like family. Of course, he was particularly glad now that she'd never treated him like one of the family. That would just be weird. Weirder than it already was.

As he came into the kitchen, he noticed Lindy shutting down her laptop and putting it away in the other room. "Thanks," she told him briefly, digging through the bags on the counter to put away the groceries. "Want something to drink? Iced tea? Beer?"

"I wouldn't say no to a beer," Dean told her. "Need some help?"

"No, I've got it," she told him, passing him the can of PBR across the counter. He looked at her thoughtfully while he cracked it open and took a sip. Maybe he wasn't the only one who had been paying attention. "You can turn on the TV if you want while I'm doing this."

"Sure, okay," Dean said.

He figured maybe he was making her nervous—or just getting on her nerves. Lately, it could go either way. He went into the living room and sat on the couch. He flipped through the channels for a minute, thinking more about being at Lindy's house and Lindy herself in the other room. He stopped on a nature documentary that caught his eye.

When Lindy walked into the room carrying a glass of red wine and a plate of snacks, Dean was already fast asleep on the sofa. She grinned at him. "Well, so much for round two."

She went over to the couch and sat the plate and wine glass down on the end table and untied the laces on his boots. She removed them and pulled the throw from the back of the couch around him. She shut off the lamps around the room and then returned to the couch. She looked at the nature documentary with interest and curled up on the other side of the sofa from Dean. She tucked her bare feet into the blanket with him, and after a moment's hesitation, reached down and pulled his legs up onto the couch. It was a long couch, and she figured he'd be more comfortable that way. She reached for the plate, a mix of the sweet and the savory she'd picked up at the deli in town, and grabbed a handful of salted peanuts. She took a sip of wine and watched Dean with interest for a minute.

It was odd to see him sleeping. She hadn't really had a chance to observe him sleeping before. He didn't snore. Actually, he hardly made a sound. She thought wryly about holding a mirror up to make sure he was still breathing. She shook her head. He was attractive. She'd never been able to deny that. And he could be sweet when he wanted. Or at least when it suited his purposes.

She imagined it suited him now, whatever this was that they were doing. And it suited her, too. After all, she wasn't looking for a relationship. She turned her attention back to the nature documentary and melted when they began talking about mothers and babies. That's all she wanted. To be a mother, to start a family of her own.

*****

Dean woke up and took a moment to orient himself to where he was. He could have kicked himself. He couldn't believe he'd fallen asleep at Lindy's. He opened his eyes slowly and saw Lindy curled up on the other side of the couch beside him. The documentary he'd turned on was just going off, and Lindy turned to him. "I wasn't sure if you were going to wake up or not," she told him with a grin.

"Sorry. I didn't get much sleep last night," he replied with a slow smile.

"I remember. Feel better?"

"Much." He sat up. "Did you take off my shoes?"

"You looked uncomfortable," Lindy said, getting up to walk to the kitchen. Dean noticed that she was the one looking uncomfortable now. He followed her.

"That was awfully sweet of you."

"It was practical anyway. I didn't want you getting your work boots on the couch," she said with a shrug. "Seth called while you were out. Mom's hosting brunch tomorrow, and he's bringing Libby. He said something about inviting you. He called your phone, so you'll probably have a message."

"Huh. Well, that's random."

"Are you going to go?"

"Would you mind if I did?"

"Why would I mind? Of course, you can go. If you want to," Lindy told him, looking inside the fridge.

"Then, I'll go. What are you doing anyway?" She'd been standing in the door of the fridge for a while now.

"Oh, I thought I would make dinner if you're hungry," Lindy told him, closing the refrigerator door. "Are you hungry?"

"Mm-hm. Maybe you can make dinner a little later? It's still early after all," Dean said, taking her hand.

"What did you have in mind?" Lindy asked with a slow smile of her own.

"What don't I have in mind?" Dean asked with a grin, pulling her toward him.

A couple of hours later, they made it back down the stairs. While Lindy was getting dressed, Dean returned the call to Seth to accept the invitation to brunch. It's not that he was never invited, but it was a rare thing. He wondered if it would be awkward to spend time around the family now that he and Lindy were—doing whatever the hell they were doing.

He'd like to say dating, but he had a feeling Lindy was trying to keep it a little more casual than that. He was usually fine with that, but he wondered what it would be like to take her out to dinner. He thought he'd quite like to see her on the other side of the table, lit by candlelight even. He wasn't exactly a hopeless romantic, but with

Lindy, he thought he could be.

She walked down the stairs in leggings and a sweater that said, The Future is Female. He grinned at her and asked, "Do you want to just order in?"

"No, I don't mind cooking. Just give me a few minutes. Want a drink while you wait? I've got Coke, beer, and wine," she said, rummaging through the refrigerator. "And orange juice."

"A Coke is fine."

He watched her and wondered how they'd got there. He'd expected it to be awkward, but it wasn't really. It was a mix of the familiar and the unknown together. He liked it. All through dinner, they talked casually and ate, but he noticed she kept glancing at the clock. At first, he thought it was his imagination, but then he grew mildly annoyed.

"Got plans tonight?"

"Not really," Lindy said with a shrug. "Just a little TV, maybe a long bath later. You?"

"I had some ideas on that," he told her with a smug grin. "I thought from the way you were watching the time that you had a hot date."

"I did have a date, actually. I rescheduled it."

"Rescheduled, huh?" Dean looked at her blankly. Well, they weren't exactly in a committed relationship. In fact, he wasn't even sure if Lindy wanted a relationship. "For me?"

"No, for me," Lindy said calmly, getting up to take her plate to the sink. "I didn't get a lot of sleep last night, and I want to call it an early night," she said, looking at him pointedly.

"Okay, message received, loud and clear," Dean said with a laugh. "I need to go home and get some sleep, too, if I'm going to make it to brunch on time."

*****

After Dean left, Lindy pulled out her laptop. She knew she would need to reserve a little time to figure out this thing with Dean. It already seemed to be getting out of hand. That first night was understandable. She'd needed to blow off steam, and he'd been there. They'd had unexpected chemistry. But to have him over the second day in a row and sitting down together at dinner like an actual relationship—well, she needed to make sure she kept the boundaries clear. Otherwise, this needed to stop altogether.

She shook off those thoughts and tried to concentrate. She still needed to choose a donor, and she couldn't do that if she couldn't focus. So here she was, scanning through the databank. There were a few solid possibilities. She made a couple of notes and thought about what it would be like to have a child of her own. She drifted off that way, her head pillowed on her arm on the table.

When she woke up a few hours later, she noticed the silence in her home and the lateness of the hour. She sat up groggily and decided to make her way up to bed. She powered down her laptop and headed upstairs slowly. She had the passing thought that she wished she'd had Dean stay over. Still, she didn't want to get in the habit of sleeping with someone else. She would miss it when he moved on, and she had no intention of getting used to it. After all, her future would be just the two of them—herself and baby. That was the plan anyway.

She made it into her bed, leaving her clothes on. She pulled the sheets around her and could smell Dean's cologne. She grinned and then caught herself. She stared up at the ceiling and wondered what she'd been thinking. His cologne had probably graced the sheets of half the town, and it was inevitable he'd move along when he had the chance. She would take it just as casually. That would be much better than getting her heart broken. Besides, in a year's time, or hopefully a little less, she'd be snuggled up in this bed with a baby of her own. She sighed happily at the thought.

She hadn't been lying about rescheduling the date. She checked her text messages and saw that she had one from Reggie. He was attractive and a real sweetheart, but she just wasn't up for going out tonight. She'd met him at the studio during a co-ed wedding shower he had grudgingly attended. Apparently, the groom was his brother, and the sister of the bride was his ex. So, he'd hung around Lindy as a buffer from the tension of the room and they'd discovered mutual interests.

Mostly, they'd discovered a mutual interest in each other. They'd been out for coffee a couple of times and he had wanted to make her dinner. She'd taken a raincheck, but now she texted back to see when a good time to go might be. She had no intention of not living her life because of the baby or because of Dean Walton. In fact, she was looking forward to the future, although she considered she'd have to step away from the dating game long before birth.

She smiled sleepily and snuggled down into the covers. So, they smelled like Dean. So what? They'd had a good time, and then they'd had a number of common interests to talk about. That's all it was. There was no harm in it, especially if she set the boundaries up early. Of course, he wasn't likely to get attached, and Lindy knew his reputation enough to know that it would be unwise for her to form an attachment there. She shrugged it off and thought about being a mother. She drifted to sleep with a soft smile on her face, holding the pillow Dean had slept on.

Chapter 16

Keely woke up early to find that Seth had already arrived and was just lining up the brunch ingredients. Libby sat at the table drinking coffee with Lindy, one hand tucked in her dress pocket. She smiled as she saw the three of them in the room. She liked to know that she was responsible for introducing Seth and Libby, but she figured it was a small enough town that they might have found their way to each other eventually. Still, it was nice to see that they were happy together, especially after the rocky road they'd traveled earlier this year. Keely could admit now that she thought Seth had royally screwed it up, but at least she'd raised a man who could admit he was wrong and try to make it right.

"Good morning!" Libby said when she saw Keely walk in. "He won't let us help. We tried," she said with a helpless shrug.

"I didn't try that hard," Lindy said with a grin.

"I bet you didn't," Keely said with a wry look. "Now what all are we having?"

"Libby made some muffins, but I thought I'd make omelets to go with them," Seth told her.

"That sounds good," Keely said as the bell rang. "Are we expecting anyone?"

"Well, yeah," Seth said sheepishly. "I didn't think you'd mind if I asked Beth and Dean to come over, too."

"The more the merrier, I always say. But this is all very suspicious," she said with a curious look. Libby hopped up and went to answer the door, motioning them to sit back down. Lindy and Keely exchanged curious glances.

"We'll satisfy your curiosity soon enough," Seth told her with a smile.

"And your appetite," Libby reminded them, coming into the kitchen with Beth and Dean in tow. "I'm starving!"

"You're always hungry," Seth said with a grin. "Eat a muffin while you wait. They're really good muffins."

"Of course they are. I made them," Libby said smugly, getting one out herself and passing the basket around the table.

"How's my best girl?" Dean asked, coming in to wrap Keely in a bear hug.

She pressed her cheek briefly to his. She often thought of Dean as her other child. He'd been such a wild thing when he'd come over playing with Seth, left to his own devices for hours and restless with it. He'd taken to their home life like a duck to water, and it would have melted her heart to know that Dean thought of her as a mother of the heart, too.

"I'm just fine. It's so good to see you." She held on a moment longer and then sat back. "Are you still charming all the ladies?" she asked him with a grin.

He grinned at her, "None of them can hold a candle to you," he replied automatically. They'd had this banter for ages, but now he wanted to glance over at Lindy. He didn't, of course, but he wanted to.

"Don't believe a word this one says," Beth said dryly. She gave Dean a pointed look as she poured herself a mimosa. "How was the date with Reggie?" Beth asked Lindy, sitting down into the seat beside her.

Dean poured himself a drink, snagged a piece of bacon from the sideboard, and sat down to listen. Lindy ignored him and kept her attention focused on the drink she was pouring. "I had to reschedule," she said with a shrug.

"Wait—is Reggie the hot guy you met at the shower or the one at the bar?" Libby asked, interested.

"You met some guy in a shower, Lindy? That's familiar," Seth tutted from the stove.

"Bridal shower," Lindy said with a laugh.

"Do men go to those?" Dean asked, looking at Seth. They both shook their heads. "Men don't go to those," Dean told them.

"Co-ed shower," Beth inserted. "Anyway, shower guy or bar guy?"

"Shower guy," Lindy said, trying to think of a way to change the conversation. "Where's Mr. Darcy today?"

"Jamie's watching him for me this morning. And don't think you're distracting me. I'm living vicariously through your love life," Beth said with a grin. "So. Reggie. Spill."

"We rescheduled for Tuesday night. I don't have any classes then," Lindy shrugged and tried not to look at Dean.

"Where's he taking you?" Keely asked, curiously.

"Actually, we're going to have an early dinner and then go on one of those full moon guided hikes at the State Botanical Gardens."

"That sounds romantic," Beth sighed.

"I agree. You're meeting him there? At the restaurant?"

"Yes, Mom. You know I'm careful."

"And what does this Reggie guy do? Does he work?" Dean asked. He really, really wanted her to say that he was unemployed. Or to do something seriously uncool for a living. Not that it was a competition anyway. I mean, what could be better than a firefighter, right?

"He's a personal trainer," Lindy muttered into her mimosa.

Libby and Beth both grinned, and even Keely cracked a smile. "A personal trainer, huh?" Dean asked. "For, like, old people? Or dogs?"

"No, like at a gym," Lindy said evenly, finally meeting his eyes. "Anyway, when am I getting fed?" she demanded, looking over at Seth.

"Coming right up," Seth told them. He plated omelets, and

Libby hopped up to help pass them around, shooing Keely back to her seat.

"Well, isn't that lovely?" Keely said, taking Libby's hand as she passed a plate over. She looked at the diamond ring winking on her left ring finger. It was a vintage beauty in rose gold with filigree and a round diamond. "I remember my mother wearing this. It was the one piece of jewelry she cared for in the world." Libby held on tightly to her hand and then leaned over to hug her.

"Oh my God, you're engaged?" Beth squealed. "Congratulations!"

"I feel like I should make some kind of ball and chain joke, but I really think you got lucky," Dean told Seth with a grin. "He doesn't treat you right, you let me know, okay?" Dean told Libby.

"Do you mind, Lindy? I told Seth you might have wanted the ring," Libby told Lindy, sitting down beside her. "If you do, we'll get another."

"Oh, Libby, a ring isn't in the cards for me," Lindy said with a shrug that had Dean aiming a curious look in her direction. "I'm so happy he gave it to you. It's perfect for you. And now I have a sister." Libby leaned over to give her a hug, and Dean walked over to Seth.

"You did good. I like this one," Dean told him.

"Yeah, I know. I do, too," Seth said with a smile. "Now who's hungry?"

*****

Lindy managed to get through brunch as casually as she'd ever done with Dean there. She simply ignored him as she always had before, although for different reasons. She booted Seth and Libby out of the kitchen afterward and did the clean-up duties herself. After all, Seth had cooked, and it was their celebration. She rinsed out each dish carefully and loaded it in the dishwasher. She turned around after wiping down the counters to see Dean watching her from the doorway. She darted a quick look around to see if anyone was paying attention to them.

"Did you need something?" she asked him casually.

"I was just seeing if you needed any help," Dean said with a shrug.

"No, I've got this," Lindy said evenly. She looked at him curiously standing in the doorway. He was tall and lean, and his blonde hair was combed carefully today. He didn't have the tousled look he normally had, but he'd always made an extra effort for her mother. She'd noticed and appreciated it, even if she'd hated herself for noticing. "What are you thinking?" she asked him, raising an eyebrow as he stepped closer to her.

"So you're really going out with this Roger guy?"

Lindy laughed. "Reggie. And why wouldn't I?" she asked him flippantly. He leveled a long look her way. "This isn't a thing," she said indicating the two of them.

"What isn't?" Dean asked, taking another step closer and coming around the counter.

"You and me. This isn't a thing. We're not dating," Lindy told him, looking around again to make sure they weren't being observed. She kept her voice down and noticed that he did the same.

"What *are* we doing, Lindy?"

"The hell if I know," Lindy muttered under her breath, taking a futile swipe at the already clean counter and turning away from him.

"Hey, what are you guys in here whispering about?" Beth asked, coming to a full stop as she entered the kitchen to Dean and Lindy standing so close together at the sink. "Dean, are you bothering Lindy?" she asked fiercely.

"Yes," Lindy said at the same time that Dean said, "No."

"Go back out there and congratulate the happy couple. Lindy and I have got this," Beth told him, shooing him back out to the dining room. She turned and gave Lindy a long look. "Do you want to tell me what that was about?"

"It's nothing. He was just asking about Reggie," Lindy said with a shrug. Beth looked at her skeptically. "You know he likes to give me a hard time about the people I date."

"Well, that's true enough," Beth said with a shrug. "He *hated* Tyler," she reminded her.

"Yeah, he did. I'd forgotten about that," Lindy said thoughtfully. "He always called him a tool."

"That was one of the nicer things he called him." Lindy snorted out a laugh. "I agree now, but it used to make me so mad when he said it."

"I always thought that he had a crush on you."

"Well, I hope he did. We were together for a long time."

"Not Tyler," Beth said with a dramatic roll of her eyes. "Dean."

"That's crazy," Lindy said dismissively, feeling the heat rise to her cheeks.

"Well, he did in high school. Some people carry those old flames for years." Seeing Lindy's skeptical look, she continued. "Ask Seth if you don't believe me. It used to embarrass him. I might have teased him about it once or twice," she said innocently.

"High school was a long time ago," Lindy said with a shrug. "If he did, I'm sure he's gotten over it."

"Are you?" Beth asked curiously. "I'm not. Well, anyway, just be careful. This is Dean we're talking about: chaser of skirts, destroyer of hearts," she intoned with a flourish.

Lindy grinned at her, but she could feel her heart sink. Surely she hadn't bought into his charm for even a minute? No, she was still going out on dates and living her life. Dean was just an anomaly in it. Besides, she really needed to focus less on dating and more on starting her family. She'd decide on a donor this week, she promised herself. It was time to get serious about this. She turned back to Beth.

"I'm not worried about Dean. So, let me tell you about Reggie ..."

Chapter 17

Keely curled up on the couch with a cup of tea and enjoyed the quiet. It had been the strangest week, really. She had, of course, filled Vera in on all the details of her first date with Theodore. She'd even told her about the follow-up calls and the flowers he'd sent. Lindy and Seth hadn't noticed the flowers when they'd stopped by. She'd accepted the delivery at home and put them in her bedroom. She enjoyed looking at them there, but she also hadn't wanted to answer any questions yet.

It was still early days, but she had met Theodore for lunch one day at his house where he'd made BLTs and fresh-cut French fries and showed her around his farm. They'd enjoyed a drive one afternoon when she'd gotten out of work earlier than expected. They'd made time for each other, and Keely could admit, although it was surely too soon, that she was falling in love with Theodore Westerman.

It seemed unlikely somehow that she would fall in love again at the age of fifty-eight after feeling nothing more than a casual liking for any man in decades. Oh, she'd loved Seth and Lindy's father. She'd loved Zeke Carver with the blindness of adolescence. She hadn't seen his selfishness or irresponsibility. She'd only ever seen his charm and his good looks and the way he made her feel like the only woman in the world. He must have made a lot of women feel like that, all at the same time. She shrugged. That was water under the bridge these days. He'd been gone for decades, and she'd managed to raise two beautiful, headstrong, wonderful humans without his help.

She never expected to love anyone the way she'd loved Zeke. She'd even hoped not to, afraid that loving again would mean being willfully blind to faults. But now she wasn't so sure. She knew that she was falling for Theodore, and yet she could still see his faults. He could be bullheaded in his opinions and deeply possessive of his private time. He had an introvert's way of overthinking problems, and it seemed like he enabled his younger daughter Layla, giving in to her every request, to her detriment. Plus, he snored.

She thought about that last fact smugly. It was something she knew about him after all. After a handful of dates, they'd made the transition to lovers without skipping a beat. Vera knew, of course, but she hadn't quite gotten the courage to tell her children that she was dating.

Of course, she knew that they had secrets of their own. She'd guessed about the engagement the moment she'd noticed Libby's hand in her pocket at brunch. She'd known for months that Seth had the engagement ring, and she'd wondered if he would give it to Libby. And she'd also noticed how Lindy had carefully avoided Dean at brunch as well. They'd been stepping around each other for years, and she wondered if they weren't finally noticing the attraction she'd noticed all along.

That gave her a moment's pause for Lindy. After all, Dean enjoyed a much-deserved reputation, and Lindy was looking to start a family. But she figured her girl was smart enough to figure these things out without her interference.

Still, she wanted to be able to tell them about Theodore. She wanted to share this experience, but she wasn't sure how—not after all these years. It was guaranteed to be a bit awkward, but she knew she'd have to get it out of the way soon. Theodore had already mentioned that he'd told Presley about them. He'd admitted with a shy smile that he'd asked her for dating advice after their first date. She'd found it charming and endearing, but she knew that he would expect that she be equally forthcoming about their relationship. After all, it was a small community. It wouldn't be long before her kids heard it through the grapevine simply because one neighbor or another saw them out at dinner. She made up her mind to tell her kids long before they heard it from someone else.

*****

Lindy looked at the time as she got home. It was well after midnight, and she had to go into the studio tomorrow. She leaned her head back against the headrest and listened to the rest of the song on her playlist. She'd programmed an Ed Sheeran vibe for date night, and she finished the song and got out of the car with a smile. She was glad she'd agreed to go out with Reggie. They'd met at a sushi restaurant in Athens, and she'd paired skinny jeans with candy apple red stilettos. She'd worn a red tunic top that suited her coloring and silver hoops that gave her a gypsy vibe. Reggie had already secured a table before she'd gotten there, and he'd stood up as she'd been escorted to the table. He was wearing a white shirt, open at the neck, and black slacks. He had hugged her when she'd come in, pressing his smooth dark skin against her own pale cheek.

"You look beautiful," he'd said immediately. Then he had grinned at her shoes, the deep spike of red, and continued, "I'm not sure how you're going to hike in those, though I don't doubt you can."

"I brought my hiking boots and left them in the car," she said with a smile.

She remembered Reggie being attractive. He'd been damn near sullen when they'd met at the bridal shower. He was missing a football game to come out and support the happy couple, but he was skeptical that he'd enjoy what he thought of as paint-by-numbers night. Besides, the bride's sister was an ex that he didn't relish seeing again. The breakup had been particularly acrimonious, and he'd dreaded spending the evening dodging her snide remarks and venomous glares.

Lindy had laughed because he hadn't realized that she owned this paint-by-numbers joint when he made that particular wisecrack. He'd lightened up as the evening went on, and she even managed to let him know the score of the game throughout the evening. He'd been so cute and embarrassed when he realized that she owned the place and didn't just work there, but he still managed to lay on the charm and ask for her number before the night wrapped up. She had particularly liked his smile, the way it lit up his whole face. He had dimples, too, which she liked to tease out of him.

Dinner had gone smoothly, and he had been charming and funny throughout the evening. They drove over to the gardens separately, and Lindy changed into her hiking boots when they got there, a less fashionable but far more comfortable concession to the evening's plan. Reggie had smiled widely when he'd noticed the change, and the date had been as romantic and charming as she could have hoped. He'd ended the evening with a soft kiss and a request for a second date, which she'd readily agreed to. The kiss had even had a spark, although she hated to admit that it hadn't compared to the fireworks of that first kiss with Dean. Still—Reggie was an attractive, intelligent, and charming man, and she enjoyed his company. This thing with Dean had been fun, but she really needed to figure out a way to end it before anyone's feelings got hurt.

She climbed out of the car and walked into the house, carrying her stilettos with her. She got ready for bed slowly, savoring the romance of the evening. She'd liked getting to know Reggie. He was seriously smart, which she found sexy as hell. He didn't have any children of his own, but he talked fondly about his many nieces and nephews. She liked to think he would be comfortable with her choice to start a family, but she admitted to herself that few men would likely support this part of the process. It didn't hurt to get to know him. After all, it was always good to have a new friend.

She got into bed and pulled the blankets up around her

shoulders. The evening had gotten chilly, and she'd spent the evening with his blazer around her shoulders. She could still smell his cologne, and she liked it. She'd given him his blazer back when he'd walked her to her car. She'd been anticipating the kiss, and it didn't disappoint. She replayed it over in her head. She began drifting off to sleep thinking of Reggie and how romantic the entire night had been, but when she dreamed, she dreamed of Dean.

*****

Dean didn't need to ask how the date with Reggie had gone. He'd heard it all secondhand from Seth who'd heard it from Libby. Apparently, Libby thought Reggie was a keeper, and Lindy hadn't disagreed. He scowled at the paperwork on his desk and tried to think of an upside to this situation. He had a long list of numbers he could call to forget Lindy entirely. Any one of them would likely be happy to hear from him. His brows drew tighter together in annoyance. He simply couldn't think of one name on his list who interested him enough to make the call. They were all great women, but he'd gotten stuck on Lindy.

He thought about her when he woke up and when he fell asleep, and he had been hoping that she felt the same. To hear about her dating exploits was grinding his gears. He'd thought about calling her and having it out on the phone, but then he'd decided he'd much rather do it in person. He hadn't heard from her since brunch. Not a call, not a text, nothing. He didn't like feeling used, and he certainly hadn't expected Lindy to be the type to treat people so casually.

He didn't see the irony in that line of thinking either, but he was too mad to care if he was being rational. Seth had even noticed his bad attitude, which he'd attributed to lack of sleep and working too many shifts. What else could he say? *Hey, buddy, I've been sleeping with your sister, and now she's moved on to greener pastures?* Oh, yeah. That would go over well.

He looked out the window and saw Lindy heading over to Brews & Blues. Well, that couldn't be better timing.

"Hey, I'm going to run across the street and grab some coffee," he said quickly, leaving his coworker staring curiously at the full cup of coffee Dean left behind as he darted out the door. When he walked into Brews, Lindy was leaning on the counter chatting with Candace. Dean thought if he heard the name Reggie one more time, he would seriously blow up.

"I didn't expect it would happen this soon, but I'm glad it did," Lindy was saying. Dean scowled.

"I knew they were perfect for each other the first time I saw them together. And that ring!" Candace exclaimed.

Dean realized they weren't talking about Reggie at all but about Seth and Libby's engagement. Obviously. It did little to cool his temper, however. Just seeing Lindy standing there so obviously unruffled annoyed the hell out of him.

"I know, right?" Lindy said. "It's perfect for her."

"Hey, Dean," Candace said casually.

Dean didn't notice Naomi coming in from the kitchen or how she stopped in her tracks to watch them, but he did notice that Lindy nearly spilled her drink when she jolted and turned around.

"Here, let me carry that for you," Dean said coolly, taking the coffee from her hand. "Nice to see you, Candace," he said casually, heading out the door. He only vaguely heard the "You, too, Dean," as he walked out with Lindy. Candace and Elle exchanged a glance before turning worried looks toward Naomi who was now watching the two of them from the window.

Out on the sidewalk, Dean walked toward the painting studio with Lindy's coffee. "What the actual hell, Dean?" Lindy asked him. "In case you didn't notice, I was having a conversation." He turned and handed her the coffee but kept walking. "Hey, wait a minute," she called to him. He finally stopped in his tracks and turned toward her.

"I'm sorry? Did you say something to me?" Dean asked angrily. "I didn't think we were talking."

"What is your deal?" Lindy asked him in exasperation. "Are you actually mad that I haven't called you?" Her tone was incredulous. "Since when do we do that?"

"I don't know, Lindy. Since when do we sleep together?" he asked her pointedly.

"Look, Dean, we're adults. What happened, happened, and I think we can both agree that we had a good time, but it was a mistake. Okay?"

She'd been texting Reggie, but she was more and more sure that it wasn't a good time to date. After all, she'd narrowed it down to five potential donors. She needed to make a choice this week. For real this time. She couldn't keep putting it off. A relationship wasn't exactly high on her agenda.

"It was a mistake," he repeated slowly.

"We're very different, and neither of us wants to hurt Seth. Look, there's no reason we can't be friends, but if you're going to act all crazy because we slept together then we definitely shouldn't do it again," Lindy told him, feeling her own anger rise to the surface. How dare he treat her like this!

"I have no interest in being your fuck buddy, Lindy," he told her angrily.

"Well, that's crude," Lindy said, coloring. She took a step back. "That's not what I meant at all."

Dean finally looked her full in the face and could see the hurt behind her eyes. He rubbed a hand over his own and lowered his voice. "I don't know what we've been doing, but I don't appreciate you falling off the face of the earth like that. You could have told me you're not interested."

"Are you seriously giving me dating advice, Dean Walton?"

Lindy asked sharply. "We didn't date. It was just a casual thing, and you have *no right* to be angry with me about it." She turned on her heel and headed for the painting studio.

Dean sighed and realized just how poorly he'd handled the situation. Now there would have to be an apology, and he'd have to make it good. He knew she was right, and worse still, she knew it, too.

*****

When Lindy got off work, she walked home trying to burn off the mad. How dare he barge in and take her coffee and frog march her back to work while lecturing her on dating etiquette! She was truly steamed, and the afternoon's session with the kids from the elementary school hadn't managed to cool off her fiery temper. She opened the gate and walked to the carriage house from the garden entrance. She'd go see her mother in a little while, but she wanted a long bath first. She'd love a glass of wine, but she'd recently decided to go off alcohol since she was about to start trying for a baby.

She turned the corner and saw Dean sitting on her doorstep waiting with a handful of flowers. "Those better not have come from my mother's garden. What would you have said if she'd seen you out here?" Lindy demanded, gesturing him angrily to get inside.

"I'd have told her I'd made you mad and wanted to say sorry, and she'd have believed me," Dean said honestly. He handed her the bouquet. "I bought them. I didn't steal them. Here."

"Thanks," Lindy said grudgingly. "Now go home." She turned on her heel and walked into the kitchen. She wouldn't have alcohol, but she could at least make herself a comforting cup of hot chocolate. She pulled the milk out of the fridge and sighed when Dean followed her in. "Why are you still here?"

"I really am sorry, Lindy," Dean said seriously. "Look, I didn't like how it felt when you went out with Richard."

"Reggie," Lindy corrected automatically.

"I didn't like it. I hated every minute of it," Dean admitted. "I don't know what we're doing, but I'd have liked the chance to take you out to dinner or even to a movie. I was jealous." Lindy looked up at him. It was rare for Dean to admit to anything as normal as jealousy.

"I don't know what to say, Dean. I didn't plan on this," Lindy said with a helpless shrug.

"I didn't either," Dean admitted. "But now that we're here, can we at least agree to some ground rules for this thing?"

"I honestly don't know if this is a good idea. The you and me thing. We should probably go back to the way things were and forget this ever happened," Lindy told him frankly.

Dean walked around to where she was pouring milk into the saucer and adding chocolate. "Lindy ..." She looked up at him. He was so close, standing there. "Do you want to forget?"

"It would probably be best. For everyone," she said, looking away.

"Lindy," he said, taking her chin in his hand and drawing her eyes up to his own. "Do you want to forget?"

"No, I really don't."

She moved then, closing the distance between his lips and hers. She couldn't resist, not with him standing so close. He wrapped his arms around her and backed her against the fridge. He let out all of the frustration of the day by focusing only on her mouth, keeping his hands in her hair and on her waist. She could feel him gripping a handful of hair in his fist as his mouth moved over hers, and she let out a sigh.

"This is probably a bad idea."

"Probably."

"We should stop"

"Okay." He started to pull away.

"But I don't want to stop," Lindy told him, pulling his mouth back to hers.

Chapter 18

In the morning, Lindy nearly jolted when she saw the time. She rolled over and saw Dean still sleeping with his arm thrown out across the bed and one covering his eyes. "Dean!" she said. "You have to get up." He rolled over and put an arm around her.

Dean muttered sleepily, "Too early."

"I've got breakfast with my mom in a few minutes, and you need to not be here," she told him firmly, peeling his arm off her.

"I like breakfast."

"Absolutely not," she said. "Go home."

He got up groggily and started looking for his clothes. She finally had pity on him. "Look, I'm going to take a quick shower. By myself," she specified when he looked at her with interest, "And run over to have breakfast with my mom. Sleep as long as you like, but then go home."

She kissed him and headed into the shower. He was asleep by the time she got out so she crept quietly out of the house and over to her mom's. It was still dark as she let herself in by the garden door and walked to the wide kitchen island to begin lining up ingredients. She cherished these breakfasts with her mom, and today it had at least been a handy excuse to send Dean on his merry way. She was just lining up the ingredients when she heard voices upstairs. Voices. As in more than one. She grabbed the skillet and headed for the stairs.

"Mom!" she called out. "Is everything alright?"

There was a pause, and then a strained. "Everything is fine, Lindy. I'll be right down."

Lindy returned to the kitchen but didn't put down the skillet. She was giving it five minutes, and then she was heading up there.

She'd only just resolved to go up anyway when her mother came down looking flustered. Her hair was in disarray, and she looked as though she'd gotten dressed in a hurry.

"Honey, you can put down the skillet," Keely said with a laugh. "This is my own fault for not saying something sooner."

"You're not making any sense, Mom," Lindy told her, putting the skillet down reluctantly. "Who's upstairs?"

"Well, I've been meaning to tell you that I've been seeing someone," Keely began, blushing to her roots. It was silly to be so embarrassed, but really it was quite awkward.

"Oh my God. This is your walk of shame," Lindy said, finally cluing in. "I am so sorry, Mom. I'll just run home, and we can both pretend like this never happened." She was so mortified she could have died, but Keely laughed and wrapped her in a hug.

"I don't think I've done a walk of shame in such a long time," she said with a laugh. "How about you just get enough ingredients out for four, and I'll make pancakes."

"Mom, if your walk of shame involves a third person I swear I will die right here," Lindy told her, covering up her own eyes in embarrassment. "Not that there's anything wrong with that, but you're my mother, and I can't—I just can't," she said, stuttering to a halt.

Keely let out a long laugh. "You credit me with being far more adventurous than I am. I think you'll remember Theodore, but while he's getting ready, why don't you call Dean and tell him there's no need for him to escape out the back way?"

"I'm sorry—what?" Lindy said blankly.

"I know Dean Walton is in your house right now. You call him and tell him I said to come to breakfast," Keely insisted, heading back upstairs. "I'm going to go fix my hair now. You tell that boy to come right on over."

"This is not happening," Lindy said, as she picked up the phone.

"This is clearly a dream. That's what it is. Just the worst nightmare." She dialed Dean's number. "Don't ask questions. Just get dressed and come over here. No, not through the front door. Come in by the garden. I'll tell you when you get here." Lindy put down the phone and prayed for patience as she pulled out the ingredients for pancakes.

*****

Dean opened up the garden door nervously, wishing he'd worn something a little nicer than a long-sleeve T-shirt and jeans. Still, he hadn't expected to play a morning round of Meet the Parents, even if he already knew Keely. He stuck his head in the door and saw Keely at the stove making pancakes. Lindy was nowhere to be seen—to his chagrin. He gingerly closed the door and prepared to turn on the charm.

"How's my best girl this morning?" he asked with a smile, going as far as the kitchen island but no farther. He wasn't quite sure of the lay of the land. He wasn't even sure what he was doing here.

"You mean Lindy?" Keely smiled smugly. "Well, you'd have to ask her. She's in the dining room with Theodore. Would you like a drink Dean?" she asked easily.

"I think I need one," Dean muttered. She laughed and poured him an orange juice. "Wait—did you say Theodore? The book guy?" he asked curiously.

"I did, indeed," Keely said, flipping a pancake. "I want a quick hug, and then you head on in and save Lindy. She looked none too pleased with me when I left them alone in there."

Dean came around the kitchen island and wrapped Keely in a quick bear hug and then walked into the dining room carrying the glass of orange juice. Clearly, this was just a dream. Or the Twilight Zone, Dean thought. None of this made sense. Only Theodore was sitting in the dining room, and Dean simply dropped into a seat beside him with a sigh.

"Do you have anything I could put in this?" Dean asked, indicating the glass. "Like some gin maybe?"

"Tough morning?"

"I would go with awkward. Definitely awkward," Dean said, sizing up Theodore. "So, you and Keely ...?" He couldn't even finish the sentence but left it hanging in the air.

"Me and Keely," Theodore confirmed. "Or Keely and I. I'm not sure what's right, considering." He gave Dean an assessing look. "So, you and Lindy?"

"I have no idea how to answer that. It's not a straight-forward thing, I don't think," he admitted. He looked around the room for a second.

"She went to the powder room," Theodore explained. "I think it was really an excuse to escape the situation."

"The situation?"

"Me," Theodore said simply. "I don't think she quite expected me this morning. And I'm guessing she didn't expect you to be here either."

"No, that one was a surprise."

"There's no gin, but there's champagne for mimosas if you'd like one," Theodore told him, finally answering his earlier question.

Dean wondered if he always meandered so casually between topics. It was interesting, certainly, and he guessed the novelist didn't do it on purpose. He looked at him curiously. He felt protective of Keely, but he didn't feel any need to interrogate her—date? Lover? He wasn't sure how to finish that sentence. He trusted she could handle herself, and he wasn't quite up to being on either end of an interrogation this morning anyway.

"I think I'm okay with this." Dean indicated his orange juice.

They sat quietly for a few minutes. Dean was in no hurry to rush Lindy along. He had a feeling things would only get more awkward when she joined them. He didn't have long to wait. He could hear her long stride coming down the hall. He sat up and tried to look calmer than he felt.

"Hey," Lindy said simply, taking a seat. "The pancakes should be done in a minute." She looked adorably flustered.

"I do love a good pancake," Dean said. He wondered if he should rattle her cage a bit, for old times' sake, and then just grinned. "I didn't expect I'd be getting any pancakes, what with you telling me to head home and all when you were done with me."

Lindy shot a quick, mortified look at Theodore, did a quick check to make sure her mom hadn't come into the room and then shot Dean an annoyed glare. "If you'd gone home last night, there'd have been no need for you to join us this morning," she told him evenly.

"Well, to be fair, we knew he was over there last night," Theodore admitted reluctantly. He had no desire to weigh into this fray, but facts were facts.

"You knew ..." Lindy began and then left off, considering the ramifications. "No, I don't want to know."

"I really should have set an alarm and left early this morning, but your mother invited me for pancakes," Theodore said with a charming smile.

"Now you can't blame a man for sticking around for that," Dean told her.

"I'm just going to sit over here and pretend like none of this is happening. You two just carry on," Lindy told them, turning to the window and picking up her coffee mug.

She looked out pointedly, fixing on a spot in the garden. Nope, this couldn't be happening. What should have been just a casual thing with Dean had now become something she'd have to explain. She wasn't sure how she was going to do that when she couldn't even explain it to herself. Now it would be awkward when she'd hoped to avoid any drama. She'd be answering questions about this now, and when they'd both gone on to other people, she'd likely have to answer questions then, too. She sighed and didn't see the curious look exchanged behind her.

Her discomfort this morning had layers. She'd already received a text from Reggie, planning their next date. She'd replied while she was in the bathroom, mostly killing time until the pancakes would be ready. When she had food in front of her, she could concentrate on eating and then get out of the door. But she was uncomfortable about Dean and uncomfortable about continuing to date Reggie while this was going on, and she felt especially awkward about her mom knowing about her and Dean. Then there was the thing with her mom and Theodore to top it off.

She couldn't blame her mom. Not for Theodore. She'd called him a silver fox herself and had even encouraged her mother to date. No, there was nothing wrong with all of that. Sure, it was a bit weird for her, but she wanted her mom to be happy. She wasn't even annoyed about all that, though she would have liked a heads up. She just couldn't imagine what her mom was thinking about her and Dean.

She sipped her coffee and pretended she was alone in the room. She tuned out Dean and Theodore's conversation behind her and thought about painting a still life, just for fun. She contemplated what props she'd use and didn't turn her attention back to the room until she heard her mother coming in from the kitchen.

Chapter 19

Jamie Radford was just leaving the gym and heading to work when he heard a familiar bark. He grinned widely and sat down to wait on the bench. He had a little time before work, and he knew the wait would be worth it. He liked that the gym was close to Lost Horizon where he'd been working full-time the last few years since his corporate job had gone bust during the recession. He didn't much look like a person who cared about antiques, with his shaved head, tattoos, and muscular physique. He looked more like a soldier, and he had been one ... once. Now, he appreciated a solid workout and a regular routine, but otherwise, he was happy with his life and his work.

His patience paid off. Around the corner came the cutest little white bull terrier with a black nose and a black ear wearing a turquoise sweater with a pattern of falling leaves. Behind him, and attached to the other end of a bright pink leash, was Beth Everett, Seth's cousin. He heard her before he saw her. She was known for having full conversations with Mr. Darcy, the dog, while she walked him around town. She didn't mind that other people talked about her; Beth truly marched to the beat of her own drummer. Her outfit today was classic Beth—an Audrey Hepburn style dress in a sort of rust color with a floral motif and a navy cardigan paired with navy ballet flats. Her red hair was pulled back in a messy bun, and her horn-rim glasses perched on a face clean of makeup. She wouldn't go in for work for another hour or so at least. They both grinned when they saw him waiting, woman and dog.

"Hey, Beth. Hey, Mr. Darcy." He gave the dog a scratch behind the ears and reached into his gym bag while the dog's butt hit the ground. He knew the score. There were bound to be dog treats tucked away, just in case. His little tail whipped the sidewalk furiously as he waited.

"Did you get a good workout in?"

"Yeah, it was okay. I almost had the place to myself."

"I bet. It's too early for most people to be awake. I'd still be asleep if it wasn't for this one," Beth said, aiming a mock-stern look at Mr. Darcy. "Do you want to come over and watch something tonight?"

"Sure." Jamie didn't read anything into it.

He could admit that he was attracted when he first met Beth, but they'd quickly become friends. She was clear about the fact that she wasn't interested in dating, and he respected her choice. He'd never asked her out, but they'd fallen into the pattern of hanging out. She'd become his best friend. While she chattered away, he gave Mr. Darcy the attention he was clearly expecting and listened with amusement.

"Oh, I almost forgot to tell you the big news," Beth said, stopping in the middle of her own sentence as the thought struck her. Jamie waited with a grin. "Seth and Libby are engaged!"

"Yeah? That's great! I'm happy for them," Jamie said sincerely. He considered Seth a friend more than a boss, and he was fond of Libby. They seemed like a good fit for each other.

"Well, if he tells you himself, act surprised, but I wanted to tell someone. It's so exciting!" Mr. Darcy danced on the leash around her. "Okay, I think I need to get him to the park. Come over later?" she asked as Mr. Darcy pulled her away.

"Sure. I'll call you after work. Want me to bring anything?"

"Grab a chocolate something. I don't care what. I'll make dinner," Beth told him, smiling helplessly as Mr. Darcy tugged her forward again. There was a patch of grass he preferred near the park, and he was single-mindedly heading toward it.

Behind her, Jamie was watching her walk away. She wasn't a bad cook, but they were both fond of takeout. They usually alternated between the few places that delivered, and occasionally one of them would go into town to pick something up. But Beth cooking was an anomaly. He wondered if she was just nuking pizza rolls or something. Of course, knowing Beth, she'd read a cookbook cover to cover and could now replicate an entire gourmet meal. She was just like that. He smiled to himself and headed over to work.

*****

Seth was in the back of the store cooking the books. He'd have to do it again at the end of the year, but he liked to stay on top of it. He made a few notes about changes he'd like to make when business was booming, and he heard the front door open and close. He looked out of his office door and saw Jamie heading into the storeroom to hang up his jacket. He'd come in carrying it so he must have been at the gym before work. He heard other footsteps in the store so he looked up to see Lindy heading his way.

"Jamie let me in," she said shortly, dropping into a chair with a sigh. "It's too cold out there," she complained.

"A couple weeks back you said it was too hot," he reminded her.

"And I was right," Lindy said with a smile. "I brought donuts," she added, plopping a box on his desk.

"What do you want?" he asked her with narrowed eyes. She was up to something. He could just tell.

"I can't bring you donuts without a reason?" she asked innocently.

"Yeah, that sentence but without the question mark," he retorted.

"Fine. Okay, a weird thing happened, and I should probably tell you before Mom does so you have a little warning. I didn't get a warning. I got blindsided," Lindy said with a snarl.

He was used to her snark so he shrugged and poured her a cup of coffee from his office coffee maker. He knew just how she liked it since he drank his the same way. He passed it across the counter to her grunt of thanks. "So what's up?"

"I should probably just say it, but you might want to sit back down."

"Okay, what's up? Is Mom okay?" he asked, only a little worried. Lindy often liked to lead into a tale with dramatics.

"Um, yeah," she said with a laugh. "She's great. So ... I came over to breakfast yesterday, and she did the walk of shame." At Seth's blank look, she laughed again. "She wasn't alone."

"Oh," he said, comprehension dawning. "Oh," he said again more flatly, horror coming on the heels of comprehension. "Anyone we know? And also: why are you telling me this?"

"Theodore Westerman," Lindy told him. "And if I have to know this, so do you."

"Theodore who?"

"The author from the book signing? Anyway, so they're a thing. It's been going on for a little while now."

"Huh. Well, okay. She's entitled to date. Is it just kind of ..." Seth fumbled for a word.

"Weird? Oh yeah," Lindy agreed. "But that's probably not the weirdest thing so I'm just going to say it. I mean, Mom probably wouldn't say anything, but I don't want you to be surprised if she does." She took a deep breath. "Dean was kind of over at my place when it happened."

"Wait—what was he doing there?" Seth asked in confusion. "Did he stop by on his way to work?"

"No, he kind of stopped by after work the day before," Lindy told him, waiting for the light to go on.

"You want to explain that one?" Seth began. He'd been shocked about his mom and Theodore, but Dean and Lindy? No, that couldn't be right. He had to be misunderstanding. "Wait—I don't want details." He rubbed a hand over his eyes. "So, are you two—

dating?" he asked, tentatively. He equally wanted to know and didn't want to know.

"No, I'm totally using him for sex," Lindy said with a grin. At Seth's groan, she laughed. "Come on, Seth. This is Dean we're talking about. It's not a serious thing. For him either. It just happened. But now Mom knows so I figured I'd tell you before she let it slip. I know he's your friend, but it's not a big deal."

"Sure, it's not," Seth said. "My sister and ... nope, I can't do it. I can't think about this right now. Or maybe ever. My brain hurts," he complained. He gave her a long look. "You do know he's had a crush on you for pretty much forever, right?"

"What? That's ridiculous!" Lindy said dismissively. "I mean, maybe in high school, but that was ages ago. Besides, we're adults. It's really not a big deal. I mean, we're both still seeing other people. It didn't mean anything."

"Okay. Well, thanks for the donuts and the high blood pressure," Seth told her flippantly, opening the box. "Want one?"

"Would I still be here if I didn't?" Lindy asked with a grin.

They ate their donuts in companionable silence, but Seth was thinking about having a few words with Dean after work. Lindy said it wasn't serious, but Seth couldn't think of a single way that this wouldn't go south. Dean had been half in love with Lindy since high school. Maybe he was over it, and maybe he wasn't, but the truth is that Lindy could really hurt Dean.

And the reverse was true as well. Dean was a player. It was an acknowledged fact. He didn't want to settle down, and he didn't do the one-woman thing. Lindy's temper was impressive, and he didn't see a good end to Dean stepping out on her either. He couldn't visualize one scenario in which this ended happily, and he'd been friends with Dean his whole life. Why did they have to go and mess that up with sex? He nearly shuddered at the thought but kept his cool and reached for another donut.

*****

Dean had spent the day at the lake house, making small repairs mostly. He had a whole list of projects that needed to be done, but he tried to tackle the ones he could easily handle alone. He usually invited Seth out to work with him, but he hadn't been able to extend the invitation today. It would be impossible not to talk about Lindy, and he wasn't sure how to even broach the subject with Seth. He wasn't used to this sort of thing being awkward.

After all, he'd always handled relationships smoothly enough. He'd stayed friends with most of his exes, and only a few of them seemed to have any hard feelings toward him. But this wasn't just anyone he was ... seeing, he thought, deciding on a way to categorize their relationship. This was Lindy. Who he'd been a little in love with for over half his life.

But now? He was afraid that he'd gone from a little in love to the big *L*. Which could not be more stupid, Dean thought to himself furiously. He'd just have to get over it. He had managed not to catch any feelings before, and he could do it again. He'd just have to make a few dates, maybe meet a few women. He'd have to keep this thing with Lindy in a nice, casual place where he could enjoy it without either of them getting hurt. Not that he could hurt Lindy, he thought in annoyance. After all, she was just passing the time.

"I think that nail is in," Seth said blandly, watching Dean beat the hell out of a cabinet he was repairing on the front porch.

Dean looked up in surprise. He'd been so busy thinking that he hadn't even heard Seth pull up. He was surprised to find that he was genuinely angry. After all, he knew how the whole no strings attached thing worked. He'd done it himself for years. But it really pissed him off that Lindy could look at him so casually when what he felt was infinitely more complex. He looked up at Seth and tried to think of something other than his sister.

"You want a beer or Coke or something?"

"Sure," Seth said, going inside to grab one. He came out holding a Coke and sat down on the porch swing. It was the one thing in this whole wreck of a house that didn't need repairs, although Seth did eye the roof overhead to make sure it would hold up.

"I didn't know you were coming out," Dean said, inspecting the cabinet he was fixing. Seth had picked it up for him at an estate sale, and he'd meant to leave this project for later.

"I didn't either." Dean looked up at him quizzically. "Lindy stopped by the shop today." Seth watched as Dean dropped his eyes back to the porch, looking for nails that had dropped and picking them up. Seth knew Dean was just avoiding the inevitable, but watching his discomfort was entertaining under the circumstances. He let the silence stretch out without filling it.

"Yeah, what did she want?" Dean asked as casually as he could. Damn Lindy for getting under his skin!

"Apparently, my mom's got a boyfriend," Seth said distastefully. "I've been trying to wrap my head around that all day. I mean, good for her, but I kind of don't want to know. I guess I'll have to check this guy out and make sure he's treating her right," he said with a heavy sigh.

"I think your mom can handle herself, and she'd kick your ass for hearing you talk like that," Dean said with a quick grin. "Misogyny and all that."

"I didn't mean it like that," Seth began. "Okay, I kind of meant it like that. Point taken. So anyway, there I am, trying to wrap my head around my mom and some guy she barely knows dating, and Lindy's brought me donuts so I know something's up. I mean, other than the thing with Mom," Seth said, leading into it. Damn, this was awkward! "And she tells me she was abducted by space aliens."

"What?" Dean asked, looking up in confusion.

"I just wanted to make sure you were paying attention," Seth said wryly. "Anyway, I'm pretty sure you know what she told me anyway. I just want to know why I didn't hear it from you."

Dean stopped what he was doing and walked to the steps and sat down, looking out at the lake. "I didn't know what to say," he began. "I mean it. I didn't know how to even start."

"How long has this been going on?"

"Not long. You know the night I went out with the guys to Athens? I ran into your sister there. It just sort of happened," Dean said with a shrug.

"And then again the night before last?" Seth asked. "I don't want details," he warned.

"Last night and most of the nights since the first one. Except when she's had a date or whatever," Dean replied darkly.

"Wait—so Lindy's still dating?" Seth asked, confused.

"Yeah. *We're not a thing.* Her words. She's seeing that Reggie guy still," Dean complained.

"Okay, let me get this straight. So, Lindy's still dating other people and you're not?" Seth asked, intrigued.

"It's not that I'm not," Dean insisted. "I just haven't had time."

"Because you've been seeing my sister," Seth clarified helpfully.

"Well, that and work and fixing up this junk heap," Dean explained, scuffing his boots against the railing of the porch with a shrug.

"Hmm …" Seth was well aware that work and the lake house had never before stopped Dean from juggling multiple romantic interests. "Well, it's weird. I'm not even going to lie. And I think one of you will probably get hurt. But you're adults. Just don't tell me about it. I don't want to know," he said with a roll of his eyes. "So, what's the next project on the list?" Seth asked, actually rolling up his sleeves to get to work.

Chapter 20

Lindy was sitting in the studio looking over her own schedule for the month. The holidays simply meant that she was busier than ever. She looked at the fully booked classes and wondered how she was going to narrow down the donors from the three she'd selected with all this on her plate.

"What's with the face?" Beth asked her. She'd popped in to pick up some new pieces to carry in the gift section of the bookstore.

"Just a busy schedule. Holidays and all that," Lindy said with a sigh. "It's great for business, but it's a little daunting."

"We've got the same problem at the tea room. I mean, it's a great problem to have, and we'll probably miss the rush in the new year, but it's a lot of work." Beth looked through the stock, selecting several items and placing them in a box. "How are things with Reggie? Is that still on?"

"I've gone out with him a few times. He's really sweet."

And he was. It wasn't a lie. But the thing with Dean wasn't exactly over like she'd expected it would be by now. After brunch, he'd kept his distance for a couple of days, and then he'd shown up at her door with a pizza one night and stayed over. They never met for lunch or went out on dates anywhere, but he spent a lot of time at her place. She spent a little time at his, but her house was more likely to be stocked with actual food versus snacks and drinks.

"Is he?" Beth asked with a note of suspicion in her voice.

"What?" Lindy tried to pay better attention and looked up from the schedule. "Is he what?"

"Reggie. Nice," Beth said shortly. "Because you're making that face again."

"He's a peach," Lindy said with a small smile. "I'm just not going to have a lot of time for socializing with all this." She indicated the schedule, and Beth nodded.

Still, the holidays would give her a good excuse to stop seeing Dean. After all, this whole thing had gone on long enough, and she didn't need to be distracted. She needed to make a decision. There were three viable candidates, and she just needed to pick one. And soon. By this time next year, she could be getting ready to celebrate her baby's first Christmas.

That thought gave her a thrill. She believed with all her heart that she was meant to be a mother. She knew that this thing was going to happen, and she'd even showed her list of donors to her mother, who had seemed interested and a little amused. She hadn't yet told Seth, but she figured she'd wait until she was actually pregnant and then explain it. It might save some awkward conversations. The one about Dean had been awkward enough for a lifetime! She'd tell everyone when she was good and ready, but for now, she kept this secret to herself. She'd choose a donor, and she'd start the process.

It might take a few months, but Dr. Kimm had assured her that there was no reason why she couldn't get pregnant. Lindy was perfectly healthy, and she was still ovulating. She hadn't run out of time after all. She hugged that thought to herself long after Beth took the items for the gift shop and left her alone in the studio that was once her biggest dream. Well, now she had another.

*****

Dean was home today. He'd worked a late shift the night before, and he'd had the chance to sleep a little later than usual. He'd woken up thinking of Lindy and wondering what was wrong with him. He'd never brooded over any particular woman before, at least not since high school and even then, it had been Lindy. He wanted to think this was all just a way to play out an adolescent fantasy, but he already suspected that his crush had grown up and become love. Not just love but capital *L* love. The kind he had actively avoided all these years.

There was no way he could tell Lindy. Even with her family knowing now, she still seemed uncomfortable with their relationship. They still didn't go out anywhere together, and she hadn't stopped dating. She'd gone out with Reggie a couple more times, and he'd even overheard from Candace at Brews & Blues that she'd had a coffee date there with someone else. He wasn't sure what to make of that.

The truth was that he hadn't dated anyone since that first night with Lindy. Not that there hadn't been plenty of opportunity. In fact, he'd even gotten messages from some of the women he'd dated in the past. He'd thought about a casual hook-up, but he couldn't quite summon the interest. Lindy continued to fascinate him. There was something about her mix of snarky and sweet, and he liked watching the way her quick mind put things together.

They'd gotten into a bit of a routine. He'd come over after work, typically to her house because of the food thing, and they would order takeout or take turns cooking something quick. About half the time, dinner had to wait until after. They'd managed to christen nearly every room of the house, and they were still insatiable. He liked that she was completely comfortable in her own body and didn't seem to have any sexual hang-ups. Other than the fact that she was keeping their relationship as discreet as possible. He couldn't fault her discretion. He even appreciated it. But sometimes he wondered if that's all this was to her, like a friends-with-benefits arrangement.

But that didn't quite line up with the rest of their time. They'd eat dinner and watch TV. They both favored medical dramas and game shows. Neither cared for reality television, and they both liked the same kind of movies. They were good with horror or comedy or a big action film. They liked the occasional romance, but they both tended to make sarcastic comments when the plot veered pretty far from reality. They would cuddle up together on the couch with a blanket and just spend time hanging out. But it wasn't all sex and TV. They spent a lot of time talking, too, and there were nights when he stayed over just holding her. That's when he'd see the softness that she so often covered up.

Was it any wonder he'd fallen in love with her like a big idiot?

He wanted this to be something it wasn't. He wanted to be able to take Lindy out for dinner without her feeling the need to make excuses or explain away their relationship. He wanted them to be exclusive, but he didn't know how to ask for that. He'd never really been in this position before, although he reflected he'd been on the other side of it often enough.

He winced when he thought back to how insensitive he had been when the shoe was on the other foot. He'd always been so dismissive of attachment and needing to make things official. He regretted having been so unkind to so many women over it, but he still didn't know what he was supposed to do when he was the one who wanted to make a relationship exclusive. After all, he knew that hinting didn't work. Or begging. Or threatening. He'd been on the other side of all of that, and he'd just found it to be a solid turn-off. It didn't matter what the delivery was; if he hadn't been feeling it, nothing worked. He reflected that it was probably the same with Lindy. If she didn't want this to be anything more than it was, there wasn't anything he could do about it.

By the time he showed up at Lindy's, his mood had gone south. He'd woken up in love with her and had slowly realized that he wasn't okay with how things were between them. He needed her to love him back and to stop dating other people. He tried to chill out and to focus on the time he got to spend with her, but that little kernel of annoyance kept popping up.

"I already ordered Chinese," she told him when he walked in.

"Should be here in just a few minutes. I'm going to go upstairs and change. The toddler class managed to get more paint on me than on the canvas today," she said breezily, heading upstairs. "Drinks in the fridge," she called out as she ran up the stairs. "Down in a sec."

"Fine," he called up, trying to disguise his irritation.

He walked around the room, picking things up restlessly and putting them back down. He looked at the books on her shelves and noticed they even read the same sort of things—biography, true crime, and mysteries. He sighed heavily and kept walking. He looked at the family pictures she had hanging up and reflected that he remembered nearly all of them. He could pinpoint how old they all were, and he had a dozen memories attached to any one picture. After all, he'd been around for most of it. He did stop and look at a picture of baby Lindy.

He noticed that she didn't have any photos of her dad, but she didn't really remember him either. When she'd been old enough to understand, she hadn't expressed even the mildest curiosity about him. Even during her rebellious years, she hadn't wanted to find him. She'd emphatically stated that he was dead to her the moment he'd left her mom. She meant it, too. So whatever pictures might have existed of Zeke Carver would never hang in Lindy's home. He could understand a grudge. Hell, he was capable of holding one of his own. Now he wondered how it would be if they didn't work out. She could as easily turn that level of anger at him, he thought, getting more irritable by the passing second.

While he prowled around, Lindy came downstairs in leggings and a UGA sweater with a bulldog on the front. She'd twisted her hair up on top of her head and was wearing some kind of snarky novelty socks. He couldn't figure out what kind of animal was on them or what they said, and he wasn't in the mood to ask.

"Beth came into the shop earlier and picked up some new pieces for the store. They all seem to be selling well," Lindy told him, pouring a glass of wine.

"Good," he said shortly.

"They're about run off their feet over there, too. We'll get the usual holiday rush with the festival coming up."

"Uh-huh."

"I won't have a lot of time to work on my own paintings, but I can catch up after the new year."

He kept answering in monosyllables and grunts, distracted by his own thoughts and his sour mood. He even walked into her studio and looked at the work she had hanging up and the projects she was working on, scattered around the room. Had he opened the sketchbook on her desk, he would have noticed all of the sketches of him. She'd done a little informal study. Dean sleeping. Dean's hands. His face when he laughed. She'd even done a full nude, completely from memory. In fact, when she noticed him roaming around her studio, she remembered the sketchbook and moved quickly to intercept him before he started flipping through it.

"What's up with you today? You seem restless," she commented, going over to straighten out her desk and moving the sketchbook into a drawer.

"Just didn't get much sleep last night," he lied. She paused, wondering if that meant he was dating again. It was entirely possible he was seeing someone else, and if that were the case, he probably wasn't getting much sleep. She knew his reputation well enough to know that his lady friends didn't exactly come over just to catch up on their rest. Lindy scowled down at the papers in her hands and moved them aside.

"The food should be here soon," she said calmly, motioning him out of her studio.

"Interesting work," Dean commented neutrally, looking at a painting hanging on her wall. It was more abstract than he preferred, but he liked anything that Lindy did. It was certainly eye-catching, but he couldn't quite make out what it was supposed to be.

"Thanks. I like it," Lindy said with amusement. She'd painted that one during one of the many sleepless nights when she'd been planning the family she was so afraid she wasn't going to have. She'd painted a seed just sprouting, but then it had become something other. She couldn't even fully explain it to herself, but she'd liked it enough to hang it up.

Dean glanced down at the buffet that Lindy used for her art supplies. Seth had found it for her at an auction and set it aside for her. She loved antiques, and it suited the studio somehow. It took up the entire wall, and it was spacious enough to hold most of her materials. Of course, the surface was littered with ongoing projects, although Lindy kept telling herself she'd clean that up soon and then really show off the buffet.

It took her a minute to realize that Dean had fully stopped in his tracks and was reaching for a printout just beneath the painting. Belatedly, Lindy realized that she'd left the family planning information out the last time she'd gone over it. Usually, she slid it into a drawer when she was done. She hadn't anticipated Dean's restless prowl through her home.

"Want to tell me what this is?" Dean said, holding up a pamphlet on the fertility drugs she was taking.

Lindy snatched the paper from his hand and shoved it into a drawer. She silently cursed herself for leaving it out in the first place.

"I don't really owe you an explanation," Lindy said angrily. Not only had he prowled around the house invading her privacy, but now he thought she should just explain her own private business.

He was quiet for a full minute, pondering the implications. "So, is that what this has been about?" Dean asked bitterly. "Have you just been trying to get knocked up? I guess you have a whole stud farm these days with me and then Reggie and whoever else you've got on the side."

Lindy turned white in shock and then her face flushed red in anger. "Get the hell out of my house!" Her fists were clenched, and she was trying to keep her temper in check.

"Seriously, Lindy, what the hell?" he asked her, putting his hands on his hips. "I don't think an explanation is too much to ask under the circumstances."

"You don't deserve an explanation," she hissed at him. "Don't let the door hit you on your way out!" she told him, spinning on her heels and leaving the room. He was following behind her, heading for the door, when she whipped around. "Has there been a single time we've had sex that I didn't insist on protection?" she asked him angrily. Dean thought back and realized that she'd been vigilant each time. She couldn't exactly get pregnant if she was protecting against it. At least, not easily.

"Well, no ..." Dean began, already wishing he'd found a different way of asking. "Then what is all that?"

"It's really none of your business," Lindy said coldly, trying to calm herself. It wasn't working, but she was trying.

"Look, we're sleeping together. You're taking fertility drugs. It wasn't an illogical leap," Dean defended himself.

"And I guess a stud farm was a logical conclusion, too," Lindy said sarcastically. Dean closed his eyes briefly in shame, thinking how nasty that comment had been.

"Look, I'm sorry about that. I just don't understand," Dean admitted, holding up his hands in a gesture of peace.

"You don't deserve to," Lindy told him flatly. "But I am planning a family. God knows I'm not planning one with you. I had a deadbeat dad already, and I certainly don't need one for my kid. I'm going to do this on my own, and I don't need you or Reggie or anyone else to do a damn thing for me," Lindy said angrily.

"Wait—you're going to try to get pregnant on your own?" Dean was confused.

"I'm going to have a baby, and it doesn't concern you. I'm doing this my way," Lindy told him, her voice dropping. "Look, this was a mistake. You and me. We need to be done now. I want you to leave," she told him.

"Look, Lindy, I'm sorry about how I reacted—"

"Leave now," Lindy told him, exhaustion in her voice. She wouldn't even look at him. She turned and left the room, going back into the studio and closing the door behind her. The doorbell rang, and Dean headed uneasily toward it.

"Hey, I didn't know you were going to be here," was the greeting he got when he opened the door. Dean thought it was unfortunate that he knew the delivery guy because the last thing he wanted to do was have a conversation. But he didn't want to be rude to the kid either. He'd gone to school with his older sister.

"Hey, Ty. How's Leslie doing anyway?" he asked as he dug out money for the food and a generous tip.

"Oh, you know. The usual. Still got a crush on you," Ty said with a laugh, passing over the bags of food.

"She never did," Dean said easily, leaving out the part where they'd had one brief and disastrous date and had both agreed never to do it again. "I heard she got married over the summer."

"You heard right. I'm going to have a niece or nephew by next summer," he said as he left with a wave.

"Tell her I said congratulations," Dean told him. He closed the door and took the takeout boxes inside to the kitchen. There wasn't a sound from the studio. "Lindy, I'm leaving the food on the counter," he called out. No response. Not that he expected one after behaving like a total horse's ass. He shook his head and left, locking up behind him.

Lindy waited until she heard him leave before she came out of her studio where she'd been sitting in the dark. There were tears running down her face. She'd walked away before Dean could see them. She wanted to blame her reaction on the ugliness of Dean's accusations, but she could admit to herself, alone in her kitchen with more Chinese food than any one person could eat just sitting on the counter, that she was heartbroken.

She knew that it would have to end eventually. She was never meant to end up with someone like Dean. In fact, she was pretty sure she wasn't meant to end up with anyone. And that was okay. She'd planned a beautiful life for herself, and soon she'd have a child of her own to love and care for. But she hadn't realized just how much she cared for Dean until now.

Well, that was over now. She couldn't forget how he reacted. Besides, what she'd said was true enough. She'd had one deadbeat dad. Her child would be spared that. Her own sperm donor had willingly left her. He'd apparently started over on the other side of the country with a whole new family. She'd looked him up once but never said anything to anyone about it. Social media was useful that way. She didn't remember him, but she could admit that she had his eyes. As a teenager, she'd toyed with color contacts to erase that one connection to him before deciding that her biology wasn't a factor. She took after her mom and her mom's family in every way that mattered. She'd realized that if she were going to start this family, she certainly couldn't do it with Dean in the picture.

He was far too casual in how he treated women, and anyone could see he had obvious commitment issues. She'd watched him over the years, the way he serially dated and so easily moved on from each one. It seemed like entertainment to him, but Lindy knew well what it felt like to be on the other side of someone's casual disregard.

After all, hadn't Tyler just been passing the time? She'd seen a future, and he'd seen a year of one-night stands with a few date nights thrown in. She hadn't been much else to him, in the end. He'd taken and left her as casually as her dad had once left her mom, and she'd been reminded that there was no man she could truly trust. Well, outside of her family.

Lindy picked up the phone and dialed the second number on her speed dial, the one she placed in immediate importance after her mom. She listened to the phone ringing and looked at the clock. It was late, but it wasn't too late. Her instinct was to hole up in her house and wallow in her own misery, but she didn't want to give in to that particular impulse.

"Hey, Lindy. What's up?" Seth's voice was warm on the line.

She trusted her brother more than any other man in the world, but Dean was his best friend. She didn't need to thrust him into the middle of this awkward situation, but she needed to talk. Normally, she'd call her mom, but this wasn't a situation she could talk out with her. The last thing she wanted was for her mom to think she had some kind of daddy issues because she was raised by a single parent. Her mom had been better than any two parents she'd ever known. She knew exactly who she needed to talk to.

"Can you put Libby on?"

Chapter 21

Libby made it over to Lindy's place in a matter of minutes. She'd been curled up in their home library with a book while Seth was watching TV. Dinner was in the oven, and she had no bigger plans for the evening than a quiet night in. When Seth handed her the phone with a concerned look on his face, she put the book face down on the table beside her. She held the phone in her hand and saw Seth mouth Lindy's name.

"Hey, Lindy. What's up?" she asked easily.

"Can you come over? Please? Just you?"

Libby didn't hesitate. She could hear the break in Lindy's voice. "Sure. Give me ten minutes?" she asked quickly. Lindy wasn't just Seth's sister. They'd become friends. Besides, Libby knew that Lindy rarely asked for help. It was a quality she understood because she was the same way. She got off the phone and went to find her shoes.

"Hey," she looked up as she laced her sneakers.

"I'll walk you over, and call me when you want to come home. I can drive over or walk you back, okay?" Seth told her softly.

"It might be late."

"That's okay. Do you think she had a fight with Dean?" There was real worry in his voice. This is what he'd been afraid of after all.

"I have no idea. Okay," she said, standing up in her sneakers and reaching for her coat. "I'm ready." Seth left her at the door with a quick kiss and started off toward their house, or what would be "their" house by the end of the month. It was still weird to think of it that way.

When she walked in and saw Lindy's tear-stained face, she immediately enveloped her in a hug. Lindy just broke down and cried, but then after a few minutes, she pulled herself together. She wiped away the tears and grabbed a tissue from the counter.

"Are you hungry?" she asked, indicating the boxes of Chinese food.

"I could eat," Libby said amicably, reaching for the lo mein and spring rolls and deciding that the dinner Seth had made could keep for tomorrow. They took the food into the living room and curled up on the sofa to eat it.

"I haven't told Seth yet, but I'm planning to have a baby," Lindy said quietly.

"You're pregnant?" Libby asked with excitement.

"No, not yet. I'm actually going to go the donor route and do it myself. I've already talked to Mom about it. I'm pushing forty, and I just don't feel like the right man for me is going to come along. I just don't want to lose my shot at a baby," Lindy admitted.

"That's understandable. So how does it work? Do you have to do IVF?" Libby had some friends who'd used in vitro fertilization to get pregnant. She knew it was expensive and often stressful. Actually, she knew a lot about fertility treatments. She'd tried and failed to have a baby herself, back when she was married.

"No, actually, it should be easier for me. I'm a little older than what's ideal, but my cycle is regular enough. I'm taking fertility drugs to increase my chances, and I just chose my donor last night. During my next cycle, I can do the intrauterine insemination. It's the easiest way." She closed her eyes. There was nothing to be embarrassed about, but it felt awkward explaining.

"That's great news, but why do you look so unhappy?"

"Dean was over here tonight. He saw the brochures," Lindy replied flatly. "It didn't go well."

"Oh." Libby thought about it. "Well, it's not something you'd really bring up with someone unless it was a serious thing I guess. How'd he take it?"

"Well, he accused me of running a stud farm with him and

everyone else I date," Lindy said, more tears falling. She was still angry about that comment, but now the hurt seeped through. Lindy saw the quick flash of anger behind Libby's eyes.

"That's an ugly thing to say! I have a good mind to …" She paused and took a deep breath, cooling the anger that had risen up so suddenly. She had gotten better at calming it over the last year. She tried to find another approach. "Besides, you've only been seeing him and Reggie. That's hardly a stud farm." Libby paused. "Though *stud* might be accurate," she said with a grin, hoping to lighten the mood. "Anyway, it's not like you were trying to have his baby."

"Exactly!" Lindy said. "He had no right to blow up like that."

"I'm sure he'll be sorry when he thinks it over. He can be flippant sometimes, but I don't think he means to be unkind," Libby suggested, thinking of the Dean she knew. He'd messed up, no question, but she wondered if there wasn't more to it.

"Well, it's over anyway. It shouldn't have gone on this long, honestly. We don't really have anything in common, and we want different things," Lindy said sadly.

Libby thought that Lindy and Dean actually had quite a bit in common, but she held her tongue. She knew that wasn't what Lindy wanted to hear.

"Do you want to be with him?" Libby asked curiously.

"No, that's crazy! You know how Dean is," she said flippantly, dismissing the idea. "Anyway, it was a mistake, and I need to focus on the baby."

"Tell me all about this donor, and where are you putting the nursery?" Libby asked, turning her attention to the spring rolls.

She could talk babies all day. In fact, she and Seth had been discussing the future earlier today. She wasn't sure she could have babies, but she was thrilled to know that Seth was perfectly fine with adopting if it came to starting a family. He just wanted to be a family with her.

*****

Down the street, Dean was pouring himself another glass of whiskey even while he considered the foolishness of drinking a second one on an empty stomach. He had blown it, big-time. He knew he'd overreacted. He should have found a way to ask without coming across like a judgmental ass. After all, she had the right to look into starting a family. He'd just jumped to the conclusion that she was using him. It was something he'd been afraid of all along. After all, she was keeping things as casual as he always had when he wasn't looking for anything serious. It had grated on him throughout the day, and he knew that he'd been spoiling for a fight when he went over there. He just hadn't expected this particular plot twist.

Lindy wanting a baby had been a shock. He could see it though. Sure, she was getting older, but he figured she had plenty of time to settle down and have a kid or two. He understood she had some trust issues where men were concerned. It'd be hard not to with a biological father who walked away and then went and had a whole other family and never looked back. He could respect the idea of her wanting to start a family, but his first reaction had been that he was used.

His second reaction? She was planning a whole future where he didn't even play a part. Well, maybe she saw the future with him as the side character who popped in at Thanksgiving and Christmas, but that was it. After he realized she wasn't using him, he had a jolt of sadness and anger that she couldn't even imagine a future with them together. Certainly, not as a dad.

Maybe his own dad hadn't been the best, but Dean had always liked kids. He assumed he'd be a father one day, although he'd taken care not to be during any of his casual relationships, and he thought he'd be a good one with the right person. It was galling to know that the right person for him didn't even see him in the picture. She'd planned a whole family, and he wasn't in it.

Now he wouldn't even be in the picture at all. She may have ended it sooner or later, but he'd lost that extra time by losing his temper. She was right: it wasn't his business. She had the right to see whoever she wanted, and she could plan her family her way. He just wished he had a place in it. Thanksgiving was coming up, and he always had lunch with her family. He didn't want it to be awkward, so tomorrow he'd call her up and apologize. If she preferred it, he wouldn't come this year. He was pretty sure Cracker Barrel did a Thanksgiving lunch. It wouldn't include Keely's special dressing or Seth's pecan pie, but it would be something to do. Or he could volunteer for some extra shifts. Maybe that would be best.

He poured a little more whiskey and wondered how he could have been such an idiot. When his phone rang, he had a pretty good idea who was calling. "Hey," he answered briefly, his tone defeated.

"Did you do some kind of boneheaded thing with my sister?" Seth was asking on the line.

"I really don't want to talk about it," Dean said quietly. In fact, he wasn't sure what he could say. Did Seth even know? It wasn't his business to tell, and the last thing he wanted to do was give Lindy another reason to be pissed at him. "Look, ask your sister if you want to know."

"You okay?" Seth asked.

"Man, I really screwed up," Dean said with a sigh.

"I figured one of you did. Guess you better fix it."

"I don't know if I can, but I'm going to try. Did she call you or something?"

"No, she called Libby. I figured it had something to do with you. I was worried about this."

"Yeah, I know." There was silence on the line.

"You want me to come over?"

"No, I'm good. I'll call you tomorrow." Dean put down the phone and poured out the whiskey. He just wanted a shower and some sleep. He wasn't sure if this could even be fixed.

*****

Lindy walked into the clinic and looked at all the pictures of babies hanging on the wall. It gave her hope that one day she might have her own picture to contribute. She'd been seeing Dr. Kimm for the last year. At first, she'd just wanted to confirm that everything was in working order. She wanted a baby, and she didn't want to lose her chance at having one. Dr. Kimm had done a workup, and they'd sat down and talked through all of her options. She was cautioned about waiting too long to start a family. She was given all the alternative options to have a child, and they'd carefully talked through them all. Dr. Kimm had become more of a friend in the last few months.

Today, she would start the donor process, officially. She could conceive in the office or at home, but she had chosen the office option. She was made comfortable in a room, and they ran the standard blood and urine tests. She flipped through a magazine patiently while she waited.

Dr. Kimm came in with a bemused look on her face. "We did decide on the office option for your insemination?"

"Of course," Lindy said with a smile. "I don't just come here for the magazines."

"I thought that's what we decided. It's just that something has come up," Dr. Kimm began.

"Is today not a good day? I've been tracking my cycle very carefully, but if it's not an optimal day, I can come back," Lindy assured her. "I just want to make sure everything is ideal. I know you said it could take a while, but I'd love to get pregnant on the first couple of tries."

"That's the thing, Lindy," Dr. Kimm said gently. "You're already pregnant." When Lindy opened her mouth, but couldn't find her voice, Dr. Kimm continued. "You're not very far along right now. I'm guessing you got pregnant right after our last visit. I'll be able to do an ultrasound in another month, but we did a urine and a blood test so you are most definitely pregnant."

"But I don't understand," Lindy began.

"You've been having a sexual relationship with someone, correct?" Dr. Kimm asked. "Well, yes, but we've been very careful." Lindy insisted. "We've always used a condom."

"That doesn't work one hundred percent of the time, Lindy. Besides, you've also been taking fertility drugs for a few months now. It might have helped increase your chances."

"But I wanted to do this by myself," Lindy insisted, not fully understanding what was happening here.

"You wanted to get pregnant. And you are. I'm not sure what the nature is of your relationship, but you can still choose to do this alone if you'd prefer."

"We broke up. Well, we sort of broke up. It wasn't an official sort of thing. I've known him forever actually, but he's not the type to settle down," Lindy explained. "Anyway, it's over."

"I'm sorry to hear that. But congratulations, Lindy. You're going to be a mom." The news finally sank in, and Lindy began to cry. "This is totally normal," the doctor explained, reaching over to wrap Lindy in a firm hug. "It's big news."

"It really is," Lindy said, pulling away with a big grin on her face. "I need to go tell my mom. I have no idea how I'll tell my brother, but this is so exciting!"

"Let's make an appointment for your ultrasound. I know you're already taking prenatal vitamins, and you can stop with the fertility drugs. I think you're good there," Dr. Kimm said with a smile. "You already have all the books so really you just need to get ready for baby. We're probably looking at a summer birth if our calendar is right."

"That soon?" Lindy said in awe. "I can't even imagine. Wait—yes, I can! I can see it perfectly."

When Lindy left the office holding her next appointment card, she couldn't stop smiling. She knew she'd have to deal with the whole Dean issue. After all, she knew for a fact, this was Dean's baby. But he knew she was doing the donor thing so if she said nothing, he would be none the wiser. At the same time, he was always around. He was Seth's best friend so he probably always would be. It would be hard to hide, and she would feel bad about lying to him. She could let him know and still insist on doing things on her own. Yes, that's what she'd do. She texted her mom to see if they could meet for lunch and headed home. She didn't have to be at the studio today, and she wanted to go home and start officially planning the nursery.

*****

Dean was waiting when she pulled up, his truck parked on the street. She pulled Frances into her parking spot and got out warily. Really, he had the worst timing.

"Hey, Lindy, can we talk a minute?" She shrugged and went and sat down on the bench outside her place and looked up at him silently, waiting.

"Okay, I'll just say what I have to say and go," Dean said nervously. "I'm sorry for what I said and what I implied the other night. It was an awful thing to say, and I was wrong. None of it was my business. If you'd rather I didn't come for the Thanksgiving thing in a couple of weeks, I'll pick up an extra shift at work. I don't want you to be uncomfortable on your family holiday."

"It's fine if you come," Lindy told him shortly. "My mom looks forward to having you there, and so does Seth." Dean wished that she would say that she did, too, but he knew that was asking too much.

"Okay, thanks. I won't stay long," Dean told her. "For what it's worth, I think you'll make a great mother."

"Thanks for saying that," Lindy said, softening a little. Dean nodded and started to walk away.

"Did you tell this Reggie about what you're doing?" Dean asked. He held up a hand. "I know it's not my business. I just wanted to know if you could tell him but not me."

"No, I didn't tell him. I'm probably going to stop seeing him. I need to get ready for a baby, and there aren't a lot of men who are going to want to date me while I do that," Lindy said ruefully. "It's okay though. I planned on that."

"Bet you didn't plan on me," Dean said with a quick grin.

"No, I really didn't," Lindy admitted ruefully.

"What would you think about just seeing me?"

"What do you mean?" Lindy asked, bewildered.

"I'm talking about an exclusive sort of thing. I know you want to start a family. I respect that. But I still want to be with you, Lindy," Dean told her, shifting awkwardly. He couldn't think of a single time he'd ever asked for a commitment. He didn't like it one bit.

"But you understand I'm trying to have a baby?" Lindy asked him, still confused.

"I know. I don't care."

"Is this some weird fetish thing?" Lindy asked him with narrowed eyes. "I'm going to be pregnant. I'll get huge."

"You'll be beautiful," Dean assured her. "It's not a fetish thing. It's an I'm-in-love-with-you-thing." He looked miserable about it.

"Okay," Lindy said slowly. "I care about you—" She stopped when Dean groaned.

"Don't say that. I can't count the number of times I've said that. Look, you want to be with me or you don't, but you don't have to say that you care about me. I know that you do. But I'm in love with you. I'd like to have a chance to be with you," Dean told her honestly.

Lindy looked at him objectively. This was the first truly serious conversation she'd ever had with Dean Walton where one of them wasn't trying to snap and snarl at the other or make a joke of everything. She'd always taken him with a grain of salt, but he looked completely earnest. Of course, maybe he always looked this way. Maybe he even meant it when he said it to whoever was important to him at that moment.

It was tempting, but she had to be realistic. She was going to have a baby in a few months. Her whole life was about to get turned upside down. She didn't need to worry about dating, and what would they even do after the baby was born anyway?

"I don't know if it's a good idea. There's a lot to think about."

"Why don't you take some time to think it over? Maybe we could go out for dinner in a few days. Maybe Thursday night? I know you have classes lined up this weekend. Or I could do lunch if that's better."

"Dean ..." she began, rubbing her temples where the headache was forming.

"It can be a friend thing if that's what you decide. I just want more time with you, Lindy." He reached into his truck and pulled out a small bag with the logo from the sweetshop in town. He handed it to her. "I'm really sorry about what I said. I'd like a second chance with you."

When he drove off, Lindy opened the bag, moving the tissue paper aside. At the bottom was a box of chocolate truffles in what she could see were all of her favorite flavors. She reached inside and pulled out a salted dark chocolate caramel and took a bite. It was nearly time to meet her mom for lunch, and she had a lot to think about. But first, she was going to think about the nursery.

Chapter 22

"I love it here," Keely said with a sigh as she sat down across from Lindy at the wide farmhouse table near the windows that overlooked a large horse pasture.

"I'm surprised we were able to get reservations," Lindy commented, looking around at the crowd that had just come in. The ranch just outside of town was a bed and breakfast that also took reservations for non-guests. Lindy had called last-minute to see if they had any openings for lunch and talked her mother into joining her when they did.

"I'm sure they'll get booked up with guests and holiday parties soon," Keely said, sipping her iced tea and looking happily around the large room with its wide-planked floors.

The room was surrounded on three sides by large windows looking out onto the property. A large red barn cleverly disguised a full working spa. Keely had been out here a time or two for a hot stone massage or facial. The large barn even boasted hot tubs, flotation tanks, and a sauna in addition to the spacious treatment rooms. She thought about booking a treatment before she left.

"Have you heard if Seth and Libby have set a date?" Lindy asked curiously. She'd been so caught up in her own news she hadn't even touched base with Seth or Libby about their plans. She felt a little guilty since they'd been so supportive of her choices lately.

"Not quite yet, but they've agreed on Florence for the honeymoon," Keely said, smiling her thanks at the server who sat their orders down in front of them. "She's asked her sister and a couple of friends to be bridesmaids, I believe."

"Yeah, Seth asked me to stand up with him," Lindy said with a grin. She didn't subscribe to traditional gender roles, a fact Seth well knew, and she'd been amused and truly honored when Seth had asked her. She was sure he'd asked Dean, too, and wondered if that would be awkward.

"Will you wear a dress or pantsuit?" Keely asked with interest.

"I'm still deciding," she said absently. She was really hoping they'd pick a date soon. What she could wear would really depend on how far along she was by then. "So, you know how I told you I was starting the donor process this month?"

"How did the appointment go? Were you very nervous?" Keely asked sympathetically. "I imagine it will take a few weeks to really know."

"Well, that's what I wanted to tell you. I went in for my appointment, and I'm pregnant already," Lindy told her with a nervous smile. "Not very far. Just a few weeks, and I won't have an ultrasound for another month."

"You're pregnant?" Keely let a couple of fat tears fall down her face. Her baby! Her baby would be having a baby. She couldn't wait to call and tell Theodore.

"I am. Dr. Kimm said I'll probably be due in July so that gives me a little time to get ready," Lindy told her. "I'll tell Seth today, and I thought I'd wait until Thanksgiving to tell everyone else."

"I didn't realize you'd started the process so early," Keely told her. "What made you change your mind?"

"That's the sticky part," Lindy admitted. "It's Dean's. It has to be. I didn't start treatment yet."

"Oh," Keely said, thinking that over. She knew she'd need to proceed carefully. "Does Dean know?"

"No. Well, he knows I'm doing the donor thing so when I announce it, he'll just assume that's what happened," Lindy explained. "We've been careful so he'd never think it was his."

"Are you going to tell him?" Keely asked, careful to keep a tone of judgment out of her voice.

"I guess I'll have to eventually. He has a right to know, I guess, but I still want to do this on my own."

"You don't see a future with Dean?"

"Dean doesn't do commitment, Mom. You know how he is. Besides, we never meant for this to be anything serious."

"Well, it's your secret to tell. I know how Dean has lived all these years. You'd have to be living under a rock not to hear the rumors. But that boy has a good heart. I know you want what you want. You always have. Just be careful not to step all over his heart on your way to getting it. I think Dean Walton would make a wonderful father!"

"Hmm ..." Lindy said, thinking. "I guess I've never really thought about it," she lied. She'd had a few passing thoughts of a future, but then she'd reminded herself this was how every other woman who dated him got hurt: imagining impossible futures. "I'll tell him sometime. Not yet, but I will tell him."

*****

Dean had given Lindy her space during the week. She'd texted him Thursday morning and agreed to dinner, and he'd texted back for her to pick the place. He grinned when he noticed that she'd chosen a burger joint in a neighboring town. They had thick-cut fries, blooming onions, and any burger topping you could imagine. They'd even added a black bean veggie burger and some kind of gluten-free option to the menu. It was a no-frills sort of place that served up large slices of pie for dessert with an ever-changing daily menu. You could always count on fresh toppings and homemade ice cream. It was far from fancy, but it was good.

When he pulled into the driveway to pick her up, she was already waiting outside in a hunter green coat over a dress that was more mustard than yellow. The look suited her, although he noticed that she'd opted for a dress over her standard uniform of leggings and a sweater.

"Hey," he said simply with a slow grin. He'd missed her, but he knew better than to lead with that.

"Hey, yourself." He opened the door to the truck for her, and she raised an eyebrow but got in without comment. He was a little surprised she'd suppressed whatever snarky thing she was going to say. When he climbed in, she was leaning back with her head on the headrest, smiling.

"What?"

"I didn't have to change the station," she said, waving a hand toward the radio. He'd left it on classic rock, which he knew she'd prefer. It was only a ten-minute drive to the restaurant, and he didn't mind the quiet. Although, quiet wasn't exactly the word for it. They didn't talk, but Lindy sang along to every song that came on the radio. After a minute of enjoying it, he joined in. When they pulled up, she hopped out before he could open the door, but he beat her to the door of the restaurant. She grinned like she knew what he was up to but went in anyway.

They ordered and then sat staring at each other. Dean had thought he wouldn't know what to say, but instead, he had trouble choosing what to say first. He had so much he wanted to tell her about the week, and he wanted to know all about how she spent her days without him. Talking to Lindy was always interesting, but he hesitated. Everything he said the last time they'd argued came back to him. She may have accepted his apology, but that didn't mean either of them had forgotten what he said. When he struggled to come up with a safe topic, Lindy took the lead.

"How was work?" she asked him easily. "Will you have Thanksgiving off next week?"

"Work was busy. There was an apartment fire, but the owner used an extinguisher before we got there so it wasn't too bad. Then we had a couple of calls that turned out to be false alarms. I am getting Thanksgiving off. A guy I know volunteered for the extra shifts to earn a little extra for Christmas. He's got four kids so I figured he needs the time more than I do. Kids are expensive."

"I know," Lindy said quietly.

"But, you know, worth it," Dean was quick to add. He didn't want Lindy to think he was discouraging her.

"Did you ever think about having kids?"

"I always thought it would happen sooner or later. I assumed I'd meet someone, and it would click. I didn't want to settle for anything less and then end up unhappy. Kids deserve better than parents who settled, you know? I grew up with that, and it wasn't fair. They should have divorced earlier, really. They kept staying together for us, but it really just made us all miserable."

"I'm sorry. That must have been terrible," Lindy said, reaching out to touch his hand.

Dean shrugged. "I didn't know there was a different way to live until Seth invited me over."

"My mom has always thought of you like a son."

"I love your mom," Dean said simply. "I just hope you don't think of me as a brother," he said with a laugh.

"No, far from it. Otherwise, this whole thing would be weirder than it already is."

"Agreed. So, do you have names picked out?" Dean asked after the server put their food on the table.

He had gone for fries and a bacon cheeseburger with a fat tomato and fried egg on top. Lindy had opted for the fries with a burger topped with mushrooms, bacon, and Swiss cheese. They had already agreed to split a slice of the pie when they were done. They were trying to decide between butter pie or the chocolate truffle. Dean suspected they'd get one of each, with Lindy eating most of the chocolate truffle.

"Names?" Lindy asked, absently, concentrating on her food.

She loved the salt and vinegar fries they served, and she always ate them before her burger. She had to remember she was saving room for pie. Of course, she was eating for two now so maybe she could eat it all and still be okay.

"You know, for when you have a baby. Do you have names you like?" Dean asked curiously. He didn't want her to think that he was in any way weirded out by the whole situation. Sure, maybe it felt a little strange, but he was determined to be supportive.

"I guess I've thought of a few. I haven't really decided though," Lindy told him truthfully.

"You think you'll go traditional or will you do one of those oddball Hollywood kid names? Like Pickle or Mustard or something," he said gesturing to their burgers.

"I like some old school names, but I like the new ones, too. Nothing crazy though. Just imagine the teasing at school," she said with a roll of her eyes.

"Do you care if you have a boy or a girl? Like, do you have a preference?"

"No, just a baby," Lindy said softly. "I don't care which kind. Do you think it matters?"

"I don't think so. Kids are fun. I'm sure you'll be happy with whichever you get."

"So where do you come in with all this?" Lindy asked him frankly. "I mean, you seem to want to have an actual relationship, but I'm planning to have a baby. Where do you see yourself in that?" When Dean was quiet, Lindy continued. "I don't mean that the way it might have sounded. I'm just curious about what you want."

"I'd like to be with you. If what you want to do is have a kid, I'd still like to be with you and support you during that. It can't hurt to have a partner to help out. You know, rub your feet, get you whatever strange food combinations you're craving. Whatever," Dean said with a grin.

"And you really want to do all that?" Lindy asked him skeptically.

"I want to do all that with you," he said evenly, holding her eyes. Lindy felt her heart leap into her throat. No, this wouldn't do at all. Falling in love with Dean would just make this complicated situation even worse.

"What if that meant no sex? I mean, what if I felt weird about it or you did? I've never been pregnant before so I'm not sure how that would work."

"I hear it works the normal way," he said with a grin. Then, getting more serious, he said, "Okay, so if sex was off the table, would I still want this? Hell yeah, Lindy. I mean, it wouldn't be my first choice. But we could still talk and read or watch TV. I could just be with you through it. And if you wanted, I could still sleep over and just be there if you wanted anything. I mean, you wouldn't be pregnant forever," Dean pointed out.

"That's true," Lindy agreed. "But you'd probably get a lot of questions. I mean, if I were pregnant, and you were with me."

"That's true, but I don't care. It's not like no one's talked about me before." Lindy cringed, thinking of times she was the one who had said something about Dean's reputation. It had been none of her business. "Let me worry about that, Lindy."

"So how would it all work then?"

"I guess like any other couple. We'd have dates. We'd spend time together. All the normal things. But we wouldn't hide it."

"Okay," Lindy said simply.

"And we wouldn't see other people," Dean reminded her, wanting that to be very clear. He really didn't want to share, nor was he interested in dating anyone else.

"Okay," Lindy agreed.

"Okay, as in you want to do this. Or just okay?" Dean asked, confused.

"Okay," Lindy said with a grin.

Dean just looked at her. "You're being really annoying," he told her with his own grin. "You want pie?"

"Okay," Lindy answered, grinning back.

"Want to take it to go so we can get back before *Family Feud* starts? You know we're supposed to go see that band at Brews tonight, right?"

"I'd forgotten about that." Lindy sighed. "I could use a night in, but I did say I'd go."

"We'll go for a little while. We don't have to stay for the whole set," Dean assured her.

"Afterwards, are you staying the night?"

"If you'll let me, I'll stay every night," Dean told her seriously.

"Okay, let's just start with tonight," Lindy said with a roll of her eyes. "And let's get both kinds of pie."

Chapter 23

Naomi lived in Rutledge, a few minutes outside of Madison. She was close enough to get to work without a long drive, although she had gone a few miles further to attend college in Athens. Of course, she hadn't done so well there. It was expensive, and she hadn't really focused on her classes in the first year. Now she was taking classes at a satellite campus in Madison. These were just basic business classes, but it would help her get her GPA back up.

She'd just left dinner with her parents when she saw Dean and Lindy come out of the burger joint across the street. She froze, not believing her own eyes. She narrowed them as Dean took Lindy's hand and actually walked around to open the truck door for her. He helped her in and then grinned as he headed back around to start the truck.

So that's who he was dating, Naomi thought angrily. Lindy, of all people. Lindy, who claimed she wasn't even remotely interested in him. Well, she'd suspected that she was lying. After all, Lindy sure had jumped in to warn Naomi off, hadn't she? All under the guise of clearly false concern now that the truth was out. Lindy was a lot older than Naomi, too. She was even older than Dean. It wasn't fair! Of the two of them, anyone could see that Naomi was better looking. She was younger and much more fun than dour Lindy. Naomi fumed as she watched them drive away.

Naomi sauntered into Brews & Blues about twenty minutes late and with a huge chip on her shoulder. Elle Lewis-Lawson, her boss, noted the arrival time and the attitude that came with it. She exchanged a look with Marissa, her chef and long-time friend. This didn't bode well, particularly on a busy night. Candace didn't spare Naomi a glance. She was used to her lateness and the attendant attitude. Instead, she walked Noah through the instructions for the evening again, just to make sure that he understood everything. She assured him that he could always ask her again if he forgot. Only when she'd finished that conversation, did she acknowledge Naomi.

"Did you know that Dean is dating Lindy Carver?" Naomi demanded of Candace, her hands on her hips. The rest of the staff paused what they were doing to shoot Naomi a quick glance. The band was coming in from the lounge in the back and heard it, too.

"How would I know that, Naomi? It's not like they tell me their business over coffee orders," Candace responded blandly, turning back to her checklist for the evening and making sure all of the tables were set for the guests due to be arriving.

Elle walked over quietly. "You'll need to change into your uniform. We have guests arriving shortly," she reminded Naomi. "Do you have any questions before we get started, Noah?" Elle asked her newest recruit.

"I think I've got it. I'll ask, though, if I get mixed up," he said with an easygoing smile.

"It should be steady tonight but not overwhelming. And I can vouch for the quality of the band," she said smiling warmly at him.

Elle was starting Noah off as a server tonight, but he'd be working alongside Marissa in the future. He was attending culinary school and had wanted an opportunity to work in a kitchen. While Elle doubted a coffeeshop was his first choice, hers was not exactly typical. Sure, they did scones and breakfast pastries, but they also served lunch and occasionally dinner when they had live music in the evenings. They varied the menu and tried new things, and Noah was eager to get started. He was a little older than the typical culinary student. He was closer to thirty than twenty, and he had dark red hair and green eyes. His height and weight were average, but he had a beautiful smile.

Elle had noticed that right off when he asked to work for her.

Well, that and the ginger hair. He'd been friendly and accommodating so far, and Naomi often flirted with him during her shift. Elle had hoped he wouldn't take it too seriously, and she could see now that he hadn't. He was diligently doing his job while Naomi continued to quiz Candace about Dean and Lindy.

"Who Dean Walton dates is not our business," Elle reminded her firmly. "Our business is getting our guests seated and fed and the band ready to play. We're fully booked so you can go change or go home because we don't have time for drama tonight," she said severely.

Naomi pulled herself up to her full height and said witheringly, "In that case, I'll go. I don't need this job."

She sailed out, and Elle shook her head in regret. She hated to see an employee quit, particularly so suddenly. She knew Naomi's mother a little and knew that she would be disappointed that she'd left yet another job. Her temper and immaturity often stood in her way. If she came back and apologized, Elle might even consider giving her back her job. She watched her walk outside and then turned to Candace and Noah.

"We're going to be a little short-staffed tonight, but don't worry. I'll come out and help serve as I can. We'll do this together."

*****

Theodore and Keely were walking toward Brews & Blues. Keely would be meeting Presley for the first time. Theodore had invited Layla, but she'd made excuses not to come. Of course, he hadn't expected anything else, but he'd wanted Keely to meet both of his girls. Still, he was happy that Presley was coming out. She was even eager to meet his new girlfriend, although that term still seemed like an odd way to describe the woman he had fallen in love with. Presley was meeting them there. In fact, Theodore could guarantee that Presley would get there early and be waiting at their table. She was dependable like that.

"I hope she likes me," Keely commented nervously.

"Of course she'll like you," Theodore assured her. "You don't have to worry about Presley. She's my sunshine," he told her. "Now, Layla. Layla's my storm. Not that it's completely black and white that way, but Presley tends to see the best in everyone."

"I'm sorry Layla couldn't make it out," Keely lied. She wanted to meet his youngest daughter, but she was also a little intimidated. Everything she'd heard about Layla led her to believe that she might be a bit difficult. Not that she was judging her in advance or anything. She just wasn't sure if she should expect a warm reception there. Apparently, she hadn't been warm to women Theodore had dated in the past. She'd mostly been dismissive of them, or downright condescending. Theodore hadn't said as much, but Keely had gleaned most of that from the stories he did tell and the conversations she'd overheard with Presley.

They walked into Brews, and Keely immediately recognized Presley from her pictures with her dad on Facebook. She wore her short, black hair down with the fringe of bangs, and her blue eyes lit up when she saw Theodore. She stood up and waved and then walked over to give him a hug and kiss on the cheek. She turned to Keely and wrapped her in a hug, too.

"You must be Keely. I'm so excited to meet you!" she said eagerly, gesturing them to the table she'd secured near the stage. "I know this will be a little loud, but this is the best spot. There's a view of downtown by the windows and the best view of the stage."

"So, this is Presley," Theodore said wryly, smiling at his daughter.

"It's so nice to finally meet you," Keely told her warmly.

Elle approached the table. "It's so good to see you, Keely. Thank you all for coming out tonight. We're a little short-staffed this evening so our service might run a little slower than normal, but we're offering dessert on the house."

"Well, that's not necessary," Theodore began. "We're in no hurry."

"Are you short on servers or in the kitchen?" Presley asked curiously.

"We're a server short, but it won't be a problem," Elle assured them.

"Do you need a little help? I can't cook at all, but I'm a decent server," Presley offered. "We won't be able to talk as much when the band plays anyway so I could help with the tables. I worked as a server back in high school and when I first started college. Do you mind, Dad?"

"That's my girl. Always helping out," he said proudly. "We don't mind a bit."

"That's so sweet of you to offer, Presley," Keely told her.

"It is sweet, but it's unnecessary. We'll be fine. But thank you so much," Elle told her firmly. "Tonight, you're our guest."

"I really don't mind. Look, if all these tables are booked, you're going to need all the help you can get," Presley said with a smile.

"If you're sure …" Elle said reluctantly.

"I just need a quick crash course, and I'll be set," Presley assured her. "It'll be fun," she said with a grin. "You don't even have to pay me," she said as she followed Elle back toward the kitchen.

"And that's Presley," Theodore said ruefully as she walked away. "She never could keep still."

"It says a lot about her character that she would pitch in to help."

"I can't say I mind having you all to myself now," Theodore said, taking her hand with a smile.

*****

"Hi. I'm Presley, and I'm going to pitch in to help out tonight," she said to Candace and Noah who were behind the counter getting ready. "I'm going to need to borrow your expertise so I'm actually a help and don't just get in the way," she said with an easy smile. "But if I do get in the way, just say that. I'm not sensitive."

"I'm afraid I can't help much. First day," Noah explained. "Candace is the expert here."

"Hardly," Candace said wryly. "It won't take long to get you up to speed. Leave the coffee orders to me. Some of them tend to be complicated. You two take the orders, get them to Marissa, and just keep an eye on the tables. Marissa will get the orders out pretty fast, but it's not fast food. If there's a wait, just keep drinks and bread baskets refilled. We can go over the menu really fast before we open, but if you're unsure of something, just ask."

Presley nodded and made a quick study of the menu. "I kind of have a photographic memory."

"That's handy," Noah said, impressed.

"Well, it helped me get through exams, and it won't hurt here, either," Presley told him.

"What kind of work do you normally do?" Noah asked curiously as Candace went to take a coffee order.

"I'm a midwife," Presley said briefly. "And yoga instructor."

"That's—" Noah barked out a laugh, "not what I was expecting. That must be interesting. Will you have to leave if one of your patients goes into labor?"

"No, I'm not on call tonight. Are you working here full-time?"

"For now. I'm a culinary student. Marissa in the kitchen? She's a real chef. She does a little bit of everything here, but she's not a short-order cook. I'll work mostly in the kitchen except when they need me out here."

"Culinary student, huh?" Presley asked. "I can't really cook. I've tried, but mostly I'm limited to breakfast foods. Bacon, eggs, a sad-looking but delicious omelet," she joked.

"No French toast?" he teased.

"Oh, I love to eat it, but I can't make it. It always comes out soggy for me." She grinned.

"Do you want me to take your parents' order?"

"Oh, that's my dad and his new girlfriend actually. I can take it. It'll give me a chance to check on them periodically," she said with a grin. "I think I like her though."

"They make a nice couple," Noah agreed.

Presley headed off to take their order, and Noah headed in the other direction. A midwife, he thought. He hadn't been expecting that at all. He was thinking accountant or lawyer for some reason. She had seemed sort of buttoned-up when she first came over, but that all fell away when she smiled. He imagined that her patients felt pretty relaxed under her care. Well, as relaxed as you could be if you were in labor, he considered.

Chapter 24

Lindy and Dean walked slowly over to Brews. "Do you think this is a good idea?"

"Look, Naomi works here. We'll probably run into her from time to time," Dean said calmly. "I'm not saying it will be fun, but I want to take you out. They're doing the live music thing. I happen to know this band is good. I just want to go out and enjoy the night with you."

"We just had dinner," Lindy pointed out.

"So we'll have drinks. We'll relax and enjoy ourselves. Rumor has it, people do that," he said with a laugh.

"We could have drinks at home. And watch *NCIS*. In pajamas," Lindy reminded him.

"You have a DVR. We can do that later," Dean said. They walked in and both took a quick glance around. "Maybe our luck is changing." No Naomi in sight.

"Hello, Dean. Nice to see you. Hey, Lindy," Elle greeted them warmly but with her eyes wide in surprise. She'd thought Naomi had been engaging in idle gossip, likely fueled by jealousy. But here they were, clearly together. It was certainly an unusual pairing. "Your mama just came in. Would you prefer to sit with them or have a table to yourselves?"

Lindy froze, unsure how to react. Her mother and Theodore had a window seat near the stage. It looked awfully cozy, and she didn't want to interrupt. "How about we go say hello and then decide, Lindy?" Dean smoothly interjected. Elle gave a nod of approval. An odd couple but not a bad match, she thought to herself.

"I guess you're not my best girl anymore," Dean said theatrically as they approached Keely.

"Dean! Lindy! I didn't know you were coming tonight," Keely exclaimed.

"Well, I had to overcome some strong objections," Dean told them. "*Jeopardy. NCIS.*" He explained when they gave him a blank look. Keely laughed.

"Why don't you join us?" Theodore invited. "And while you're here, you can meet my daughter, Presley. Apparently, a girl quit earlier so Presley volunteered to help out."

Dean and Lindy exchanged a look. They guessed the girl was Naomi. They'd both seen her as they left the restaurant earlier but had hoped she'd not seen them. When Presley came over, Keely handled the introductions. She grabbed them some extra chairs, and Lindy tried not to feel weird about actually, you know, *dating* Dean. People dated. That was a thing. She had nothing to feel embarrassed about. It wasn't serious anyway. Besides, at least she wasn't showing. That would add a layer of discomfort to this whole situation. She hadn't quite worked up the courage to tell Dean yet. So far, they were "taking things slow."

"Can I get you a drink?" Presley asked.

"You want wine, Lindy?" Dean asked. "I'll take a PBR if you have it. A Blue Moon if you don't."

"Actually, I would love a spiced apple cider if you're still serving it," Lindy suggested. "It was a bit cold outside," Lindy explained when Dean looked at her curiously.

"Do you want my jacket?" he asked her, already shrugging his off.

"It's plenty warm in here," she told him, but she accepted the jacket anyway, twin blooms of color coming to her cheeks when she noticed her mom's speculative look.

"So I hear congratulations are in order," Theodore began jovially. Lindy was pretty sure Keely stepped on his foot, but she couldn't be a hundred percent sure. She kept her face neutral.

"Oh? What for?" Lindy asked while silently praying he wouldn't announce the pregnancy for her.

"I heard you sold out on all of your holiday classes. Your mom has been so proud," Theodore said smoothly.

"I'll probably have to add a class or two to the schedule to accommodate the overflow, actually. But it's nice that business is so good. Are you working on a new book?" she asked him with interest, grateful he'd been so quick on the uptake. She was sure he'd been about to spill the beans.

"I have an idea or two, but it's not gone any farther than a handful of chapters. The last one took me years to write, but my publisher is hoping that I'll manage a little faster with a second book," Theodore said with a shy smile. "I like that they think there will be a second book."

"Are you coming to Thanksgiving dinner next week, Dean?" Keely asked, hoping to move the conversation away from any further congratulations.

"If I'm still invited," Dean said with a grin.

"Theodore, you should bring the girls," Keely suggested. "We'd love to have you. He has another daughter who couldn't make it today," Keely explained to Dean and Lindy.

"I'll ask them. We usually just do something at the farm, but they might like a more exciting Thanksgiving."

"Well, it'll be hectic anyway. Seth and Libby will be there, and Beth will come over. You remember Beth, my brother's daughter. He may not show up, but she'll bring Mr. Darcy, which is always exciting because he's a character. And a couple of the other cousins might stop by during the day on their way home from other places," Keely explained.

"We'll start the day with the Macy's Thanksgiving Day parade," Lindy added.

"Then we switch to football," Dean explained. "And if you

survive all that, we sometimes make it to a Christmas movie."

"Or a nap," Lindy said with a laugh.

"We're pretty laid back at the holidays," Keely said with a smile.

"Should we bring a dish, if the girls agree?" Theodore asked.

"I think we'll have it covered. Unless you want to bring an extra dessert. My horde never lets any of the desserts go to waste," Keely told him.

Lindy sipped her apple cider and let herself relax. She pulled Dean's jacket around her and secretly enjoyed that it smelled like his cologne. She'd always liked to wear a boyfriend's sweater or jacket. It had been a long time since she'd enjoyed that level of intimacy, and right now, it was only a little weird because it was Dean. Otherwise, if it had been anyone else, it would have felt perfect.

When dinner arrived, everyone tucked into their plates with enthusiasm. Even after eating the burgers and fries, Dean ordered an appetizer.

"Not hungry?" Dean asked Lindy when he noticed she was fiddling with the breadbasket but little else. "I'll share," he said, pushing his plate of pita chips with spinach and artichoke dip toward her.

"I'm too full from lunch. This is fine," she told him. She'd felt fine at the burger joint. She'd eaten her food with gusto, and now that she thought of it, that probably was a mistake. She'd likely eaten too much. Her stomach had been a bit queasy on and off since then, but she dismissed it. It had to be way too early for morning sickness!

Besides, her mother had said she'd never had a day of morning sickness during either of her pregnancies. She just needed to proceed with caution rather than gobbling up everything in sight. She sipped the apple cider and eyed Dean's dip and chips jealously. It looked delicious, but she just couldn't manage another bite. She excused herself and made it to the bathroom before she threw up.

As she exited the stall, she nearly ran into Presley. "Are you okay?" she asked Lindy. "Was it the food?"

"No, it was fine. I barely touched it. I think I ate too much earlier," Lindy explained shortly.

"Did you eat before you came?" Presley asked curiously.

"Yeah. We really just came for the band. I just haven't felt great."

"Queasy? Sensitive to smells?" Presley asked, routinely.

"God, yes! How did you know?"

"I guess my dad forgot to mention I'm a midwife." She paused. "Could you be pregnant, Lindy?" Lindy darted a quick look around, making sure the bathroom was empty.

"I am. But only a few weeks," she admitted. "Look, my mom knows, and I'm guessing she told your dad, but no one else knows. Yet. I'm supposed to tell everyone at Thanksgiving."

"Secret's safe. But let me give you a couple of tips with the nausea." Presley went over a few things that would help and a few things to avoid, and Lindy found herself calming down.

"I really like your dad," Lindy admitted.

"I really like your mom," Presley replied with a smile.

"I appreciate the information. I read about it, but I just didn't know it would hit so suddenly."

"It does that. Look, just follow those instructions if you want to keep the secret a little longer. And sometimes you can pour juice into your wine glass before your boyfriend comes over so he thinks you're both drinking. That might delay the knowledge for a while."

"That's innovative!" Lindy said with a laugh. "I like it."

"Well, I deal with a lot of pregnancies. Not everyone wants to announce it right off for one reason or another. Especially before the twelve-week mark."

"Do you think it would be smarter to wait?"

"I understand why some people think so. But I don't see anything wrong with an early announcement either. I'm so happy for you," Presley said, giving Lindy a hug. "Sorry!" Presley said with a laugh. "If you haven't noticed, we're kind of huggers."

"I hope you'll come to Thanksgiving next week. My mom invited you guys, but your dad said he'd talk it over with you and your sister."

"Well, I can't promise Layla will come. Or how she'll act if she does. But I'd love to," Presley said. "Now I'm heading back to work, and don't forget what I told you."

Lindy came out of the bathroom and returned to the table. She felt much better. She took a slice of bread from the basket and chewed on that. It did seem to help settle her stomach a bit. She even managed to steal a couple of Dean's chips and dip and felt perfectly fine. She gave her mom a quick squeeze of the hand to let her know that she was okay. They turned their attention to the band that had started another set. Dean reached for her hand, and she held it in hers, thinking all the while about the baby they'd made together.

Chapter 25

Seth and Libby headed over to Lindy's early on Thanksgiving morning. He'd told her she could sleep in, but she'd already gotten up. She hated to miss the beginning of the Macy's Thanksgiving Day parade. Lindy had asked them to come over early, and then they would all go help their mom with Thanksgiving. Of course, Seth knew that meant that he would actually be the one helping with dinner. His fiancé and sister would handle the other guests and set the table. But mostly they would pick marshmallows off the sweet potato pie and discuss their favorite parade balloons.

Lindy was dressed and waiting when they arrived. She wore a sweater that said, "Ask me about my feminist agenda" with leggings. They'd taken bets on which of her sweaters would make an appearance at dinner, and Libby had won. Seth handed her a $5 bill as they walked in. He'd guessed she'd go with "Feminist is my Second Favorite F-Word." After all, he'd gotten it for her on her birthday. She looked more nervous than sassy today, despite the sweater.

"Everything okay, Lindy? Hey, Dean's not here, is he?" Seth asked, slapping a hand over his eyes.

"No, he's not here, and it's not like he'd be walking around naked. Usually," she added.

Seth uncovered his eyes and rolled them. "So what's up?" he asked as Libby came in and gave Lindy a hug.

"Okay, so there's a thing I need to say today, and I needed you guys to hear it first," Lindy began.

"You were abducted by aliens," Seth suggested.

"No," Lindy said with an eye roll.

"You and Dean eloped to Vegas," he threw out.

"No," she said with a scowl.

"You're joining the circus," he suggested, enjoying himself.

"No. What's with him today?" Lindy asked Libby.

"We picked a date. He's excited," she said with a grin. "But your news first," Libby said firmly, cupping her hand over Seth's mouth.

"Okay, I'll be quiet," he said in a muffled voice. Libby slowly lowered her hand.

"I'm pregnant," Lindy said.

"I'm sorry, what?" Seth asked, looking baffled.

"Oh my God! That's so exciting!" Libby enthused. "When are you due?"

"Well, it's early yet. I have an ultrasound in a week. But we're thinking mid-July."

"Wait—is this Dean's? Oh my God, you and Dean are having a baby," Seth breathed. He looked completely flummoxed.

"What's wrong with you?" Lindy asked Seth sharply, as he struggled to take in the information. His face had gone kind of white, now that she thought about it.

"Nope. I'm okay. Just ... absorbing this," Seth said, shaking his head abruptly. "Nope, still not absorbing it."

"My plan was to get a sperm donor and do this family thing myself," Lindy admitted. "Stop making that sound, or breathe into a bag or something. It's not a big deal," Lindy snapped at Seth when he gasped aloud. "Anyway, when I went in, I found out I was pregnant already. So. No donor needed." She paused. "Yes, it's Dean's. No, he doesn't know yet. No, you're not going to tell him. I'll tell him. Probably not today," she qualified. "But soon."

"You're really going to have a baby?" Seth asked her skeptically. "Dean's baby," he said, slowly, trying to wrap his head around it.

"Yes. Mom already knows. I told her first," she admitted. "She knew about the donor thing, too, so the pregnancy wasn't a surprise. Just the timing—and the father."

"I'm going to have a niece or nephew," Seth grinned broadly, deciding to focus on the baby and not the parents. He looked from Lindy to Libby. "And we picked a date!"

"It's October 20. I know that's nearly a year away, but we didn't want to rush. Plus, we have to decide on a lot of things," Libby explained.

"Big or small. Local or destination," Seth added.

"Colors. Music. Vows. Dress. Cake," Libby intoned. "It's a lot."

"But we know who we want standing by us," Seth told her. "So you're still in for that."

"October should give me a little time to lose some baby weight, too," Lindy considered.

"It's incredible to think about. I'm so happy for you," Libby told her, tears falling down her face.

Lindy knew that Libby had difficulty conceiving with her ex-husband. She reached out to take her hand. "Is this hard for you?"

"No. I never look at it like that. One day, I'll have babies, too. We might just have to adopt. I'll love my baby just the same. I'm just so happy for you. I'll have a niece or nephew, too," she told her. "God, I love playing with babies! Rachel won't give me any more," she said, referring to her sister who already had a houseful. "And I don't think Faith is going to give me any babies to play with any time soon," she said, referring to her other sister who worked on a cruise ship and seemed to have little interest in a family of her own or settling down.

"I didn't want to show up your engagement news," Lindy admitted. "Is it okay if I tell everyone today?"

"Sure, just maybe leave out the sperm donor stuff, and you should probably tell Dean before you announce it," Seth suggested, wryly. "Like now because he's coming through the garden," Seth added, standing quickly with Libby. "We'll just get out of your hair," he added with a grin.

"Hey, man," Dean said in passing to Seth as they came out of Lindy's. Seth gave him a big hug. Dean looked at him. "Why are you being weird?" he demanded.

"We picked a date," Libby said quickly. "October 20th. Yes, it's nearly a year away, but it's a date."

"I'm going to help Mom with the food. You should go talk to Lindy," Seth added before Libby steered him away.

"Your brother is acting weirder than normal," Dean told her as he came in.

"That's not a newsflash," Lindy said with a grin.

"The parade's going to start soon. Are you ready?"

"Almost," she told him. "I need to tell you something before we go." She paused. "Just give me a minute," she said quickly, turning on her heel and leaving the room.

Lindy rushed into the half bathroom and threw up. She thought she'd been doing okay with the morning sickness, but it seemed to hit her at the oddest times. She'd had a morning sickness peppermint tea earlier and had even sucked on one of those lollipops for pregnant people. She was fine up until the moment she wasn't. Dean followed her back.

"Are you okay?" he asked outside the door.

"I'm fine," she told him, waiting to see if she was going to throw up again or if it had passed. "Go away. I'll be out in a minute."

"Do you have the flu? Or maybe food poisoning?" he asked through the door.

"No," she replied shortly.

"Are you sure? Can I get you anything?" he asked. "Crackers, ginger ale, anything?"

"I'm fine," she insisted.

"Throwing up isn't fine, Lindy," he insisted back.

She opened up the door and looked at him. "I'm pregnant," she told him flatly, waiting for his reaction. She didn't have to wait long.

His eyes bugged out of his head.

"Already?" he asked. "Okay, how far along are you?"

"Maybe a month or a month and a half. I have an ultrasound next week," she explained. "Look, I'm going to tell the family today so that they don't hear it from someone else. It might cause some questions."

"You mean everyone will assume it's mine," he said bluntly.

"Well, yeah," she answered evenly.

"Let them. I wish it was. I want it to be," Dean told her, holding her hands. "Congratulations, Lindy. You're going to be a mama." He pulled her in, and she sighed. It was done. She'd told him, and he'd actually handled the news so much better than she could have wished. "You're going to be such a good mom," he continued.

"Now you've done it," she told him in mock anger. "You're ruining my mascara," she said, wiping a tear from her cheek with a short laugh.

"Come on. Let's go and watch the parade. When do you want to tell everyone?"

"I thought you could put grape juice in a wine glass on the sly, and I could make the announcement while everyone thinks I'm drinking," she said with a mischievous grin.

"I like the way you think," Dean said with a laugh. "Maybe something less shock-inducing?" he suggested. "Someone could have a heart condition."

"I'll just tell them," she said simply.

"We'll tell them," Dean told her. "Is that okay?"

"I guess. Look, we're going to need to talk about all this," she began. "You know, later."

"I know. I already bought a book." Lindy gave him a mystified look. "About pregnancy and babies," he explained. "We've got this."

"I've got this," she grumbled, trying not to be impressed that he'd actually bought reading material to prepare himself.

"Look, just signal me if you get the morning sickness stuff," Dean told her.

"And what do you think you're going to do about it?" she asked him curiously.

"I'll hold back your hair."

He said it so earnestly that Lindy laughed.

"Yeah, okay," she told him with a roll of her eyes, and they headed inside to see the family.

Chapter 26

Beth was drinking a glass of wine and waiting for the parade to start. Mr. Darcy was happily sleeping in her lap, but he jumped to his feet when he heard Beth greet Seth and Libby. Bored with wedding talk, he jumped off her lap and found a nice warm corner of the room to sleep in. By the time Dean and Lindy came in, he was fast asleep on his side, snoring lightly. Lindy grinned when she saw the dog's sweater today. It was blue and covered in a turkey pattern that said Happy Thanksgiving. Lindy sank down on the couch beside Beth while Dean went to get drinks.

"So, you and Dean are an actual thing now?" Beth asked curiously.

"Apparently," Lindy said dryly.

"Hmm ..." Beth said, considering. "I'd heard he wasn't dating anyone. I don't think he's been dating anyone but you this whole time," she said. "That's not—" She stopped abruptly and colored. "Sorry."

"No, I know. That's not like him. I don't think either of us anticipated this particular situation," Lindy admitted. "I certainly didn't."

"Yeah, it kind of came out of left field," Beth agreed.

"Does it bother you? I know you went out with him that one time ..." She trailed off. Dean had asked Beth to a movie some years ago. She'd gone thinking it was a date but had quickly realized that Dean had only asked her as a friend since he flirted with every woman he came across the entire night. She'd been steamed and had told the story far and wide, warning other potential victims.

"No, it's completely cool. Look, he's great looking so I was flattered when I thought he wanted to go out. But he's not really my type. Don't worry yourself on my account," Beth said breezily. She meant it, too. She didn't want to be just one of many for Dean Walton. Besides, she had given up on dating. She was going to happily live her life with a pile of books and Mr. Darcy. It sounded like a good life to her. "Are you happy with him?" Beth asked.

She still couldn't quite see it, but in a way, it made sense. They both had similar personalities even if their interests appeared diverse. And they'd known each other for ages.

"Yeah, I really am. I'm not saying it will last or anything, but things are good. I'm good with this right now."

Lindy smiled when Dean brought her a wine glass filled with what she could only assume was juice. He had her dark sense of humor, too. She saw him lean over to Seth and Libby and mouth "grape juice" for their benefit. He was funny when he wanted to be. She sat the glass down. "I'm going to go see if Mom needs any help."

Lindy walked into the kitchen and caught her mom and Theodore engaged in what could only be described as a steamy kiss. She rolled her eyes but smiled widely. Okay, so it was a little awkward for her, but it was also really sweet.

Zeke, she never thought of him as *Dad*, had left her mom a long time ago. She must have been heartbroken, but she never showed it. Instead, she'd jumped into work and single parenting with vigor, never letting them feel the lack for a single moment. Lindy's grandfather and uncle and even family friends had pitched in on Father's Day and Daddy-Daughter dances. When a male couldn't stand in, her mother had no problem being the one to come along and endure the questioning looks. But she was never ashamed of it, and she never made excuses. In fact, she'd been the one to play catch with them and take them camping and fishing. There was nothing that Keely Ann Sanderson Carver couldn't do.

She waited until the kiss wound down before clearing her throat. Her mom looked flustered, and Theodore quickly made himself scarce. Both women watched in amusement as he scurried toward the living room making excuses about checking on the parade.

"I like him," Lindy said honestly. "He makes you happy."

"He really does," Keely agreed. "How are you feeling?"

"The morning sickness is still brutal. I keep thinking it will pass. I mean, I know it's just the first trimester, but I'll think it's gone, and it starts back up again," Lindy explained with a sigh.

"Did you tell Dean?"

"About the pregnancy, yes," Lindy said. "Not about the other thing yet. He doesn't care if people think it's his."

"Well, that's promising then," Keely said with a smile. "I told you he has a good heart."

"I never doubted the good heart. Well, not entirely," Lindy admitted. "But we know how he is."

"People can change, Lindy," Keely reminded her.

"I don't believe they really do. Not really. But it's a moot point for now. We're … dating, I guess, and he's okay with the baby stuff. He even bought books. You know, pregnancy books," Lindy said with a baffled laugh.

"That's the sweetest thing," Keely said with a sigh.

"I don't know what's going on in here, but I need both of you out of my kitchen. You're going to get things salty with your tears!" Seth ordered from the door in mock-fierceness. "Besides, you're needed in the living room. Theodore's daughters are here. Introductions all around." He waved them out the door and then turned back to the stove, checking to make sure they hadn't touched anything. His mom was a great cook, but there was general agreement that the student had finally bested the master. Seth put on the apron he kept at her house and turned back to his list.

Lindy and Keely headed into the living room. Presley and Beth were already chatting away about the parade on the sofa, and Layla stood uncomfortably in the corner with Theodore, looking distinctly out of place. Lindy looked at the sisters with interest. She'd always wanted one, even though Libby assured her it wasn't always what it was cracked up to be. Presley's short black hair was brushed to the side with barrettes. It made her look younger than she was, and she'd kept the makeup light. She wore a dress shirt and jeans with boots and seemed comfortable.

In contrast, Layla seemed like she was about to come out of her own skin, alternating between crossing her arms at her chest and shoving her hands into her pockets. Both sisters were petite, though Presley's build was curvy but toned and Layla was mostly slim. Presley's short black hair contrasted with Layla's chestnut curls. Layla also wore darker lipstick and smoky eyes, a look that made a dramatic contrast to Presley's fresh-faced appeal. Presley had those baby blue eyes, like Theodore, but Layla had hazel eyes with long lashes. They were both lovely girls who shared a couple of similar features, but their personalities were night and day. She wouldn't necessarily have pegged them for sisters at first either if she hadn't anticipated them.

Lindy appreciated friendly, bubbly people, but she *understood* people who came across as prickly. She'd been judged for that a time or two herself, so naturally, she waved at Presley and made a beeline for Layla. She noticed Theodore's smile when she approached lit up his whole face. This was clearly a dad who was proud of his daughters, even the one most people would have termed "difficult."

"You must be Layla. I met your sister the other night. I'm Lindy."

"Nice to meet you," Layla said dutifully. "I couldn't make it the other night. Class," she explained, briefly.

"What kind of classes are you taking?" Lindy asked with interest.

"This one is bookkeeping. I'm taking business courses to become a CPA," Layla told her with pride.

"I was never much good at math, but I did enjoy business

classes. Of course, put a dollar sign in front of anything, and I can figure it out," she said with a grin. "Do you want anything to drink?"

"Sure, that'd be great." They walked together to the dining room where Lindy offered her a choice of beverages. Layla chose a sweet tea, and they headed back to the living room. "I hope it's okay I invited my boyfriend to come," Layla offered, hesitantly. It was clear she was preparing for it to be a problem.

"We're a the-more-the-merrier kind of family," Lindy replied lightly. "Besides, my brother is cooking enough for an army. He always does," she said with a roll of her eyes. "Don't be surprised if you leave here loaded down with leftovers. His fiancé bought all of these environmentally-friendly leftover containers weeks ago when she saw the menu he was planning," Lindy told her ruefully. "But he's a good cook so you'll be glad."

"That's nice. Your mom doesn't cook?" Layla asked curiously.

"She cooked when we were growing up. Then she taught Seth, and he kind of took over. It gives my mom a break. She raised us by herself so she always did everything growing up. We like giving her a chance to just enjoy the holiday these days." She paused. "Did your mom cook?" She knew from her mother that theirs had died when they were teenagers. She remembered losing her grandfather just shy of her own teenage years and couldn't imagine dealing with losing her mom then.

Layla paused and shifted uncomfortably. "Yeah, she was a good cook. Well, actually, she was terrible except for a couple of recipes. My dad did a lot of the cooking, but she had a couple of things we really loved," she said frankly. "I always wished I'd learned them, you know, before it was too late." She shrugged.

"My grandfather used to make those ships in a bottle. You know the ones? Anyway, he did when I was a kid, and I never did learn how to make them. I planned to, but I just never did. Kind of couldn't see the point after he was gone," she said, understanding the loss. "Anyway," Lindy continued, striving for a lighter tone, "prepare to eat until you're stuffed, rest, and then eat some more. After all that, he'll still send you home with leftovers. I think I heard the door, though, so maybe that's your boyfriend," she said brightly, moving toward the front hall. Layla followed behind.

On the front porch stood an attractive man with red hair and a familiar face. Before he could speak, Lindy demanded, "Have we met? Sorry, but you look familiar," she exclaimed, trying to place him in her mind.

"I think you were at Brews & Blues the other night?" he asked, phrasing it like a question. He remembered her now. She'd been sitting with Presley's dad and girlfriend. "I'm Noah James," he said, formally introducing himself.

"Lindy Carver," she replied, shaking his hand with amusement. If she could have imagined a boyfriend for Layla, it wouldn't have been this guy. Maybe for Presley. They seemed like a study in opposites.

"Am I dressed okay?" she heard him whisper to Layla behind her as she led them back to the living room.

"The sweater's kind of weird," Layla muttered. "It's fine though."

"My Nana gave it to me. I've got to go to dinner with her after this, and it'll kill her if I'm not wearing it," Noah explained. "She made one for all of us."

Lindy stayed out of the conversation, although she was frankly eavesdropping as she walked them into the house. The sweater was a bit startling. It was a dark green knit with a turkey appliqued crookedly across the front. The turkey even had googly eyes. Lindy grinned as she led the way, but she thought it was sort of charming that he'd wear that ugly thing out just to please his grandmother.

"Okay," she began briskly as she approached the room. "I'll make the quick introductions, and you are free to roam," she said with a grin.

"Thanks," Layla and Noah said together. "I'll get you a drink," Layla told Noah and headed off.

*****

Presley looked up from where she was sitting when Lindy came in and registered a small shock. Noah. Layla's boyfriend was Noah. Huh. Well, that was a plot twist she hadn't anticipated. After the introductions, she got up and decided to get this over with. There was no need to feel awkward. So maybe she had felt a vibe. It might have been all in her head. He seemed like a nice guy, and Layla needed one of those.

"Hello again," she told him. "I didn't realize you and Layla were dating when we met the other night."

"I didn't realize you were sisters. I mean, I knew she had a sister, but you don't really look that much alike," he said, raising an eyebrow.

"Have you two been dating long?" she asked, curiously.

He didn't seem like Layla's type, but maybe she'd left behind the kind of guys she used to date. One could only hope, Presley thought in relief. She'd hated the string of boyfriends her sister had brought home. They were clearly players, addicts, and even abusers. All had commitment issues and seemed to treat her sister as if she were a plaything more than a person. It had made Presley's blood boil. Which is why she should feel happy her sister had met Noah. Happy was the right emotion, Presley told herself. Disappointment was not.

"A few months. Three next week," he said, briefly. "Is your boyfriend here?"

"Oh, I don't have one of those," Presley said flippantly. "I probably work too much."

"I thought Layla said you were seeing someone," Noah said apologetically. "I must have gotten that wrong."

"I was, earlier this year," she said with a forced smile. "It's been over for a while though."

She hated to invoke Derek at all on a day reserved for gratitude. He was probably enjoying turkey with Amber and her family, or worse, she nearly blanched at the thought, with his. She'd never met them, but she'd heard a lot about them. They seemed so warm, and Presley had often imagined a future where they met her and loved her. She'd even imagined a special relationship with his mom who shared a love for her favorite movie. She shook off the thought, looking down into her drink. Today was not about Derek. Or Derek and Amber. Or about her at all. It was about getting to know Keely and her family.

"Hey," Layla said, coming up and handing Noah his drink. "What are you two talking about?" she asked shortly. She wasn't sure how she felt about Presley chatting up her new boyfriend. People tended to like Presley better. She wasn't sure why. They just did. They gravitated to her and away from Layla. It had been that way for as long as she could remember.

"I was just asking about this, um, interesting sweater he's wearing," Presley deflected, although she was curious.

"Oh, I told him he didn't actually have to wear that," Layla said with a roll of her eyes in his direction.

"My grandmother gave it to me. I'm going to see her later," Noah explained in embarrassment.

"Sweet of you then," Presley commented. Then she turned to Layla. "I actually met your boyfriend here the other day at the coffee shop. I went with Dad and Keely to have dinner, and Noah was working. I pitched in a little when they were short-staffed," Presley said casually.

"I thought you worked at a restaurant?" Layla asked Noah abruptly, turning away from Presley.

"Well, they do coffee, too. Actually, they do breakfast, lunch, and dinner now. Well, dinner some nights of the week anyway."

"Oh. Okay. Anyway, I couldn't make it. I had a class," Layla said defensively.

"It's fine. You'll like Keely. She's really sweet," Presley said, looking over at her dad and Keely.

"She's older than I thought she'd be," Layla said, begrudgingly looking at her father and his "girlfriend."

"They're the same age—or nearly the same age," Presley said with a grin. "Anyway, I think she's lovely. And her family is great, too. Well, I guess Seth is. I haven't really talked to him much, but Lindy's a peach," Presley said.

"I met her. She seems nice enough," Layla acknowledged. The conversation stalled.

"I'm just going to get another drink," Presley said, holding up her near-empty glass.

She headed for the dining room and thought about switching to wine. She'd noticed Lindy had a cup, although Lindy had whispered earlier that it was grape juice and not actual wine. She'd responded in a whisper that a glass of wine would have been okay, too, if she kept it to a single glass. When Beth had looked at their whispered conversation curiously, they'd broken off and turned the attention back to the parade. Some boy band had been singing on top of a float for a kids' show none of them had heard of. It wasn't the highlight of the parade by any means.

Chapter 27

Seth called everyone into the dining room, and Lindy's prediction proved accurate. There was enough food to feed hordes of people, and Libby immediately started making boxes after they were done in case anyone wanted to take some to go later. There was still plenty of food out after dinner for them to pick at while they watched the game. Actually, a handful of them gravitated toward the game and the others gravitated toward the now-clear dining room table where Lindy had set out a few board games.

Lindy had made her announcement over dinner without dramatics and had explained the wine glass trick when she noticed Layla furrowing her brow in judgment at the glass in her hand. It had gone smoothly enough. There were well-wishes all around, some outright surprise, and a lot of congratulations toward Dean even though Lindy hadn't specifically said he was the father. Everyone had assumed, just like they'd figured. Dean had taken it in stride and had reached for Lindy's hand and kissed it, a gesture that had embarrassed her more than the announcement.

Now that dinner was done, and everyone was relaxing, she could talk easily about plans for the baby. Over a game of Scrabble with Presley, Libby, and Theodore, they'd easily alternated between wedding and baby planning. Presley chimed in with her knowledge from the medical perspective, and Theodore offered to show Libby some places on the farm if they decided on the outdoor option. He explained that he'd had a few couples ask to marry there over the years, and he himself had been married there ages ago. Of course, Presley and Lindy were outgunned on Scrabble, what with playing against two writers. They finally gave up, although Presley managed to win on a Triple Word Score with only two letters.

"I'm pretty sure that's not a word," Lindy argued.

"It really is," Presley twinkled at her in glee.

"Use it in a sentence," Lindy demanded.

"I can't. Look it up though," Presley said with a laugh.

"I thought we said we can't use our phones this round," Libby said in confusion. "You said we couldn't," She pointed out to Lindy.

"Yes, I said the two of you couldn't," she said, pointing to Libby and Theodore. "You're both writers. It's like playing with a walking talking thesaurus. You don't need the help," Lindy insisted, to Presley's amusement. "What does it mean then?" Lindy asked Presley, looking at the "qi" that had edged them all out of the competition.

"Energy. I think," Presley said. "It's been my secret weapon at many a Scrabble competition," she added smugly.

"Well, then, fine. I call for a rematch!" Lindy insisted. They switched up this time, Libby bowing out to play a game of Pictionary at the other end of the table, and Noah joining them from the other room.

"Halftime," he said in explanation.

"Just be careful—she cheats," Lindy warned, pointing at Presley, who gave a mock-innocent look.

"I win," Presley said smugly.

"I think I'll leave you to it," Theodore said, as Dean came into the room. "Dean, you take over for me now." Theodore headed over to play Pictionary with Keely, Libby, and Layla.

Dean sat down with a sigh. "We're winning," he said with a grin. "But I can take a break long enough to play a round."

"Not with as long as this one takes," Presley said with a nod toward Lindy.

"I wouldn't take as long if we could use our phones," Lindy shot back. They exchanged a look and nodded in agreement. "Okay, phones are back in since the writers are gone."

They settled down to play, and Lindy observed their little group with interest. She would definitely have put Noah and Presley together if it were up to her. They seemed natural with each other. There was an immediate rapport. She'd noticed it even at Brews. Still, it wasn't her business, and he wouldn't be with Layla if he didn't like her. She was a beauty. She was easily more eye-catching than Presley, but Presley had a sort of, I don't know, aura, Lindy thought. Or something less woo-woo. She had charisma, Lindy decided. Anyway, she wouldn't have paired herself and Dean together either, so she shouldn't be so quick to judge an odd couple. After all, what did they have in common?

They liked the same shows. So what? And, yeah, they were into the same music and stuff, but who didn't like classic rock? Anyway, they were totally different even if they had grown up in the same town and sometimes even in the same house, as much as Dean came over to play with Seth over the years. They were probably the oddest couple here, Lindy thought, looking around at her mom and Theodore who seemed so perfectly suited and Libby and Seth who she could see canoodling in the hall. Sure, Layla and Noah were different, but they made a kind of cute enough couple. Layla was prickly, but she was also smart. Noah seemed super laid back, but sometimes opposites attracted. And sometimes, they just collided, Lindy thought looking over at Dean.

*****

Jamie hefted the box he was carrying to one arm while he wrestled open the door. He'd come in late on Thanksgiving to prep the store for Black Friday. Of course, as an antique store, Lost Horizon wouldn't get the booming business of the big box stores with their huge discounts, but they planned to stay open anyway. Seth had worked up a few solid sales and an early bird discount, but they'd be opening at ten in the morning and not some crazy time before the sun came up. They'd rely on local and visitor traffic and the after-lunch browsers downtown. They usually had a pretty good day on Black Friday, and Jamie didn't mind coming in early to set up.

Beth had called earlier after she'd finished dinner with Seth's family, and asked if she could help. She knew his routine as well as he knew hers. She'd pitch in to help him out, and then he'd go over to the bookstore and help her get everything in order for their big day tomorrow. It was nice to have a little help, and the steady stream of conversation would make it feel less like working on a holiday. Beth and Jamie just volunteered to do it so no one else would need to come in on Thanksgiving. Besides, they didn't really mind it.

He could hear the jingle of the door as Beth came in and the jingle that meant she'd let Mr. Darcy off the leash. He smiled, knowing that the dog would immediately head to the bed they kept for him behind the counter. After all, it was near the front where they kept the treats.

"I'm back here," he called out. He could hear her footsteps coming toward him. She rounded the corner, and he took in today's ensemble. She'd gone fairly conservative, for her. It was an old-fashioned dress with a Peter Pan collar. It was short so she'd paired it with thick leggings and boots. She'd plaited her hair into two braids and looked kind of adorable. Or like Pippi Longstocking. He couldn't decide which. He grinned at her.

"How was Thanksgiving at Keely's?" he asked curiously.

"Oh my God, Jamie, it was filled with announcements. So, get this," she began, while Jamie unloaded another box and checked prices. "Dean and Lindy are together. Like together-together. It's an official thing. And Lindy's pregnant!" She didn't consider it gossip. Jamie was one of her best friends after all, and he knew most of the players in this story.

"And Keely and her new guy are super adorable together. Like lovey-dovey adorable. His daughters joined us, and one brought her boyfriend who somehow already knew her sister. That was kind of random. Anyway, we already knew about Seth and Libby's engagement, and they even picked a date. But don't get too excited because it's almost a year away. Anyway, I think Dean and Lindy kind of stole the show this year," Beth finished.

"How was your Thanksgiving?" She liked to hear about Jamie's family. Her own was pretty small these days. There were no little kids running around, although there would be soon.

"Not quite as exciting as yours. Mostly loud. And busy." He'd driven over to Buford and had dinner with his parents and siblings. They were a pretty big family. "Of course, I got the usual interrogation about when I'm going to meet someone and settle down." They both rolled their eyes and sighed.

"Holidays are like hell for single people sometimes," Beth said dramatically.

"I did sign up for online dating again. I didn't volunteer that information though," Jamie said with a laugh.

"If you had, they'd have just loaded you up with relationship advice," Beth pointed out.

"That's true. Anyway, it was still fun. Jodi asked about you," Jamie told her. Beth had met Jodi once leaving Jamie's place late one night after a movie marathon. Actually, it had been sort of funny. Jodi had assumed they were dating and then had been amused when they'd both rushed to explain that they weren't. I mean, people were always assuming that because they were both single. Everyone just liked to pair people off, Beth thought with a shrug.

"Isn't it weird, the whole thing with Dean and Lindy?" Beth asked him as she picked up a music box and looked it over.

"Why would it be weird?" Jamie wanted to know. Beth set the music box back down and called for Mr. Darcy. Jamie went straight to the counter to get a couple of treats and grinned when Mr. Darcy sat patiently waiting after Beth to put on his leash. Satisfied with what he was given, he turned expectantly toward the door, and they all walked companionably out of the antique shop, locking it behind them.

"I don't know. I guess I never got that vibe from them. And anyway, he's liable to break her heart," Beth explained. She held Mr. Darcy's leash as they navigated down the sidewalk. He walked along happily enough in his little sweater, and Beth was glad she'd thought to bring her own coat and sweater with the cold front that had moved in.

"Or she'll break his," Jamie reasoned.

At Beth's dismissive "*Pfft,*" he continued. "It's not outside of the realm of possibility that he has one," he said with a grin. "Are you … jealous?" he asked hesitantly.

Everyone knew of the failed "date" between Dean and Beth, mostly because she'd let everyone know that it hadn't been a date after all like she'd thought. They went into the bookstore and shrugged out of their coats. Mr. Darcy immediately went behind the front counter to find his bed and favorite toy.

"Why does everyone keep asking me that? I'm not into Dean. I just think they're very different. And anyway, they've been sort of friends for a long time," Beth pointed out.

"You don't think people who've been friends can date?" Jamie asked casually, concentrating on the box of books in front of him.

Beth paused before responding, considering. "I think it makes for a nice book plot. I mean, I get it. I've read those, too. And it works for movies. I just don't know that it really works that way in real life. Wouldn't it be weird? Or maybe ruin the friendship?" she asked him uncertainly. Maybe she'd thought about it a time or two, you know, in passing.

"I don't think it has to," Jamie said casually. "Anyway, if they're happy, that's what matters."

Beth reminded herself they were discussing Dean and Lindy.

That's what this was about. "That's true. They do seem happy. Dean seemed positively thrilled about the pregnancy. And Seth was surprisingly cool about it seeing that we're talking about his best friend and his sister," Beth added.

"Well, he loves them both. And he's easy-going about most things. I'm sure he just wants them to be happy. And the baby stuff is exciting," Jamie said with a grin, looking up from his box. "Do you ever think about having kids?" he asked. Beth was pretty firm about her desire to stay far, far away from relationships.

"You know, I thought about that today. Lindy was going to go the sperm donor route. You know, use science and all that. Though I don't actually think everyone knows that, so maybe don't tell anyone," she said as an afterthought. Still, she could trust Jamie. "Anyway, I've always kind of seen myself as a mom someday so maybe when I'm ready I'll just do it that way. Give Mr. Darcy a brother or sister," she said with a mischievous grin.

"I'm sure Mr. Darcy will be thrilled," Jamie said with a roll of his eyes. "If you have a girl, you could name her after Mr. Darcy's sister in the book. What was it again?"

"You're so right!" Beth exclaimed. "That's genius! It's Georgiana. But what about if it's a boy?" she asked, wondering what he'd think of next.

"You could still do George and keep it close to the book. Or even do Fitzwilliam from his first name. Call him Will or something. That'd be cute," Jamie said. He had a ton of nieces and nephews. He wasn't unfamiliar with the ins and outs of naming kids. He'd heard it debated often enough.

"Okay, well, if and when that time comes, you are officially helping me name it," Beth declared.

"You're on," Jamie told her.

It was a nice idea, but he wondered sometimes if they would still be in each other's lives by then. Even if Beth persisted in this idea of staying single, he likely wouldn't. After all, he had no intention of being celibate, and he enjoyed being in a steady relationship. If he met someone he fell in love with, he'd want to do the whole marriage and kids thing. He could see that as easily as he could see being there for Beth when she went through the whole pregnancy thing. He just couldn't see doing both.

Chapter 28

Keely woke up on Black Friday at Theodore's house for a change. She didn't often stay the night there, although she did occasionally. She loved his property. He had acres of land, and some of it abutted the lake. He had a little golf cart he'd take to get there on the days when he didn't feel like walking quite that far on the trails around the property. They'd gone to the lake a number of days just to sit and talk. When it had been a little warmer, they'd taken the canoe out a couple of times. Keely was determined to learn to kayak in the spring when the prospect of flipping it over and going in the water wasn't quite so daunting.

She found it very telling that she thought about still being with Theodore in the spring. Actually, if she were completely honest, she thought about being with him at all times of the year. Sure, it had only been a couple of months, but she felt like she'd always known him. When she'd been with Zeke, she'd been caught up in the thrill and the romance, but she'd never known him like this. In fact, she'd only really gotten to know his character after she'd had two babies and no job and no idea how to end a marriage she never should have begun in the first place.

She had told Vera, and now Theodore, that her first reaction when he'd up and left had been relief. She'd been so happy to have him gone and to be able to plan a life for herself and her kids without him. Her second thought, of course, had been pure panic. She had no job, a work history that had only ever included working at her father's store, and two babies to take care of. She was stuck in a house with a payment she couldn't manage, and she'd never even learned to drive.

Of course, it had all worked out in the end. She'd called her

Daddy and poured out the whole ugly story—her mama had been suffering from one of her headaches then—and he'd moved her right in that very week. She'd stayed in the guest cottage where Lindy lived now for the first little bit, but as her mother's health failed in earnest, she'd moved them into the big house. That's the only place her kids would remember. She'd started working at her father's store, although she suspected he didn't need the help. She found that she had a good head for business, and she had a way with the customers, too.

Everyone thought she'd remarry, after all, she was attractive enough—the one quality everyone seemed convinced was worth its weight in gold—but she never had. Not for lack of offers. But she was determined not to make the same mistake twice. She wasn't willing to settle for less than absolute true love and friendship. While she'd met some nice men over the years, none had made her reconsider that vow.

Until now anyway. She enjoyed being with Theodore, and she suspected that he felt the same. In fact, she knew it because he had no problem communicating his thoughts or feelings. She felt like he was a real friend in addition to being, well, a lover, Keely reflected. She looked out the window and wondered what part of the farm he was working on today. Sometimes, she could hear a tractor—or was it a backhoe—running on the property. That usually gave her a clue where to start looking. Instead, all was quiet.

She started downstairs and nearly fell the last few when she saw his legs at the bottom. She could only see his blue jeans and socks. It looked like he had on one boot. She thought then that he must have fallen or been taken ill while he was putting them on. She froze before she jumped to action and checked.

"Dear God, don't be dead. Don't let him be dead," she said aloud, over and over. She kept calling his name as she checked his breathing and looked for a pulse. She wasn't sure about the pulse.

Her own was racing, but he was breathing at least. She was afraid to move him, but she grabbed the phone on the counter, grateful now that he had a landline although she had joked that it was pointless since it rarely rang, and he always used the cell phone to talk. Her own phone was still on the bedside table, and she didn't want to leave him for a moment unattended to grab it. She called for an ambulance and then sat beside him holding his hand while she waited.

Keely rode in the ambulance with the paramedics. She'd dug his insurance card out of his wallet and grabbed his phone and keys—although she couldn't remember now if she'd actually locked up. When the paramedics arrived, she'd remembered she wasn't dressed yet and was still wearing her pajamas. She'd raced upstairs to change and grabbed her purse and phone on the way back down. When they got to the hospital, she sat in the waiting room and shakily entered the password on his phone. He'd given it to her some time ago. A picture of the two of them, faces pressed together, popped up as the background.

She squeezed her eyes shut in grief for a moment before looking through his contacts. She'd call Presley and then Layla since she knew Presley lived and worked nearby. Then she'd need to call Seth and Libby. Beth could take care of the bookstore, but she'd need to find help with the tea room. Lindy would be busy at the studio with a Black Friday workshop she'd offered as a special, but maybe Libby could fill in. Keely knew for certain that she wouldn't leave this hospital without Theodore. And if he didn't make it—she shook her head firmly. She wouldn't even consider that thought.

*****

Presley doubled over when Keely told her what had happened. She could hear the older woman's voice shaking on the line as she tried to describe what she'd seen and how her father had been and how long she thought he'd been there before she found him. She wasn't next of kin so she had limited access to information. Presley straightened and collected the necessary information for the hospital and assured her that she would meet her there and call Layla on the way. After all, Layla should hear it from her. That's how she'd found out her mom had died.

Presley had been in the room when it happened, although it was pure coincidence. She'd decided to take her book into her mother's room to read, mostly to get away from the noise of the TV where Layla and her latest boyfriend were watching some show. Her mother had taken that one gasping breath and then nothing. Presley hadn't thought anything of it at first. But she'd waited, afraid to look up from her book. She hadn't heard anything else, and she had prayed it was because her mother was finally resting.

Well, she was resting alright. She would never stop resting. Presley had come running into the living room with tears on her pale face, and she'd just blurted it out. Her dad came in from the kitchen where he'd been getting her medicine together. The home health nurse they'd used had just come out of the bathroom where she'd only been for a matter of minutes, and Layla had sat in silent shock while her boyfriend mumbled excuses and left the house.

Presley was dialing Layla's number, but it kept going to voice mail. She finally left a terse message saying Dad was sick and the address of the hospital. She was busy sending a text message that said the same when she plowed into Derek near the exit. It was natural that they'd eventually run into each other. Well, not literally, but it had been bound to happen figuratively anyway. Amber worked in the same hospital. He probably came by to have lunch with her now. Presley looked up and felt the color surge into her face and then fall away again. She sidestepped around him, saying nothing.

"Hey, Pres, can we talk a second?" he asked her.

"I don't have time for this," she said bluntly, walking around him and heading for the door.

"Yeah, I know. You're always busy. But just for a second," he said, walking alongside her as she headed to the parking lot.

She turned to him angrily. "My dad collapsed this morning, and he's in the hospital right now. I don't have time for whatever half-assed apology you have planned or to listen to whatever is going on with you and Amber right now. Let's pretend you said whatever you have to say, and I responded with 'You're forgiven' or 'Congratulations' or whatever socially acceptable thing you're hoping I'll say so I can go." She kept walking briskly, digging for her keys.

"They're in the side pocket," he reminded her, keeping the pace.

She glared at him, hating that he knew anything about her, even something as small as where she kept her keys. She found them, they were in the side pocket, and made a beeline for her car in the parking garage. At least she'd gotten a decent spot today, and it was early enough that there wouldn't be traffic. She'd given a quick explanation to her supervisor and gotten out of there as fast as she could. Her shift had nearly been over anyway, and it was a slow morning. The next midwife on duty could come in a little earlier.

"Let me drive you," Derek offered. "You're shaken up. I'll give you a ride."

"I'm fine," Presley insisted.

"You're really not. Look, I don't want you getting in an accident because you're upset driving," he insisted stubbornly.

She looked up at him in shock. He was short and compact with sort of curly blonde hair that he wore in an old-fashioned sort of style that suited his face. It was a long face, but attractive. He had lots of smile lines and soft brown eyes that used to strike her as so sincere. She'd spent hours studying that face, asleep and awake. Now she just looked at it, baffled.

"How do you think I drove home when I found out about you and Amber? You don't think I was upset then?" He looked hurt, but she was furious. "Everyone knew but me. The people I worked with.

The people you worked with. Some of our friends. I don't have time for a post-mortem with you. This is done. I can drive upset. Believe me when I say I've done it before." She walked around him, got into the car, and started it. She lowered the driver's side window. "You might want to move because with the mood I'm in, I could easily run your ass over," she told him, watching him quickly step to the sidewalk and out of her way.

She could see that he looked surprised and hurt, but she didn't care. She just kept thinking that if Keely wasn't such an early riser— my God—if she hadn't been there, her dad could have been lying there for hours. Or even days!

On the way to the hospital, another thought struck her. She used Google voice to search for the phone number to Brews & Blues in Madison. She even had it call the number for her. Elle answered, and she explained quickly that she needed to get in touch with Noah if he was available. After a couple of minutes, he came to the phone.

"Hey, it's Presley. If you talk to my sister before I do, tell her our dad is in the hospital," Presley said briskly, angry still that she couldn't even get a response from Layla. She knew Layla was usually glued to her phone so she had a feeling if messages were being ignored it was because it was from Presley and not one of Layla's many friends.

"I think she's in class, but I'll make sure she knows. I'm sure she'll get there as soon as she can. I'll text you my number, and you can send the hospital information to me. I'll take care of it," he said calmly. "Are you okay?" he asked in concern. "I mean, all things considered ..." He trailed off.

"Am I okay that my dad could be dead for all I know? No, I'm not okay. He's all I've got. Tell Layla to get here," she said and hung up. She knew she'd feel bad for snapping at him later, but right now, she could only think of what it was like to lose her mother, that absolute fear and grief between that one rattling breath and the moment when Presley had looked up to confirm what she'd suspected.

She'd always felt guilty that she hadn't looked up before. Maybe something could have been done? She'd started studying medicine even more than she had before, wondering if she should have acted quicker to save her mom or to at least have shared that last moment with her. Were her mom's eyes open for that last breath? Had she seen Presley sitting there, absorbed in a fantasy a world away? She couldn't lose her dad, Presley thought. She just couldn't.

When she made it to the waiting room, she was shocked at the change in Keely. She was holding a cup of coffee and looking out the window blankly. She hadn't had time to put on any makeup, and even her clothes looked like they had been put on in a hurry. Her hair was pulled back severely, and she had tear tracks on her face from crying. The hand holding the coffee cup was trembling slightly, and she sat it down with a splash when she saw Presley.

"Thank God for you," Presley told her, crossing the room and wrapping her in a hug. Keely was much taller than Presley, but she clung to her crying. "If you hadn't been there, my dad could have died," she said shakily.

"He's not …" Keely began in wonder.

"No. I phoned a friend on the way in. I know some of the nurses here. I interned at this hospital a few years back. Anyway, he's in surgery. They think it was his heart. But he's okay, and he's got a good chance because of you. They don't think he was there long, and if you hadn't found him when you did, he wouldn't have a chance at all," Presley said, tears falling from her eyes as she squeezed Keely's hand. "Anyway," she said, managing a laugh, "he's always been healthy as a horse so they're being cautiously optimistic." They hadn't been very optimistic at all, but Presley needed to believe that everything would be fine and so, obviously, did Keely, who sat shakily back in her chair. "You've been here for hours. Do you want to go and get something to eat?" Presley asked. "I can wait and call you if there's any news."

"No, I'll stay," Keely insisted. "But maybe I'll just run to the restroom since you're here and clean myself up a bit," she said, looking down at her hastily-assembled outfit. "I don't want to scare him looking like this after he's had a heart attack," she added with a small smile.

Keely began to head to the restroom, then she turned around. "Is Layla on her way?"

"She better be," Presley said darkly. She was having a hell of a day between her dad, her sister, and that angry run-in with Derek. She kicked the seat in front of her and wished that she had hit him with her car. You know, not too hard. Just a little.

"You look like you could use this."

Presley looked up in surprise and saw Noah standing there with a coffee in hand. In fact, he was there with a bunch of different coffees in a drink carrier and a box of what she could only hope were pastries. She'd planned to grab breakfast after her shift, but she hadn't had a chance.

"What are you—" she started, but he waved the question away.

"I've got a break, and the boss said I could take a few extra minutes, considering. Anyway, I couldn't get Layla to answer the phone. She had an exam this morning so she's probably got her phone off. I figured you guys could use some coffee and something to eat while you wait, and I'm sure Layla will be over just as soon as she can," Noah told her. He was wearing his uniform from Brews & Blues and had obviously rushed over as soon as she called. She looked down in shame.

"I'm so sorry about the way I talked to you earlier," Presley began.

"Forget it," Noah said calmly. "I understand. Anyway, I wasn't sure how many of you would be there or what you liked so I brought a few different kinds and a variety of the pastries, and actually, I have a few more in the car," he explained shyly.

"There's Keely now. I'll come out and help you bring it in," she offered, grateful to make up her earlier actions.

Keely walked over to them transformed. She had applied a light coat of makeup, turned the shirt she was wearing around so it wasn't both inside out and backward, and had a flush of color on her face. Part of it was the liberal use of blusher and the rest was hope. He was alive. She kept repeating those words to herself. He was alive now so he'd be fine. She was in love with him. He just had to be okay.

She smiled warmly at Noah and hugged him hard when she realized what he'd done. She gratefully accepted a cup of coffee and dismissed the hospital coffee as sludge. She waved Presley and Noah off as they went out to get the other kinds Noah had selected. She'd have to remember to send Elle a thank you card and a floral arrangement since Noah had insisted it was all on the house.

Presley followed Noah out to his car. She'd expected something sedate and practical, but he stopped instead at a vintage Mustang. She could read the model on the car, but she couldn't begin to guess the year. Maybe 1960s or '70s. It was cherry red, and Presley wondered uncharitably if Layla had seen the car before the man. She always did like flash. Still, it seemed an odd choice for Noah who seemed more down to earth. She looked at him quizzically.

"It was my dad's. Anyway, I've been fixing it up for years. We used to work on it together." He shrugged and unlocked the doors. He handed her another box of pastries, and he took out another selection of coffee, all carefully labeled.

"It's a lot of coffee just for us," Presley commented.

"I get the sense Keely's kids might come out. I don't know. They seem the type. Or even if it's just you guys, you could have a couple each or share it with someone else waiting. It's hard to wait, and the coffee there really is garbage," Noah told her. He said it like someone who'd know.

"Was it your dad?" she asked. She knew he'd once waited here with someone.

"No, my dad's fine. He just lets me fiddle with the Mustang myself these days. Claims arthritis won't let him help, but he actually was never really into cars. He just thought he had to be. Anyway, it was my uncle. Bad heart attack last year."

Presley looked at him. "I want to ask you if he made it, but I can't right now. I just can't. Can I ask you another time, once we know if my dad's going to make it out?" Presley asked him softly, holding the box of pastries close to her chest.

"Sure," Noah said easily. "Don't crush the donuts." He told her with a small smile, gesturing to the box.

"There are donuts in here?"

"There's a little bit of everything. Marissa's been experimenting with a few donut recipes. I think maybe a few cronuts, too, since that was a big thing for a while. I don't think it ever quite made its way to Madison. Anyway, there's a good selection, and I've been sampling the menu to make sure everything's up to par," he said with a wide smile. "It's good. Trust me."

They walked into the waiting room to a crowd. Seth and Libby had shown up before work, and Dean and Lindy had come out, too. Beth explained that she had dropped Mr. Darcy off with Jamie on her way, and Keely's friend Vera had dropped in as well. Theodore's friend Doug had come, and he said his wife Laura had just stepped out to take a call. Most of them had busy days ahead, but they'd all made time to stop by the local hospital to be with Keely and wait for news of Theodore.

Presley came to a full stop and nearly dropped the pastries. Tears ran unchecked down her face. She forgot that she was wearing scrubs and that she'd been up most of the night. For the first time, she felt a real surge of hope. She looked gratefully at Noah.

"Thank you for bringing all of this. Really," she told him sincerely. "Looks like the coffee won't go to waste after all," she said with a smile.

"Good," he said shyly. "I've got one more thing in the car, and then I promise I'm done. I thought you guys might want some plain coffee as well. Candace remembered to tuck in some cream and sugar, too." He headed out again, and Presley watched him walk away. She could see what Layla saw in him, but what he saw in her was a mystery. Sure, maybe she had an exam, but all of these people had come as soon as they heard, and yet she wasn't here at all.

Around lunchtime, Layla rushed in, filled with apologies. Presley took one look at her tear-stained face and let the anger fall away. Dad was all she had left, too. Besides, she could still remember the look on her sister's face when she'd realized that Presley had been with her mom when she died. The loss had hurt, but she'd been haunted by her own guilt that she'd opted to spend the afternoon watching TV with her boyfriend rather than sitting with her mom. They took a long look at each other and seemed to remember that they were still sisters. They met in the middle and wrapped each other in a hug.

"He's still in surgery," Presley told her. "It'll be a little while longer, but they said he's fighting."

"That's our Dad," Layla said with a shaky smile. "Noah said he brought some coffee?"

"Coffee's gone, but you should try these cronuts. They are insanely good," Presley said enthusiastically. "And there are a couple of muffins that I thought were going to start a fight earlier."

Chapter 29

"Can you believe they call this coffee?" Keely looked up from pouring herself another cup of the sub-par hospital brew and met the woman's eyes.

"At this point, it's more cream and sugar with a little coffee thrown in," Keely admitted. The coffee Noah had brought hadn't lasted long. Theodore was in surgery until later this afternoon, and then he'd been moved into the ICU for recovery.

"It's the only way to stand it," the woman said, shaking her head in disgust. "What are you in for?" she asked, walking back toward the waiting area with Keely.

"Heart attack," she said simply.

"Husband?"

"Boyfriend," Keely said with a small smile. She couldn't quite make herself go home. Not yet. "You?"

"My sister," the woman said with a grimace. "We're not too close, but she called me when she had the pains."

Keely took another sip of the coffee and wondered if another shot of creamer would be excessive. She made a note to herself to organize a hospital outreach group that would deliver good coffee and pastries in the event of an emergency. No one should have to suffer through a scare with coffee like this, she thought in disgust, taking another small sip. But it was caffeine. A very poor excuse for caffeine though.

"You know what? I'm just going to get a Coke. Do you want one?" she asked politely.

"I wouldn't say no. I'll pour out this garbage," she said, taking Keely's cup and her own to go dump out in a sink.

On her way to the vending machine, she stole a glance at the sisters sitting side by side in the waiting room. Body language said everything. Layla leaned on to the opposite arm of the chair and scrolled through her phone while jiggling her foot impatiently. Every now and then she glanced up and around the waiting room before returning to her mobile device. Occasionally, she looked at her sister as if she wanted to say something but wasn't sure what. Each time she gave up and returned to her phone.

Presley, on the other hand, was deep into a book. She had crossed her feet in the seat, and Keely noted that even in total relaxation she kept her spine straight and long. Yoga training, she assumed. Still, she was engrossed in the book, turning one page after another. She'd come out of it a few times, each time blinking as if she'd been far away and then looking around the room with interest. She had made conversation with Keely each time but had little to say to her sister.

She came back from vending with two Cokes in hand and passed one to the woman waiting who nodded her thanks. "Those your girls?" she asked, nodding to the other side of the waiting room.

"My boyfriend's girls," she explained. "My kids came earlier."

"Nice of them. So, why aren't they sitting with you?" Keely didn't mind the questions. There was little else to do in a waiting room other than pass the time with strangers. "Y'all don't get along?"

"They don't really know me. I've only met them a couple of times. It's still new," she said with a small shrug. "They're nice enough. Just very different."

"That's me and my sister," the woman said. "Night and day."

"I have a son and a daughter. They're not so much alike, but they've always been close."

"They close to their daddy?"

"He left when they were babies. It was just the three of us." She looked over at Presley and Layla. Losing their mother at such a tender age must have been terrible. Plus, not all siblings were friends.

"We grew up in a big family," the woman said, glancing up at the TV in the waiting room and then around to watch a new group come in and head for reception.

Keely took a big drink of Coke and wondered if she should pester the nurse again about Theodore or if she should make an effort to sit with the girls and talk. She wasn't sure if they would welcome time spent with their father's girlfriend. Or, if she was honest with herself, she wasn't sure Layla would welcome it. She had been a bit abrasive when she'd gotten here as if her arrival should automatically mean Keely's exit from the family scene. It was a good thing her feelings weren't easily bruised, Keely thought. She was in love with Theodore, and she intended to stay right where she was until she could be sure he was okay. She turned her attention back to the woman beside her.

"Guess by the time we got grown, we just didn't see the point in crowding each other. We'd shared rooms all our lives, so the second we got out of school, we all went off and made our own homes. You know how it is. You grow up and drift apart."

Keely nodded. "It was like that with me and my brother."

Of course, she and her brother Miles had never been close. She'd always been Daddy's girl, and Miles resisted the thought of ever having anything to do with the store, much less take it over. Not that their father had expected him to in the first place. He wasn't a man to consider retirement, much less passing on the reigns to someone else. When Miles had told him he wouldn't be taking it over, their dad had just laughed. He'd known all along. Miles didn't get the big argument he'd been spoiling for over the years, the one he expected.

For some reason, the lack of drama seemed to annoy him to no end, and it only got worse when Zeke left her and she took over the store. He hadn't wanted it, but he'd never expected his kid sister to take over either. When he began to lose a string of jobs, he liked to blame her for "stealing his inheritance." She didn't see him much these days. Just for weddings and funerals. His wife was a stranger to her, although kind enough. She just seemed a bit distracted and rarely came around. Beth had been her only link to Miles all these years.

"That's families for you. Me, I say you gotta make your own family," the woman said, nodding her head sagely. Her phone vibrated, and she answered it, excusing herself to go outside.

Keely had done a lot of thinking since she'd found Theodore. She'd experienced a flash of fear when she'd seen him lying there that she'd found him only to lose him so quickly. She'd experienced pain when Zeke left and even when other boyfriends and lovers had gone on their way, but it hadn't felt anything like this. Her full life looked a lot emptier without Theodore sitting by her side with his quick-witted commentary and easy smile. She never would have thought that she'd be nearly sixty before she found a love like this, but none of her life had been what she'd expected. It had been far better.

Even the fact that he'd survived surgery felt like a blessing. Every moment of his recovery was a moment more than he might have had if … She shook off the thought. It hadn't come to that. Lots of people had a faulty ticker and lived years longer. He would just have to be one of them, she thought to herself resolutely, taking another drink of her Coke. She got up and walked across the waiting room.

"I'm just going to step outside to make a call," she told the girls quietly. "Can you come to get me if there's news?" she asked, directing the question at Presley when Layla refused to meet her eyes.

"Of course," Presley replied. When Keely walked out, she looked over at Layla. "It wouldn't kill you to be nice."

"Why is she still here anyway?" Layla asked in annoyance as Keely walked outside.

"If she hadn't been there, you know Dad would probably have died, right?" Presley said tearfully. "Maybe you should remember that when you're being so rude to her." Presley stalked over to the window to look outside, but mostly she was trying to cool her temper. This wasn't the time to have it out with her sister. She rested her forehead against the cool glass and closed her eyes for a minute.

Layla rolled her eyes, but inside she cringed. She had been rude, and Presley was right. If Keely hadn't been there, their Dad probably wouldn't have made it this far. She checked her phone again. Noah hadn't responded to her last text, but he was at work and was scrupulous about not texting on the clock.

She'd been happy that he'd come by and brought coffee. She wanted her family to think well of him after the string of losers she'd brought home over the years. She wanted to shout from the rooftops, "See? I can get a good man!"

Of course, they'd always been friendly to whoever came around, but she could read the disappointment on her father's face and the judgment on Presley's. She shifted in her seat, uncomfortable knowing that she was in the wrong. It seemed like she was always on the wrong foot with her family, the one who always seemed to screw things up.

Presley came back over and picked up her book without a word. Layla glanced at the cover of the book Presley was reading. She wanted to ask her what it was about, but she'd likely earn that annoyed look she always got if she interrupted Presley's reading. So, she didn't. She played a game on her phone and scrolled through social media and wondered how pissed her family would get if she went to her classes in the morning. She couldn't just stay here. The smell of sickness made her feel nauseated and reminded her a little too much of her mom's hospice care. She wondered how Presley could stand it every day. She thought it was disgusting.

She sighed. Clearly, she'd sighed louder than she'd intended because Presley looked up, annoyed. Layla thought back to when it had been the two sisters against the world. They'd aligned themselves against their parents, always sticking together and covering for each other. All the way up until their dad had sat them both down to say that their mother wasn't going to get any better. She hadn't had strep throat or tonsillitis or anything like that. It was throat cancer, a likely result of all those years of smoking. It had spread, and the prognosis wasn't good. The shock had been immediate. Presley had gotten quieter, and Layla had spun out of control. When Layla started smoking, the fissure in their relationship became impossible to bridge.

Layla had quit smoking in the last year. Not that her family took any notice of it, but Noah was proud of her. She didn't want to end up like her mom, hurting with every single rasping breath all the way up until the end. Not that Presley had ever described that moment at the end, but she could guess. Anyway, she wasn't spinning out of control anymore. Maybe it had taken her too long to get back on track, but she was going to live a good life and to hell with anyone who still judged her for the choices she'd made, she thought angrily.

Anger was her default setting, although she wouldn't admit it. It was so much easier than feeling uncomfortable or in the wrong. She glared over at Keely as she walked back in and then went back to scrolling on her phone. She knew she should apologize, but she didn't know how to say the words so she sat and stewed instead.

*****

Presley could almost hear Layla's internal argument. She'd only become aware of it with that heavy sigh, but she knew her sister well enough to know the general direction of her thoughts. Layla had been stuck in a victim mentality since their mother's diagnosis. Of course, then she'd gone off and started smoking like she could vanquish her mother's cancer by getting it herself.

Presley had been angry more than heartbroken. She'd had all this fierce love for her little sister, the curly-haired brat who had trailed her like a shadow for as long as she could remember. She'd wanted them to stick even closer together to get through it all, and instead, Layla had gone out and got an older boyfriend to buy her a pack of cigarettes. Presley had gotten tired of watching her mother die, her father grieve, and her sister spin out further and further from them all. It had been too much.

She and Layla had never gotten past it. She wasn't sure they ever would. She could see that Layla was trying to turn over a new leaf, but she didn't have a lot of confidence that she would sustain the effort. After all, she'd done it plenty of times in the past. She'd straighten up and start to take control of her life, and then someone would piss her off at work, and she'd burn every bridge she'd so carefully built. Her temper and impulsivity kept her out of good jobs and even stable relationships.

Though maybe Noah was different. He was nice anyway, which wasn't her usual type. Layla had dated all kinds of men, but they'd typically shared good looks and fecklessness in equal measure. The unemployed. The live-with-their-mothers. The mooches. The cheaters. None of them were ever good enough for Layla, but try telling her sister that, Presley thought in disgust. After all, Layla kept picking them. She did that whole "stand by your man" thing better than anyone, even when the man was a total ass-hat, she thought with a roll of her eyes. Presley knew she could do better, and she'd finally done it. The question remained if she could keep him. She couldn't see Noah sticking around if she started back to those childish behaviors.

When Layla got up, ostensibly to use the restroom, Presley decided to go check on news of her father's condition. Visiting hours were limited, but they all wanted to be close by just in case. She needed to convince Keely to go home and get some rest. She'd already been waiting longer than any of them, and she was likely exhausted. She shouldn't feel bad for getting a little rest. After all, she lived just minutes away. They could call her if anything changed, good or bad. Still, it was nice that she wanted to stay.

Chapter 30

"What's with the heavy sigh?" Beth asked frankly.

Lindy looked over at her, unaware she'd sighed so loudly. "Sorry. The Black Friday painting class was a little exhausting. Fun, but exhausting," she explained. She'd come into the tea room to have a cup of herbal tea and a little peace and quiet after the rush of the early class she'd offered for kids whose parents wanted to get a jump on Black Friday deals. She really just wanted to sleep all day, but she was grateful for the business and for something to think about other than her mom and Theodore.

"Any word on Theodore?" Beth asked. They'd both gotten the early morning call. Beth had assured Keely she'd handle the tea room and not to worry. Lindy had headed straight to the hospital to sit with her mom before the early classes were scheduled to begin.

"He's in surgery still. Seth went over at lunch, and we'll both go check on them this evening," Lindy said, taking a sip of her tea.

"Shouldn't you be resting?" Beth asked, eyeing her carefully. "You seem tired."

"I'm tired all the time these days," she said with a shrug. She'd told her family she was pregnant, not ill, when they'd cautioned her about coming by the hospital. They'd agreed to take the visits in shifts but only if Lindy would agree to shorter shifts than the rest of them. She'd agreed, but only because she'd been too tired to argue.

"Is Dean any help?" Beth asked, sitting down for a minute. They'd had a quiet morning but a busy lunch rush.

"He's been great, actually," Lindy said, drawing her brows together.

"Um, tell that to your face," Beth said with a laugh.

"No, really. He's been amazing. It's just weird," she explained.

"Mom said she'll probably stay with Theodore a while during the recovery," she said, changing the subject. "She's keeping positive by planning his rehabilitation. I almost wanted to remind her not to get ahead of herself, but I didn't have the heart."

"I wouldn't have either," Beth admitted. "Still, it's nice to see how much they love each other." She waited a beat. "So, can we talk baby showers yet?"

Lindy smiled at her. "It's a little early, but sure," she replied easily, glad for a break from worrying about her mom. Keely was clearly besotted with Theodore, a term she'd never used before but suited the situation perfectly. "Everyone's already heard the news anyway. I only told the family, Nina, and Marnie, but the staff at the store knew before I told them," she said with a shrug.

"How is Marnie?" Beth asked. Marnie had been Seth's high school and college girlfriend. After the breakup, she and Lindy had stayed close.

"Planning her wedding, mostly," Lindy said with a smile. "They're doing one of those destination weddings, but she wants a big reception when she gets back."

Marnie had been excited to hear about the baby, but the plot twist that it was Dean's had left her in stunned silence for a full minute before the laughter had begun. Lindy was afraid the news was causing that reaction in a number of people who knew them both, she thought ruefully. After all, they'd spent their lives fighting and now this. No one was surprised Dean had a baby on the way, but they were more than a little surprised it was going to be hers. Of course, she'd anticipated talk when she started planning for this. Just not about her and Dean. She sighed again.

"Why don't you go home and take a nap?" Beth asked kindly.

"Because I'm not a child?" Lindy snapped.

"Whoever said naps are just for kids?" Beth asked curiously, unconcerned with Lindy's tone. A snapping Lindy was fairly normal, and she figured pregnancy didn't help. "Looks like you have a visitor," Beth said, looking out the window where Dean was passing by heading for the studio. She walked over to the door and opened it up, calling his name.

"She's in here," she added and walked off, not bothering to see if he was following behind but grinning when she heard him come in behind her.

Lindy rolled her eyes from her seat at the table. He'd taken to stopping by to check on her lately. Dean kept inserting himself into her plan, even as she assured him it wasn't necessary. Every time she did, he just shot her a cheeky grin and went right back to it. She kept looking for a good time to tell him that it was actually his baby and not just a donor's, but one thing or another got in the way. Like Theodore's heart issue. Or the other day when she nearly told him, but he'd been so cute going on about breastfeeding versus formula that she'd lost track of what she'd been about to say and kissed him.

There was the day she'd come home to find he'd painted the nursery for her. She'd left the paint chip sitting out, and he'd gone to the store and bought everything himself as a surprise. He'd even drafted Seth to come help. She wanted to tell him then, but Seth had called Libby over, and they'd ordered pizza. They hadn't been alone until late, and she'd felt she sort of missed the chance. He was tired after working and painting all day so it wasn't really a good time to bring it up.

Then, there was the ultrasound. She was going to go with her mom, but with everything going on with Theodore, she didn't really want to ask her to take the time for something so basic. There would be more ultrasounds later. Lindy had promised to bring both pictures and video if she could, and she'd planned to go alone. Dean showed up first thing that morning, ready to go with her. He'd asked, of course, and she couldn't quite work up to saying no. When the image of the baby, no more than a peanut, had popped up on the screen,

Dean had said, "See that little alien? That's your baby, Lindy." He'd grinned wide when they listened to the heartbeat, and she'd wanted to tell him then. But then the ultrasound technician started talking, and Lindy didn't think an audience was appropriate for that conversation anyway.

When he sat across from her and smiled, she tried to shut down the automatic smile that tried to cross her face and scowled instead. "What are you doing here?"

"I thought I'd walk you home," Dean offered, breezily, unperturbed by her tone.

"What if I wasn't done yet?" she asked belligerently.

"Then I'd have waited until you were," he said evenly. "Have you eaten? Want to get some dinner?"

"I just want to go home," Lindy replied, trying and failing to check her irritated tone.

"Want me to pick up takeout or cook?" he asked gamely. She looked up at him, considering.

"You'd cook." She said it more as a flat statement than a question, but he answered anyway.

"Sure, if you want," he said with a slow smile. "Then I can rub your feet after."

Lindy rolled her eyes automatically but still felt warm as he said it. Dammit, he was ruining her bad mood, just as she was really getting into it. She eyed him across the table. The dating thing was weird with the pregnancy thing. Dean kept trying to make it seem less weird, but Lindy still thought it was the oddest thing. She'd dreamed of nesting and spending all her time planning for the baby, but she hadn't imagined dinners out and foot rubs and all of the *romance* that Dean seemed to be inserting into her carefully ordered life.

She didn't need that kind of thing. He'd taken to bringing flowers home for no reason. She could see how all those other women had fallen in love with him. But just because she could see it didn't mean she had to do it, Lindy told herself severely. He was just a smooth kind of guy, and he probably was like that with everyone while he was with them. Then, he moved on.

Lindy told herself not to count on him. After all, it was one thing to date her while she was still small. She wouldn't start showing for a couple of months or more. He'd probably feel different when it looked like she'd swallowed a beach ball, and he'd definitely feel different when there was a baby crying at all hours in her house.

Even that line of thought failed to get her back into the mood of a good sulk. She decided she'd enjoy it for now. That was the healthy thing to do. When he moved on, as he inevitably would, she'd concentrate fully on the baby. She'd pick names and buy tiny clothes once she figured out what she was having, and she'd paint a mural over the background color she'd chosen for the room. She would miss the foot rubs and conversation, but she'd restore order to her life and move on. Everything would be about the baby, and that would be okay. They'd be just fine on their own, she told herself.

"So, what do you want?" he asked, patient with her long silence.

"I want pizza," she decided.

"Any weird toppings?" he asked with a smile.

"Every topping," she insisted, seeing if he'd argue.

"Anchovies?"

"Of course not," she snapped.

He picked up her hand and kissed it. "I love it when you're angry."

"Oh, shut up," she said, finally laughing.

Chapter 31

Dean had found himself standing in the baby section at the store earlier that morning. He hadn't intended to go in that section at all. To be honest, he was only vaguely aware that such a section existed. Still, he'd passed it, and it had caught his eye. He found himself looking at all the odd things they made for babies. There were breast pumps that looked like instruments of torture. There were teething rings that seemed to inexplicably have animals attached to them. There were slings and pouches so parents could wear the baby like a fashion accessory. Or a kangaroo. But it was all kind of cute. They had cloth diapers, which he couldn't quite figure out. That seemed a little gross.

Then, he found his way to the baby clothes section. He was holding up a tiny onesie and eyeballing it when he heard the voice.

"Dean Walton, what in the world are you doing?"

He turned around and grinned at Candace who was pushing a cart and looking at him in amusement. "Babies cannot be this small," he told her, waving the onesie in her direction.

Candace walked closely and checked the size. "That's 0-3 months. You'll want to get a few, just in case the baby is big, but this is the size you're looking for," she told him, handing him a newborn onesie.

"It's like doll's clothes," Dean told her.

"Haven't you ever been around babies?" she asked him, her voice filled with amusement.

"Not ones this small," he said, shaking his head.

"I heard congratulations were in order, but I didn't believe it," she told him frankly.

"Well, it was certainly a surprise. The good kind though," he quickly added.

"Do you need any help?" Candace asked him, correctly guessing that he was out of his depth here. "What are you looking for?"

"I don't know. Something helpful, I guess. There's some weird shit back here; I'm not going to lie," he told her, nodding to the breast pumps and some kind of weird device that, if you believed the package, had parents doing something incredibly nasty to help with stuffy noses. He'd blanched when he saw that, but he was sort of hoping it was a gag gift and not a real thing.

"Well, what does she need?" Candace asked practically, looking at him as if he had any idea.

"According to her, nothing," Dean said with some irritation.

He was busy convincing Lindy that she needed him these days. She so clearly didn't. And not just financially. Lindy did pretty well for herself so she didn't need help with that. Apparently, she'd saved for medical costs and a number of other baby-related expenses before choosing to start a family. She didn't want or need his help with that, as she'd told him a number of times. She was quite competent at putting together baby furniture and painting and registering for what the baby would need. She didn't need his help there either, although he had taken the initiative and painted the nursery so he could at least feel useful. The truth was that Lindy didn't need him for any of this. She was perfectly capable of managing without him.

But he wanted to be a part of their lives. Not just hers. Already, he could see the three of them together—him, Lindy, and this baby that wasn't his but could grow up calling him Dad. He didn't know that he wanted that until it was a possibility. He'd never envisioned a future with anyone else he dated. He hadn't even been sure it was in the cards for him. Being a confirmed bachelor wasn't something that made him shrink back in horror. But now he could only see himself with Lindy. Maybe she'd even want another child, later. He didn't have to have one of his own. It wasn't a big issue for him, and he'd love her child just the same. But if she wanted another, he could see making a baby with Lindy. He just didn't know how to make *her* see it. She never saw anything she didn't want to, Dean thought darkly.

"Look, don't get overwhelmed. Some of this you'll need, and some you won't," she told him, guiding him past the gross nose thing he'd eyeballed earlier. "You'll get a lot at the baby shower, I'd imagine, so maybe you should just stick with something sweet right now."

"Sweet?" he asked her skeptically. "Like what?"

"Like one of those outfits you were looking at or something like this," she held up tiny bunny baby booties that he had to admit were pretty cute but impossibly small.

"That could work," he mused. "Thanks," he told Candace gratefully.

"Dean Walton with a baby," she said in amusement, shaking her head. "You might just surprise us all," she told him as she walked away.

"Might just surprise myself," he muttered, looking around to see what else he could pick up. Maybe he wasn't Lindy's type, he thought. And maybe he'd dated too casually and none too discreetly before. He could own that. But he'd never been unfaithful. He'd just avoided commitment.

Unfortunately, that's how Lindy still seemed to see him. It was hard to convince someone you could be different who'd watched you be sort of the same for years. He brooded about the situation more than he cared to admit. It wasn't easy loving someone like Lindy. He didn't care that she was headstrong. He was, too. He tossed a couple of items into the basket he'd picked up and thought that it was hard to love someone who could easily live without him and be just fine. He'd gotten used to the women who had worked so hard to keep him whether he wanted to be kept or not.

His thoughts slammed to a sudden stop. Could he be that person for Lindy? Was he really becoming the person that kept trying to keep someone who didn't want to be kept? What about what she wanted? He picked up a couple of things off the shelf with a frown. He added one to the basket and put the other back. Anyway, was it wrong to try to get someone to fall in love with you if you loved them back? He'd never had to wonder because he'd never fallen in love before. He might have tripped here or there on one attachment or another, but he'd always easily disentangled himself long before it could get serious.

Dean walked out of Target shaking his head, carrying an armful of bags and a receipt that was longer than he had intended. Every single time, he thought. Still, Lindy would enjoy the chocolates, and she might get a kick out of the teeny tiny baby booties he'd found. And the matching hat was pretty cute, too. He'd gotten one that looked sort of like a boy and one for a girl and one that was a gender-neutral sort of yellow. He figured she could use whichever one she liked.

He was pretty sure that whatever she was doing wouldn't conform to any societal standard of gender norms, he thought with a smile. In fact, he'd already bought a set of black baby onesies embroidered with some of her favorite snarky feminist phrases. He'd surprise her with that closer to time. He knew how she thought, even if he wasn't entirely sure what she thought about *him*. He looked at her across the table from him as she started to laugh. He'd give her the chocolates tonight. If her mood didn't improve, he'd spring the booties on her, too.

*****

Theodore managed to get up and go to the bathroom and back, but he found it infuriating that he couldn't just do the things he wanted when and how he wanted to do them. He found the rehabilitation insufferable, a word that Keely was probably using to describe him about now, he thought with irritation. Still, he'd never had to worry about his health. He barely ever caught a cold, and he could probably count the number of severe illnesses in his life on one hand.

He'd never anticipated heart trouble. After all, there was no family history of it, and he was still active. His diet wasn't strict, but it wasn't terrible either. It had just been one of those things, the doctors had said calmly. He'd had a coronary artery bypass, and they were optimistic about his recovery. They'd tried to give him a lot of medical detail, but he'd passed them off to Presley. He knew she'd tell him exactly what he needed to know and do it in a way that didn't seem overwhelming.

When he'd come to in the hospital, Keely, Presley, and Layla had been there. Keely's family had been in and out, and some of his own friends had stopped by. There was a steady stream of visitors during his stay, but Keely was the most faithful. She'd even moved into this drafty barn of a farmhouse he lived in to help him recover, and he'd been nothing but a bear lately. Every time he realized how irritable he sounded, he'd try to check himself, but it was hard being on his best behavior all the time when he felt so lousy. Keely had waved off his apologies. She'd ignored his ill-temper and continued to care for him calmly.

Of course, Presley said she hadn't been quite so unflappable when she'd found him. Theodore couldn't imagine how difficult, and downright scary, that must have been for her. He'd only seen her calm and collected, busy with the tasks of taking care of him, but Presley had described a grieving woman, shaken and devoid of makeup, who had sat at the hospital through the surgery and recovery eager for any news.

It was that knowledge that made him feel deeply ashamed of

himself for behaving so badly now. He just wanted to be able to get around without assistance and do things around the house and on the farm without having to hire help to do it for him. He missed going out for long hikes around his property, and he missed being able to do for himself and move around without thinking about it. He didn't want Keely to have to be his nurse, but he also didn't want her to leave, for a couple of reasons. First, he was in love with her. She'd been an absolute peach through the whole ordeal. But he was also afraid to be alone now. Had Keely not been here, he wouldn't have gotten help in time. He was in love with her absolutely, but he was also afraid that if she left, it might be one of his daughters that found him next. Presley, in all likelihood, and she'd already been the one to find her mother.

He sighed, a heavy sigh similar to the one Layla often employed, although he wouldn't have cared for the comparison. He heard Keely's footsteps in the hallway and tried to assemble a pleasant expression. She stopped in the doorway and gave him the oddest look.

"Are you okay?" she asked. "Can I get you anything?"

"I'm fine," he groused. "I'm smiling, aren't I?"

"Is that what you're doing?" she asked in amusement. "I was afraid you'd had a stroke. Well, you don't have to fake a smile on my account. I know you must be feeling awful," she sympathized.

"You have no idea!" he told her with a tone of irritation.

"I think I can imagine. My daddy went through the same thing once. He was as mad as a hornet until he was able to get around for himself," Keely said with a wry grin.

"Did your mom have to take care of him?" he asked in curiosity. Perhaps Keely had learned care-taking from her mother.

"No, she'd always been too ill. It was mostly left up to me and to a nurse friend we knew," she said with a shrug, thinking that Miles had gotten out of sick duty easily enough.

"It must be terrible for you to take care of another sick old man," Theodore said in self-pity, but Keely only looked at him with compassion and grabbed his hand.

"Stop calling yourself an old man, seeing as you're a few years my junior. It's insulting," she told him blandly. "And there's nowhere else I want to be other than right here beside you. No matter how grumpy you get or how much care you need."

"Maybe you should just permanently move in. Here, with me," Theodore suggested, feeling calm for the first time since he woke up in the hospital.

"Maybe you should marry me first," she told him evenly, not blinking an eye.

"Are you asking me?" he demanded with a delighted grin, maybe his first real one since he left the hospital.

"Are you saying yes?" she countered with a small smile.

"Of course I'm saying yes—though I'm a little disappointed that I don't get a ring," he joked.

"Well, there is a sort of ring," she said with an embarrassed smile, going to her purse to get it out. "It was my dad's." She showed him the antique ring her dad had worn for as long as she could remember. "It's not his wedding ring. He gave that to Seth with my mom's rings. It's just a ring he loved and wore most of his life."

"You got me a ring," Theodore said in wonder.

"You don't actually have to wear it," Keely said, looking mortified. "It was just a silly idea," she said, standing up to put it back in her purse.

He grabbed her hand. "That's my ring, and I'm wearing it," he said smugly. "I'm going to show it off to all my friends," he said with a laugh. "Isn't that what I'm supposed to do?"

"But you'll marry me?" Keely asked him, unsure if he was taking it all seriously.

"I'd marry you tomorrow. We'll worry about the details later," he told her seriously. Keely squeezed his hand and passed him the ring. He took it and leaned over to kiss her. "I'm not sure how long I have. I didn't know I had a tricky heart. But whatever time I have left, I want to spend it with you." She smiled through a gleam of tears and laid her head on his shoulder. "And I'll get you a ring to show off, too," he said, which made her laugh as he knew it would.

Chapter 32

Beth decided that today would be a good day for a longer walk. After all, the Georgia weather had veered from bitterly cold back to pleasantly mild. It wouldn't last long, but while it was here, she planned to enjoy it. She didn't even need to put Mr. Darcy in a sweater today, although he had an assortment of Christmas sweaters for the upcoming holiday. She walked out of the house with a spring in her step.

"I adore Christmas," she told Mr. Darcy. He kept walking, clearly unimpressed. Or maybe just used to her banter by now. Beth didn't take it personally. "I mean, you've got to admit, everyone did great with the lights." Lights, wreaths, ornaments, pretty baubles, and nativity scenes—the neighborhood was decked out in them. The styles ranged from severely elegant to campy fun, but she loved them all.

Jamie had come by the first week of December to help her hang up holiday lights, and they'd even decorated her tree. She'd insisted on a real one this year, although Jamie had mournfully shaken his head and declared it a goner. She'd elbowed him aside and gone back to tending her tree, ignoring the implication that she would kill it stone dead well before Christmas.

"I did not kill the tree," she muttered to Mr. Darcy who had stopped to sniff around his favorite tree before marking his territory. Beth was pretty sure he thought all of downtown Madison was his territory with the number of times they'd stopped so far. She shook her head ruefully and then continued her one-sided conversation. "We checked holiday lights off the list with Seth and Libby. We've already had your picture with Santa at the groomer's. We, well, you didn't, but I did," Beth clarified before continuing. "I got to see *A*

Christmas Carol at the Fox. What else? Oh, Rudolph! Can't forget my annual nod to my inner child's love of puppets."

She'd talked Lindy into the Center for Puppetry Art's annual Rudolph performance since she'd have a baby to take one day. Dean had tagged along, too. Beth wasn't sure how that would go, but it actually made her feel better about the whole situation. Sure, Dean was still as charming as ever, but he didn't check out the ticket taker, and even Beth could see that she was stunning. He didn't flirt with anyone but Lindy, even though a couple of women had made fairly obvious overtures. She wouldn't go so far as to say he'd changed. He was still a big flirt, but he really did seem invested in Lindy.

"You left out the popcorn thing," Jamie pointed out, as he approached from the direction of the gym.

"I'm sorry—what?" Beth asked, losing her train of thought. Jamie was wearing jeans and a long-sleeved shirt, and he was carrying a gym bag, which he immediately began digging around in to get her dog a treat. She'd been so deep into her conversation with Mr. Darcy that she took a minute to register what he was saying.

"The popcorn thing? We did that stringing popcorn thing for your tree last week and watched old Christmas movies—*It's a Wonderful Life* and *Miracle on 34th Street*," Jamie reminded her. "You forgot to add that to your list," he said with a smile.

"That's right. I feel like I'm leaving something out," Beth admitted. "Like there's something I wanted to do this year that I haven't done."

"You did Santa pictures?"

"Of course."

"Christmas lights?"

"Did it."

"I know you've done Christmas movies and tree decorating since I was there. And we've watched almost all of your Hallmark movies for the season. What's left? Christmas shopping?"

"No, I started that way super early this year. I'm good."

"Did you get me something?" he asked with a grin.

"Have you been good this year?" she joked. "I've done Christmas cookies and a gingerbread house, and I think I've made ten gallons of hot chocolate already. What else is there?" she asked him more seriously.

"I know you want to squeeze every bit of joy out of the holiday season and all, but I think you might be overthinking this, Beth," Jamie told her wryly. "But I'll tell you what, let me know what your next day off is, and I think we can go squeeze in one last Christmas extravaganza," Jamie offered.

"What did you have in mind?"

"You'll find out," Jamie said with a smile. "Let it be a surprise."

"I like surprises," Beth said with a grin. "Okay, deal. So, what's new with you?"

"Nothing, really. Business is good. Mostly, the store is buzzing with gossip lately. Seth's engagement and Lindy's baby and all. Pretty exciting stuff, I guess," Jamie said with a shrug. "How about you?"

"Same," she said with a smile. "When people aren't talking about the holidays, they've been quizzing Keely about Seth's wedding plans and the baby. She's finally back to work pretty regularly, although she's taking a long weekend just before Christmas. Theodore's getting better, but she takes breaks to check on him anyway. It's really sweet."

"Love is in the air, and all that."

"I know. It's usually pretty annoying, but this year it's kind of inspiring." Beth said thoughtfully.

"In what way?" Jamie asked, sitting down beside where Beth had dropped to a bench and putting Mr. Darcy in his lap.

"Well, you've got Keely who's been single forever meeting her dream guy, and then Seth and Libby walk around with hearts over their heads over the whole wedding deal. Considering that a couple of years ago Libby was stuck in a bad marriage, and Seth was avoiding relationships altogether, it's pretty sweet. Then you've got Lindy actually walking around with a big smile and planning for a baby. Not that she's any less, you know, *Lindy*, but she seems so much happier. And Dean? Who would have thought he'd settle for one woman, much less someone we know? It's kind of nice to see that sometimes things work out. I don't know," she said with a shrug.

"I know what you mean," Jamie agreed. "It makes me think if things can work out for them, they can work out for me, too."

Beth sighed. "I know they'll work out for you. I don't usually miss all that stuff, but every now and then I get a little twinge. Maybe a little envy or something. It always passes though," Beth said with a dismissive wave of her hand.

"Are you thinking about dating again?"

"Um, no. I think I'm fine living vicariously through the Hallmark Channel. I mean, I still go out sometimes when I feel like it. But I like it being just me and Mr. Darcy," Beth told him honestly. "We're happy."

"Well, don't forget to tell me when you're going to have a day off, and we'll go do something," Jamie reminded her. "I better get over to the store and see what's going on today." Jamie gave Mr. Darcy a last pat on the head and sat him softly on the ground.

"I have Friday off, but isn't this the weekend you're going out of town to spend the holidays with your family?"

"I'll head over there afterward. Friday sounds good," Jamie said with a smile. "We'll get started early so just dress for the weather."

"Well, I'll wait until Friday and see if we're having winter or spring here," Beth said with a laugh, heading off with Mr. Darcy.

Chapter 33

Lindy sat on the floor of Seth's house and looked through the boxes of ornaments. Some were Seth's and some were Libby's. Dean was in the kitchen talking to Seth while he cooked, and Libby was wrapping lights around the tree. The whole house smelled like cinnamon, and Libby had put on a Christmas record, which Lindy was pretty sure was Bing Crosby.

"Well, none of them broke in the move. That's a relief," she told Libby.

"I'm glad. I was a little worried about it the way Seth was tossing the boxes on the floor. I guess I should have written fragile on every side and not just the tops," Libby replied, walking over to look in the box. "I'm not sure what I should do with some of these," she admitted, picking up a First Christmas Together ornament she'd bought with her ex-husband Colin. There were a few in the box from her marriage. A trip they'd gone on, a special memory they'd made. They were a part of Libby's life, but they didn't belong on a tree hanging beside Seth's ornaments and the ornaments Libby and Seth selected together.

"There are two schools of thought on that," Lindy told her. "You could throw them away if you wanted to, or you could keep them and either hang them on the tree or just save them."

"Which do you think is right?" Libby asked with interest.

"I had a couple I'd bought with Tyler. They were handmade by a friend of ours, and it really meant a lot to me at the time. After it ended, I really wanted to crush them. Like maybe with my car," Lindy admitted ruefully. "But they're actually really lovely pieces. And they happened to me, you know? So, I hung them on the tree, but I didn't give them pride of place. I stuck them toward the back.

They're still a part of me, but they don't get to be the most important part, you know?"

"I think that's lovely," Libby said. "I'll talk to Seth and see what he thinks. Does he have ornaments from when he was with anyone else?"

"I probably have a couple," Seth admitted from the doorway. "I'm still cooking, but I thought you might like some apple cider," he offered, bringing in two mugs. Dean waited behind him, leaning on the doorframe. "Marnie and I had several Christmases together. I stopped putting up the ones with our picture, but the rest are around here somewhere. Other exes didn't really make it to the tree after it was over," he said with a shrug. "But I can go either way. Hang whichever ones you want, and we'll put the rest aside."

Libby walked over and kissed him softly. "I like what Lindy said. The ones from the past just don't get the focal point, but we'll still put them up. Not this one though," Libby said, putting her first Christmas ornament with Colin softly back into the box. "But some of the others I'd like to keep," she said, running a finger over one they'd bought at a glassblowing workshop on a trip up the East Coast one year.

Dean looked over at Lindy, surrounded by all the boxes. She still didn't look pregnant. She would be right around twelve weeks at Christmas, and she still looked as slim as ever. Of course, her color tended to go from glowing to pale when the morning sickness hit. Right now, she just seemed happy, which is why he decided not to address his very strong feeling about having one of Tyler's ornaments on *their* tree. Well, technically it was her tree, but he'd helped decorate it. He'd even hung up lights on the little cottage. He followed Seth back into the kitchen.

"What's with you?" Seth asked him, keeping his voice down.

"I didn't know any of the ornaments we put up were from him," he said with a shrug.

"Careful there," Seth cautioned. Dean gave him a questioning look. "She has a past, but so do you. If you're going to poke at hers, it's only fair she gets to do the same." Seth laughed. "I see you didn't think of that."

"I just hated that asshole," Dean muttered.

"Yeah, you weren't subtle about that," Seth said with a grin, checking each of the dishes on the stove.

"I took Lindy to see the lake house," Dean said, changing the subject.

"Did she notice the nursery?"

"Be hard to miss," Dean said with a shrug.

He'd taken Lindy over to see it when she got curious about where he was spending all his time when he wasn't with her or at work. He didn't want her to think that he was dating anyone else so he drove her up to the house and let her see what he'd done. She'd gotten out of the car slowly and gingerly walked up the stairs, testing the rails for stability. She'd gone around the cottage quietly and then asked about the renovations he'd been doing. If she'd noticed the nursery he'd been working on, she didn't say a word. Of course, it would have been hard not to notice. He'd painted it the same color as her own, and he'd even bought one of those glider rocker things. They were ridiculously comfortable so he'd taken to having a beer in it after he finished working around the house.

"She hasn't said anything more about it," he continued.

"Is that why you're scowling over there?" Seth asked with a perplexed look at his closest friend.

"It's just ... this whole thing ... it wasn't what I expected," Dean admitted. "I mean, not just the pregnancy. She's planning this whole life." Of course, what he didn't say but certainly thought was that she was planning it without him.

"And she's planning it without you." Seth knew exactly where his mind had gone. They knew each other too well for Dean to think he could hide it. He sighed.

"Well, I'm not going anywhere," he said stubbornly, heading back to the other room. He moved a few boxes to sit down on the floor beside her. She leaned back against him, which was a small improvement. She didn't seem to mind as much if people knew they were together, although she kept telling him that he might mind when she started showing.

"Dinner's almost ready," Seth called from the doorway. "Give me a few minutes."

"We'll start with ornaments after dinner," Libby told them. They'd invited Keely and Theodore to come over, but they were seeing a ballet in Atlanta and then taking a long weekend before Christmas in the mountains.

"Okay, you've got to tell me the story behind this one," Dean said with a grin, pulling out what was arguably the ugliest ornament any of them had likely ever seen.

While they talked, Lindy let her mind wander. She leaned back against Dean's legs and sipped her cider, letting her thoughts drift. They were all busy at work with the holiday rush, but that would slack off in the new year. In fact, Seth and Libby were discussing a cruise in January or February, and even Lindy was tempted to book a little tropical getaway once the busy season died back down.

Of course, she thought grimacing, she'd need a maternity bathing suit if she didn't go soon. Already, it was uncomfortable to button her pants. She was glad now that she had a healthy supply of leggings and yoga pants with enough stretch to cover her expanding abdomen. Dean claimed not to notice any weight gain, but he'd always been a charmer.

She looked at him discreetly while he talked about the holidays with Libby. She'd always found him attractive, not that she would have admitted it before. She'd never really allowed herself to study him, but lately, she found herself admiring the fall of his lashes on his cheeks when he looked down or the way his eyes crinkled at the corners when he smiled. She found herself doing more studies in her notebook of his hands or his profile when he sat beside her watching *Jeopardy*. She was a little afraid that she'd already fallen in love with him when she'd been determined not to.

She reminded herself that you could love someone and still let them go. After all, she'd loved Tyler with a ferocity that had astounded her, but she'd let him go when he wanted to leave. Or, to be more accurate, she'd booted his sorry ass out the door when she'd realized he'd been unfaithful. But just because she'd been the one to end things didn't mean that she didn't love him anymore. She still did but in more of an abstract sort of way.

Falling in love with Dean didn't have to mean a change to her carefully constructed plans. After all, it wouldn't be long now before the baby would be here, and she fully anticipated he'd move on by then. She turned back to the box beside her and lifted out the tree skirt that was tucked inside. Right now, she needed to focus on her health and the holidays. Everything else would work out in the end, she thought as Seth came into the room with a wide smile.

"Dinner's ready. Y'all are on clean-up duty though," he warned.

"I'll be playing the pregnancy card," Lindy told him, gingerly getting off the floor.

"Aren't you always telling us you're not ill, you're pregnant?" Seth demanded.

"Not today," she said with a laugh.

"Well-played," Dean said into her ear, and it didn't matter that she was pregnant or that this situation had grown more complicated than she knew how to manage. The quick surge of desire wasn't unexpected. They had more chemistry than they knew what to do with, but the surge of love she felt for him surprised her.

Affection, she corrected herself, as she turned toward him and kissed him in a way that had Seth dramatically groaning and calling for hot pokers to be applied to his eyes. She ignored her brother but broke off the kiss. After patting Dean's cheek and walking away without a word, she sent a wink Libby's way.

"I don't know what that was about," Dean said, sitting down in a chair beside her. "But we're going to finish that conversation later."

Chapter 34

Naomi scowled as she left the boutique. It was less than a week until Christmas, and she still hadn't found another job. She really wanted to stay local. After all, it was already a drive from Rutledge, and she didn't want to lengthen her commute. But unfortunately, every place she'd gone already had plenty of holiday help, and some had even reminded her that they'd be losing seasonal employees after the new year because of slower business.

She glanced across the street at the brisk lunch business at Brews & Blues. Maybe it hadn't been the best job, but it had been steady. Her pay had been decent, and Elle was fair even if she was a hard-ass about being late. Still, she wished she hadn't quit so impulsively, especially right before Christmas. She'd spent her last check on presents, and she wasn't sure how she was going to be able to afford her utility bill when it came due.

She looked at the handful of resumes in her hand and assessed her options. She couldn't really work at the dog groomer's. She wasn't an animal person. She wouldn't mind working at one of the restaurants, but they all seemed to be fully staffed. She'd die before she'd ask Dean's girlfriend for a job. She was still steamed that he had actually settled down and even updated his relationship status online with someone else when he'd been so dismissive of relationships before. She was sure it wouldn't last long, but she wasn't so desperate she needed to beg for work from her. She sat down on a bench and wanted to cry, but instead, she looked hard at the resumes, holding back tears.

Beth plopped down on the bench beside her with a sigh. "I keep telling myself that the holidays are almost over, and then I can rest. I just keep finding more gifts!" she said with a grin. She was wearing thick tights under an Audrey Hepburn-inspired dress, and she had her red hair pulled back in a messy bun at the nape of her neck. She was carrying bags from the store where Naomi had just asked for a job, and it made Naomi blush to her roots in embarrassment. She'd probably been rejected in full view of an audience and hadn't even noticed.

"Looking for holiday work?" Beth asked casually.

"Yep," Naomi said shortly. She didn't exactly want to make conversation about how she'd quit her job in a fit of temper and now couldn't find anything else. It didn't make her look mature or responsible, and Beth probably knew anyway the way gossip spread around this town. She'd never find a job at this rate!

"Do you like to read?" Beth asked curiously.

"I guess," Naomi said with a self-conscious shrug. The turns of this conversation seemed increasingly random. "I like certain books."

"I read everything. What do you read?" Beth asked, resituating her bags and looking at Naomi with interest.

"I like romance and dystopian stuff. Sometimes I read mysteries," she shrugged. Who cared about all that? She couldn't even afford to buy a book right now.

"How are you with computers and social media and all that?"

"I'm pretty good," Naomi said. "What's with all the questions anyway?" She didn't want to be rude. After all, she'd burned enough bridges lately. But geez!

"Come on. I might have a job for you," Beth told her, hefting her bags off the bench.

"Really?" Naomi squeaked in surprise. She cleared her throat and tried again. "What kind of a job?"

"So, I manage the bookstore at Utopia, right? Well, we're a little overrun right now with the holidays. It'll settle down soon, but I could use some help. After the holidays, we're losing one of our servers in the tea room. A few are just here seasonally, but we really need someone who can come in part-time on a more regular basis. If you're interested, you could help out in the book and gift shop and do a little serving, too, when you're needed," Beth said. "If you work out," she qualified. She'd heard from Candace about Naomi quitting, and Elle had reached out around town to see if anyone was hiring who might be willing to give her another chance. Perhaps she was firm with her own employees, but she solidly believed in second chances.

"I, um, quit my last job," Naomi admitted. "I don't know if I can get a reference," she said uncomfortably.

"If you're willing to work and do your best, that's all I'll ask. But I have to level with you about something, and it might be sort of personal. I just think it's best we get this out of the way," Beth said, looking Naomi dead in the eye, as she sat her shopping bags down by the bookstore counter with a thud. "Keely owns the place. I run this side of things, but if Keely feels like you're not working out, that's it. She's Lindy's mom, and I know you don't exactly like her, but Keely won't hold that against you. Now if you make trouble for Lindy, then she won't stand for that. Is this going to be a problem?"

"Does everybody know about me and Dean?" Naomi asked in embarrassment.

"It's a small town," Beth said with a shrug. "And I knew you had words here with Lindy at the book signing a few months back. I just want to make sure that you know that it won't be appropriate to bring that personal stuff here."

"I wouldn't do that," Naomi said with her eyes wide. "Okay, so I have in the past, but I won't do that again. I really need a job," she admitted, blushing to her roots.

"Okay. I just needed to make sure. Lindy doesn't need to be upset with the baby and everything so I thought I'd get the lay of the land before we made any decisions," Beth said, heading over to get an employee application.

"What baby?" Naomi asked in confusion.

"Uh-oh," Beth said, stopping and turning around. "Okay, I thought you'd have heard. Lindy and Dean are having a baby."

"Oh," Naomi said in surprise. She crossed her arms at her chest. "I didn't know that."

"Well, it's new news," Beth said. "Is that going to be a problem?"

"I mean, it's just the icing on the cake of my life right now, but I'll be fine," Naomi said shakily, trying not to cry.

"Look, I get it. You wouldn't be the first heart he's broken, but Lindy is also a good friend of mine. Whatever feelings you have, you're going to need to deal with them off the clock. But if you have a minute, we can sit down and go over pay and hours and what's expected. There's a dress code, too, and you'll want more comfortable shoes," Beth said, looking at the stilettos Naomi was wearing.

"Okay," Naomi said humbly, sitting down. "Thanks."

"Don't thank me," Beth said with a smile. "Elle heard I needed help and said you might be looking for work. Seems she thinks you're a good worker when you put your mind to it."

Naomi looked down, ashamed of herself for all of the ugly thoughts she'd sent Elle's way since she quit. Elle had acted professionally in the situation, and Naomi hadn't. It was uncomfortable to think of how badly she'd behaved and that Elle still had reached out to help her. It looked like she'd need to make one last stop before she drove home today.

*****

Keely sat downstairs in her house Christmas morning sipping a cup of hot chocolate. She'd made a fresh batch in the crockpot and was enjoying the early morning quiet. It was dark still, and the only light came from the lights on her Christmas tree and of her own home and the neighboring homes lit up for the holiday. She curled her feet under her and thought about all of the Christmases spent in this home. She thought about her parents following her and Miles sleepily down the stairs while they ran to open their presents. She thought about those years when Zeke had gone, and she'd shared holidays with her parents and her babies. All those Christmases and all those years, and now everything was changing. This time next year, what would Christmas be like? Lindy would have her child, and Seth and Libby would be married. She sighed.

"I hope that was a happy sigh," Theodore said behind her.

"I thought you were sleeping in," she told him, placing a hand over his own on her shoulder.

"I could hear you thinking from up there. Are you sorry for the way things have turned out?" he asked her softly, coming to sit down beside her.

"No. Not at all. I was just thinking of all of the Christmases we spent right here in this house," she said. "Not just me and the kids, but me and my brother with our parents. Everything will be different next year. I guess it's sort of bittersweet for me," she said with a small smile. "But mostly sweet."

"That's understandable," Theodore said calmly. "When will the kids be over, do you think?" he asked, looking at the time. It was just shy of 7:00 a.m.

"You'd be surprised," she said wryly. "Seth and Lindy are both still like kids at Christmas."

"Presley and Layla may be a tad bit later if that's okay," he told her. "They don't get out of bed quite this early," he said with a smile.

"Neither does Beth, and she's coming over for a little while with her dad. You'll get to meet Miles. He probably won't stay long, but it's nice to see him," Keely said softly. "Seth will get busy with breakfast, and Lindy will put on a Christmas movie. We'll wait to open presents until everyone gets here."

Chapter 35

Beth got up early and pulled out the tacky Christmas sweater she favored for the holidays. It was truly hideous, but that's what made it fun. She paired it with fleece-lined leggings since the weather had veered back to cold in the last couple of days. She was excited for Christmas this year, and Mr. Darcy danced around her feet while she got ready in his own version of doggie anticipation for the holiday. She had gone into the living room to load up the haul of presents she was taking over to Aunt Keely's when she heard the doorbell.

"Can't be Santa," she told Mr. Darcy with a grin. "He already came," she said gesturing to the pile of presents under the tree for her dog and her family.

"Hey, Jamie!" Beth said in delight. She reached out and gave him a hug before she could think about it. "Merry Christmas!"

"Merry Christmas, Beth," he said with a laugh at her enthusiasm. "I just wanted to stop by with something before I head to my parents."

"You're the best!" Beth told him, pulling him inside. "Look who it is, Mr. Darcy!" she exclaimed.

Currently, Jamie was Beth's number one favorite human. On Friday, he'd taken her to Stone Mountain Park's Snow Mountain for a Christmas village and sledding adventure. Even though the day had turned out warmer than winter warranted—she liked the alliteration there and had used it more than once during the day—they had played in the snow and gone tubing down the artificially created slopes. They'd ridden a train and sung Christmas carols and even stayed for a Christmas parade. Jamie had bought her an ornament with her name and Mr. Darcy's on it, and he'd even bought a new stocking for her dog. (Yes, he had an old one.)

It had been one of the best days Beth could remember. She finally stopped feeling like there was some holiday celebration she'd missed out on this year. They had enjoyed the entire outing and then come back to her place to watch Christmas movies. It might have been the perfect day, Beth thought. She was sure a slap-happy Christmas smile was stuck on her face all week, but it had made her happy. Leave it to Jamie to know exactly what she needed, Beth thought with a grin.

"I brought presents," Jamie said with a grin. "First, for you." He opened a bag and handed Mr. Darcy the large bone he'd gotten him, and he pulled out a bag of pig ears and assorted treats. Mr. Darcy sat eagerly, thumping his tail until they gave him permission to enjoy his present.

"And for you," Jamie said shyly, handing Beth a small box.

Beth carefully peeled back the wrapping paper. She usually liked to rip into her presents, but this one was so small. Inside was a small bracelet with an inscription. She held it up to read it and gasped aloud. It said *I will honor Christmas in my heart and try to keep it all the year.*

"Will you help me put it on?" she asked with a smile. As Jamie fastened it, she admired the way it twinkled in the light. "Where did you find this?" she asked him curiously.

"I found the bracelet at an auction. Then I took it somewhere to get it inscribed," he said with a shrug as if it were no big deal.

"I love *A Christmas Carol*," Beth said with a happy sigh, referring to the quote.

"I thought it would suit you," Jamie said with a smile.

"I really love it, Jamie. It's the sweetest thing!" she enthused, clasping it to her chest. "But wait because I got you something, too." She dug around in her big pile of presents until she found it. She handed him the medium-sized box with a grin.

He opened it up slowly. Inside was a large tartan throw blanket tied in twine. She'd tucked three books into it and a handmade scarf. He looked through the books. She'd included *A Moveable Feast* by Hemingway, a collection of poems by Pablo Neruda, and a best-selling mystery that she knew he'd been interested in reading. Her memory for what people liked to read was legendary around here, Jamie thought with a grin.

"You can use the blanket for movie night," Beth said with a smile.

"Thank you. I love it," Jamie said simply. "Did you make it through your holiday list?" he asked. "I think we covered everything on it, but this is the last day so be sure," he teased her.

"Hmm ... I think I've checked it twice." Beth went over to the counter and picked up an actual list, which made Jamie laugh. He followed and took it from her to look. It was a long list of every type of Christmas activity one could imagine, and she'd actually crossed them all off. Ice skating outdoors. Christmas lights. Make a snow angel. Have a snowball fight. Decorate a gingerbread house. Make gingerbread cookies. Go to a Christmas play. He read the long list with a grin. He'd picked the right gift for sure. She was sure to have a list like this for every time of year.

"You missed one," Jamie pointed out.

"No, I didn't," she argued. "I don't even think that's possible." She grabbed the list. "Where?"

"Look at the end," he directed.

"Oh. Mistletoe. I crossed that one out," Beth told him with a grin. "Mr. Darcy gave me some love the other day under one, so it counts," she said in amusement.

"Does it count?" he asked her with a smile.

"It better count because I don't have time for anything else today," Beth said with a laugh.

"I've got to run to my family thing, but give me just a second," Jamie said, running out to his truck. Beth shooed Mr. Darcy back inside and went to wait for him on the porch. She admired again her beautiful bracelet. When she looked up, she nearly did a double-take and then laughed out loud.

"You keep mistletoe in your truck? That's pretty bold!" she said with a grin.

"I take it to tease my nieces and nephews," he admitted. "They mostly run away, but the baby lets me kiss her. Anyway, I don't want you to miss out on anything on your list."

"You're sweet, but I don't have time to find someone to kiss today. I'm meeting my dad at Aunt Keely's in a few minutes, and we'll be swamped doing Christmas stuff all day," she said. "But you're very sweet."

"And you're very slow," Jamie said with a roll of his eyes. "It'll be painless I promise," he told her, holding up the mistletoe over her head and giving her a questioning look. She quirked an eyebrow and grinned.

"Fine. Let's cross this one off." She offered up her cheek, and Jamie stepped in to kiss it when they both turned. Beth's lips were a breath away from Jamie's, and she thought, why not? She wasn't sure after who closed the distance, but someone did because his lips were soft against her own. It was the lightest of kisses, more of a tease really, but Beth nearly swayed when his lips left hers. Thank God for the post on the porch, she thought, as she leaned back against it. "I think we can check that one off the list now," she said shakily.

"Yeah," Jamie agreed. "Look, I've got to go. Talk later?" he asked, heading for the truck.

"Of course. Merry Christmas," she told him as he hurried away.

"Merry Christmas," he replied automatically as he got in. He drove nearly on autopilot to his parents' house wondering what he'd been thinking. He'd opened Pandora's Box alright, and he should have kept it firmly shut.

Beth walked back into the house in a daze and noticed Mr. Darcy sitting on the back of the couch staring out the window. "You didn't see anything," she told him firmly and headed to gather up the holiday presents to go to her aunt's house.

*****

By the time Beth arrived, the driveway and street were packed with cars. She recognized her dad's. He was parked in the most convenient place to leave early. She knew Seth and Libby had probably walked, and Dean would be parked at Lindy's if he hadn't come on foot. The other cars were likely Theodore's and his daughters. She walked in and hoped the blush that had stained her cheeks all morning would be attributed to the brisk walk in the cold and not to anything else. No one would have a reason to suspect anything else. If it came to that, she thought, she'd just say she was sick. It could be a fever, she thought distractedly.

Christmas morning, other than the unexpected kiss, was the same as all the others except with more participants this year. Beth had sort of expected everyone to be paired up, but Seth and Dean were talking in the kitchen, and Lindy was sitting with Layla on the couch. Libby and Presley were looking through the selection of Christmas movies, and Keely and Theodore were talking to her dad. Everyone seemed to mix and mingle easily enough, and they enjoyed brunch and gifts in equal measure. It wasn't until the last present was opened that the bombshell hit.

"We have a little news," Keely began hesitantly, glancing over at Theodore.

"I don't know if my heart can take another pregnancy announcement," Seth said with a laugh.

"Haha," Keely intoned. "This may seem a bit sudden, but Theodore and I ... well, we ..." She paused.

"What your mother is trying to say is that we got married over the weekend," Theodore said with a grin. The room went absolutely quiet for a minute before pandemonium broke out in the form of questions from every side. "Wait—we can't hear you all at once," Theodore told them with a smile.

"I can't believe you'd get married and not tell us first," Layla said angrily.

"We didn't exactly plan it. Well, not this soon," Keely began, hesitantly.

"And we have pictures. The place we went to took loads of pictures for us, and there's a video, too," he said proudly, failing to notice Layla's flushed angry face.

"How nice for you," she said coldly. Lindy put a hand on her knee in a warning, shaking her head quickly. This wasn't the time, the gesture said.

"We want to hear all about it," Libby said with stars in her eyes. "Was it incredibly romantic?"

"Well, we certainly thought so," Keely said, looking at Theodore with a smile.

"We're so happy for you, Mom," Seth told her, exchanging nods with Lindy. "We're so happy for both of you."

"This is great," Presley said, joining in for the first time now that she saw Layla wasn't going to make a scene. "Let's see the pictures."

"Wait—are you going to live here or at the farmhouse?" Miles asked, speaking up from the back of the room. He'd been about to make a quiet exit when the announcement was made. Now he'd have to stay through the congratulations before he could go. He could at least be the voice of reason while he was here, he thought pragmatically.

The room got quiet. Seth and Lindy looked at each other in alarm. They hadn't thought of that. "Well, we discussed that," Keely began. She looked at Theodore who nodded in encouragement. "We'd like for both houses to stay in the family, but there's no need for us to live in two places. We decided I would move to the farmhouse," she said tentatively.

"And we were thinking Lindy might want to move in here," Theodore continued. "Seth, we know you and Libby just moved in together, and we thought that you wouldn't want to move again. Besides, Lindy's going to have the baby, and the carriage house is so small. We thought you might like to make your home over here," he explained, looking at Lindy. "Then you could rent out the carriage house for extra income if you want or use it for a studio one of these days."

"I don't know what to say ..." Lindy began.

"You don't have to say anything now. You and your brother talk it over and figure it out between you. We're happy with whatever you choose," Keely said calmly.

"But our breakfasts, Mom?" Lindy asked, tearfully. "Pregnancy hormones," she said in explanation, wiping away the tears.

"We can have breakfast before work still. Any time you want. You just say the word," Keely told her, coming around to wrap her in a hug.

"Hey, can we see the ring?" Presley asked suddenly, hoping to distract from the heavy emotions that had just settled in the room.

"Here it is," Theodore said, wiggling his ring finger.

"Why are you showing us yours?" Presley asked with a laugh.

"Because this is what she gave me when she proposed," he said with a grin. "Ask her if you don't believe me. She's got a ring, too, though."

They all gathered around to hear the story, and most of them were amused by the tale of Keely's proposal and the decision to elope over the weekend. They looked at pictures of a mountain ceremony that had even included a horse-drawn carriage and a honeymoon cottage lit with Christmas lights. Keely had worn a red dress she'd chosen for Christmas festivities, and Theodore had found a red tie to match it. They'd decorated with poinsettias and greenery, and she'd carried white and red roses down the aisle for the quick ceremony.

Only Layla sat silently through the pictures. She couldn't quite settle her emotions. She wished Noah was there to help her. She felt calmer when he was around and less likely to get agitated by some small something that didn't bother anyone else. She knew that the pictures were beautiful, and the story was even romantic. She could acknowledge that to herself. Her dad even seemed happy. She wasn't sure why she begrudged him that happiness, but all she could think about was her mom. She still missed her, even after all these years. She looked down at her hands gripping the mug of hot chocolate. She felt rather than saw Presley sit down beside her.

"I miss her, too," Presley said quietly. Layla looked up into her eyes. "At Christmas. On my birthday. On her birthday. Every time I hear Elvis on the radio, which is pretty much for a month solid on the radio at Christmas. Every time I hear Eric Clapton or an artist that reminds me of Eric Clapton. Every time I enter the hospital and have to pass the oncology floors. I miss her all the time."

"Yeah, me, too," Layla admitted. "I don't know why it feels worse right now."

"I don't either," Presley said. She was happy for her father, and she could see that Layla wanted to be but didn't know how. "I think Mom would have liked her," Presley said, looking at Keely.

"I know," Layla said. "She seems really nice," she offered. They sat quietly watching the group and after a minute Layla spoke up quietly to Presley. "Thank you."

"Any time."

Chapter 36

Lindy looked around her little cottage. She'd been thinking of her mother's offer since Christmas. She'd discussed it with Seth who was happy for the house to stay in the family but not to live in it himself. He loved his own house too much to want to move, and Libby felt the same. Her Uncle Miles hadn't seemed bothered by the suggestion. He hadn't wanted to move back to Madison anyway, he'd said with a rictus grin. He'd been terribly awkward about it, but Lindy suspected it was because he'd stayed far longer than he intended to and was ready to go home. Her Aunt Susan hadn't come at all. She'd gone to see her own family and had told Beth she'd see her there later. Lindy doubted she'd want the house either, as she'd never been keen on the town. Still, Lindy felt weird about moving back into the house she'd grown up in as a child.

But raising a child where she'd been raised? The idea did have an appeal. She could even make her old room the new nursery. Of course, it was more house than she needed, but she could always adopt later and add to the family if she decided that's what she wanted. Right now, she just wanted to concentrate on this baby. She'd made it past the twelve-week mark and into the second trimester. The morning sickness had finally eased up enough where it wasn't daily. She was even starting to show. She didn't really want to move, but at the same time, moving wouldn't be any easier when she had an infant at home.

Lindy opened the door to go out into the garden and nearly ran into Dean who had clearly been pacing right outside the door. "Come in or stay out, but stop being weird," Lindy told him snarkily, heading over to the hammock on her mother's porch. Her porch, she wondered? Dean followed behind her. "Any reason you're wearing a path in the garden today?" she asked him, settling into her favorite spot. The porch was screened in so she could rest bug-free all year long. She sighed as the hammock gently swayed under her.

"I had two ideas, but I don't know that you'll like either of them," Dean began.

"Well, then you're probably right so no need to tell me," she said with a smile, her eyes closed as she swayed.

"Lindy, I'm being serious."

"So am I," she said wryly, thinking of the peace and quiet she'd planned to enjoy daydreaming about her baby gone up in a puff of smoke at Dean's sudden arrival.

"Just hear me out," Dean began again, clearly frustrated. "I was thinking that we'd get you moved in here before the baby was born, and I could rent the cottage from you. It would pay you some rent, and I'd be right here for anything you or the baby needed." She opened one eye to look at him and then shut it.

"I don't think that would really work," Lindy told him. She certainly didn't want the revolving door of girlfriends when they were done to be in and out of her old place while she got a rent check from her ex.

"Then I was thinking that you could marry me, and we could live together here," Dean suggested calmly.

"You what?" Lindy asked, carefully. She didn't want to react too strongly and flip the hammock. "I must have heard you wrong because it sounded like you said something insane."

"I'm in love with you, Lindy. I've always been in love with you, and I always will be. We could get married and raise this baby together," Dean said persuasively.

"Look, there's something you don't know," Lindy began, uneasily, gingerly sitting up.

"Are you already married?" Dean deadpanned.

"No," she said witheringly.

"Then, I don't care," he countered.

"Look, you're very sweet, but I'm not looking to get married," Lindy told him as kindly as she could manage.

"I know. I wasn't either. But I want to marry *you*," Dean insisted.

"I think you just like the idea of us," Lindy told him frankly. "This whole you and me thing probably isn't going to work long-term, and we both know how that scenario eventually ends."

"Do you still think so little of me?" Dean asked in frustration.

"I don't think little of you at all. But you are who you are, and I am who I am."

"And I don't see why who you are and who I am can't just get married and be together," Dean said stubbornly.

"You're talking crazy," Lindy said dismissively, laying back down.

"I am in love with you," Dean said honestly, looking down at his feet. "You probably don't believe that, but there it is."

"I love you, too, Dean, but I'll get over it," she said with a shrug. "Don't get mad," she warned him. "I'm just trying to be practical. This probably won't work out, and we should be mature about it."

"You be mature about it then," Dean said coldly. "I'm going to go now."

"Are you still going to the appointment next week?" she asked him as he walked off.

"The gender thing?" he asked. "I wouldn't miss it." He started to walk away but then called over his shoulder. "I love you, Lindy."

"Uh-huh," she replied as he walked away.

She heard the screen door slide open. "Now I didn't mean to eavesdrop ..." Keely began. "But who says *uh-huh* when a man says he loves you?" she asked, sitting in the chair Dean had vacated.

"I do. Especially when the man who says it has a string of girlfriends in the past and probably a whole string more lined up for his future," Lindy said coolly.

"Are you slut-shaming Dean Walton?" Keely asked her with interest.

"Where did you even hear that term?" Lindy asked in amusement.

"Oh, I pay attention," Keely said dismissively. "Are you though?"

"Not exactly. I don't judge him for that. I just don't think he's the kind to settle down, and I'm just trying to be ready for that," she said honestly.

"Honey, most of us aren't the kind to settle down until we meet the right person. You're it for Dean. Has he done one single thing since you've been dating that's made you think he views your relationship as a casual thing or a way to pass the time?"

"Well, no."

"Has he flirted with other women or made you feel like he wanted to?"

"No," Lindy admitted grudgingly. He'd been great. They'd actually been far better together than she and Tyler had ever been.

"Then why won't you marry him?" Keely asked. "And, yes, I heard that part, too."

"It's not just about me anymore," Lindy said, a hand resting on her abdomen.

"I know. And I know that your father left you, honey, but not all men will. Zeke and I weren't right for each other. For a time, I wanted us to be. I let that blind me to who he was. I know you're cautious, and you've got a good head on your shoulders. Just don't be blind to what's in front of you because you're afraid that you might get hurt. That's the risk we take when we love," Keely told her kindly.

"Theodore's not going to hurt you," Lindy assured her.

"Lindy, he already has. Walking down the stairs and finding him lying on the floor is one of the most hurtful, terrifying things that has ever happened to me. And we're not getting any younger. He could have another heart attack and die. Or I could. Nothing is guaranteed except that one of us eventually will go first. But I don't think he'd hurt me on purpose. The question is if you think Dean would do that to you. You don't have to answer, but you should think about it," Keely suggested. "Now come on in. I made soup, and you've got to be getting chilly out here."

"I don't think I'll ever be chilly again," Lindy grumbled, referring to the pregnancy hormones that had already made her sweaty in the cool January air. "I love you, Mom."

"Uh-huh," Keely said with a grin and reached to help Lindy out of the hammock.

Chapter 37

Noah came out of the kitchen and hung up the apron he'd been wearing. His shift was over, and he needed to go home and change before picking Layla up for dinner. She hadn't been happy lately, and he hoped a dinner out would cheer her up. He wasn't sure exactly what was wrong, but he knew her dad had gotten married over the holidays without telling her first. She'd been hurt and angry about that. She did seem to be getting along better with her sister, but even that didn't explain her continued difficult mood.

She hadn't been argumentative with him when they first started dating. Sure, she'd been a little sarcastic, but only in a humorous way. Could she be impulsive and overreact? Well, yeah, but everyone had flaws. Still, she'd been consistently sad or angry nearly every day in the last month. He had to admit that his patience was wearing thin.

He headed to the door and noticed Naomi and Elle talking quietly near the door. He stalled, hoping to avoid any awkwardness. The last time Naomi had been in here she'd made a big scene and quit. He didn't relish any more of that drama. The talk seemed amicable enough, but he still waited until it was over and she was leaving before he made his exit. Of course, he might as well have gone ahead and left because the first thing he did when he stepped outside was to nearly run over her.

"Sorry," he said, automatically holding up his hands.

"No, it was my fault. I was daydreaming a bit," she replied with a shrug.

"I didn't expect to see you here," Noah admitted.

"Oh, I made up with Elle about a month ago. She actually helped me get the job I have now. I'm sorry I made a scene on your first day and left y'all shorthanded," she said sweetly. "I'm really embarrassed that I acted that way. You know, made a big scene."

"It happens," Noah said with a grin. Naomi noticed just how attractive he was. She normally wasn't attracted to red-haired men, though she couldn't think why. She returned his smile. "No harm, no foul," he said casually.

"I like my new job so it worked out. I just try to stop in and say hello from time to time. I'm a little old to be burning my bridges," she said with a shrug.

"You can't possibly be old at all," Noah said gallantly.

"Well, I'm old enough," she said with a laugh that was friendly with just a hint of flirtation. She couldn't help it. He was cute and being really nice, and she liked to flirt after all.

"I've got to get home and change for dinner tonight with my girlfriend, but it was really good seeing you," Noah said.

Naomi gave him a wry smile. What a sweet guy, she thought. He'd noticed she was flirting with him and made it clear he had a girlfriend. Well, she might have been a lot of things in her life, but a cheater wasn't one of them. She'd never even tried to poach. She gave him a friendly smile. "You both enjoy that," she said sweetly.

She walked away, and Noah noticed the hypnotic sway of her hips. Of course, he'd have to be dead not to notice it, but he was glad that she'd started dressing less flashy. He hated to see women do that. It got them involved with characters like that Dean guy who had broken her heart and then gotten that other girl knocked up.

Not that Dean wasn't a good guy. I mean, he'd been perfectly friendly to Noah when they met, but he knew the type. And that type tended to target a girl like that who looked innocent but dressed in a certain way. It wasn't right, but there was little he could do to stop it. Still, he'd never been attracted to the showy girls.

In the beginning, Layla had been a bit flashier than she was now. She'd never tried to be the center of attention, but she did wear a lot of makeup. She dressed up, but she was petite enough that short skirts were never a real concern. He'd been attracted to her hair first. He'd noticed the full, pretty curls and her candy-pink lips. He'd liked that she was more of a loner than a party girl, and he thought he could see right through that whole misunderstood persona she'd adopted. People really did misunderstand her. Not him though. He saw who she was and liked it. He just wished she'd feel better and not be such a drag all the time.

He winced as he thought that. It didn't sound very charitable, but he was tired of trying to get her to cheer up all the time. Still, maybe a nice dinner out at a new restaurant would help her feel better. He'd even stop and get her some flowers on the way.

*****

Dean showed up early for the appointment. Maybe Lindy still didn't see him as her forever person, but he was going to prove to her that he would be there for both her and the baby. He would keep showing up as long as it took to convince her that he didn't want to be with anyone else.

"Are you talking to yourself?" Lindy asked him as she came outside.

"No," Dean said, wondering if he had been. "No," he said more firmly. "You ready?"

"Yes and no. I want to know what I'm having, but then it makes it so real. But then I can pick names and buy more clothes. So, yeah, I'm ready. Let's do this," Lindy said more confidently.

"What names do you like?"

"I was thinking Maya for a girl or Davis for a boy."

"Um. Maya Angelou?" he guessed. She nodded. "And what's the Davis for?"

"Angela Davis," she explained with a grin. "How'd you know?"

"You don't do anything without a reason," Dean said. "I love that about you. Anyway, I like the names."

"I haven't decided on middle names yet. I'm still thinking," Lindy admitted.

They sat in the waiting room flipping through magazines, and Lindy took Dean's hand nervously when they were called back. A few short minutes later, they were walking out of the office in a daze. Lindy was still holding Dean's hand, but he wasn't going to point that out to her in case she'd forgotten she was doing it.

"Can you believe it?"

"So, it's Maya then," he said with a big smile. "You're having a little girl."

"We're having a little girl," she corrected slowly.

"Wait—are you saying you will marry me?"

"No, I didn't say that," Lindy said sharply.

"So, what did you mean?" Dean asked. "Are you going to let me help raise her?"

"I mean … she's just … she's yours, too," Lindy told him awkwardly.

"I hope she'll think of me as her dad. I'd love that. I mean, I know we'd have to tell her the truth when she's older—"

"That is the truth," Lindy interrupted.

"I'm sorry—what?" Dean asked blankly.

"I hadn't had any treatments when I went in. I found out I was already pregnant. It's yours. I mean, ours. Maya's ours," Lindy said carefully, waiting for a reaction.

"Were you going to tell me?" Dean asked her, still in shock.

"I've been trying to find a way. You just assumed, and I kept trying to tell you, but … Yes, I was always going to tell you."

"We're having a baby?" Dean asked. "She's actually mine?"

"Ours," Lindy corrected firmly. "She's ours."

"And you still won't marry me?"

"Nope," Lindy said, watching him carefully for his reaction. Whatever she'd expected, this wasn't it.

"You're so mean," Dean told her with a roll of his eyes. "I still love you though," he said as they walked to the car. He squeezed her hand. "Our baby," he said in wonder.

"Maya," Lindy said with a smile.

"Maya Walton has a nice ring to it," Dean suggested.

"Um, no, it doesn't," Lindy said with a laugh as she climbed into the car.

"Maya Carver-Walton?" he suggested.

"We'll see," she told him with a small smile.

Chapter 38

"It looks so good," Keely said, squeezing Beth's arm.

Beth took a final look around the tea room. They'd closed it for the day for a private party. She scanned the decorations and had to admit that it was pretty perfect.

"Well, we stayed up late enough doing it," she replied with a grin. "I couldn't have done it without all of you."

Keely and Libby had helped, and Libby's sister had stopped in to lend a hand. Seth's ex and Lindy's close friend Marnie also dropped by to help, since she was in town for the shower. Beth figured it would be weird for Libby and Marnie to work together, but instead they were over there comparing engagement rings and talking about their respective weddings. Beth smiled at them and was pleased when she didn't feel a drop of envy.

"That's nice to see," Keely commented, following Beth's gaze.

"I wasn't sure if that would be awkward or not," Beth admitted. "You should go over there and show off your ring, too."

"I just might," Keely said with a grin.

Beth watched the three of them coo over rings and couldn't help a grin of her own. She had the occasional moment of hating the single life, but for the most part, she was content. Of course, that Christmas kiss had shaken her up, but she just attributed that to the shock. She was sure that Jamie meant to kiss her cheek, and she'd just moved the wrong way. Embarrassing but an easy mistake.

They hadn't mentioned it since, but they'd both been busy with work. It wasn't a big deal. She didn't even want a relationship, and she certainly didn't want one with a good friend. This wasn't *When Harry Met Sally* after all. This was real life where sleeping with your friends only ruined the friendship. God, not that she was considering sleeping with Jamie, she thought to herself quickly. Because no. Obviously, no.

"I would love to know what you're thinking about," Libby said. Beth blushed to her roots. "You look like you're rehearsing an argument."

Beth smiled. "Only with myself."

"I do that, too," Libby said conspiratorially. "Are we all set?"

Beth looked around and checked the room again. Everything was perfect. There was nothing left she could do.

"I think we're good. I'll go get Lindy, and you can organize the troops." She'd talk Lindy into coming over, and they planned to surprise her. It would be great. She hadn't wanted to do a gender reveal because of misogyny—hey, Beth agreed completely so she hadn't insisted—but she'd be excited about this very gender-neutral, brightly colored baby shower.

She'd been going for a rainbows and rain showers sort of theme with bright umbrellas, flowers arranged in colorful rain boots, and puffy clouds with colorful raindrops hung from the ceiling. She'd enlisted Lindy's studio staff to help with the artsy stuff, and she'd taken care of the theme ideas. Keely and Libby had collaborated over food and games, and Marnie had made sure to invite all the necessary friends. Dean and Seth had groused about being included in a co-ed shower until they mentioned cake, Beth thought with a roll of her eyes, as she hurried across the street to the studio.

It was quiet when she walked in, and Lindy was just propping a canvas on the stand. "Hey, can you come by and look at something for me? I'm doing this display in the bookstore, and it just looks off. Come give me your professional opinion."

Lindy looked at her skeptically. "You've never wanted my opinion before."

"This is a super important one," Beth insisted.

Lindy was done in the studio, but she had a sneaking suspicion that Beth was up to something. Getting anything coherent out of an excited Beth would be impossible so she decided to go along to get along, but that didn't mean she couldn't have a little fun with it. "Why don't I stop by later and take a look?"

"Later will be too late," Beth squeaked. She hadn't thought it would be this hard. She had to think fast. "Plus, your mom was baking cookies, and you'll want to snag one while they're hot."

Lindy grinned. She'd known there was something going on. "You really buried the lead on that one," she said, getting up and grabbing a jacket. "Always lead with cookies," she reminded her.

Beth smiled. Well, that wasn't so bad. "Look at the display, too, but yes, there are cookies."

"You never could manage to keep a secret. Which did she make? And did you let Seth know?" Her mom's Christmas cookies were damn near legendary, and she usually only made a batch or two.

"He's already there," Beth told her.

"Are you serious? I can't believe you'd call him before me. That's not even fair," Lindy said, irritated now. "And I am pregnant if you'll recall. You'd think I'd get first dibs," she muttered, looking down at her boots as she walked.

"We better hurry then," Beth told her, picking up the pace.

Lindy stopped when she walked in, more shocked by the profusion of rainbows than anything else at first. Rainbows, floral displays in rain boots, and umbrellas everywhere. Then she realized how many of her friends had come out, on a weekday no less, to celebrate her baby. Even Dean was there, standing in the back with Seth, grinning like a fool. He'd told everyone who had ears that he was going to be a dad, which amused everyone because they'd assumed that when Lindy had made her own announcement.

"You kept a secret," she said to Beth as everyone shouted Surprise! at her.

"First time for everything," Beth said smugly. "But your mom did make cookies, so I wasn't entirely lying."

"And I waited for you," Seth said with a grin.

She'd made it to spring and to thirty weeks so quickly. She couldn't even think where the time had gone! As she went around to greet everyone, she marveled at how quickly everything was coming together. Seth and Libby had gone on their cruise already. Her mother and Theodore had taken a belated honeymoon. She was only ten weeks away from her due date, and they'd just finished moving in the last of her stuff to the main house. Her house, now. She was still considering moving Dean in, too, but maybe only on a trial basis. Or maybe just during her maternity leave so she wouldn't be alone during those first few weeks.

"You're going to need this," Beth told her, handing her a crown and pointing her to the glider rocker decked out like a thrown. Lindy shook her head ruefully and looked for Dean in the crowd of friends and family.

"Where are you sitting?" she asked him.

"Right by you. No throne though," he said with a cheeky grin. "And no crown."

"My feet hurt, so I'm not even going to complain about that," she said as she lowered herself into the chair.

"I'll rub them later," he said with a smile. "And I'm going to go snag you a plate."

A couple of hours later, she looked around at the profusion of gifts. They'd told her she wasn't allowed to help with cleanup, so she took a moment to just soak it all in. She and Dean opened up the absolute cutest little outfits, and they seemed to have gotten every item they'd registered for and then some.

Her last gift was from Dean himself, and it was for a spa day that included a prenatal massage. It had been her favorite gift by far, and Dean had actually scheduled for all of the party guests to have a chair massage while they were there. She'd thought that was a little over-the-top, but they'd all left the party happy. Of course, the rest of the guests were probably a little tipsy on the champagne Beth had brought, but Lindy had just sipped her tea and dreamed baby dreams.

Chapter 39

Presley left the baby shower still grinning. Of course, it was probably a smile brought on by lots of champagne. She was so happy that she'd been invited. She really liked Lindy, and her friends were fun. They'd had a great time playing silly games, and she'd even won a door prize. It was a single-serve teapot and cup combo with a bestseller she'd been dying to read and a certificate for one of the paint studio classes. She thought she'd ask Layla if she wanted to go with her.

She and Layla had been getting along better since Christmas, but then she'd sort of been distant over the last couple of months. She tried not to read anything into it. After all, Layla had moved in with Noah, and they were probably still in that honeymoon period. Still. She wanted to be closer to her sister, but she didn't want to rush things either. She thought she'd ask her to the paint night and just play it by ear.

She saw Noah coming out of Brews just as they'd agreed. She'd gotten a ride with one of Lindy's friends to the shower, and Noah had agreed to bring her back home afterward. Carpooling just made sense, and it was so easily arranged that she hadn't thought twice about it. Now as they drove to Athens, she tried to think of something to say. The silence was getting awkward, and she'd thanked him twice already for the ride.

"Has Layla been okay lately?"

"Yeah, why?" Noah asked sharply.

"No reason. I just haven't heard from her much," Presley explained.

"Oh, she works a lot, and then she studies for hours when she's not at work," Noah explained with a genial smile. "I was afraid the two of you had some sort of falling out again."

"Not at all. Anyway, don't say anything to her. I don't want her to think I was being nosy. I just wanted to make sure she was okay," Presley told him.

"Secret's safe," he said with a smile. "That's a pretty dress," he told her. "I think we're all glad for a little warmer weather after all this cold."

"Thanks," she said. "I think Layla gave me this dress, actually. I'm certainly glad for the warmer weather. I'm hoping to spend more time outdoors now that it's staying warm."

"Layla doesn't get outside much, but she uses the gym at our apartment complex all the time."

"I don't really like the gym. Too many mirrors and people watching themselves and everyone else work out. I prefer to run outside, but that's tricky with the weather."

Presley thought he'd glanced at her legs a moment, but his eyes were now fixed firmly on the road so she must have imagined it. She shifted in her seat a bit in discomfort. She'd probably imagined that vibe between them when they first met. She was embarrassed to recall it now. She was so happy that Layla had found someone nice and settled down.

The car in front of them put on a turn signal and slowed down, but Noah didn't seem to see. Presley absolutely hated to backseat drive so she tried not to say anything. She gasped as they drew closer, and Noah slammed to a stop throwing an arm across her chest as he did. They missed the car in front of them by inches and both let out a shaky breath.

"Mind if I pull over a second?" Noah asked her, removing his hand from where it had crossed her chest. "Sorry about that. I was afraid we were going to crash," he explained. He let his hand fall, and it rested there on her knee as he pulled off the road and into a driveway of a house that was for sale. He sat quietly for a moment just breathing.

Presley was just getting her breath back, too. He'd been going so fast, and the stop had been so sudden. But she'd also been surprised by his hand across her chest, that quick flash. Her mom used to do that when they were kids, and it had always hurt. Presley thought she was going to have a bruise across both breasts, but she was grateful for his quick thinking. Still, as she finally calmed down, she realized his hand was still on her leg. Well, sort of on her thigh if she were going to be exact. When she'd scooted back, her skirt had come up, too. An inch or two more, and this whole thing would be a lot more embarrassing. She looked down at his hand.

"Oh, sorry. Sorry. I'm so embarrassed. I just can't believe I almost hit that car. I should have been paying better attention. Are you okay?"

"I'm fine. That was a close one," she said with a relieved smile, inching her skirt back down.

"I'll be more careful from now on," he told her with a smile. "Trust me?" he asked playfully.

"Of course," she said with a smile. He looked so embarrassed about the whole situation. At least they hadn't wrecked. That would have made a long day so much worse. "How are you liking Brews?" she asked him, changing the subject away from their near-collision.

"It's great. I ran into that Naomi girl that used to work there. The one who quit on my first day?"

"I heard she was working over at the bookstore."

"Yeah, that's what she said. I guess she made up with Dean, too," he said with a shrug. "Is he still ... I mean, isn't he with Lindy?"

"Dean and Lindy are together. I don't think he ever sees Naomi, but I don't really know either of them well enough to say. Maybe you misunderstood," Presley said, worrying for Lindy. Lindy and Dean had seemed so happy together. She didn't want to think he'd cheat, but then again she'd never expected Derek to cheat either, she thought wryly.

"I don't know much about her, but I get the impression she has a little bit of a reputation so maybe I assumed and read the whole thing wrong," Noah offered. "I'm still getting to know everyone. Maybe it's someone he works with."

"Are you sure it's a firefighter?"

"I think so. But I don't know for sure. It was just something she said, and she'd just come from that way. Forget it," he said uncomfortably. "I'm sure that I got it wrong."

*****

Naomi ran a bath and gingerly waded into the water. She'd brought a book with her that Beth had recommended, but she hadn't opened it yet. The fire station had been a mistake. It had started innocently enough. She'd just wanted a tour. Dean had never given her a tour when they were dating. Besides, didn't every girl have a little bit of a firefighter fantasy?

She hadn't meant to flirt. Well, she'd meant to flirt a little, but in a playful way. She hadn't meant to be so suggestive. And then she'd thought there'd be no harm to it. It was kind of sexy to fool around back there. Sneaking into the firetruck had seemed like a lark, and no one was around anyway. Plus, things had been pretty hot, and she'd forgotten all about the fact that he had a girlfriend. Honestly, she had.

His mouth had been on hers, and when his hand had moved up her skirt she hadn't mind at first. He'd been a little rougher with her than she'd expected, and she'd been shocked and then seriously turned on. She liked the take-charge attitude, although she hadn't really expected things to go in that direction when she'd stopped by. She was just being friendly. She'd gone a little further than she'd intended and then further still. It was only when she realized that they were sort of in a public place that she'd put a stop to it going any further.

Of course, when she'd stopped him, he'd finally realized what he was doing. He was horrified and ashamed, and he actually looked like he was going to cry. He apologized so many times that she assured him it wasn't a big deal and that she'd never mention it. It was a mistake. She wasn't anyone's side-piece. It just couldn't happen again. In fact, they would just pretend he hadn't happened at all.

She sank deeper into the bath. Of course, his girlfriend could never know. She couldn't even say her name aloud in her own head she felt so guilty. It was awful, and they should never do it again. She'd be so embarrassed the next time she saw her so she'd just have to forget about it so she didn't give anything away. I mean, he'd made a mistake. They both had, Naomi thought. But it didn't have to ruin the relationship.

Despite what anyone thought, she really didn't want to break them up. She wasn't that kind of person. At least, she didn't want to be anymore. Beth had given her a fresh start, and she wanted to make the most of it. It's why she'd tried the friendly approach when she'd seen him outside the firehouse. She sank down in the bath and noticed the marks on her skin where he'd actually bitten her. She'd been surprised but not unpleasantly so. She'd have to keep them covered. That would be difficult to explain and make it hard to pretend that nothing had happened.

Still, before he'd gotten all freaked out over what they had done, he'd been sexier than he'd ever been before. He'd gone beyond charming to something else. She couldn't quite put her finger on it, but she was disappointed she couldn't find that with someone who was available. She sighed. It was hard to regret something that had felt so good, but wrong was wrong.

*****

Dean went home and took a long shower. He'd go over to Lindy's in just a little while. The baby shower had been fun. He hadn't expected to enjoy it quite as much as he did. They'd had a great time, and Lindy had wanted to stay longer and spend some time with his friends. Dean had agreed to meet her at the house later, not the guest cottage these days, and so he'd headed over to work to grab some paperwork he'd forgotten. He'd left some notes on things he wanted to fix at the lake house on his desk. He put his hand over his eyes and let the hot water run down his body. He really shouldn't have gone to the station. None of this would have happened if he'd just gone home or even waited at Lindy's for her to get home.

He wasn't sure what to do now. It definitely put him in an uncomfortable position. Should he tell Lindy or just forget it had happened? I mean, if he forgot the whole thing and just pretended like it didn't happen, no one would get hurt. Besides, Lindy was pregnant and didn't need the stress of the whole situation. On the other hand, if she found out from someone else, it could get ugly. This was one of those situations where you lost no matter what. On the other hand, Dean thought, what were the chances she'd actually find out? Sure, it was a small town, but if it was a one-time thing, no one would ever have to know.

He turned off the water in the shower and dried himself off. It would probably be best just to forget it for now. They'd had such a good day, and Lindy was in a great mood. They'd spend the evening putting the baby stuff in Maya's room and planning for the delivery. Libby had already baked about a thousand entrees that they could thaw out during maternity leave. She'd brought them over earlier in the week, and Keely and Beth had promised to contribute more. He and Lindy had agreed to make a list so that they could easily meal plan for those first few weeks.

Anyway, what happened, happened. It couldn't be undone. But it probably wouldn't happen again either so there was no need to say something and cause a big scene over a one-off. Still, it had been embarrassing. He'd left the station in a hurry, and Naomi had left shortly afterward, her clothes still in sort of disarray. They hadn't been very discreet, but she seemed too flustered to notice. He just needed to forget all about it. There was no positive outcome of telling, and if Lindy found out later, he'd deal with it then. These things happened, right?

Chapter 40

Beth walked over to find Naomi reading on the clock. She was pretty absorbed in it so Beth leaned down to sneak a look at the cover and nearly scared Naomi's pants off.

"Sorry! Sorry!" Naomi began, jumping up from the sofa and putting the book down hastily.

"This is a bookstore," Beth pointed out. "You don't actually get in trouble for reading on the clock. I told you I wanted you to familiarize yourself with as many titles as you could. I just wanted to know which one you were reading."

Naomi held it up. "*The Woman in Cabin 10*—Ruth Ware."

"That is a page-turner," Beth agreed. "No wonder you jumped," she added with a grin. "Do you like it?"

"I really do. I thought I would suggest it for the book club if you haven't done it already. Or if you have, maybe one of her other books?"

"Sure, that sounds good. I like to see you take an interest. Actually, I wanted to talk to you about something else."

"What's that?" Naomi asked nervously. Lately, she'd been really skittish around the shop, practically darting into the back office every time Keely came around. Maybe she wasn't over the whole Dean and Lindy thing yet because she sure was acting weird.

"I was thinking that if you're interested you could help me when you have some extra time. It would be extra hours and pay, and we might even be able to make it into a regular thing," Beth explained.

"Help you with what?" Naomi asked, puzzled.

"Oh, didn't I say?" Beth laughed. "Sorry. I was distracted. I'm planning more author events, and I thought you could stay and help me set up. You've got an eye for design, and I thought you could help me set organize everything and put out the refreshments. It would be at least once a month, and I think we could see to raising your salary a bit, too, in addition to the hours since you've been coming to work on time regularly now. I think you're a great fit here, but if you don't want the extra responsibility, that's okay."

"No, I mean, I do want it. Thank you," Naomi said gratefully. "I'll work really hard."

"I know you will. I'm not worried about that. Hey, is everything okay?"

"Everything's fine," Naomi said firmly. "You know, same as usual."

"Okay, well, I just wanted to make sure. We're really glad you're here," Beth added. Keely walked into the room, and Naomi mumbled something about the bathroom and walked off. "Was that weird or is it just me?" Beth asked her aunt.

"The fact that she's been avoiding me? I wondered about that, too. It's hard to do when she's serving, but she somehow manages it. Do you think I should have a talk with her?" Keely asked with concern.

"No, I think I'll give it a little more time. I don't want her to feel like we're ganging up on her, but it seems like something's wrong. I don't know. Maybe she's just uncomfortable because you're Lindy's mom, and she's with Dean," Beth said with a shrug.

"Maybe. Maybe it's just the age. Layla's been acting strange lately, too. Theodore says she goes through these moods and always has, but I worry about her. I think sometimes she might be depressed. It would explain the moods and a lot of her history actually," Keely said thoughtfully. "But it's not something I can really talk to her about. And I don't want to get involved in their family business when they haven't asked for my help."

"Well, you're family now. If you think there's a problem, maybe there is. Have you asked Presley about it?"

"They aren't very close so it's hard to know the right thing to do. I don't want to just idly gossip. Anyway, let me know if I can help with Naomi. She's a good worker. I'm glad Elle recommended her," Keely said as she left the room.

*****

Layla finished her test in a hurry. She really shouldn't have stayed up so late. She should have skipped dinner and a movie and studied for the exam instead. She'd hated to disappoint Noah though. He'd made reservations and bought the movie tickets already, and he really was trying to cheer her up. She hadn't dated many men who even cared if she felt tired or depressed or anxious. They only liked her when her mood stayed up.

Noah wasn't like that. He was even more solicitous when she was struggling. He'd bring her breakfast in bed and go out and get her favorite magazines. Once, they'd taken a weekend and watched every episode of *Downton Abbey* just because she'd had a tough week. They'd stayed in bed and alternated between making love, watching the show, and eating pizza. They'd turned their phones off and just spent time enjoying each other's company.

Still, she really should have stayed up late studying for the exam, but she'd been tired when they got home. They'd had sex, which kept her up even later, even though she really didn't feel like it. It's just that he did, and he'd gone to all that trouble just to show her a good time and cheer her up. She hadn't wanted to use the "I'm tired" excuse, and she didn't want to bring up the exam and ruin his mood either. In the past, she would have been spoiling for a fight about now. She was famous for self-sabotage. Every time she dated someone nice, she'd get depressed and then end up lashing out at the person who was trying to make it better. She was determined not to do it this time.

She'd have time to do a little studying tonight. Noah was going to do a little extra work in the kitchen, practicing some new recipes after Brews closed, and she had the night off from work. She'd take the time to get ahead for the next exam so that she wouldn't have to worry about studying in the few evenings she and Noah both had the night off. Her phone rang, and she glanced at the screen. It was Presley. Again.

"Before you even ask, I'm fine," she began as soon as she answered. Presley had been calling a lot lately.

"I never thought otherwise. I guess Dad's probably been checking up on you, too?" she asked.

"Yeah. Wait. You said *too*. Has he been checking up on you?"

"You know he likes to worry about us. But that's not why I called. I've got tickets to do a paint night thing in a couple of days. Do you want to go with me?"

"I don't know if that's my thing," Layla told her, chewing on her lip as she thought about her schedule.

"They'll have adult beverages," Presley pointed out. "It'll be fun."

"Yeah, sure. Let's do it," she agreed.

When she got off the phone, she wondered if she should have checked with Noah first to make sure he didn't have any extravagant plans. He liked to make reservations to new, fancy places to eat. Of course, he was often critical of the food, but that was natural with his career and all. Sometimes he got tickets for concerts or plays and liked to surprise her with them. She wasn't used to everything being a surprise so she stopped making so many plans. She'd really disappointed him once when she'd made plans with friends for a day that he'd had an elaborate surprise laid out. She'd canceled her arrangements, but he'd still been a tad touchy about it. Still, she wasn't used to such romance, and she intended to enjoy it. She'd just make sure the painting class wouldn't interfere with anything he might have planned.

*****

"Girlfriend problems?" Candace asked as Noah looked down at his phone and made a face.

"No, we're good. She just texted me to see if she can go to a thing with her sister. I don't care if she goes. I'm just glad she's spending time with her family," Noah explained. They were taking a quick break out back on the stoop in the alley behind the coffeehouse. It had gotten stuffy inside. Summer was coming, and already the humidity was brutal. Still, there was a little bit of a breeze out here.

"I don't see my sister much these days. But my family's not close. Not even a little," Candace admitted.

"Mine either," Noah confessed. He stood up to go back in and noticed Dean at the fire station across the street. He narrowed his eyes. "I really don't like that guy."

"What, Dean?" Candace asked surprised. "Why not?"

"I don't know. There's just something about him," Noah admitted.

He already regretted saying anything. He'd liked Dean when he first met him. Sure, he seemed to be one of those great looking, athletic, charmers that the ladies liked, but he'd also seemed genuine. Now he just struck Noah as sort of smarmy. He wasn't sure why, but he always looked guilty as hell when Noah saw him. What was that quote? What's past is prologue, he thought.

"He hasn't been stopping in to get coffee in the morning lately. It's kind of weird," Candace told him. "But he's a good guy. He's probably just working too much."

"Yeah, maybe that's all it is."

He texted Layla back to have fun with her sister. He'd just pick up an extra shift that night or go see a movie. It was no big deal. He'd even go out and get a couple of bottles of wine to send with her, and he'd offer to drop her off and pick her up so she wouldn't have to worry about the drive home. If he had to work, he'd pay for an Uber for her, but it shouldn't come to that. He'd likely get off work before she would get out of her paint night.

"I can't believe you don't like him," Candace said. "He's one of the friendliest guys I know. Did he hit on your girlfriend or something?" she asked, curious.

Noah was coming to regret what he'd said even more. He should leave well enough alone. "No, I probably just misunderstood something. I mean, you're right. He's probably just really busy. I'm sure he's a nice guy," Noah said, not believing it but not wanting to seem like a jerk either. He knew he should go in, but he took another couple of minutes outside.

He scrolled through his phone and saw a message from Naomi. She'd been sweet that day she'd apologized for making a scene, but that didn't mean he wanted to be friends with her. He'd even been clear and told her that he had a girlfriend. He shook his head. She was clearly used to a certain level of attention, but he wasn't going to respond to it. He just deleted the message and blocked her number. The last thing he wanted was drama.

*****

Naomi put her phone down and wondered what was wrong with her. It wasn't like her to text guys with girlfriends, and this was the third time she'd done it this week. She was just feeling insecure and lonely. She'd just been off since the whole slip-up. She'd been avoiding Keely at work and had been jumpy around everyone else. She reminded herself that he had far more to lose than she did if he told anyone so, clearly, he wouldn't tell. And she sure as hell wasn't going to tell or even let it happen again.

She needed to make that clear the next time she saw him. She'd gone by a couple of times today, but then she hadn't worked up the courage to go in and say anything. Instead, she'd changed direction and found herself buying something in a gift shop she cared nothing about. But at least it had looked like a normal thing to do.

She decided that maybe what she needed was to dress up and take herself out tonight. She deserved a night out. She hadn't been spending much since her raise, and she wanted to celebrate. She'd check and see if any of her friends were game, but if not, she thought she'd go out and enjoy herself on her own. Like a date, sort of. She chose a dress that showed off her generous curves and decided to go without a bra. It would be warm enough outside that she shouldn't need a jacket.

She applied her makeup with an expert hand, going dramatic on the lips and eyes. She played up her features and made sure her freckles showed through. The dress might have been a little on the short side with a clever little slit up the side, but it showed off her legs to great advantage. The dress also showed enough cleavage without risking a nipple slip. That was a very real thing and had happened to a friend of hers. She made sure the straps were secure. She found a flirty pair of heeled sandals and carefully painted her toenails.

She decided she'd show up at Brews for some live music, and then everyone would see her out and know that she wasn't some loser who stayed home every night by herself. She'd have a drink, listen to the band, and then maybe go out somewhere else if she felt like it. Now that she and Elle were on good terms, she could drop in at any time. She'd even had a word with Candace and apologized for how she acted. She was pretty sure she apologized to everyone, which was awkward and embarrassing. The good news was that everyone had been really nice about it, and now she didn't have to be afraid of going out in her own town.

Chapter 41

"What have you got there?" Presley asked, reaching to take the two bottles of wine out of Layla's hands.

"Noah sent them," Layla explained, feeling nervous. She should probably be home, and she didn't know how to just hang out with her sister anymore. She looked at the table and noticed the snacks. "That looks good."

"We need to pick which painting we're going to do," Presley told her, looking critically at the choices around them. "Wine glass, spring tree with a swing, or the love birds?" she asked.

"I like the love birds," Layla told her decisively.

"For you and Noah?" Presley asked. Layla shrugged. "Okay, I'll do the same one but in different colors and give it to Dad and Keely."

"Is it hard, being on your own now?" Layla asked her abruptly.

"What do you mean? I've been on my own for years," Presley asked absently, mixing her colors together carefully the way Lindy had shown them to do.

"I mean, without Derek. You know."

"Oh," Presley stopped and looked up. "That's been over for a while."

"You didn't say what happened," Layla said curiously.

"There was someone else. A nurse I worked with. I introduced them, and he started seeing her while we were still together. Apparently, I was the last to know," Presley said flatly.

"How humiliating," Presley looked up sharply, but Layla looked genuinely upset. "That must have been terrible for you."

"What's worse is I run into them a lot since I work with his new girlfriend. And I ran into him the day Dad had his heart attack,"

Presley told her.

"What did you do?" Layla asked breathlessly.

"I almost ran him over with my car. He moved though." They both giggled. They hadn't laughed together in years. Presley felt the squeeze in her heart that had tightened when Layla had mentioned Derek loosen. She'd missed her sister.

"How are things with Noah? He seems really nice," Presley said.

She wondered if he'd told Layla about their near accident. It had been such a shock, but they'd been able to laugh when the danger was over. She had sustained a bruise across her chest, but she'd realized it must have scared him pretty bad to react like that. It had scared her, too.

"He does, doesn't he?" Layla said thoughtfully. "He does all these grand romantic gestures. It's hard to get used to," she added. "He surprises me all the time."

There was an odd tone in her voice, and Presley really hoped that she wasn't going to self-sabotage this one. "That's really sweet. Well, sounds like he's a keeper. He's got a great job, too. I tried their new lunch menu the other day, and it's pretty great."

"I didn't know you had lunch there," Layla said curiously, wondering why that would bother her a little.

"Oh, I didn't. I stopped by to drop something off for Lindy, and she ordered us lunch and then made Dean go get it for us. It was good though. Anyway, her nursery is almost done, but I knew she was looking for a very specific lamp. I came across one at a good price so I snagged it for her," Presley explained.

"They seem really sweet together."

"They really do. Well, speak of the devil," Presley said as Lindy approached. "You should sit when you can and get off your feet."

"I know. I look like I swallowed a basketball. But I'm so close to the end. I'm afraid if I sit down I'll notice that my feet are wearing two different shoes," Lindy said with a grin.

"They're not," Layla said helpfully.

"Good thing. I did go out the door the other day with two entirely different shoes on. They slipped on so I didn't notice they weren't the same color. I tried to pass it off as Punky Brewster-inspired style, but I don't think anyone bought it," Lindy joked.

"Who's Punky Brewster?" Layla asked.

"Millennials!" Lindy said in mock disgust. "That's it; we're officially having an '80s cartoon morning one day soon, and you both have to come. Though, technically, *Punky Brewster* is not a cartoon, although there is a sort of cartoon in it. Never mind—you're coming," Lindy said firmly.

"Sounds fun," Layla said.

"Sounds like we have no choice," Presley laughed.

*****

Naomi got into her car with shaking hands. The night had not gone anything like she'd expected. She'd never even made it to Brews. She'd been nearby when she'd seen him. To be fair, she'd tried to pass unnoticed for once. After all, he had a very serious relationship, and they had agreed to forget what had happened. He wasn't the last attractive man on Earth, and she had no intention of trying to flirt with one who was already taken. She straightened her shoulders, screwed up her courage and confidence, and sauntered toward the restaurant.

"Hey, Naomi," he'd called out. "Can we talk?" After ignoring her messages, she was surprised by the offer. She'd walked to the far side of the parking lot to speak with him. "Look, let's go for a drive, so we can talk in private," he suggested.

"You totally ghosted me," she pointed out, feeling more angry than hurt by this point.

"I know. I'm sorry. I was just … I didn't know how to handle what happened between us. I totally freaked out."

"Yeah, me, too," she admitted, softening. "It can't happen again."

"I know. Look, just get in so we can have this conversation somewhere else. I just want to get something off my chest, and then we can pretend like none of this ever happened." He was being sweet and seemed sincere. He'd agreed it was a mistake, so she didn't feel worried when she got in the car. "I haven't told anyone what happened," he said, as she put on her seatbelt. "I wouldn't do that."

"I appreciate that," she said honestly.

"Did you tell anyone?" he asked, as they idled in the parking lot.

"No one. I mean, we agreed it never happened," she reminded him.

"Yeah, we did," he said, as he put the car into drive and pulled out of the parking lot.

As she settled into the seat, she noticed that her dress had slid up a couple of inches from getting in the car. She wanted to pull it down, but she didn't want to seem self-conscious either. "Where are we going?" she asked curiously.

"Just somewhere quiet to talk," he said. "Do you want to listen to the radio?"

"I thought we were going to talk," she said, perplexed.

"I thought we'd talk when we got stopped somewhere so I'm not distracted. But, sure, we can just talk now," he said easily.

"No, the radio is fine," she said, selecting a station. "Is this okay?"

"It's fine," he said. "You look amazing. I know I shouldn't say it, but you know it's true," he said aiming a charming smile in her direction.

"Thank you," she said primly. She wasn't going to flirt and encourage him. She'd already promised herself that this situation wouldn't repeat itself. They would just talk it out and then everything could go back to normal. She could stop being so damn jumpy and just enjoy her life.

"What is that? Satin?" he asked, reaching over and touching the edge of her skirt while he drove.

"Silk, actually," she said, shifting uncomfortably in her seat. His hand was stroking the silk, but the skirt had climbed higher with the movement.

"Soft," he said, quietly. "Smooth."

"I like it," she said evenly, shifting her thigh away. He went from holding her skirt to holding her leg, tightly, his fingers stroking higher. "Look, we said we're not doing this anymore," she pointed out firmly.

"We're just taking a drive. There's no one here to see us. And I'm not going to say anything. We'll go somewhere and talk this out, and then that's it. Okay?" he asked, climbing his hand slowly still higher and sliding back her skirt.

"Don't," she said, her voice sounding weak even to her own ears. "We shouldn't."

"You don't like it?" he asked quizzically, sending a seductive look her way.

"I didn't say that," she said breathlessly. "We just shouldn't—"

"Naomi, we're not doing anything. I'm just driving. See? I'll stop." He took his hand off her leg and grabbed her hand instead. He moved it firmly between his legs and held it there.

"We really can't ... I'm not comfortable ..." Sure, she was tempted, but this was wrong. Was he sexy? Of course, but they just couldn't do this again. She'd already felt ashamed of herself for getting in his car. This wasn't going the way she'd hoped.

"I'll just pull over here, and we can talk," he said smoothly.

Later, when she was driving herself back home, she began crying so hard she had to pull off the road. She pulled into an empty church parking lot and parked as far from the street lights as she could get. She sat in the car and cried. They had talked alright. Or he had. He'd pulled over on a dark road in the country. She wasn't sure where. He'd unsnapped her seatbelt so fast it had surprised her. She'd turned to speak to him, trying to pull her hand away from his jeans where he had held it, and he had his mouth on hers.

She could admit she'd been sort of turned on during the drive, but in that uncomfortable way where she knew what they were doing was wrong. When he kissed her, she had just a moment where she'd enjoyed it before she remembered having to face his girlfriend on a regular basis and practically her whole family. She'd cringed in shame and tried to move away, but he'd already worked the silk sheath she'd been so proud of over her breasts. It pooled around her waist, and her skirt had slid up to join it. He'd left it there, and pulled her panties down to the floor. She'd tried to stop or get out, but he'd bitten her breast hard. She had a feeling that her body was covered in bruises and bites, mean little ones that wouldn't show outside of her clothes. He'd wanted to talk and he had, whispering filthy things into her ear and telling her how much she deserved this and how much he knew she liked it. He'd taken her braless state as an invitation and said anyone would have. He even talked about his girlfriend while he touched her and told her about what they did together.

Naomi was shaking like a leaf. Who could she tell? Who would believe her? With her word against his, she'd look like a liar, and he'd look like his normal, charming self. Besides, this wasn't a thing that happened. This was an urban legend to make girls like her cautious. It wasn't something that could happen to someone you knew, not really. She admitted that she'd liked the kiss and had been really turned on up until the moment he'd started hurting her. It wasn't just the bite. It was the pinches and slaps and the roughness of the entire encounter. And the filth he'd spewed at her. She never would have expected someone like that to act like this. She'd even trusted him!

He hadn't raped her. Thank God it hadn't come to that. But it had been awful and humiliating. He'd driven the rest of the way back singing along to the radio as if nothing had happened. He'd almost pulled away before she was even completely out of the car, leaving her a good mile away from where he knew her car was parked. She'd hurried to the car, and then she'd cried in the church parking lot. She'd made it home and gone straight to the shower to wash this whole night off. While the water ran, she cried and tried to remember why she'd been attracted to him in the first place.

*****

Noah's car pulled up at the curb. Layla was coming out laughing with Lindy and her sister. He stepped out for a minute to chat and then went around and held the door open for Layla. She slid in with a laugh, waving goodbye to her friends.

"Did you have a good time?"

"It was fun. Look, I even painted something for us. We don't have to hang it up or anything, but I thought it was fun," she told him, showing the lovebird painting.

"Of course, we'll hang it up! We'll put it right in the living room. Or, better yet, in the bedroom."

"Did you have to work?"

"I got off a little early so I just hung out and listened to the band a while. Hey, was Dean heading here to pick up Lindy?"

"I think he's working. Why?"

"It's nothing. I just thought I saw someone else get into the car with him earlier and drive off. It must not have been Dean," he said with a shrug.

"Like some other girl?"

"Forget it," Noah said with a smile. "I'm sure it was someone else."

Chapter 42

Braxton-Hicks contractions are no joke, Lindy thought. She was so close to the end now. She was eagerly counting the days, and her friends and family had started a little pool on the date she'd actually give birth. Someone had every day from now until her due date. She was pretty sure Keely had chosen tonight because she'd brought over an eggplant parmesan, citing its ability to induce early labor. Lindy had laughed but taken the food. She was hungry all the time these days. Hungry and aching. Her back ached, her feet ached, and the baby moved constantly.

Dean hadn't left when she'd started showing. He hadn't even left when she got bigger and bigger and bigger. He'd rubbed her feet and run to the store to satisfy her cravings—she hadn't had any weird ones, just specific ones like salt and vinegar chips or cracker jacks—and he'd continued to read through all the pregnancy books with her. Of course, he had started acting jumpy lately, but he was probably nervous about having an actual baby in the house. They'd decided he would go ahead and move in and stay during those first few weeks. Lindy thought of it as a trial run. If it went well, maybe he could just stay.

She'd started to think about what a future might be like with him in it. Him and Maya. The idea of an actual family, a regular one with two parents, still felt vaguely foreign. She knew what it was like to grow up in a single-parent household. She had had a happy childhood, but she could see the advantages of two parents. They'd just need to decide if one of those parents lived in the house or out of it.

She was in love with Dean, not that she'd told him yet. She was afraid he'd propose again. He was up to three proposals so far, and she didn't think he was done yet. It wasn't even that he couldn't take no for an answer so much as he just kept getting his hopes up that she might have changed her mind. She sighed. Men thought persistence was sexy when sometimes it was just aggravating.

Of course, everything aggravated her lately. She had to pee about every five minutes. She was hungry and thirsty all the time, which didn't help. Her lower back ached, and every time she got a look of discomfort on her face everyone freaked out and asked if she could be going into labor with a mix of terror and hope on their faces. Then there were the classes. Standing up to teach had gotten tough. The only weight she'd put on was around her belly, but she wasn't sure it could pop out any further. She already had her belly button pop back out, and she didn't care what Presley said, it probably wasn't going back in ever again.

Presley had been a godsend. She wasn't her midwife, but she was her friend, so she gave Lindy helpful tips to survive those last few weeks of the pregnancy. Every time Lindy had called with a question, Presley had answered calmly and with confidence, assuring her she had nothing to worry about. Dean, on the other hand, had no chill. He overreacted to the smallest pregnancy symptom and seemed to share some of her pain. He'd even developed back aches right along with her, to her amusement. She assured him only one of them needed to carry the baby, and it really needed to be her.

Still, the twinges in her back had been worse today. She wouldn't tell Dean yet. It was likely a false alarm. He was too likely to call in the cavalry because she thought she might be closer to labor now. She rolled her eyes but smiled, too. She had to admit it was pretty cute.

She was so excited to meet Maya. She'd been talking to her and singing to her and reading her stories. She'd introduced her to classic music—like classic rock, her kind of classical music. She'd told her all about her family, even the great-grandparents Maya would never get to meet. She'd felt her kick and squirm, and she'd dreamed of holding her very own baby in her arms. Maybe the dream hadn't included Dean before, but she squeezed him into the picture now.

"Jamie and Seth are here," she called to Dean. They were going out for what they were calling a fatherhood celebration. The baby was due any day now, and they told Dean he wouldn't get many more chances to go out and party.

"Don't worry; I'm DD tonight," Jamie told Lindy while they waited.

"I'll pick up your slack," Seth told him with a grin.

"I thought you'd never get here. Are we going out or what?" Dean asked as he came down the stairs.

"All of you get out of my house, so I can have a little peace and quiet," Lindy said with a laugh. "I'll get the hangover cure ready for you," she told Dean, giving him a quick kiss.

"Ugh! My eyes," Seth said with a groan.

"Think he'll ever get used to this?" Lindy asked Dean with a grin, kissing him again.

"No, he won't," Seth answered for him. "And no more kissing tonight."

"Who made these rules?" Jamie asked with a wide smile. "He's only saying that because Libby's doing the Taco Tuesday thing."

"It's Friday," Lindy pointed out.

"Needs must," Seth said.

"What?" Lindy asked, perplexed.

"That's what she said when I asked her why Taco Tuesday was moved to a Friday. Needs must," he said with a grin. "She's adorable, right?"

"Now I'm going to be sick," Dean said with a laugh. "Let's get out of here."

Jamie drove to a bar in downtown Athens. They parked and planned to just bar hop until they were tired and wanted to go home.

"What are you doing?" Jamie asked Dean as they got out of the truck.

"Texting Keely and Libby to make sure the labor plans are in place," Dean said absently.

Seth rolled his eyes. "I'm going to confiscate your phone."

"And if Lindy goes into labor, it'll be your head that rolls," Dean reminded him.

"Good point. Text away."

"I'll grab drinks," Jamie said, heading to the bar.

Dean snagged a table near the back, and then he saw a familiar face as he was sitting down. "Hey, Shelby," he said easily, leaning over to give her a hug. "It's good to see you."

"Hey, Dean," she said uncertainly. "How are you?"

"I'm really good," he said awkwardly, wondering how he'd left things with her and suspecting it hadn't been good.

"Good? He's great. He's about to be a dad," Seth said, cutting into the conversation.

"Seriously?" she asked him, a smile blossoming. "Congratulations! This is Maddox," she told him as her boyfriend walked up with their drinks. "This is Dean. He's about to be a dad."

"You're Dean?" Maddox asked curiously. "Nice to meet you. Boy or girl?"

"Girl. We're thinking Maya, but we're still debating," Dean explained. "My girlfriend can't decide which name she likes best so we decided to wait until we see her to see what she looks like."

"That's a good idea," Shelby said with a small smile. So, Dean Walton had a girlfriend these days. And a baby on the way. She congratulated him again and watched as he made his way back to his table with his friends.

"That's the guy who broke your heart?" Maddox asked, wondering if he should be relieved the guy seemed off the market now.

"He was. You're the guy who put it back together though," she told him with a grin.

"You did that yourself," he reminded her. "He didn't seem like an asshole."

"He's probably not with her. Maybe he wasn't with me either as much as he was … careless maybe," she said with a shrug, turning away from Dean to find a table where they could sit.

*****

"You know, we're both spoken for, but feel free to pick someone up if you want," Seth told Jamie after a couple of beers. Jamie looked amused.

"Nice of you, but I'm fine."

"Don't see anyone you like?" Dean asked. He looked around the room. There were nice enough women here if Jamie was looking. "There's a group over there checking you out," he added helpfully.

"I'm not really looking tonight. Seriously, guys, I can get a date if I want to," he said with a grin. "No help required."

"Unless you're looking at the gym—hey, that's an idea—I don't know that you're going to find one," Seth told him with amusement.

"Unless you're seeing Beth now," Dean pointed out. "Is that a thing?"

"Nope. Just friends," he said. Seth and Dean both snorted out a laugh.

"Me and Lindy? We were just friends, too," Dean added with a wry grin.

"There's nothing going on with me and Beth," Jamie insisted. "She's not looking for a relationship."

"Ah! But if she were, would you then, in fact, be interested?" Seth asked.

"Yeah, there's the question," Dean agreed.

"Look, I'm going to get more drinks, and you can answer your phone, Dean," Jamie pointed out, nodding to the phone lighting up on the table.

*****

Beth and Naomi were working a little late on promotional material for an author event. Naomi had designed the flyers, and Beth was working on the text for some of the social media announcements Naomi would post leading up to the event. They'd been working on the project for a couple of hours when Beth announced it was time for a break.

"The good thing about working here is that Amie always leaves us goodies in the staff fridge for late nights. There's even a just-for-us cookie jar," she enthused. They walked companionably to the kitchen and got out a few cookies and poured some glasses of milk. They sat at the counter and tried them.

"Heaven!" Naomi exclaimed.

She loved this kitchen. She didn't normally hang out here because she was even more uncomfortable around Keely now, but she felt comforted around the large stove and counters with the smell of baking scones and cookies constantly in the air. She sighed, happily. She lived for the moments now when she didn't feel those hard slaps and pinches and bites. She'd been having nightmares since it happened, and she'd even experienced a little hair loss, although it embarrassed her to remember how she'd brushed out those chunks of hair. She'd pulled it up in a messy bun and hoped to hide it. Not that it had been a lot, but it was more than she'd ever seen come out at once.

"Can we talk about something?" Beth asked.

"Sure. What's on your mind?" Naomi asked curiously. She assumed Beth had another wacky idea for the promotion that would probably be wildly successful, like most of her ideas—no matter how weird—ended up being.

"You want to tell me why you're avoiding Keely?"

"Um." Naomi looked down at her lap. The bruises were gone now. They'd faded away some time ago, but the second Beth asked, she'd brought that night into this room, too. "What would you do if you knew something bad about someone, but you didn't want to say how you knew?"

"Seriously, Naomi, I'm worried about you. I know something happened. I really just wish you'd tell me. Is it Dean? Is he bothering you in some way? Or Theodore? I notice you leave the room when he comes in, too," Beth asked in a hushed tone.

"If I tell … if I say what I know, no one will believe it," Naomi said, tears falling down her face. She looked up at Beth and even with the makeup, she suddenly looked just as young as she was.

"I'll believe you. Whatever it is, I'll believe you," Beth said firmly, taking one of Naomi's hands, which were clutched together in her lap.

Chapter 43

Dean answered the phone and had to take it outside to hear. He was gone only for a minute when he rushed back in.

"We've got to go now. Lindy's in labor," he said in a panic. "And I'm drunk."

"You're only a little drunk, and I'm driving, remember?" Jamie reminded him.

"We can stop for coffee on the way," Seth suggested.

"We don't have time!" Dean told them. "We've got to go." He threw too much money down on the table for the tab and ran out. Seth and Jamie grinned at each other behind him.

"He's going the wrong way," Jamie pointed out.

"Hell, yeah, he is," Seth said with a grin. "He's a daddy now."

*****

Lindy had called Keely and started the chain reaction of phone calls right before she called Dean. She'd wanted someone close by to know before she told him. It would take him at least half an hour, depending on where they parked downtown, to get here. It would likely be closer to an hour. She was glad they'd taken Jamie. He was a safe driver, and he wouldn't let Dean get them killed by speeding here.

She'd tried to ignore the twinges, but when the first actual contraction had hit, she'd changed her mind. Waiting any longer suddenly seemed like a bad idea. But thirty-eight weeks was good, right? I mean, it was full term. She called Presley and let her walk her calmly through the breathing until she heard Keely at the door.

"Theodore left the car running," Keely said as soon as Lindy opened the door.

Lindy carefully slipped her feet into her shoes while Keely helped support her. She was down to flipflops now, the only shoes that would accommodate her swollen feet. They were ugly as homemade sin and didn't match anything she wore, but at least she had shoes on. Dean had treated her to a spa pedicure a couple of days ago so at least her toes were pretty. Not that she could see them, she thought, as she gingerly sat in the car. She grinned when she noticed the seats were covered in towels.

"My water hasn't broken yet," she pointed out.

"See?" Theodore told Keely. "Better safe than sorry," he chuckled, heading toward the hospital.

*****

Beth was still shaking when she made it to the waiting room. She would explain it away as excitement about the baby, but she wanted to tell someone. She actually wanted to hit something, or more accurately, someone. And she knew just who she'd hit if she had the chance! She told Naomi she would believe her, and she did. She couldn't believe she'd actually trusted him! Or that he would do something so insidious!

Except she could actually believe it. She'd assured Naomi that none of it was her fault, hugged her firmly, and promised to call when there was news of the baby. Naomi had left looking lighter, and Beth had headed to the hospital in a fury. She paced outside for a moment and then got herself under control. She couldn't do anything about it tonight. It wasn't the time or the place.

She headed into the waiting room and realized that she was one of the first to arrive. Keely was back with Lindy, and Theodore was waiting. He caught Beth up on who was on the way, and they sat together flipping through magazines.

"It's okay if you want to go back and check on Lindy. You don't have to keep me company." Theodore said with a kind smile.

"I like to keep you company, but I will pop back and say hello real quick," Beth agreed.

Theodore smiled. It probably wouldn't be really quick, but it was sweet she thought so. He picked up his phone and texted his girls again. Presley already knew, of course, but he just wanted to check in and let them know that Lindy was in actual labor and was being admitted now. Presley was heading over after her shift, and Layla and Noah said they would stop in a little later. He went back to the magazine, content to wait for news.

*****

Keely was sitting beside Lindy talking to her softly. "I know it hurts, baby. It won't hurt for much longer."

"I think we call that a lie here in the South," Beth pointed out, as she walked in. "Can't it take hours?"

"Not helpful," Lindy said between gritted teeth.

"She's getting the epidural just as soon as they hurry up and get in here," Keely explained. Lindy closed her eyes, and they all watched the monitor to see how long the contraction lasted.

"That was a big one," Beth said, her eyes as round as saucers beneath her glasses.

"Tell them I'll put it in myself if they'll just bring it in here," Lindy said urgently.

"They'll be back in a minute. We got here right at a shift change, honey. It takes some time," Keely pointed out, smoothing back Lindy's hair.

"Can I get you something?" Beth asked.

"An epidural," Lindy said flatly. "That's all I want right now."

"I can put on my bossy boots and go make trouble if you think that'll help get it here any sooner," Beth said cheerfully.

"I already have," Keely said calmly.

"I bet you went all imperial though," Beth commented. "Look,

Lindy. You've got this. You're the strongest person I know," she said encouragingly. She'd have made a great cheerleader if she hadn't had her nose stuck in a book every year of high school, been completely uninterested in football, and if she hadn't found the uniforms sexist and generally objectionable.

"Is Dean almost here?" she asked tearfully.

"He's on his way," Keely told her. "Though I think he might have had a little to drink."

"I miss drinking," Lindy said weepily as another contraction hit. "It hurts, Mama."

"I know, baby," Keely told her, holding on to her hand. "The whole crew is on the way. Presley already let us know she was coming, and Layla and Noah will be by. I already talked to Libby, and she said all of their group is moving from the Mexican place to here, sans margaritas I'm afraid. Your brother and Dean are headed here now. Everything will be okay."

When the anesthesiologist walked in, Beth made her excuses and left. It was one thing to know a thing intellectually. It really was. But to have to know it and then see the person responsible? She was haunted by Naomi's story. It was so sordid and ugly. It was clear he'd manipulated the whole thing and then made her feel responsible for it. How was she supposed to act even civil with all of this going on? She couldn't exactly out him here, with all their friends and family around and Lindy in labor. That wouldn't be right. But letting him get away with this? That wasn't okay either.

She headed to the waiting room and sat down beside Theodore. Who was the right person to tell? Should she say anything? It was Naomi's secret after all, but she had a terrible feeling that Naomi wasn't the only person who was being hurt. If she didn't say anything, he could keep right on hurting someone else. She took a deep breath and had started to speak when Presley rushed in.

"I got here as quick as I could," she said, leaning over to hug her dad. "How's Lindy?" she asked Beth.

"She's holding up. They just brought in the epidural."

"Good. That'll give her some relief."

"I thought midwives didn't like epidurals," Beth said, a question in her voice.

"I'm of the opinion that if I'm not the one having to deal with the pain and pushing out a baby, then I don't have the right to make that judgment call on the one who does. What my patients want, within reason," she qualified. "my patients get."

"You're a good person," Beth said seriously.

"Um, thanks," Presley said with a laugh.

"I'm going to go grab a soda. You girls want anything?" Theodore asked.

"No, I'm good, Dad," Presley told him. Beth shook her head. They both watched him walk away. "What's up with you tonight? You seem restless? Like maybe you've got a bee in your bonnet," Presley continued.

"I found out a thing. Like, a bad thing. And I don't know who I should tell," Beth began.

"Wait—it's not about Dean, is it?" Presley asked nervously.

"Why would it be about Dean?" Beth asked carefully.

"Nothing. Just something Noah said in passing. I probably misunderstood," Presley said with a wave of her hand.

"Oh, no, you probably understood it correctly," Beth said darkly. "Can we go somewhere and talk? Maybe to the cafeteria or something?" Beth asked quickly, darting a look around to make sure no one else had come in.

"Yeah, sure. Let me tell Dad. He can text us if anything happens," Presley said, assessing the seriousness of the situation.

"So, what's up?" she asked as they got into the elevator.

"Did Noah tell you something about Dean?" Beth asked frankly.

"Not exactly. He'd kind of implied that maybe Dean was seeing someone else," Presley said uncomfortably. "He said he was probably wrong though. Or maybe just misunderstood."

"Was it Naomi?" Beth asked simply.

"Wait, it's not true, is it?"

"We need to sit down for this," Beth muttered, leading her to a table in the back of the cafeteria where they wouldn't be overheard. "Look, you can't fly off the handle, and you cannot say anything to anybody while Lindy's in labor, okay? Or even in the hospital. It's her big day," Beth reminded Presley.

"Of course," Presley said, waiting to see what this was about. "But Dean's not cheating, then?"

"No. It's so much worse."

*****

Dean got to the hospital, backseat driving all the way. He was so afraid he was going to miss the birth. Jamie obeyed too many traffic laws, and it had taken forever to get here. He jumped out of the car before it had come to a full stop and run wildly into the building. Seth and Jamie exchanged a look.

"Want to come in and watch the fun?" Seth asked.

"Sure, but just from the comfort of the waiting room. I've got a big family, so I've seen childbirth. I'll just warm a chair and run errands if you don't mind."

"Maybe you can talk with Beth while you're here. Ask her out," Seth said with a sly grin.

"Shut up," Jamie retorted. "Friends, remember?"

*****

Noah and Layla were the last to make it in, but they were only just behind Libby and her friends who had turned the waiting room into a bit of a party. They hadn't gotten far on the margaritas, but Jenna's husband Finn had gamely picked them up in their van and driven them to the hospital. He promised to come back and get them later when there was news.

"Hey, Dad," Layla said, hugging him and looking around the room for her sister.

"Where's Presley?" she asked as Noah walked off to talk to Jamie about baseball.

"She went downstairs to get something to eat," Theodore explained.

"I think I'll go find her," Layla told him. "Do you want anything?"

"No, I think I'll wait here for Keely and news on the baby," he said easily. "And I'll keep your man company," he said with a smile.

*****

In the room, Lindy was finally feeling the full effects of the epidural. She started to relax, but she still held her mother's hand. When Dean entered the room, she was even able to give him a tired smile.

"Do you want me to stay or go?" Dean asked softly.

"I want you both to stay," Lindy told Dean and her mom. "I got the epidural."

"I'm glad. Are you okay?" Dean asked her, slowly approaching the bed.

"I'm okay now," she said seriously. "It really hurt."

"I'm sorry, baby," Dean told her softly, kissing the top of her head. "Are you going to marry me now?"

Lindy laughed. "No. I'm busy giving birth," she pointed out. "Or about to anyway." The nurse who had come to check her vitals grinned at their banter.

"After she's born? Marry me then?" Dean whispered.

"Nope, we'll be too busy taking care of her," Lindy told him.

"Did we decide on Walton or Carver? I can't remember," he claimed.

"We decided on Carver-Walton. But not a middle name," she pointed out.

"Well, we have a little time to think," Dean said, taking her other hand.

Chapter 44

Presley sat back in her chair in shock. "What are you saying? Are you sure?"

"If you could have seen her face when she told me ..." Beth said. "That girl was terrified. And ashamed and hurt. It was awful. I'm only telling you because I think we should do something," she admitted. "Not now, obviously. But something."

"There was this thing that happened the other day," Presley began. Beth had a bad feeling about where it was going. Presley detailed a car ride, a sudden stop, and a hand thrown across her chest when she could have sworn it felt up her breasts for just a split second while it was there. It had been a hard hit that left her bruised, and then his hand had sat high on her thigh for a few beats too long. Beth felt sick. "To be honest, from the day I met him, he made me feel like we had this connection. Even after I found out he was dating my sister. I felt ashamed of myself for being attracted, and I kept telling myself that he wasn't flirting at all."

"Do you think he's hurting Layla?" Beth asked seriously.

"Yeah," Presley said softly. "She won't make plans in case he plans a surprise for her. She asks him if she can go places and then checks in with him the whole time she's out. She's been really jumpy since they moved in together, and I just thought it was her normal moody thing. But I think he could be hurting her."

They both looked up as Layla walked into the room. "Dad said you were getting something to eat," Layla said, looking at the empty table in front of them. Beth and Presley exchanged a look, and Beth nodded slowly.

"I think we need to talk," Presley said. "Can you sit down a second?"

*****

Noah sat in the waiting room uncomfortably. He'd talked baseball with Jamie for a few minutes, but that hadn't lasted nearly long enough to kill the time. He had no interest in talking with a group of drunk women, and he'd already ascertained that Seth had been out drinking, too. Not that it was a big deal. A beer or two didn't hurt anyone. Still, Seth was sitting over with his fiancé and her drunken friends having a fine time. Noah walked over to speak to Theodore instead. He wasn't drunk, and he was intelligent enough. They could pass the time together.

Layla had been gone for a few minutes longer than he expected, but she was always slow like that. The first time he'd pushed her he'd just wanted to go to the bathroom. She was moving too slowly in front of him, and he'd just reacted. When he'd come out of the bathroom, he'd claimed it was an accident, that he hadn't meant to bump into her at all.

That was after Layla had moved in. He realized quickly that she was messier than he'd expected. She never made a bed, and she was perpetually behind on laundry, throwing her clothes over every available surface when she took them off. The sex was good, at least. She was pretty much game for anything, and if she didn't like something, she didn't really stop him from enjoying it himself. Well, maybe she told him to stop, but then she seemed not to mind when he didn't. It was those mind games again.

Just like Naomi. She'd walked right by his car wearing that short, thin dress. She hadn't bothered with a bra, and she must have seen him when she parked. It was the fire station thing all over again. He'd just been dropping off some coffee when she'd walked by. He'd talked her into a tour of the empty station and a private tour of one of the fire trucks in the back of the garage. He hadn't intended to see her again, but when he saw her walking by in that slip of a dress, he knew what she wanted. She'd gotten into his car so easily and had even slid her dress up a few tantalizing inches as she sat down. He would never actually date a girl like her, but he had a few other things in mind. She'd enjoyed it, too, even if she had done the fake tears thing in the end. He'd taken things a step further, and he was sure that the next time he got her in his car or at her house, they'd go all the way. He liked to take it in stages after all.

Layla was perfect though. She didn't like going out much anyway, and she didn't have a lot of friends. She wasn't close to her family really, and she wouldn't talk to them about this. She was seriously pretty but didn't seem to realize it because she was hung up on her sister being prettier. Then on top of that, she was so easily impressed just by being nice. All he had to do was pay for a meal or hold open a door, and her legs fell open. She moved right in, thinking he was her Prince Charming. And he was.

Girls like Naomi passed the time when he got bored, but he planned to marry Layla. She hadn't once said a word about the bruises or mentioned anything they'd done in the bedroom when they weren't doing it. There was nothing he could do to her that she wouldn't take and still come home the next night after work and do it again. He sat companionably beside her dad and talked about summer vacation plans while he thought about everything he would do to Layla again when they got home.

*****

Layla turned increasingly pale through the story, her hands clenched in her lap. "Do you know who we're talking about?" Presley asked.

"You probably think it's Dean," Layla said softly, remembering how Noah had tried to convince her that he was cheating on Lindy. "But it's Noah, isn't it? Noah did that?"

"You know he did, don't you?" Beth asked compassionately.

"It sounds like something that happened to me a few times,"

Layla admitted. When she laid her head down on the table and cried, Presley laid her head down beside hers and did the same.

*****

"It's time, baby," Dean told her. Lindy held tight to her mom's hand on one side and Dean's on the other.

"On the next contraction, you're going to need to push. A couple more, and we're there," the nurse told Lindy with a smile.

"Are you going to marry me now?" Dean asked nervously.

"Are you going to shut up and let me push?" she asked on a laugh.

*****

Presley had texted her dad and asked him to come to the cafeteria alone. She was specific about not telling anyone where he was going. It wouldn't take long after all. When he got out of the elevator, the first thing he saw was Layla in Presley's arms sobbing. He was across the room in a few strides and sat down in a chair heavily.

"Is it Noah?" Theodore asked. "Did something happen?"

"Why would you think that?" Beth asked curiously.

"I had this feeling when he was talking to me, and then I saw Layla crying. What did he do?" Theodore asked, fear in his eyes. Layla shook her head and her eyes met Presley's.

"He's hurting her, Dad. He needs to leave now. We'll move her stuff later," Presley told him.

"He'll burn it all or throw it out," Layla cried.

"Then we'll buy you more," Theodore told her softly.

"I don't have anywhere else to go," Layla wept into her hands.

"You could live with us," Theodore offered brightly.

"No, Dad," Presley countered. "You'll live with me, Layla. Okay?"

"Really, Presley? You don't mind?" Layla asked, wiping away her tears with the back of her hand.

"You're my sister. And nobody messes with the Westerman girls," she said fiercely.

Theodore walked back upstairs and motioned Seth aside. Theodore was well aware he was an older man about to confront a much younger one. He apprised Seth quickly of the situation in general terms, and they agreed to get Noah out of the hospital before the baby was born.

"It's time for you to go, son," Theodore said firmly.

Noah looked up from where he was playing on his phone. Theodore and Seth stood side by side. Even though they had been quiet in their request, a hush fell from Libby and her friends as they sensed something important was happening. Noah's face flushed an unbecoming shade of red.

"I don't understand—sir," he added as an afterthought.

"Don't you?" Theodore asked severely. Behind him, the elevator doors opened, and Layla came out with her sister on one side of her and Beth on the other. She was trembling, but she wasn't backing down. They all looked at him coolly, and Layla even raised her chin up a degree as he returned her stare. He said something ugly to them all and stomped out the door.

Libby wasn't even able to ask Seth what had happened before Keely rushed into the waiting room. "She's here! She's born!" the new grandmother cried with a laugh. "Eight pounds, eleven ounces, and twenty-one beautiful inches long."

Theodore hugged her tightly, and the room erupted in cheers. "Did they decide for sure on a name?" Seth asked.

"It's Maya. Maya Eleanor Carver-Walton," Keely said with a grin. "And that's not all," she told them, getting their attention. "Lindy proposed," Keely announced to another chorus of cheers.

"Well, like mother, like daughter," Theodore said with a grin. "I can't wait to see his ring."

*****

In the room, Lindy and Dean sat side by side on the bed looking at the most perfect, most beautiful baby they had ever seen. Lindy was holding her, but she'd agreed to let Dean have her next, before even her mom. It was his baby, too, after all. When the head had finally crowned, Lindy had let out a jubilant laugh. After the final exhausting push, when they saw their beautiful baby in the doctor's arms, Lindy knew. She just knew. She knew she was in love with Dean. She knew that she was even more in love with this baby. She knew that they could be a family, and she could trust him.

Whatever black cloud had been hanging over her, all the doubts and insecurities, simply evaporated. They'd put the baby in her arms, and she'd looked up and asked Dean to marry her. She hadn't planned to do it now. She thought she'd see what kind of father he turned out to be. But she'd looked up and seen the tears running down his face and the joy in his eyes and already knew.

"Maya Eleanor. That's a mouthful," Dean told her.

"She'll just have to live up to her big name, that's all. And she'll just be Maya anyway," Lindy told him smugly.

They counted all of her perfect fingers and perfect toes. She'd cried out once and then calmed down and stared up at them in wonder. They knew from all the books that she couldn't see well yet, but they chose to believe that she could see them as perfectly as they could see her. They talked to her and kissed her, and they let the hospital staff do their jobs efficiently so that they could return Maya to their waiting arms.

"Did I say yes?" Dean asked. "When you asked me to marry you? I was so caught up in the moment I can't be sure."

"Yeah, you did," Lindy said with a grin. "No takebacks," she warned him.

"Good," Dean said smugly. "Are you ready to meet your family, Maya?" he asked the baby softly. He kissed her head and handed her back to Lindy, "I'll go get them."

Preview of Book 3

Deep in the Heart of Madison

"Friendship is certainly the finest balm for the pangs of disappointed love." ~Jane Austen

Chapter 1

"It is a truth universally acknowledged that a single woman over the age of thirty has already met her soul mate. She just wasn't paying attention." Beth Everett grinned at the book club as they settled down and turned their attention her way. A couple of them were already grinning. "If you're going to rip off an author, at least let it be the late, great Jane Austen, right? What single woman doesn't identify with Jane?" Beth paused and let her gaze wander the room. She fiddled with the book in her lap. "This is just one of many adaptations of Austen's work, and we'll discuss it in a minute. But I wanted to talk about Mr. Darcy first."

"Mr. Darcy!" Amie, friend and tea room chef, sighed his name. "The McDreamy of Austen men."

"More like McSteamy," a new group member added. Beth thought her name was Kirsten, but she couldn't see the name tag from her seat to confirm.

"A little of both, right?" Beth continued. "There's only one Mr. Darcy, but generations of women read these books."

"And then go out into the dating world to get disappointed by real men," Vera said wryly to nods around the room. Vera was the innkeeper for a local bed and breakfast and a family friend.

"Right?" Beth agreed.

"I swear, for every one Darcy out there, there are about twenty Wickhams," her Aunt Keely chimed in, as the group nodded in agreement. The lone man in the room tentatively held up one finger and indicated himself. They all laughed.

"My cousin, Seth," Beth said with a smile, knowing her cousin had only come out because his fiancé couldn't make it for work. He'd fill her in later. It's not that men didn't come to the book clubs, but it wasn't typical. "Definitely a Darcy in a sea of Wickhams."

"Thanks," he said with a grin, sitting back in satisfaction and then half-eyeing the dessert table to see if he could justify seconds. Well, thirds would be more accurate. Beth looked at him as if reading his mind, and they both exchanged smiles as he got up and filled up a third plate. She turned back to the group.

"Every woman and most men I know are frustrated by the whole dating scene. We start to think about the one who got away. You know, our chance at love that we missed because we weren't paying attention."

"Or there was a timing issue. Or they were with someone when you were with someone," Amie agreed, as Seth sat down beside her and started in on a variety of petit fours.

"So, I wanted to start out telling you about how I met my own Mr. Darcy, and then we'll pick up with the book," Beth said with a grin. Vera and Amie grinned, too, looking away while Seth shook his head knowingly. They were familiar with the story, but most of the group tonight was new and hadn't heard it yet. After all, this was their first Austen-inspired book club pick. "It took a while to find him, and we didn't meet in what anyone would consider a traditional sense. It was most unexpected and right when I'd given up all hope. I feel like I should give you a little basic history.

"My first crush was a few months before my eleventh birthday. His name was Jonah, and he had freckles and a wide smile. He was kind of adorable with his blonde hair always sticking up and his wide, goofy smile." She smiled fondly as she remembered him.

"Me? Well, I don't know if anyone would have called me adorable. Feisty, for sure," Beth grinned and brushed her red hair off her shoulders and regretted that it was still straight as a stick, no matter how often she'd try to make curls stay. Her blue eyes were covered by horn-rims, and she kept her makeup limited to mascara and colored lipstick most of the time. "But anyway," Beth told them, continuing her story and reigning in her thoughts. "Jonah was a textbook *cute boy*. I had a crush before I even knew what a crush was, and I followed him around until he got sick of me and told me to "drop dead" or something to that effect. So, I did what any other self-respecting nearly-eleven-year-old girl would do when thwarted by her man: I booby-trapped his treehouse like *The Parent Trap* and hid with my girlfriends to watch it all go down."

A laugh rippled around the group, and Beth grinned.

"You did *not*," one of them said with a laugh.

"She did," Seth told them with a grin. "There are pictures. Somewhere."

Beth grinned at him and shrugged. "Well, I was a little sorry when he sprained his wrist falling off the ladder, even if I did laugh at first, but he didn't rat me out, so we were able to eventually resume our friendship. Of course, fast-forward four years later and Jonah decided to ask me out, but I just laughed and told him to "drop dead" and he never asked again. Anyway, when I was single later on during college, and lonely with it, I thought about Jonah. I wondered if he was the one who got away, you know—the actual *one*—and I had been too proud and—gasp! —prejudiced to pay attention. I would weave these daydreams in my head about how we'd run into each other, and it would all come together. Or I'd think about what would have happened if I hadn't shot him down so thoroughly, how maybe we'd be together even now." A few of the women nodded knowingly.

Her aunt Keely came in from the kitchen with another tray of cookies. The first had disappeared quickly, and Seth had cleared out most of the tray of petit fours claiming it took about a dozen to make one regular piece of cake. Beth smiled at her and continued, "But the truth is that every single person I know—man or woman—plays that game. We get lonely, and we start to wonder if Mr. (or Mrs.) Right wasn't someone from the past we just overlooked." Beth paused to take a sip of her drink and looked around the group.

"Anyway," Beth continued, trying to stay on track. "I kept taking myself out on dates, hanging out with friends, enjoying my awesome job, and generally loving my life. I dated a little, but after a few hard knocks, I decided to take a little dating moratorium and use the extra time that I'd used to focus on dating to volunteer at the animal shelter in town. Mostly, I would take the dogs out for walks. And that's how I met him ... Yes, him. Mr. Darcy. The love of my life. Handsome, charming, well-mannered with that hint of bad boy persona under the surface. You know the type." Most of the women in the group grinned knowingly, and the lone man at the book club rolled his eyes. Beth let the appreciative murmurs settle before continuing. "Anyway, there I was, being dragged back to the shelter by a lab mix when I saw him. You could say it was love at first sight if you believe in that sort of thing. I just know that I was immediately smitten.

"There he was, just waiting for me: the most handsome bull terrier you'll ever meet." Beth caught the grins and groans from the group. "He was so little, and he was only a year old at the time, give or take a few months. He sauntered up to me and gave me what I swear was the biggest grin. And I was sunk. My heart? Gone! He was solid white, my white knight, except for a black nose and one black eye. It was love at first sight and completely mutual—just like all the love stories you've ever heard."

From the backroom, Keely brought Mr. Darcy out, and there was a chorus of coos and sighs. He went straight to Beth and laid down at her feet. She reached down to pet him, continuing her story. "I named him Mr. Darcy because I didn't need any other man. I had my perfect guy, and we were going to be very happy together. Well, anyway, if "the one" had two legs instead of four, I've never met him. Anyway, that's the story of how I came to meet my Mr. Darcy. I'd love to hear your own love stories, and then we'll talk about what we all thought about this particular adaptation." She held up *Pride and Prejudice and Zombies* for the group to see.

Beth sat back and listened as each group member shared a story of finding true love or failing to find it. Then they segued into a heated discussion of the book and how it compared to the classic. Beth was glad that she'd started the book club. For a while, it had floundered, but lately, it was a runaway success.

She thought about how much life had changed in the last year. Beth wasn't lonely, and she's stopped playing the game where she imagined every past lover might have been the one that got away. These days, she wasn't even sure she believed in that for herself. Anyway, Beth thought to herself, reaching down to scoop Mr. Darcy into her lap, it's not like the story is over. She had plenty of time for exciting things to happen.

About The Author

'Right On Walton' is Crystal Jackson's second novel in the Heart of Madison series, an ongoing southern romance set in the charming real-life town of Madison, Georgia, where she lives with her two wild and wonderful children. A former therapist turned author, her work has been featured on Medium, Elephant Journal, Elite Daily, and The Good Men Project. When she's not writing for Medium and working on her next book, you can find Crystal traveling, paddle boarding, running, throwing axes badly but with terrifying enthusiasm, hiking, doing yoga, or curled up with her nose in a book.